THE SEEMINGLY IMPOSSIBLE LOVE LIFE OF AMANDA DEAN

"A beautifully unique and captivating love story! I was on the edge of my seat as I followed Mandy through the many twists and turns that led her to the altar, and I turned the final page with a happy sigh."
—Rachel Lacey, author of *Cover Story*

"A heartwarming story of love and self-discovery that's sure to be a reader favorite. The unique style of storytelling Rose implements makes *The Seemingly Impossible Love Life of Amanda Dean* one readers will never forget."
—Mariah Ankenman, author of *Falling for You*

"Sparkling with humor and heart, *The Seemingly Impossible Love Life of Amanda Dean* sweeps readers along the enthralling romantic journey of a main character you can't help but root for. I ached and cheered for Mandy to find her ultimate joy and this happily ever after more than delivered. Ann Rose is a bright voice in romance, and this queer celebration of a book is not to be missed."
—Courtney Kae, author of *In the Case of Heartbreak*

"*The Seemingly Impossible Love Life of Amanda Dean* is a warm hug in book form. You will enjoy going along for the ride as Mandy chooses a happily ever after that is perfect for her."
—Sam Tschida, author of *Errands and Espionage*

"Enjoy Mandy's up and down journey toward happily ever after. You'll love it for real!"

—Kelly Farmer, bestselling author of *It's a Fabulous Life*

"Readers are treated to an intimate, vulnerable portrait of a complicated woman who is trying to apply all she's learned into building a life with someone. . . . The result is equal parts heartbreaking and heartwarming."

—*Publishers Weekly* (starred review)

"The unique structure makes Rose's charming adult debut stand out, and readers will fall for bighearted Mandy and her messy love life."

—*Booklist*

Titles by Ann Rose

The Seemingly Impossible Love Life of Amanda Dean
A Hexcellent Chance to Fall in Love

A Hexcellent Chance to Fall in Love

ANN ROSE

Berkley Romance
New York

BERKLEY ROMANCE
Published by Berkley
An imprint of Penguin Random House LLC
1745 Broadway, New York, NY 10019
penguinrandomhouse.com

Copyright © 2025 by Ann Rose
Readers Guide copyright © 2025 by Ann Rose
Excerpt from *The Seemingly Impossible Love Life of Amanda Dean* copyright © 2024 by Ann Rose
Penguin Random House values and supports copyright. Copyright fuels creativity, encourages diverse voices, promotes free speech, and creates a vibrant culture. Thank you for buying an authorized edition of this book and for complying with copyright laws by not reproducing, scanning, or distributing any part of it in any form without permission. You are supporting writers and allowing Penguin Random House to continue to publish books for every reader. Please note that no part of this book may be used or reproduced in any manner for the purpose of training artificial intelligence technologies or systems.

BERKLEY and the BERKLEY & B colophon are registered trademarks of
Penguin Random House LLC.

Book design by Alison Cnockaert

Library of Congress Cataloging-in-Publication Data

Names: Rose, Ann (Ann M.), author.
Title: A hexcellent chance to fall in love / Ann Rose.
Description: First edition. | New York: Berkley Romance, 2025
Identifiers: LCCN 2025010361 (print) | LCCN 2025010362 (ebook) |
ISBN 9780593815977 (trade paperback) | ISBN 9780593815984 (ebook)
Subjects: LCGFT: Paranormal romance fiction. | Lesbian fiction. | Novels.
Classification: LCC PS3618.O782823 H49 2025 (print) |
LCC PS3618.O782823 (ebook) | DDC 813/.6--dc23/eng/20250319
LC record available at https://lccn.loc.gov/2025010361
LC ebook record available at https://lccn.loc.gov/2025010362

First Edition: September 2025

Printed in the United States of America
1st Printing

The authorized representative in the EU for product safety and compliance is
Penguin Random House Ireland, Morrison Chambers, 32 Nassau Street,
Dublin D02 YH68, Ireland, https://eu-contact.penguin.ie.

To everyone who's ever loved and lost, and loved again . . .

                                                    again . . .

                                            and again.

A Hexcellent Chance to Fall in Love

The Dead of Night Keeper Agreement

1. If you are in possession of the amulet at midnight inside the store on November 2nd and you agree, you'll become the Keeper of the Store. This will stay in effect until a new person holds the amulet at the designated time and place.

2. As Keeper, you forgo all rights to the life you had before your term.

3. As Keeper, you will not physically age and any ailments you may have had before will vanish, so that you can always be in tip-top health to run the store efficiently.

4. As Keeper, you are able to travel outside the store during its operation but ONLY during its seasonal operational period.

5. You will be permitted to use the company vehicle during the store's operational period. No other employee is permitted to use it.

6. All your expenses inside and outside the store will be covered and a special credit card issued for your use. (Some conditions may apply.)

7. You will not be designated any specific working hours, but all staff will consider you management, and all knowledge of store functions will be provided at transfer of power. You are required to maintain the image of being in a leadership role of the store—meaning you must maintain a high level of professionalism.

8. You will be provided with a company phone so you can be reached at any time during operation. You are REQUIRED to answer at all times. A new phone will be provided each year to stay up-to-date with the most current technology.

9. Room and board will be provided on-site no matter where the store is located. Other store employees will be unaware of its existence.

70 DAYS
UNTIL THE STORE CLOSES

Pepper

One of the best things about having my soul eternally tethered to a seasonal holiday store was that I could eat anything I wanted. The bag of Skittles crinkled as I reached deep into my pocket and grabbed a couple before popping an orange one in my mouth as I stood in the center aisle.

    The Dead of Night wasn't your typical Halloween store. Aside from the fact that it needed a human soul to operate, it wasn't just a place to buy costumes but an experience. People were always in awe as they walked through the doors—even the employees gaped at the decor the first time they entered—but they never asked any questions about how it got there. Plus, it was nice that I didn't have to put in all the manual labor to make it happen, unlike the weeks and weeks of work when I'd been in charge of the town's annual haunted house—magic was cool like that. Too bad I didn't really have any of my own.

In the moments before the first employee arrived, I took it all in. Holiday-appropriate music played quietly overhead. The scents of plastic and cinnamon swirled in the air. Most of the shelves were already filled, and all types of costumes, from seasonal favorites like zombies and witches to more elaborate things like kings and queens, hung in every aisle. Halloween was by far the superior holiday, and now I celebrated it full-time. Some people would likely argue that Christmas mornings were the best—but no way. On Christmas once the morning was over, everything kind of settled down. Whereas with Halloween, the anticipation rose from the moment you opened your eyes—waiting for the first glimmer of darkness that lasted well into the night. On Halloween, you could be anything you wanted—no matter how old you were, costumes were always appropriate and candy was handed out freely. What wasn't fun about a fun-size Milky Way? Nothing. That was what. And today was the first day to get ready for the holiday, which meant it was the first day in a long many I got to exist at all.

As far as curses were concerned, I considered myself pretty lucky.

Questions about all the adventures that awaited me spun through my head faster than an electric mixer. Which of our regular staff would come back this year? How long would it take for them to warm up to me? How much had Clover Creek changed since last year? I could hardly wait to find out the answers.

Being Keeper of the Store was never a dull moment.

A door in the back creaked open.

It was showtime.

PEPPER

Twenty minutes later, everyone had arrived, and the energy of opening day was palpable.

"Pepper! Why does Molly get to work the prosthetic and mask counter today and I'm on general cleanup?" Caleb, one of the other Dead of Night employees, whined, his tawny skin taking on a much more pinkish tone.

Even with all the pros of this job, listening to employee complaints was definitely on the list of cons, but it was better than the complaining I had to endure before I got stuck here—at least these complaints weren't directed toward me—so it also wasn't terrible.

"Well, what did Dewy say?" I popped a few more Skittles into my mouth—breakfast of champions. The chaos had already begun as staff rushed this way and that, trying to prepare the store for this season's grand opening.

"They said I have to do general cleanup."

"So then—"

"Can't you do something about it?"

This was the common misconception that came with being the Keeper of the Store. All the staff instinctively recognized me as upper management, but I really didn't have any say in scheduling—I didn't have much say in anything at all. "Look, I know it seems like you got the short end of the stick, but what if I told you we're getting a huge shipment today and someone is going to have to count and tag every scab, scar, and wart that comes into the place?" Being Keeper, however, did mean I knew everything about the store. *Everything.*

Caleb glanced at Molly, sitting on a stool behind the glass case of fake blood and vampire teeth—dressed as an angel, her pale cheeks painted with pink hearts, a halo perched on top of her red hair, and wings secured to her back with some elastic straps—and his thick dark eyebrows rose. "General cleanup sounds amazing."

"I agree." I winked. "A few for the road?" I offered him some Skittles, and he opened his hand while I poured a pile inside.

"Taste the rainbow," he said as he shoved them all in his face, straightened his giant clown bow tie, and scampered away.

Wearing costumes was highly encouraged, but even pieces of costumes with the signature Dead of Night polo and khakis were preferred to nothing Halloween related at all.

Caleb grabbed a broom and started sweeping. He was a good kid. Even if he didn't remember me. He'd been tentative the first day he walked into the Intro to Theater class I'd taught at Clover Creek High School—he shuffled his feet and stared at the ground the entire time he introduced himself—but that didn't last long. There were those kids whose only knowledge of "theater" was a bucket of popcorn and a reclining chair, but when they got on a real stage—even the small one we had in the classroom—they bloomed right before your eyes. That was Caleb. That was also five years ago. My stomach clenched.

That was the toughest part of this job—remembering people and things about them when I was nothing but a stranger to them. There were always the awkward moments when I "knew" something they didn't think I should. But it was especially hard when I wanted to celebrate their accomplishments with them.

PEPPER

Dewy—standing there behind the register dressed as a scarecrow—had been the manager of this store for the past three years. They weren't the kind of person who trusted easily, so it took them a couple of weeks to open up. Last year they confided in me that they and their partner were looking to adopt—they hadn't told anyone about it but me. I'd been dying to know what had happened on that front since then—if anything at all—but there was no way I could straight up ask. How could I possibly know something so personal when we hadn't ever "met" before? And from experience, I knew they weren't one to share personal things with people they didn't know. So I would have to take my time with them.

Then there were people like Molly who were new to the store, but not new to the town—so while she had no idea who I was, I remembered that last year her hair was blonde, not the fiery red it was today, and that she had the most obnoxious boyfriend—who made quite a scene in the store last year. Did she finally see what the rest of us saw in him? There wasn't a ring on her finger, so that was a good sign. And did she ever register for cosmetology school like she had wanted?

So many questions I still needed to find the answers to. It was all so exciting. Nearly ten months had passed since I'd seen any of these people. Or the sky.

Looking back at how it all went down, I couldn't help but wonder if the woman who'd duped me into this got the life she wanted or what took place exactly when she passed it on to me. All I knew was that as soon as I started fulfilling my Keeper duties for the first time, the last Keeper was nowhere to be found in Clover Creek. That's one thing they don't mention in the rules—the after. So if I did break this curse, what would happen to me? To the people who knew me before? How would they reconcile the time I'd been away? Did I want to subject them to that even if it were somehow possible?

Perhaps they were all better off. One less thing to worry themselves about. I was fine before, just as I was fine now. Maybe even better in some ways. I dumped a handful of Skittles into my mouth, the mixture of flavors dancing across my tongue. Caleb was really onto something.

"What do you think, boss?" Dewy came up from behind, rubbing their hand over their head. Last year their hair had been in twisted locs; this year it was cut short and colored teal blue.

"Not your boss." I shook my head, and Dewy laughed. "Still waiting for more teen costumes, but they never decide until the last minute anyway, so I think we're in pretty good shape."

"Prosthetics are looking a little thin." They gestured toward Molly.

"Shipment should be here before noon."

"Corporate said you were good." They adjusted their name tag with the title STORE MANAGER clearly written across the top. My name tag had no title, just my name—PEPPER WHITE—not that it mattered. "I'm glad to have you around this year. It'll be nice to have the extra hands for once. New corporate initiative, is it?"

"Yep." My throat was a little thick—probably from all the Skittles. "So what's your story? Do you have any special Halloween plans this year?" Like taking a little one out for their first Halloween? It took everything in me to resist grabbing their arm and jumping up and down to find out if there was any news.

The corner of Dewy's lip tugged upward. Was that a good thing? Were they thinking about that first costume? "That's real kind of you to ask, but I know you have more important things to do than chitchat with me." They tipped their head toward some boxes that still needed to be unpacked. "We should get back to it."

"Sure," I said, but they were already walking away.

My watch chimed. It was almost opening time for us, which meant the entire town would also be opening up soon.

Everything—as chaotic as it seemed—was running on schedule. Shelves stocked, costumes hung, and the decor this year was excellent if I did say so myself.

Everyone was busy as I made my way through the back of the shop, grabbed my sweater from over one of the office chairs, and exited for the first time in 294 days.

The chilly fall breeze pushed my hair into my face as I stepped out the back door of the store. It always took me a moment to orient myself. Clover Creek wasn't a big town, but I never knew exactly where the store had set up shop for the year until leaving for the first time. A line of trees and wooden fence separated me from the back side of the town bank. To my left was Glazed & Confused, and to the right, across what had to be Apple Street, was Queenie's Burgers. Meaning we were in the old pharmacy. Did they relocate? Or did Dr. Fisher finally decide to retire?

PEPPER

Regardless, I was on the edge of downtown, so I wouldn't have to take out the "company car." Having the option was great even if I did hate driving it.

Another gust of wind sent the sugary scent from early morning apple fritters swirling around me, and I raised my arms, allowing the breeze to lift my magenta cardigan like wings. People probably thought being cursed was all bad, but one upside was that whenever I did finally get to go outside, it was always fall. My favorite season. The time for pumpkin everything, and hayrides around Baker's Farm, and hot apple cider. The time for colorful sweaters and boots and scarves. There was something special about fall. As if dormant magic woke up this time of year and it felt like anything was possible. Because for me, at least, it was.

Bing.

      Bong.

           Bing . . .

The clock started to ring. Time for me to get going. I only had seventy days to live my best life, and I couldn't wait to see what new experiences this year would hold.

PEPPER

70 DAYS
UNTIL THE STORE CLOSES

Christina

The handle on the toilet jiggles as I try to flush. Great. Just great. Next it won't flush at all, and then we'll all have to use the porta potties that haven't been delivered yet for this year's event—or they might not show up, and we'll have to cancel the haunted house altogether.

As soon as I exit the bathroom, I jot down **fix toilet handle** on my ever-growing to-do list. Patty will fix it. She can fix anything. The school is lucky to have her on staff. There's absolutely zero need to freak out. I quickly write down **confirm porta potty delivery**—just in case.

I take a deep breath. Okay, you can do this. It's just another Halloween—only the most important event that everyone expects to be wowed by, used to raise money for the arts programs at the school, and if it fails, it will be all my fault—but absolutely zero pressure. Dread rolls around deep in my stomach as I take my first real glance around the staging room for what will be this year's main Halloween attraction in Clover Creek. A tradition that brings in people from towns near and far. My high schoolers are up to the challenge—they always are—just like they have been for the nineteen years this event has taken place. The real question is, Am *I* ready this year?

As a way to signal the start of the season, I hang a special black apron with skeleton bones printed on the front from a hook on the wall, which happens to be right next to BREAK A LEG painted in bright purple with a rudimentary-looking flower. Five petals, swirly middle, nothing fancy. Not sure how the two things go together—nor have I ever bought into the breaking-a-leg thing as good luck. The historical reason is relevant, but keeping the tradition of the phrase has never really sat right with me and has my thoughts spiraling faster than Alice down the rabbit hole. Generally speaking, breaking things is bad, and let's face it, the insurance policy the school offers isn't that great.

Darn it. I stop rubbing my arm—the spot with the scar—and focus back on the task at hand.

It's time to get the initial walk-through of the house started, but, of course, I have to circle back once I'm outside because I forgot my pen inside, and it'll be extremely difficult to write a list without it.

The staging building is completely separate from the house itself—which is smart and gives us a lot more storage room to work, and a place for the kids to get ready when it comes time. It's still hard to believe that someone gave acres of land and these buildings to the school to use like this. Most haunted houses are hodgepodged together with plywood and zip ties

---

CHRISTINA

and a lot of hope that the weather holds out—at least that's my understanding of them, as I haven't made it a habit to actually go to them myself for fun or anything. But this "house" was constructed for the sole purpose of this event for the town. A gift by some well-to-do person years ago who loved Halloween way more than I do—which isn't saying much. It's not that I hate Halloween or anything, it just isn't my favorite—it's like a sugar rush: Sure, it tastes great going down, but then when it's over, you feel kind of terrible. At least that's how it's been for me, especially these last couple of years.

The last time I remember thoroughly enjoying Halloween—and not having a Halloween "hangover"—was when I was five. Mom had loaded me and my big sister, Ashley, into the car to go back-to-school shopping, and as we were driving along, Ashley called out, "I want to be Julie for Halloween."

Mom glanced at her in the rearview mirror. "It's not that time yet."

It might not have been, but as soon as the word "Halloween" was spoken, my mind swirled with ideas. The previous year, I'd been a dragon princess, and the year before that, a space cowgirl. What would I be this year?

Ashley let out a long breath. "Yeah. But that's what I want to be."

"Julie?" Mom repeated. "From that hockey movie you watch."

"*The Mighty Ducks*. Yes. Exactly. I want to be Julie."

"Whatever you want, honey," Mom said—that's what she always told us. That we could be anything we wanted to be.

Ashley smiled so big, her whole face lit up—she looked so beautiful.

CHRISTINA

"Me too," I called out. "I want to be Julie, too."

"You can't be Julie if I'm Julie," Ashley said.

I scrunched my lips real tight. If Ashley was going to be Julie, then it had to be the coolest costume, and I wanted to be cool like Ashley, but before I could say anything, Mom said, "Your sister can be whatever she wants. Plus, it'll make finding costumes easier—"

"But, Mom!" Ashley complained.

"Let's not worry about it now," she said. "School shopping first. Who needs new shoes?"

Ashley crossed her arms over her chest. "I do."

"I do, too," I said.

Mom flipped on her turn signal.

A few months later, Mom bought our costumes and got us the same trick-or-treat bags, and she even got Ashley a blonde wig—just like she had wanted.

"I want a wig, too," I had told Mom.

"You already have blonde hair," she said back, and while I was disappointed, I couldn't argue with that.

Everywhere we went that night, people asked if Ashley and I were twins, and they all gave us "a couple extra pieces" of candy for being so creative. It had been the best night ever. Dad had to carry my trick-or-treat bag with Ashley's wig all the way home because it was too heavy for me. And even though Ashley was too tired to look at her candy, Mom and Dad let me stay up late, and I laid all my goodies out on the living room floor, dividing them into chocolate and not chocolate and giving all the Whoppers to Dad because those are disgust-

---

CHRISTINA

ing, but it wasn't the same without Ashley. She didn't trade me my Reese's for her Milky Way. We didn't play dress-up in our costumes for the weeks to follow. We didn't talk about that night at all again.

A lingering scent that's both sweet and acrid at the same time mixed with the stagnant smell of a house sitting unused for months greets me as I enter the haunted house and wander from room to room, leaving my memories behind. I've got too much work to do, and thinking about the past isn't going to help me with this task in the present.

It seems like last year's cleanup crew did a good job, and the fresh spiderwebs in the corners really help add to the overall ambiance— Oh god, please don't let any unwelcome friends come home with me. I should've double-checked where I left my purse. *Maybe have the house treated for bugs?* I quickly jot that note down and continue on my way.

All in all, everything seems to be in order. Most of the lights still work, there isn't any visible damage, and there isn't even a single candy wrapper on the floor. I'm finishing up when my phone pings.

> **EMILY:** Still waiting on your RSVP
>
> **EMILY:** You ARE planning on coming, right?

My little sister's engagement party. In a few short weeks, she will be announcing officially to all our family and friends that she's getting married. Making me *officially* the spinster of

---

CHRISTINA

the Loring household. She's happy, and I love that for her. I just wish it didn't have to mean that I will once again be the disappointment.

Why can't you be more like your sister? Don't you have an architecture degree? Why are you teaching high school? Haven't you found a boyfriend yet? That last one always annoys me the most. My entire family knows I'm bi.

> **ME:** This is my busiest couple months, but I'll try

It isn't as though we haven't talked endlessly about my job and all the extra hours I do that I don't get paid for. She also knows all about this event and how important it is. I enjoy teaching and it's rewarding, but it isn't easy like everyone likes to assume—usually those are people who have never set foot in a classroom and have never been responsible for twenty-plus hormonal teens.

> **EMILY:** Titi! I need my big sister there!

Even in text I can hear the whine in her voice. She always knows how using her special nickname for me makes me feel.

> **ME:** I'll do my best.
>
> **EMILY:** Ashley is going to make a speech, and Mom thinks you should too

And there it is. Another reason I don't want to go. Not that I don't love my big sister. I just hate what our relationship has

---

CHRISTINA

become. And the worst part is that it doesn't have to be this way.

I love both of my sisters; that's never been the question, and I would do anything for either of them. But if I let the thoughts about Em's engagement sit in my stomach, they'll curdle like sour milk. I can count on one hand the number of serious relationships I've been in. Something always seems to go wrong before anything turns long-term, but for the few times they did, none of them lasted: I'm too ambitious, or I'm not ambitious enough; I work too hard, or I need to focus less on my career. It seems no matter what I did or didn't do, the common denominator was always the same: me. What is it about me that makes me so unlovable? I wish I knew so I could change it. Actually, I wish someone could love me for who I am—flaws and all. But what if they don't like me that way either?

I'd give anything to find my person.

Instead of responding to Em, I take a breath, slide my phone into my pocket, and go back to my lists. There's comfort in them—in creating something that I can check off one by one—a sense of accomplishment, and right now I could use that.

There are so many things to build and buy. The endless revolving questions about everything that needs to be done spiral in my head, unlike the toilet drain because of that broken handle.

We haven't picked out a theme yet, but knowing my students, it'll be something wonderfully disgusting. That's another reason why I'm not a super-fan of Halloween. All the blood and guts—ironic that I'm in charge of the haunted house.

CHRISTINA

There are enough things in the real world to be afraid of; I don't need someone jumping out at me from the dark in a mask to do the job. At least being a part of the planning process means I know all the jump scares before they happen.

I add fake blood to my list of basic items for the event. Whatever we do, it will include the gelatinous goop—that I'm positive of.

My alarm goes off, reminding me if I don't get started on the shopping now, I'll be eating dinner at nine o'clock again. My memory has been getting worse these last couple years and always seems to be worse around Halloween. Maybe it's just the joys of getting older, or perhaps it's the impending stress of the upcoming holidays, or it could be all the added stress of this event; but whatever the reason, lists and alarms are a must to keep me on track.

I look around one last time and let out a long sigh. Why did I ever think I should be a high school theater teacher?

CHRISTINA

70 DAYS

UNTIL THE STORE CLOSES

Pepper

At Patty's Pancake Parlor, I gorged myself on perfect pumpkin-pecan pancakes with cinnamon and bourbon maple syrup, and then slowly made my way back to the store, trying to take in as much of the town as I could along the way. It always amazed me how much the trees seemed to grow year after year but many of the buildings and the people stayed the same. How did those Keepers in big cities do it? Places where things changed so rapidly, and people were constantly moving around. At least here there was still a lot of stability from season to season.

Tina's Hair Salon was still painted bright pink with a flower box under its large picture window. The cow statue still stood on the corner outside the local supermarket. And Simply Stationery seemed to be under new ownership, with a new name—Classy Quill. I couldn't wait to check it out, but there would be plenty of time to explore later.

Part of my "job" was giving off the illusion that I was part of the team, so this meant actually working and putting in some face time with customers when all I really wanted to do was basically anything else. Not that the job or the people were terrible or anything; just with limited time, there were a million other things to do.

I grabbed a caramel apple cider on my way back and savored it until it turned cold while I puttered around the store, trying to look busy.

"Okay, who left the body in aisle five?" Dewy walked toward the front registers dragging a mannequin by the leg and a CAUTION WET FLOOR sign.

Caleb raced forward and took the body from them. "I was coming back for it. That's why I left the sign, but I got sidetracked." Meaning he decided to help Molly with some of the inventory he hated doing instead of taking care of his cleanup duties—which, to be fair, also wasn't his favorite, but he preferred it over anything with counting. Not that I could blame the kid. Molly was a sweet girl, they were close in age, and they were both interested in the film industry.

"Sign or not, it's a tripping hazard," Dewy scolded. "Where did this come from anyway?"

"I found it in the back. And I was thinking, there's that space between yard decorations and the"—he cleared his throat—"adult section that was looking kind of bare. I thought I could set something up. I probably should've asked first, though."

Dewy glanced at me, and I raised my eyebrows in response. "That's taking some good initiative," they said. "It would be best to run your ideas by management first, but I like the enthusiasm."

"Really?" Caleb asked as he hoisted the mannequin over his shoulder.

"Really," Dewy confirmed. "If you want, I have a moment now. We can discuss it."

"Sure, that'd be great." Caleb nodded.

"Some not-so-great news, though," Dewy continued. "Our newbie is a no-show, so we'll be one person down this afternoon."

"That's boosheet," Lisa said, and she swooped her black hair up and under a bubblegum pink wig for her shift. Ever since she was reprimanded for swearing within earshot of customers a few seasons ago, she'd gotten creative.

Dewy let out a deep breath. "It's not ideal, but we can manage, right, team?"

"Yes!" Caleb enthusiastically answered.

"We'll be fine," I said. First day and already a no-show; this was going to be an interesting season.

As Dewy and Caleb scampered away, I pulled some more receipt paper from the register and kept doodling. There'd been a steady stream of customers, but Lisa had everything under control, so I used my time to make a list of all the things I wanted to do in the next seventy days. Then I listed all the places I wanted to eat—which was just as important—and when I was done with that, I started to draw—not that I was any good at it—to pass the time until I could officially leave for the day and check some things off my new lists.

Ah. Ha, ha, ha, ha, ha. The cackling witch—the trademark

sound of The Dead of Night no matter where the store was located—sounded at the front door as a group of teens pushed their way inside. They were loud and rowdy the way teenagers were. One ducked behind another at the sight of dancing skeletons that greeted people when they entered. Theater kids. I smiled. It was always easy to pick them out of a crowd; they had a way of making everything overdramatic, and I loved them for it.

It was one of the things I missed most from my life before. Teaching theater at Clover Creek had been my dream job—one I never would've left by choice. The kids were always the thing that made every workday better. Their creativity and enthusiasm were contagious. There was nothing like the buzz that energized a cast from curtain up and lasted longer than the final curtain call. Planning and running the town haunted house was a bonus. Even before all of this, Halloween had been my favorite holiday, and there was nothing more invigorating than a good jump scare.

Seeing them now also reminded me that I could officially leave for the day and not feel guilty about it.

"Caleb's got some good ideas," Dewy said, pulling me out of my head and back into the store. When I didn't respond, they said, "His plan for near the back."

"Yeah, right," I said.

"It's pretty elaborate, but I think it's going to make an impact."

"We seem to be good up here. Why don't I see how I can help him before I take off for the day," I told them before crinkling up the receipt paper I'd doodled all over and shoving it in my pocket—it looked like Caleb also forgot to bring the trashcans back up front.

"That'd be great. I've gotta shift the schedule around now, it seems." Dewy rolled their eyes.

The no-show, right. Yeah. I was glad I didn't have to do any of that work. Setting up a display wasn't as satisfying as putting together the annual haunted house, but it was at least something I enjoyed.

I turned down aisle five to make my way toward the back of the store when I slammed into someone. The woman stumbled backward, fumbling the package in her hand. Her crisp black shirt and slacks screamed banker or executive of some kind. Her hair hung just below her ears and was so blonde, it was almost white. Aside from the red lipstick that was carefully applied over full, pouty lips, she looked like she was ready to attend a funeral or a board meeting more than go on a shopping excursion—but it ironically was very Halloween appropriate. "I'm so sorry," I said.

"No, it's my fault. I wasn't looking. My kids . . . Well, not *my* kids, I don't have any kids, but I'm a teacher, right? So my students are here and . . ." She glanced at the pumpkin-spice-flavored lube in her hand, and her face flushed to the color of her lips.

"And this isn't a product you are wanting to purchase," I finished for her.

"No, it's not. Not that there's anything wrong with it or anything, I actually really like pumpkin spice, even though

---

PEPPER

an ex-girlfriend said it made me basic, but whatever, I just don't need it." Her ears turned red, too, which was just adorable. "You didn't need to know all of that about me. I'll shut up now."

I held out my hand. "I can take care of it for you if you'd like."

"Yes, please." She handed it to me. "You don't sell shovels, do you?" She laughed nervously.

"Not functional ones, but on aisle three—"

"No." She shook her head. "It was a joke. Like I should probably just dig a hole in the ground and crawl inside . . . Never mind." Her cheeks got red again, and she glanced at the ground.

"That's funny," I said.

She lifted her head, her brown eyes locking with mine, and my heartbeat tripped over itself. "You're just being nice."

"Maybe." I smiled.

She smiled back.

Then we both started laughing.

She rested her hand on a cart full of plastic pumpkins and fairy lights and a bale of faux hay. Did Caleb leave this here when he forgot his mannequin? What was this plan of his? "I'm not usually this awkward," she said. "I'm just a little out of my element."

"Oh, this cart is yours." My voice sounded as surprised as I was.

"I'm getting stuff for the haunted house."

The haunted house. In this town there was only one. "Wait. You're the theater teacher at Clover Creek?" The last few years it had been Harold Wetherby—a bald guy who wore suspenders and insisted people call him Dr. W. Granted, he was a little overly enthusiastic about almost everything, but it was kind of sweet. What happened to him?

"I am." She scrunched her brow. "I guess that's common knowledge around these parts."

Shit. Being a local no one knew was really hard to explain, which was why I normally didn't fuck up this badly. "They mentioned it in a meeting. Said to be on the lookout and to help however we can."

"Oh, thank god." She let out a breath. "I've never done anything like this before. I actually don't really like Halloween that much, so I'm in a little over my head."

I held up a hand. "I'm sorry. You don't like Halloween?" How had this woman gotten the job, doing the most important event in Clover Creek, when she didn't even like Halloween?

"It's just never been my thing." She shrugged.

I glanced at her and all the random items she had picked up, and I pinched my lips together. "I'm going to pretend you didn't say that and help you out." I took the cart and pushed it into the main aisle to get it out of the way. "First, let's start over."

"So no pumpkin-spice lube, then?" She smiled.

"The candy apple flavor is much better," I said, and those cheeks of hers flared red once again. Did they feel as hot as they looked? Instead of reaching out to touch one—which would've been completely inappropriate; what the hell was I thinking?—I said, "Come on. I got you."

I led her back to the front, where we each grabbed an empty cart to get her started off on the right foot. "I know I said I wouldn't bring it up, but I gotta know. How does someone who hates Halloween get this job?"

She chewed on her bottom lip. "Honestly?" She glanced around. "No one else applied. I guess this teacher shortage thing is a really big problem."

Ouch. "But I'm sure they wouldn't hire you just because of that. I bet you have some awesome qualities. Where have you taught before?"

"Nowhere."

I blinked at her. You needed certificates and training. What the hell happened in the last year that created this big of a problem that they would hire anyone to teach kids? Granted, I didn't follow politics much—especially since I wasn't able to vote anymore—but still. Teaching was an important job. It couldn't be left to just anyone to do. Not that she didn't look professional; she just didn't look like a teacher.

"It's temporary, for now. Unless I take some classes—which I'm doing—and then finish all the requirements, and then it'll become permanent." She let out a breath. "I didn't know what I wanted to do. I needed a change, and when I saw all the news about needing teachers, I wanted to help. And the kids are great. I love them, and I minored in theater in college." She shifted from one foot to the other—her black oxfords were stunning and expensive. If there was one thing I knew, it was shoes, and those were direct from Europe.

"I'm sorry," I said. "I'm interrogating you. That's not cool. I'm sure you're an amazing teacher even if Halloween isn't your favorite." I straightened my name tag. "I do know a thing or two about Halloween and haunted houses so I can help." And god, could she use it! Her next two months were going to be jam-packed with everything about the holiday, so she needed to be prepared—and she also needed some clothes she could get paint on, but that wasn't something I could help her with.

"That would be great, Pepper White." She gestured to my pin. "I'm Christina Loring."

I grinned. "Well, Ms. Loring, it's nice to meet you."

"Christina's fine. I'm still not used to the kids calling me Ms. Loring. I keep looking for my mother." She giggled, and it fluttered in my chest.

"Are you ready for this?"

Her brown eyes lit up, like this was the lifeline she needed. "I'm so ready." She reached into her purse—also designer—and pulled out a piece of paper. "I started a list." She seemed tentative about handing it over.

Things for the haunted house was scrawled at the top.

> *Pumpkins*
>
> *Hay*
>
> *Candles? (Or is this a fire hazard?)*
>
> *Twinkle lights*
>
> *Spiderwebs*
>
> *Fake bugs*
>
> *Fake blood (I can buy this, right?)*

PEPPER

> Fog machine? (Does it make fog itself or does something go in it?)
>
> Body parts? (Can you buy fake body parts? Or do I need to get a mannequin and chop it up?)

I laughed. Oh, she was completely in over her head. "Sorry. It's the questions you left yourself."

Her cheeks flared red again. I didn't think I could ever get tired of seeing that.

"This is a great start. And yes, you do put stuff in fog machines, candles are a fire hazard, and we can find you fake blood and body parts."

"So you're saying I didn't completely fail, I just failed a little." Her lips bunched up on one side in a shy kind of smile, which looked so cute on her face. As ill-prepared as she was, she was trying, and I had to give her an A for effort.

"Not at all." I shook my head at her. "I'd give you a B-plus," I added.

"In that case, let's do this." She gripped the handle of her cart. Her determination reminded me of myself during my first year of teaching. Maybe she'd be cut out for this after all.

An hour later, Lisa and I worked on two different registers to get Christina all checked out. She didn't have everything she would need, but this would be a good start for the task she had ahead of her. I told her they "probably already had a fog machine, but knowing kids, they'd likely used all the juice up for it." Oh, how I remembered they were never happy unless the whole house looked like it had been set on fire because of all the fog from that thing. I was able to offer her a very generous discount. The exact thing the last Keeper did for me, but this wouldn't end the same way for Christina—I'd make sure of it.

"I can't thank you enough," she said. "Both of you."

"Don't worry about it," Lisa responded. "That's what we're here for." She must've been gunning for the Prestigious Pumpkin Award—a bonus of two thousand dollars that was given out at the end of each season for the most outstanding employee. I didn't need it, that was for sure.

"If you don't mind, what is that smell? Like cinnamon or something?"

I lifted my very cold and mostly empty paper cup, which I'd left at the register earlier. "Could it be my caramel apple cider?"

She took a big sniff and closed her eyes for a moment. "That's it. I didn't know Déjà Brew made those."

"It's not officially on the menu, but if you ask, they'll make it for you."

"You've been here less time than I have and already have this town figured out better than me. Any other secrets you want to share? Or is there a book at The Book Burrow that I missed or something that could tell me about this town?" She leaned forward, setting her elbows on the counter and resting her head on her hands.

"Brew's is the best; don't go to that other place—which shall not be named," Lisa jumped in, thankfully. I can't believe I almost messed up *twice*. Put a cute girl in front of me and suddenly I've completely lost myself. "Take It Cheesy has the best tachos— Oh, if you don't know what that is, it's basically loaded nachos using tater tots instead of chips. They're amazing, and a local favorite. And Peach Street Boutique gives discounts to residents all through Halloween—you just have to show your ID."

"Those are really helpful, thanks," Christina said as she handed her card over to Lisa to finish her second transaction. I had already finished my half. Then it was quiet for a moment.

I glanced down. Oh, shit. Without realizing it, I'd doodled all over her receipt. "I'm sorry." I folded the paper in half. "I wasn't thinking. Let me print you a new one. I'm sure you'll want these to submit for reimbursement."

She looked at me a second like she was considering what I said. "Oh yeah. I guess I can do that."

"I can help you down here," Lisa said to the following person in line as she shifted to the next register over. It would take Christina a moment to get all her stuff. Yep. Lisa wanted that extra cash. Not that I could blame her.

"I think I heard that there's a special account for the haunted house." They'd set aside money each year from what the haunted house brought in to help fund it for the next year, and all the rest was used for other theater and arts programs. As much fun as the haunted house was, it was also the biggest fundraiser the school had, and many of the classes there needed the extra funding. Some years there wasn't enough in the budget to get all the things the kids wanted for the event, and I'd dipped into my own account on a number of occasions to help cover expenses—hoping we'd make it up in the end.

I handed her the new receipt and shoved the old one in the

bag sitting on the counter since the trashcan still hadn't made an appearance.

"Thanks," she said again.

"We'll be here all Halloween if you need anything else." And she would. She'd make at least a dozen trips here over the course of the season—it was inevitable.

"No. No. No," a frantic mom said as her little one tore open a pack of gobstopper "eyeballs" and sent them scattering all over the floor.

"See you around," I said to Christina before heading off to help the mom clean up.

"I'm so sorry," the mom was saying as her little one plucked one of the eyeballs off the floor and popped it in their mouth. "It's not free candy." She sighed.

I stifled a laugh. "Happens all the time." Okay, so that was a lie, but the relief that washed over the woman's face made it one worth telling.

With the two of us on the job, we had the mess cleaned up in no time. I dumped the candy into my pocket to throw away later and headed back up to the register. Sitting on the counter Lisa had been working at before was one of Christina's bags.

Shoot.

I grabbed it and took off.

Maybe I could still catch her.

PEPPER

70 DAYS

UNTIL THE STORE CLOSES

Christina

My great attempt at playing Tetris with all the things I purchased from all the different places is turning into a ginormous failure as I stare at my car in the parking lot in front of the Halloween store. Why I thought I could do this all in one trip, I'll never know. I should invest in a pickup truck.

"Hey, you left this." The woman who just helped me in The Dead of Night runs out of the shop with a bag in her hand. She looks like she should be on the front of a sugary cereal box or on the cover of some kind of beauty magazine, not working at a Halloween store full of creepy clowns and decomposing body parts—even if they are fake. Her bright sweater and the mix and match prints of her top and skirt do not in any way go with her place of employment—although the tiara is a nice touch, even if she doesn't look like any princess I've seen before. The only thing that truly seems on point is the color of her hair—black as ink. "I'm glad I caught you," she says, a little breathless. PEPPER WHITE, her name tag reads—that's right. Not sure how I could forget such a contradictory name as that. Then again . . .

"I'd lose my head if it weren't attached some days." I laugh. Real smooth, Christina. Why don't you just admit to this total stranger that you are a complete and utter disaster?

"No worries. I got you," she says. Her hand grazes mine as she passes over the bag, sending gooseflesh rippling up my arm. She gives me a tentative smile. "You have quite the conundrum here, it seems." She gestures to my car.

The wood I swear I'd secured to my roof has somehow taken a tumble, and part of it has fallen forward onto the hood, and a few other pieces have slipped behind, blocking me from being able to get into my trunk. Which doesn't matter much anyway, seeing as it's full of paint cans. "You know the hardware store guy could've delivered this for you, right?"

Ritchie mentioned that, but I didn't want to take any chances. "He seemed busy, and I thought it'd be easier . . ." I'm wrong. As usual. Maybe I can leave some here and come back for it.

She reaches her hand into her pocket and pulls out a couple of keys with a very unique key chain that sparkles in the dwindling sunlight. "If you want, *I* can help. There's plenty of room in the company car."

I shift my gaze away from Pepper and the mess in front of me to a bird perched in a tree nearby. It quietly tucks its head under its wing. Same, bird. Same. "You don't have to. I'm sure I can figure this out. Do you think anyone would take this if I left it here for a little while?" I kick one of the boards and it

---

CHRISTINA

falls to the ground with a loud *slap*, almost hitting Pepper in the process.

I jump back, but she doesn't react even though it scared the bejesus out of me. Can I make this any more awkward? It seems the answer is yes. She watches me with her denim blue eyes—her eye shadow shimmers more out here than it did under the fluorescent lights of the store, and her peach skin glows. Peaches are one of the sweetest fruits . . . Get it together, Christina. I tug the sleeve of my jacket.

"I bet you could figure it out. You seem like a really intelligent woman. I mean, you did just make a lot of smart purchases for your event." She looks at the bags from the store. "But truly, it's no trouble at all."

I glance from her to the mess. It would save me so much time, and I wouldn't have to worry about anyone taking this wood until I could come back for it. My budget is already tight enough for this event. I can't waste it rebuying things I've already purchased. Plus, she's being so nice, and her compliment—no matter how small—warms my insides, which is a sensation I haven't felt in a long time. "If you're sure." I let out a breath of relief.

"Let me just . . ." She points toward the store as some college-age boy in khakis and a polo sprints across the parking lot. "You're late!" she yells at him, before turning back to me. "Just give me a second." She winks, and my cheeks immediately heat up. I hate that my face is a neon sign announcing my emotions—but there's no controlling it.

"Of course, no problem," I say as she walks away.

My futile attempt at making the situation better only makes

CHRISTINA

things worse by the time Pepper pulls into the parking place next to mine. She wasn't kidding about the company car having room—although I wasn't expecting a hearse. A truck maybe, but then again it *is* a Halloween store. THE DEAD OF NIGHT is painted across the side, and a fake hand hangs out of the back.

"Nice wheels," I tell her as she climbs out.

She flashes a grin. "If you like this, you'll love how spacious it is."

My cheeks flare once again. She means for the wood—for hauling things around, so why did that comment make me feel like a teenager getting caught making out with my high school boyfriend in his car?

She opens the back—and just like she said, it's quite spacious. Not that I've seen inside any hearses before, but this one is plush—you could even say cozy—with deep red carpeting and bloodred curtains, which I suppose you could close for privacy if you wanted. But why would someone in a hearse need privacy? I glance at Pepper, who still has that smile on her lips, and my face feels like it's on fire. Oh, I wish it was just, like, a hot flash. That would be easier to explain. How old are people when they go through menopause? It's older than early thirties, right?

"Got a lot on your mind?" she asks.

"Always. I'm sorry." I reach down to pick up one edge of a board, and Pepper goes to reach for the other side.

"Want to talk about it?" She asks it so casually like we're already friends, and even though we've just barely met, I want to answer her.

CHRISTINA

"You ever have that thing where you start thinking about one thing and then you're thinking about something completely different, and you aren't even sure how you got there?"

She chuckles to herself and nods. "I think we all do that."

I laugh with her. It comes so easily. "Yeah, maybe."

"So what was it about?" she asks as we keep lifting the wood and sliding it into the back of the hearse.

"Menopause," I say.

"You're a long way off from that," she says without missing a beat.

I stop for a moment and look at her. "How would you know? I could just look very young for my age."

She shakes her head like she doesn't believe me. Which of course she shouldn't. "You showed your ID in the store when you used your credit card."

Did I? I guess it does say "C-ID" with my signature—not that anyone really ever asks, but it does happen occasionally, and it's not like I've been great at paying attention today—the failure to secure all these boards is evidence enough of that.

"It's bullshit, though, what we have to go through," she says.

I tilt my head. Oh, menopause. That's right. "For sure. Bleeding and cramps every single month—which started for me when I was ten—and then it's hot flashes and who knows what else. Hormone therapy?" I shrug.

"I honestly haven't looked into all the details yet."

"I know, why, right? Like, it's not something to look forward to. I think I'd rather be unhappily surprised when it all starts happening."

CHRISTINA

She nods. "There are upsides, too, though."

"Upsides to being closer to death?" I brush some hair that's fallen in my face out of the way from our strenuous activity. "*This* I've got to hear."

"I mean upsides to being a girl. Like we smell better. And we have so many more shopping options—"

"And all the guilt because we don't fit into a certain size pants." I laugh, but Pepper doesn't join me.

"Every body is beautiful," she says without a hint of sarcasm or irony in her voice. "We should never measure our self-worth by some number inside our pants or on a scale."

I blink a few times. "You're right." She is. Even if I am guilty of doing just that, but it's easier said than done. And likely a lot easier for someone who radiates sunshine from her pores—does she even have any pores? And someone who smells like incense and vanilla—she's right about that, too; girls smell much better.

That grin of hers is back, and it releases a swarm of moths in my stomach. Did I eat lunch today? Tuna salad. Or wait, was that yesterday?

She giggles like she knows I'm once again not focused on the task at hand, and to be fair, I'm not—I'm just standing here while she holds the last of the boards on one side. "Not still menopause?"

"Food," I say.

"I'd love to have dinner with you," she says, and my stomach launches itself up into my throat. "How do you feel about tacos?" she asks like it really isn't a question—and to be fair, she's right yet again.

CHRISTINA

"How does anyone feel about tacos? Very positively, of course."

"Good. I know a place." She slams the back door of the hearse and jingles her keys. "Wanna follow me?"

Her blue eyes are wide like she's hoping I'll say yes. How did this even happen? I didn't technically ask her out, and she didn't technically ask me, but here we are. I glance between my car and her again. I have so much work to do—not with just the haunted house but I have grades and dishes and—so much that if I don't get it all done, who knows what kind of shit will hit the fan. But she's looking at me with beautiful, hopeful eyes, and my heart is pushing me to say yes, which is in direct conflict with my head. "Is it far?" I ask.

Her eyebrows raise. "Don't worry. I got you." Her lips curl up on one side, and my heart skips a beat.

I really shouldn't. I have so much to do, but—those eyes, that smile—I say, "Okay," anyway.

CHRISTINA

70 DAYS
UNTIL THE STORE CLOSES

Pepper

While technically a "small town," the city of Clover Creek was actually pretty big and had basically everything anyone could want or need without having to leave. I loved driving through the streets as the sun was setting—a blanket of night settling over the quaint city like it was telling people it was time to slow down, take it easy, and relax for the night. I had no plans of relaxing yet, but the sentiment alone warmed my soul in a way I'd been yearning for over the past ten months.

There were so many things I had wanted to do, but sometimes it was hard to decide where to begin. Tacos felt like a good start. There was a place I loved to get them at, but would it still be in the same location? Changes didn't happen often in Clover Creek, but when they did, there wasn't anything I could do about them. But it also meant that each Halloween season was like an exploration. What new hidden gem of Clover Creek would I find this time around?

The light on the corner of Plum and Kale turned red, so I eased to a stop. It took me all of ten seconds living here to understand that fruit streets ran east to west and vegetable streets ran north to south. According to Mrs. Turner, the school librarian, a long time ago this had all been farmland—or at least much of it was—although they didn't grow all the things these streets were named after.

It had been a little over five years ago that on the corner here there had been Earl of Grey—a little tea place that tried to re-create that British feeling of a "posh"-style tea at any time of day. They had these little cucumber sandwiches and petit fours that were all ridiculously overpriced, and the host was always dressed in a tuxedo complete with white gloves and a top hat and tails. That should've been my first clue. No one who didn't really want something in return would take a stranger there, but that was exactly where Kitty Jones had wanted to meet—her treat, she said, and I had wanted to check the place out, so I agreed. After all, what could be the harm?

"Isn't this place adorable," Kitty had said when I walked inside. She stood and pulled me into a friendly hug. It wasn't the first time I'd talked to her or met her out and about in town. I'd gone to The Dead of Night so many times that year, we were practically best friends. I just didn't know that she had already known me so well. Probably for at least the three years I'd been in this town—not that I remembered her.

The reason we were even having that silly high tea was because she had confided in me about her family and the stories she told—oh, how I could relate. Her situation sounded similar to mine—the whole reason I had moved to Clover Creek to begin with, hoping the space would help give me some peace, but it didn't. Kitty had to have known.

"It's so nice to see you," I told her as I took a seat. She was wearing a plain T-shirt and pressed slacks. Her mousy brown hair was pulled up and away from her face.

"Yeah, this is what I look like when not at work." She laughed a real hearty sincere kind of laugh. Her attire was a far departure from the costumes she'd been wearing all season. They were all quite elaborate affairs, too. Willy Wonka, the Queen of Hearts, and her rendition of Glinda the Good Witch should've been the biggest clue as to who she really was.

"I bet this is more comfortable," I said. I took advantage of getting to dress up more than usual and sported my tulle pastel pink tea-length skirt and black-and-white polka-dot top, complete with elbow-length gloves and a vintage flower fascinator. It was cute, and when would I ever have the chance to wear something like that again? Well, except for on Halloween, of course—but it was fancier than a costume, so it completely worked for this occasion.

"My family wants me to move home," she said abruptly as she poured us both a cup of tea, the scent of orange, cinnamon, and clove escaping as the clear amber liquid filled the cups.

I couldn't help myself, and after removing my gloves and laying them fashionably on the table, I immediately reached for a little pink confectionary and took a bite. White cake with a strawberry and white chocolate filling was my reward. Perhaps the British were really onto something with this whole afternoon tea thing. "What did you tell them?"

PEPPER

"That they need to let me live my life. I know they mean well and all, but I'm happy here. This seems like a great place to live, you know. And I'm sure once the season is over, I'll be able to get a job."

That was what she had told me. It was her first year in Clover Creek, and she fell in love with it the moment she got there to help open the store. Again, I knew the feeling. Clover Creek had so quickly become my home, so nothing she said made me question her. "Didn't you say you had marketing experience? I think Grant Lai could probably use some help."

Being a teacher allowed me to know a little more about the town and who all lived there since I'd see their families at open houses, and the yearly haunted house, and all the performances my students did throughout the year.

"The owner of By Association?" she asked, and I nodded. "You really think?" Kitty's eyes grew two sizes. That should've been another clue that something was wrong with her. Her facial features were small, almost ratlike, and her name, "Kitty," I bet that wasn't real either. But it was a happy, friendly name. Who doesn't trust a mousy girl with a name like Kitty? "You don't think it would be weird to talk to him about it?"

"Nah," I said. "Plus, then we could do stuff like this"—I gestured to the little spread in front of us—"more often." I had thought I was welcoming her to town the way people at the school had welcomed me when I first got here. I had thought she could be a good friend—and if I had been really honest, I did like her, a lot.

"That would be fun, wouldn't it?" Her smile was too big on her face, but I didn't notice that then; I just smiled back.

PEPPER

"My mother told me I need to find a therapist." I rolled my eyes.

"Is she still on about that?" Kitty took a sip of her tea, pinkie finger extended.

"Always." I followed her lead and took a sip, too. Needed sugar—so I grabbed a couple cubes and dropped them into my teacup. "But I'm fine. It's been years now, and I'm just fine. She thinks it's weird that I never broke down and sobbed for weeks and weeks like she did."

"Not everyone handles grief the same way."

"That's what I told her." That was what I'd been telling Mom for years, so the fact that Kitty repeated those exact words should've hoisted the red flag all the way up the flagpole, but in the moment I felt vindicated.

"It's like you wish they could just forget about it for at least a couple days, am I right?"

"Exactly. Like, can we talk about anything else for once?" I shook my head. Sure, Mom and I had other conversations, but it always came back around to that one thing—Mitchell.

"I might be able to help with that," Kitty said.

I laughed. "Are you a witch now?"

She grinned. "Didn't I tell you?" She laughed with me.

"Excellent. Then you can cast a forgetful spell on my mother." I played along. "Maybe get me the winning lotto numbers, too, while you're at it."

"Midnight, November second, at the store. Be there," she said.

"Sure," I said.

"I'm serious," she told me.

PEPPER

I shrugged. "Fine. What have I got to lose anyway? You break out the Ouija board, and I'll bring the sangria."

Her smile seemed real—it wasn't forced or fake. "Perfect."

A light horn tap brought me back to the street corner where Earl of Grey wasn't anymore and now stood a bakery with perfect cupcakes in the window. I'd never been inside.

I waved, signaling I got the message, and pressed on the gas.

I'm sure the cupcakes there were fine—better than fine since that store had been there a few years now. A much more reasonable option than a "posh" tea shop in a small town where espresso was definitely king.

The pumpkin patch was ahead of me now, and then there'd be the haunted house. So many memories of that place and the hours I'd spent there swirled in my head. Now it was Christina's job to ring in the holiday. A girl who said she didn't even like Halloween.

I might not be remembered, but no one in town would forget if this year's haunted house was a flop. It would ruin the holiday for everyone, and what would that mean for fundraising efforts in years to come? People counted on the haunted house and what it did for Clover Creek.

No. It couldn't fail. I couldn't let that happen. Halloween was too important to Clover Creek.

I had to do something about it.

PEPPER

70 DAYS
UNTIL THE STORE CLOSES

Christina

The sun is starting to touch the tops of the distant mountains as I follow Pepper and her Dead of Night hearse through town and past the haunted house—where I should be going but I'm not because a pretty girl said "tacos," and, well, who am I to refuse an offer like that?

I'm getting way ahead of myself as usual. She's probably hungry and doesn't know anyone else in town but the people she works with, and they're all obviously working so why not ask out the lonely-looking girl? I don't look lonely, do I? Note to self: Make that hair appointment. Maybe I should get bangs. Or maybe I should let my hair grow out longer. Right now, it sweeps along the tops of my shoulders, the color of tofu. Maybe I should consider dyeing it?

I check my reflection in the rearview mirror. Sure, a trim would be nice, but there's nothing glaringly wrong about my appearance, and luckily there isn't anything stuck in my teeth. Wouldn't that have been the icing on the cake?

Even though this is probably a case of being the closest available person when the hunger urge hit her, at least I won't be having cereal for dinner, so I guess I should consider that the upside. Knowing my luck, I'll probably end up with food poisoning, though, and I do *not* have time for that.

Why do I insist on doing this to myself? A question I likely will never know the answer to unless I get that therapist my best friend and colleague, Cami, says I need, but I haven't had time to look into it yet.

The last time I'd even been out to a meal with anyone had been with Cami a couple of weeks ago. She'd gotten one of her pregnancy cravings—this time for Thai food—and those are something you never want to stand in the way of.

"What do you mean, you've never had mango sticky rice before? How have you never had it?" she had asked me as we walked up Persimmon Street.

"I don't know. I guess I didn't know it was a thing until just now," I told her.

"*You* of all people? I thought dessert was your thing." She swept her long, thick, dark hair back and wrapped it up with a clip as we passed the ice cream shop—the purple neon light reflecting off her stark white top. It was unseasonably warm for an autumn evening. I was glad I hadn't even bothered doing anything with my own hair, instead wearing a baseball cap.

"Is fruit really dessert, though?" I asked.

At this she paused and spun around to look at me just as we'd gotten to the restaurant. The streetlight above us flick-

---

CHRISTINA

ered. "Fair point. But we're getting it." She grabbed the handle and stumbled forward before jerking it back. "I hate this door." She laughed.

"Or we could go get ice cream," I countered.

"Or both." She held the door open for me to walk inside.

That night Cami had taken the lead and had done all the ordering for us. Tonight, I don't even know where Pepper and I are going. Will I like the food? Will I freeze up when it's time to give my order like I did on the last date I went on? It'll definitely be weird if I turn around now, so I take a deep breath and keep driving.

A dusky sky and a crisp breeze greet me as I step out of my car on the far edge of Clover Creek. I've never been over this way before—pretty much everything I ever need is right downtown. Off the side of the road nestled among towering redwoods is a quaint little taco truck that has a healthy line waiting outside, a few picnic tables, and strings and strings of twinkle lights. It's actually kind of romantic in a way. But that is definitely *not* what this is—I haven't dated in years, and I'm sure it's not this easy. Other teachers in the lounge are always talking about the cesspool that is dating these days and how hard it is, so this definitely can't be that. I shake my head.

"Holy Guacamole," I say as Pepper comes up to meet me, my voice a little more high-pitched than usual. A sign nearby announces: SAME GREAT FOOD, NEW LOCATION. Maybe that's why I've never heard of it before. "Why'd you park so far away?"

She quirks her brow up at me. "Would *you* want to eat anywhere a hearse was parked out in front of?"

CHRISTINA

"Fair point. But it's got the store name on it."

She shrugs. "It'll be easier to get out. Now come on, I'm starving."

See—she's just hungry. I don't know why I work myself up so much.

Our feet crackle against the gravel and dried leaves as we make our way across the lot. Another breeze rushes past, this time bringing with it the smell of an array of spices and cooking onions. Aside from the truck, though, there's nothing around. No houses or stores. It's almost as remote as you can get. I assumed she was new to town—I've never seen her before today, but no one's told me about this place. Not that I have that many friends, but still. The word has obviously gotten around from the queue that's gathered.

"Lisa at the store said I had to come here," she says like she can read my mind. "Said they have the best tacos and that I had to try the piña colada horchata—but not to worry, because it's nonalcoholic. Since it's a school night and all." She winks. "And the kimchi enchiladas are supposed to be amazing—if you like enchiladas and spicy things, that is."

"I love both of those things actually." I stop next to her at the back of the line. For a new location, this place seems pretty popular. Weird no one at school has mentioned it; although a number of the people here look like college students. There is a community college nearby—I just haven't gotten around to visiting it yet. Not that it hasn't been on my ever-growing list of things to do for a while now. Teacher of the year material over here.

"So, Christina." The way my name rolls off her tongue like

CHRISTINA

she's memorized the feel of it in her mouth makes my toes tingle. "Tell me what you do when you aren't trying to scare the general public on the greatest holiday of all time." She smirks, probably recalling our conversation from earlier on how Halloween isn't my favorite.

I study the chalkboard that lists all the things the truck has to offer, including chicken chorizo risotto and Mexican coleslaw. Oh, they have flan. "You mean teachers are supposed to have a life outside of the classroom?"

She chuckles like how Cami laughs at my jokes—like she really gets it. "I'm pretty sure we're all supposed to have a better work-life balance these days. That's what the young people call it at least, right?" She winks again as she glances around. Oh good, I'm not the only one who's noticed we just increased the average age of the people here by at least ten years.

I grab hold of her arm. "We were never this young when we were in college, were we?"

"God, I hope not."

And we both laugh. Any tension I had in my shoulders before slowly releases. It's just so easy—so natural—to laugh with Pepper.

Her gaze shifts to my hand, still attached to her arm. Her skin is warm and soft under my grasp.

"I'm sorry." I unwrap my fingers, my cheeks heating up. What the heck came over me?

She places her hand where mine just was, then pulls down her sleeve. "It's okay." Her eyes connect with mine, and it's not embarrassment that has my tongue tied inside my mouth. She has the lightest freckle under her left eye just in the corner—or

CHRISTINA

maybe it's a little eye shadow that's fallen out of place. My fingers itch to find out. Another breeze passes, blowing her dark hair away from her face and showing off a pair of skeleton earrings—little bones dancing in the autumn air.

"Next," the woman in the window calls, and Pepper steps forward.

"Kimchi enchiladas, an order of the falafel tacos, a side of chips, two piña colada horchatas, and a limoncello flan, too, please," Pepper says. "You'll share that with me, right?" she asks over her shoulder.

I nod, not that she's looking in my direction as she hands over her card. It's exactly the flavor I would've ordered from that list. Did I say out loud that I liked flan?

She collects her card and hands me one of the horchatas as she steps out of line. "I was in the mood for something sweet," she says. "You don't have to have any if you don't want it, though. No pressure." She seems unsure of herself. Maybe a little hesitant. Did I make things weird by holding on to her like that?

"No, I love flan," I practically shout. OMG, be normal, Christina. What the heck is wrong with you? It's like I've never been out with another adult human before. Yes, she's beautiful, but that's no reason to be weird. She might not even be into girls like that and just looking for a friend. Okay, now I'm being really weird. I take a deep breath and slowly release it. Although dating would be so much easier if everyone wore pins or something. Could that be my million-dollar idea?

There's a small grin on her face—like maybe she knows I'm

CHRISTINA

lost in my thoughts again—as she gestures to a table off to the side and away from teens tossing chips at one another. "Shall we?"

I nod and follow her.

Pepper knocks a few dried leaves off the bench and sits down, totally oblivious to my social awkwardness. She takes a sip of her drink and closes her eyes. "Yummm..." The sound of her voice sizzles in my chest. She opens her eyes and there's something serene in them, and she almost seems startled to find me watching her. Staring isn't weird at all. Maybe I should excuse myself now before I make this any worse.

I take a sip of my drink, and damn, it's good. Like so good, it's bad. "What's this called again?" Either her friend has really good taste or Pepper is psychic. It's absolutely the perfect drink for me—creamy and sweet but not too much.

"Horchata. This particular one is piña colada."

I take another drink, letting the flavor of sweet pineapple and coconut with a hint of cinnamon fill my mouth before swallowing it down. "My bank account will not be happy about this. I may have to come and get one of these every day."

"So what you're saying is that we're gonna have to come back to taste all the different flavors." She winks and something flutters in my stomach. I guess I'm hungrier than I thought.

"Good thing," I reply, which makes no sense. "I mean, sure. Yes." I bring the cup back up to my mouth to stop talking.

A woman and two small children sit at a table two down from ours. As soon as her butt hits the bench, she opens a very large canvas tote bag and pulls out paper and crayons. Both kids immediately get to work.

CHRISTINA

"Can I use the pink first?" the one with pigtails—who I'm assuming is the little sister—asks the boy.

"Yeah." He hands the girl the pink crayon.

"Cute," Pepper says. "They probably fight like hell, too," she adds low enough so there's no way anyone could accidentally overhear her.

"They probably do." I can't help but think of Ashley and how much that's true for us. If there was anything she had, I wanted it, too—because that meant it was cool, and why wouldn't I want to be cool like my big sister?—but then she'd get mad at me for copying her, which would turn into a fight. And as we got older, we grew further and further apart until we were what we are now—which is complicated. "Speaking from experience or . . ."

She shakes her head. "Nah. I'm an only child," she says. "You?"

"I've got two sisters. One older, one younger. I'm the one in the middle."

She leans forward. "How does that work out for you?"

"Emily, that's my little sister. She's great and we get along awesomely. But my older sister . . ." I sigh. "Everything is a fight with her. I don't get it. Nothing I do is good enough or she has to do it better. I don't understand why she hates me so much."

"It's like she's competing with you, but you aren't competing with her."

"Exactly." I tilt my head at her. "Are you sure you're an only child?"

"Positive." She nods.

CHRISTINA

"Well, that's a good thing for you. I can tell you firsthand having two overachieving sisters is exhausting."

"But I thought you weren't in competition with them." Those eyebrows of hers quirk up again, and I swear this woman can see right through me. Never in my life has someone gotten me this quickly before. It's almost a little spooky.

"I'm not. But tell that to my parents. I know they want what's best for me"—something they tell me all the time—"but it's exhausting." I roll my eyes, and when I glance back, Pepper is watching me—her head perched on her hands like she's really listening. "I'm sorry. I'm dumping all of this on you, and we don't even know each other."

Pepper's nose wrinkles, and she sits up straight. "It's fine. I like hearing about it. Family is important. I know I miss mine. Because of work, I mean," she quickly adds. "I just don't get to see them much is all."

"I think I see mine more than I want to, but I'd probably feel different if I couldn't see them."

"You would." She sounds so sure of herself.

"How long has it been since you've seen yours?"

"It's been a long time." Pepper takes a deep breath and gazes up at the sky for a moment.

"And they are okay with this? You being away and your job and everything?" That didn't sound condescending, did it? "My parents just don't understand why I'm teaching and not doing 'something more important' because I'm 'so much better than that.'" I use finger quotes to emphasize what my parents love to say to me. It's nice to have people who believe so much in

---

CHRISTINA

me, but at the same time, my entire worth isn't wrapped up in what I do for a living, and I wish they'd understand that.

"Teaching is one of the most important jobs. Teachers should be the highest paid profession." Pepper's voice gets a little louder. "We wouldn't have doctors or lawyers or computer programmers without teachers." She sits back and takes a breath. "Sorry, it's just something that has always bothered me."

"No, I get it." I really do. "Your parents must be teachers or something, right?"

She shakes her head, but doesn't say anything, and I don't push the topic any more. Even though I'm here treating her like I'm an overeager Bumble date—not that I've used that app in ages—it doesn't mean she feels the same. She seems to actually know how to talk to people, unlike me. Once Cami has her baby, we need to get our girls' nights back on the books. Hanging out with teens all day and then going home to my cat has obviously stunted my ability to speak with other adults. "I like your earrings."

Her hand flies up to the side of her face, where she fingers the little metal bones. "An old girlfriend got them for me. They're one of my favorite pairs."

"Old girlfriend." I clear my throat. "So you don't see her anymore?" Real smooth, Christina, but at least it clears up the question of whether or not she likes girls.

"Not like I used to, no."

I haven't known Pepper long enough to say there's something sad in her eyes, but for a moment the sparkle just doesn't seem to be there.

CHRISTINA

"One fifty-three," someone calls from the truck.

"That's us." Pepper stands. "I'm gonna . . ." But she doesn't say anything else; she just walks away to get our order.

Way to go, Christina, really fucking this one up as usual. She's the first remotely interesting girl who asks you out in this town, and you're royally blowing it! Not that she really *asked me out* asked me out—but this is the closest thing I've had to an actual date in way too long. That's the one downside of a small town—the dating pool is very shallow. I can't even remember the last time I've *been* with someone, which is just sad. Maybe I did look lonely, and that's why she suggested this.

Pepper sets a tray down and interrupts my pity party—thank god. "I've been thinking," she says. "I want to help you with this haunted house thing."

I scrunch my brows. Is that what this has all been about? She needs some kind of side hustle? "Oh. Well. I can't, like, hire people—"

"No. That's not what I mean. I have a job. I'd volunteer." She slides my enchiladas in front of me, and oh my god, they smell so good, my mouth immediately starts to water. "I obviously love Halloween. You seem like you could use the help, and I have the spare time being new to town and all, so . . ." She shrugs, then unwraps the little twisty tie from around the chips, rolls the plastic down for easier access, and sets them in front of me. "To dip in your enchilada sauce. I thought it would be good?"

I can't help but smile. That's exactly what I always do with enchiladas. "You're really easy to hang out with and talk to, you know that?"

CHRISTINA

"Girl, I got you." She smiles back, and little fireworks explode up my spine. "So . . . yes, I can help you with the haunted house?"

This really pretty girl is asking if she can hang out with me more, isn't she? I swirl a chip in the enchilada sauce and attempt to regain my cool. "Only if you want to. All the theater kids work on it, too, so there are a lot of hands." Her shoulders fall, so I quickly add, "But you know how teens can be."

She glances up, her eyes connecting with mine, and my breath catches. "It'll be fun."

CHRISTINA

68 DAYS
UNTIL THE STORE CLOSES

Pepper

Christina. Since spending time with her, I couldn't stop myself from watching the door each time that witch cackled, waiting to see if it might be her. Hoping to catch a glimpse of ashy blonde hair and cherry red lips.

It seemed silly—I mean, I barely knew her. But I wanted this girl to like me. I didn't want her to think of me as the weirdo girl who practically begged to do free labor for her—but the fun girl, the nice girl, the girl she could maybe also want to spend more time with.

She crept into my thoughts even in moments I wasn't thinking about her. The way her hair fluttered in the breeze. The way her cheeks lit up like bowls of sweet red fruit. How she seemed to let out a deep breath before divulging something personal about herself—or sometimes after she'd rambled on—like she was releasing it from her body for the wind to carry away. In those moments she seemed lighter, more relaxed. I loved that she shared with me.

Christina was like a beautifully layered crepe cake, and I couldn't break through each layer fast enough—always wanting more.

To say there was something different about her wouldn't have done her justice. It wasn't just her, but me when I was with her. She had this way of making me forget and live in the present—no thinking of the past or planning the however many days I had of the future. But the *now*. It was a gift—a feeling, a lightness in my heart that I hadn't had for a long, long time.

Which was why that day, I found myself out in the hearse, driving over some odds and ends—things I'd found in the depths of The Dead of Night storage—to the haunted house, just to see her again.

It was quite the predicament I'd gotten myself into—this wanting to see her and also being scared . . . no, more like excited . . . about what that meant. I'd been stuck to the store for five years, and in all that time I'd been through all the stages. Denial. Anger. Depression. Bargaining. But I'd done it. I'd reached acceptance about my predicament.

I'd been an only child, so I reasoned it didn't hurt my parents much to think I'd never been born. It was one less thing for Mom to worry about—and worrying about me was her favorite hobby. My friends had other friends. And Mitchell was already gone anyway. None of them ever had to grieve for me. They forgot all about my existence. They were fine. And if they were fine, I convinced myself I was fine, too. There weren't

---

PEPPER

many people who could eat, and do, and buy whatever they wanted, and all I had to do was pretend I worked at a Halloween store. I was basically the CEO of a company. Yes, there were downsides, but did those cons really outweigh the pros? I didn't have anything to worry about. At all. Ever. No bills to pay. No expectations. No one I could let down.

But there was Christina.

Was it even reasonable to think I could spend time with this woman without wondering what it would be like to kiss her?

And how could I possibly think of wanting to start anything with her when there was no way I could finish it?

Then again, sixty-eight days from now she wouldn't even remember I existed, so where was the harm? It wasn't like I'd be forcing myself on her. And if it was clear she had zero interest in me, I'd back off.

We could at least be friends for a short while, couldn't we? It would make my limited days here more interesting and exciting, that was for sure. Plus, she did seem in over her head with this whole haunted house thing—and maybe I could convince her Halloween wasn't as terrible as she thought; then maybe she'd be better off when she had to do this all again next year, and the year after that, and the year after that.

Now I was really getting ahead of myself.

As I turned off Peach Street, I decided helping the town by helping Christina was the right thing to do. And if we also happened to become friends in the process and then she happened to forget all about me, it wouldn't really hurt her. She'd be none the wiser, and I'd have much more purpose in my current situation—something more than just fall days and tachos at Cheesy's. And maybe even someone to spend my time with. It had been so long since I'd had a real friend.

When I had Christina's job, they'd given me an end-of-the-day planning period, so I'd have time during this event to get to the house and get things prepped for when kids arrived after school. It seemed reasonable to think that much hadn't changed since my time there, which meant I'd have the chance to be alone with her before her attention would be needed elsewhere.

I wasn't, however, prepared for the rush of emotions to hit me as I pulled into the parking lot next to the pumpkin patch and took the short drive to the front of the haunted house. Like everything else in town, it looked exactly like it used to and yet completely different at the same time. The paint on the outside was a little duller—which really helped with the ambiance. The hedges on the far side of the house had been only knee-high the last time I was here, but they had to be at least waist-high now. It was strange measuring the passage of time with how much the foliage grew.

This had been my happy place, which was likely why I avoided coming back during the day—instead opting to drive by from a safe distance on the street from time to time—until Halloween, when I couldn't *not* come and see what they'd done. But that felt safe. I was just a person enjoying the show. This, being here now, reminded me of the before—of how much I loved being a part of the process. The engine rattled along with my nerves.

This was for the town. For the kids.

PEPPER

I couldn't believe how silly I was being. Coming here was a good thing. I took a deep breath, double-checked that my pigtail French braids were still perfect and that there was no lipstick on my teeth, and exited the car. I had a few bags of old costumes and things the store would never sell, and the kids would for sure go wild for them. Hopefully it wouldn't be weird to try and hang around long enough to see the looks on their faces when they rummaged through these bags. The way they would light up always brought me so much joy. I couldn't wait for Christina to experience that as well.

The buzz of a power saw greeted me the closer I got to the house. Whoever it was had to be around back, likely between the staging house and the actual haunted house itself, so that was where I went. It seemed strange that the school would hire a carpenter, but maybe the house needed some repairs before the big event.

The *buzzzz* got higher pitched as I came around the corner, and there was Christina—hair pulled back with a headband, safety goggles on—using a big-ass saw. My stomach did a somersault. I wasn't sure if everyone looked that hot using power tools, but I guessed that they didn't. Butterflies started a full-out party in my belly as she swiped an arm across her brow.

She lifted the handle on the saw, and she glanced up in my direction. I didn't want to alarm her, so I raised the bags like being here was totally and completely normal.

"I hope I didn't startle you," I said.

She flipped a switch on her table saw. "What are you doing here?"

PEPPER

Not exactly the welcome I'd hoped for, but I couldn't blame her. It probably did seem a little odd to do a pop-in. But small towns meant sometimes people just showed up. She'd get used to it living here. "I've been doing inventory and came across some things we can't sell anymore that I thought you all could use."

"That's awesome. I'm glad you caught me."

Yes, because how was I supposed to know she was here? Real smooth, Pepper. "What are you doing?" I asked to steer the conversation to safer territory.

"The kids want to have someone basically strapped down to a dining room table like they would be eating a live human sacrifice, and it's not as if tables with straps like that are common, so I'm building them one."

"So aside from being a culinary expert"—I winked, remembering how the last time she was in the store, she told me about her boxed mac and cheese catastrophe—"you know how to make that? Impressive."

She rolled her eyes. "Butter-to-milk ratios are hard. This..." She shrugged like it wasn't a big deal. "I'm good with my hands is all."

My whole body heated up. The temperature today was unusually high for this time of year. "Maybe we should take these inside." I gestured at the house.

"Oh yeah." She removed her safety goggles, grabbed one of the bags from me, then we both headed toward the back door of the haunted house.

She walked in before me. "Watch your step."

As soon as I crossed the threshold, I was slapped in the face

---

PEPPER

with the familiar scent of someone overusing the fog machine, and the back of my throat got thick. God, how the kids loved to overuse that dumb machine.

It was still early in their construction, but already the space was transforming. A couple of tree cutouts stuck out from the wall, and more were leaning against it.

"You want to put those here?" Christina motioned toward a space at the side of the room where a pile of different Dead of Night bags already lay.

"You've made a few more trips, I see."

Her cheeks turned red like candied apples. "Every time I think I have everything, it seems like I forget something else and have to go back. I wasn't, like, stalking you or anything. You weren't even there the last time I went." She pressed her lips together and turned away.

I giggled to myself. "Totally relatable," I said, and she swiveled back in my direction with a smile playing on her lips.

"Do you know how many types of vampire teeth there are?"

"I do." I laughed out loud this time.

"Of course you do." She rolled her eyes at herself.

After I set the bags down, I couldn't stop myself from really checking the place out. The number of hours, days, weeks I'd spent in this very room painting and prepping was immeasurable. A rush of emotions hit me all at once like a tide crashing onto the shore. Working here, I didn't realize how important those moments would become until now, when they came flooding back as memories. I wished I'd have taken the time to cherish them more when I was here.

The room was still in chaos—paint cans pushed up against

one wall; a few mannequins, some without heads, sat in a mound; and sawdust galore—but this was part of the process. Where a blank canvas became a work of art. Or a bloody mess in this case. I couldn't make furniture, but we always had parents who would come and help out. And we always had donations that we could repurpose. Beside the trees pushed to the side of the room was an unfinished wooden chair. "Did you make this, too?"

"It was a little more challenging than I expected. But then again, I've never made an electric chair before."

"And why would you? Unless you were some kind of serial killer." I stopped inspecting her work and spun around. "You aren't, are you? Because this would be a really great place to murder someone." I glanced at the concrete floor, which was stained with all the different kinds of paint and fake blood from years past. They'd even installed a drain when the house was constructed, likely knowing it sometimes took a lot of water to get the floor clean—and then there was always the occasional kid accidentally peeing in their pants. "With the black lights on, I bet it already looks like a crime scene."

"Oh, I bet you're right. I'd never thought about it."

I glanced up at the ceiling. The same light fixtures were there from before, so I headed to the wall and pressed a couple buttons on the light switch panel. It immediately got darker and then the black lights flickered on. Just as I expected, splatters were illuminated along the floor and walls, some bright puddles while others dim and dark. The tree cutouts Christina had made looked even more menacing in the special lighting.

Christina spun around like she was taking it all in, her hair glowing and her skin a deep blue. She'd switched out her corporate dress for a simple black tank top and jeans, which were speckled with glowing white dots. Even her black Hunter boots were covered in sawdust. "How'd you know to do that?"

Crap. Not even five minutes with her and I'd already slipped up. I was not supposed to know more about this place than she did. "Would you believe magic?"

She turned toward me, her eyebrows raised.

"My job title could be Halloween expert." The lie came out so easily as I pointed up. "I noticed the bulbs and saw the switch and put two and two together is all." I shrugged casually—like this was, of course, the perfect explanation and not that I had been the one to write the instructions on how to use all the gadgets in the house.

"So, Halloween expert and electrician." She smiled, her teeth glowing a bright violet.

"Definitely not." I shook my head. I really needed to be more careful, though—there was too much that I couldn't explain, and the last thing I wanted was to scare Christina away. I flipped the switch again, turning the world back to its normal colors. "How'd you get into building stuff?"

"My grandfather actually. My parents would drop me and my two sisters off, and while my older sister, Ashley, baked in the kitchen with my grandmother, and my little sister, Emily, either watched cartoons or helped them, I would hang out with my PawPaw in the garage and help him build things."

"That's really cool."

"You think?"

I walked back over to the chair. "Yeah." I sat down and it

didn't wobble or shake at all. She'd even gone as far as carving in little details to make it look like something that had been used before. "This is really good. Do you make any furniture that isn't torture related?"

"Ha," she said. "I made my own dining table and chairs."

"I'd say that checks."

She smirked. "I also made my bed frame and dresser and a couple of side tables."

"Hold up, Jonathan Scott. If you can do all of that and I'm betting they're just as amazing as this is, why aren't you, like, I don't know, doing this for a living?" As soon as those words hit my own ears, I cringed. "That sounded bad, didn't it? I swear I didn't mean—"

"No, it's fine. Part of me would love to build things for a living, but, like, I'm one person, and people have IKEA, and why would they pay me more for something they can build themselves?" She let out a long breath. "And then I'd have to hear about how I wasn't putting my degree to good use." She rolled her eyes. "Architecture," she clarified.

"Gotcha," I said. "Still, I bet some people would pay for quality stuff like this, or these." I walked over to the tree cut-outs. "These are so cool. And if building things brings you joy, isn't that what's most important?" At least that is what Mom always said to me—find your joy, do what you love.

"We're doing a deadly forest theme, and I thought the kids could hide between them and jump out, so I set a couple up to see if they'd work. And now that I know how to turn the lights off, I think they could actually do the trick. I was going to show the kids today when they got here."

PEPPER

"They'll love them. Plus, they look supercool." A deadly forest theme was such a simple idea, but there were so many things you could do with it. I was a little jealous I'd never thought of anything like it before. Christina may have not liked Halloween, but she had good instincts. She needed to believe in herself more.

She bit her lip. "So what did you bring me exactly?" she asked, clearly wanting to change the subject. She started going through the new bags, pulling items out.

"Mostly mix and match costume pieces, but some of this stuff you could cut up and, I don't know, pour blood all over it."

Christina glanced back at the stained floors, which only a moment ago were glowing. "I'm gonna need a lot of fake blood, aren't I?"

"There is still that murder option."

She laughed. "Might be cheaper."

"It's the ten to life that'll get you." I laughed with her. It was so easy to laugh with Christina. "You know what? I have a bunch more stuff back at the store. If you wanna stop by sometime, you can have whatever you want."

"You won't get in trouble, will you?"

"Not if it's like this, and we would toss it anyway." I couldn't exactly tell her that it was impossible for me to get in trouble. A few years ago, I tried to get myself fired, and it didn't work. "Come by whenever and ask for me, and I'll show you what we have," I said. "I got you. I promise."

"Just come by and ask for you. It's that easy?" She licked her bottom lip.

A flush of heat raced through me. "Yep."

PEPPER

67 DAYS
UNTIL THE STORE CLOSES

Christina

The scent of roasting coffee beans swirls around me and helps ignite my soul as I walk into Déjà Brew after a long day—and it won't be ending anytime soon. At least I'm inside and away from the wind whipping around outside and the temperature dropping like a storm might be on its way.

I've known the haunted house was coming since before school started, and I thought I'd prepared properly, but I was so very wrong. Per usual. And then I went and scheduled the kids to do monologues this week for a grade—they must be recorded and then posted—so I'm extra behind on all the things now. Whoever said those who can't do, teach, was a damn liar. I've never done this much work before even in my corporate life.

Coffee. I need coffee. And maybe some pad Thai so I can get through the night. I haven't had it since I went with Cami a few weeks ago, and ever since, I haven't been able to stop thinking about mango sticky rice.

"Hey, Ms. L," Steffi—a student in my second period—greets me at the counter of the coffee shop and pulls me out of my thoughts. "The usual?"

"I'm gonna need something a little stronger tonight, I think." This is my usual weeknight place when I'm on the hunt for an extra pick-me-up—and today I *need* it. I glance up at the menu. What has the most caffeine but also won't make me have a heart attack, and will still allow me to go to sleep when I need to? "Let's do the Toasted Marshmallow White Chocolate Mocha."

"Oh, that's my favorite. Good pick." She types on the register, and I search in my bag for my wallet. Crap. Where did I put it? Last night I'd been scrolling on social media when a well-targeted ad convinced me I needed a blanket that's also a hoodie.

"Everything okay?" Steffi asks.

I set it on the pillow, and then Licorice jumped up, and then . . . "I left my wallet on the couch, it seems," I tell her.

"Do you have your phone?" she asks.

"Oh my gosh. Yes. You're brilliant." I pull out my cell and open my wallet, tapping it against the card reader.

"I've lost my wallet twice this month already." She laughs, but I'm not sure this fact makes me feel any better. "It'll be up in a couple minutes; we just got hit with a huge online order."

"No problem. I'll be doing some grading while I wait." I gesture to the seating area with my head as I slide my phone back into my bag.

"Does that mean the grades will be in tonight?" She leans forward, pressing her hands into the counter.

CHRISTINA

"If I get them all done, yes." Which is why I'm at the coffee shop and not going home. If I were, I'd likely fall asleep as soon as I hit the couch.

"I'll find you," she says.

"Thanks," I say, and head toward the back of the shop to grab a seat hopefully near an outlet. The school-issued laptop has the battery life of a fruit fly. Fruit. I also need to hit the store for more bananas.

Just like usual, the tables are full of kids, drinking things topped with loads of whipped cream. As I scan the area I usually post up at for the evening, there's a familiar face sitting along the one wall close enough to enjoy the fireplace but not so close that it makes you get overheated.

Pepper raises a hand, smiles, and gestures to the empty seat at her table.

I smile back and make my way toward her. "You save the day again," I tell her as I sit down. If she weren't here, I'd be forced to go home tonight, and I have way too much work to do. I just wish the grading system weren't so wonky and didn't take forever.

"This is the hot spot in town, it seems," she says as she glances around. Her smoky eye shadow really accentuates the blue of her eyes. Maybe she could teach me how she does that.

"Always is. And you picked the best table." I drape my coat over the chair, reach into my bag, and pull out my laptop, plugging it in. "Not working tonight?" I ask.

"They occasionally let me out for good behavior." She winks and something in my chest flutters. I'm more excited for my coffee than I thought. "Funny running into you," she says.

CHRISTINA

"Small town," I tell her. "It has its perks."

"It most certainly does." She smiles and it lights up her whole face—her cheeks are round like apples; I should get some of those at the store, too. "You have a lot of work to do?" She nods at my laptop and helps me refocus.

"Grading," I say. "It's never-ending. And this program we use makes it even more painful."

"How so?" She takes a sip of her drink, her eyes watching me from over her mug.

"To post one grade, I have to click on each student individually and go into the assignment and then post the grade, which doesn't seem like a lot, but it always takes a minute for each page to load, and then when you multiply that by the number of students I have..." I let out a long breath. "It's painful. And takes forever." That didn't sound like whining, did it? Real cute, Christina. Unload all your work stuff on the pretty Halloween store girl.

She presses her lips together like she's debating if she should say something or not. "That does sound annoying." Her brow wrinkles. "Are you sure there isn't an easier way?"

"Not that I'm aware of. But it's not like this program came with a user manual or anything." Who'd have thought that using teaching software would be more difficult than CAD tools? It would be nice if there were some online tutorials or something, but so far I haven't found any for this specific program.

She scrunches her nose. "Could you show me? I'm pretty good with computers, so maybe I could help?"

Is that allowed? I have no idea, but maybe this is one of

CHRISTINA

those moments where you ask forgiveness later. Plus, she isn't a parent hoping to see her kid's grades. So if she really can figure it out, it would be worth it. "Promise not to tell my principal?"

She zips an imaginary zipper across her lips. "I don't know anything."

I scoot my chair over, open the laptop, and pivot it toward her so she can see the screen. After logging in to the program, I show her what I have to do. "See, it's a pain in the butt, right?"

She studies the screen for a moment. "May I?" She gestures toward the laptop but doesn't touch it.

"As long as you don't delete everything."

"I got you," she says. She pivots the keyboard a little more toward her and navigates back to the home screen. "You see this?" She points. "If you change the view, I think"—she clicks, and a moment later there are more options on the screen—"this'll let you see the whole class at once." She clicks again. "And then you should just be able to go down the line."

On the screen is my entire first period class in a grid view with the students lined down the side and the assignments across the top. "How did you know how to do that?"

She shrugs. "It's not much different from the software we use at the store. I bet it's made by the same company, too." She chuckles.

"I mean, I wouldn't be surprised." I shake my head and study the screen again. I can't believe it's that easy. "You have no idea how long I've been doing it the hard way. This is going

---

CHRISTINA

to save me so much time." I pivot the laptop my way and scroll through. "I could totally kiss you right now."

Pepper's eyebrows shoot up, and my face heats to the temperature of a thousand suns. What in the heckity heck would make me say such a thing?

"Here you go, Ms. L." Thank god for Steffi. She sets my coffee on the table. "And sorry about the wait on this." She places a plate with a slice of some kind of chocolate cake on it next to my large mug.

"No problem," Pepper says. "I'm just glad you had a slice left."

"Thank you," I tell her—for the coffee and for the interruption.

"Steffi," someone calls to her from the counter.

"Gotta run. Good luck with grading." She struts off to the front of the shop.

Pepper is still looking at me—her expression unreadable. "You wouldn't want to share this with me, would you?"

"I don't know how much sharing will happen. Cake is one of my weaknesses." Especially chocolate cake.

"There are worse things," she says.

"Than a giant sweet tooth? I suppose."

She grins. "You do have really nice teeth."

"Braces when I was a teen." I give her my best toothy smile. "Hated wearing them, but I'm kinda glad now that I did."

She flashes her teeth at me. Her lips are a lovely shade of raspberry. "Same. Eating popcorn was a pain."

"You weren't supposed to eat popcorn with braces."

CHRISTINA

"What can I say? I'm a rebel." She pushes herself up. "I'll go get us some forks."

I didn't even notice Steffi had forgotten that, but they're really busy, plus it's basically free cake, so who am I to complain?

By the time Pepper gets back to the table, I have all of first period graded and have started on second. This is seriously the best thing to happen to me today.

She hands me a spoon. "They were out, so this is what they gave me." She sits with her shoulder bumping into mine—the connection sizzling down to my fingertips. Our chairs are still pushed together, but it would be rude to move away, plus we have cake to share.

Since I don't want to seem too eager, I wait for her to cut off a piece first, then I dig in, getting just the right ratio of cake to what looks like buttercream frosting. The spoon disappears into Pepper's mouth, her eyes close for a moment, and then the spoon slides back out—her lipstick still in place. "Mmm," she says, and it sends tingles down to my toes.

I pop the bite into my mouth, and it's like a chocolate explosion with a hint of what has to be Biscoff. "This is so good," I say.

"Chocolate cake is one of the truest joys in life," she says, and then she takes another bite.

"What kind of lipstick is that? If you don't mind me asking." Oh god. I just admitted with my whole chest to being fully invested in watching her eat. Not a weirdo thing at all.

The corner of her mouth perks up. "It's called Juicy Berry by SHE Persists."

CHRISTINA

"Oh, I love that brand." I used to wear it all the time. "I've never seen that color before, though."

She shakes her head and scoops up another spoonful of cake. "Must be new."

I take another bite, and she sips whatever she has in her mug—chai maybe, with the sweet scent of ginger. The chatter of conversations echoes around us. Outside, the wind seems to have died down a bit, and the clouds have started to move on—turning into the best kind of night, where the crispness in the air makes you feel alive.

Inside Déjà Brew the chairs are comfortable, there's a fireplace in the middle for when—like today—it's cold. A woman closer to the fire slowly sips her coffee, paperback book in hand. In the summer here, they open the back doors to an expansive patio and garden, where you can sit and lounge for hours. They've also been known to partner with The Book Burrow and host story hour out there when the weather is nice. Not that I've been to it, but I've always wanted to check it out—even if it is mostly for kids. It felt weird going on my own, but maybe if Pepper is still in town, she'd want to go with me.

"What are you thinking about?" she asks.

My cheeks heat up. Oh crap. Fantasizing about spending more time with her when we hardly even know each other sounds like the most embarrassing thing in the world, so I blurt out, "Tattoos," which makes no sense at all.

Her brow scrunches up. "As in thinking of one you regret, or wanting to get one?"

"Oh, I don't have any. I think they're beautiful, but I'm so indecisive. Like what if I get something here"—I touch my

CHRISTINA

shoulder—"and then I figure out I should've gotten something else and now I can't? Although I have been considering getting some ivy around my ankle."

"Really? Why?" Her head jerks back. "Sorry. I just . . . Would you . . . ?" She takes a breath. "Ivy. Around your ankle, you were saying."

I take a sip of my drink, my mouth feeling a little dry. "My grandmother's name was Ivy, so I thought . . . It's stupid." I rub my forearm where the crescent-shaped scar is.

"Was?" Her voice sounds tentative.

"She passed away six months ago."

Pepper presses her lips together, and either it's the lighting or her eyes have gotten a little glassy. "I'm so sorry. That must've been tough."

"Thanks. Yeah. We were pretty close, so I thought of maybe an ivy tattoo to remember her. But it's a big commitment, you know?"

And there those brows go again.

"Not that I'm not committed to things." Regardless of what my father says. "I commit to lots of things. Like relationships, I'm fully committed to those. Too much sometimes if you ask people about my ex." Just stop talking, Christina.

She nods like she understands. "You're loyal."

"Exactly." I'm not entirely sure how she was able to decode what I was trying to say so easily, but I'm glad she did. Maybe she's some kind of magician. Or she's used to talking to rambling fools who are really good at tripping over themselves. I let out a long breath and lean back a little more in my chair.

CHRISTINA

"That's not a bad thing," she says.

"No. It's not." I take another drink of my mocha, mostly to stop the verbal diarrhea spewing out. It's not that Pepper makes me nervous; it's like when she's around, I can't stop myself from oversharing.

"Anyone you choose to be with is very lucky," she says, and my mouth is once again dry. "Are you seeing anyone now?" The question comes out so naturally, but her gaze never disengages from mine.

"No." I cough and take another drink. "No. I haven't dated for like forever. Small towns also have their drawbacks."

She lifts her mug but doesn't bring it to her lips. "Are you thinking about moving?"

I shake my head. "If it were up to my family, I'd already be gone, but I like it here. How about you? Are you planning on sticking around?" That sounded casual, right? Not like I'm hoping she'll say yes, or anything.

"It's possible." Although her mouth is hidden behind her mug, the corners of her eyes crinkle. "The people here are really interesting." She looks directly at me when she says it, and then she keeps her eyes connected with mine as she takes a drink. Her lashes are long and hit her brows with ease.

"I'm glad I ran into you."

"That seems to be our thing." She smirks, reminding me of how I literally ran into her at the store when we first met. "How are things going with your haunted house? Anything I could help with yet?"

"I'm still kind of just organizing, but soon, I promise." I take

---

CHRISTINA

another sip of my coffee. "Be careful what you ask for. There's a lot to do."

She chuckles. "Well, I wouldn't have offered if I didn't want to help. Plus, I have the time, and I like being around you."

The fire is extra hot in here tonight. I take off my sweater and try to ignore the heat growing inside me and the way that comment makes me feel. "You probably don't have to take your work home with you." I point to the open laptop.

"Not like this, no." She shakes her head. "I'm not keeping you, am I?"

"Not at all." I do have to get this work done, but I don't want her to leave. Except it's more than just that. Aside from Cami, I don't really hang out with anyone, and this has been nice—more than nice. Plus, she said she likes being around me. I take a deep breath. "Actually, I was thinking about getting some Thai food. And since you got the tacos the other night . . . Or if you don't like Thai—"

"I'd love to." Her whole face lights up.

"Then maybe we should . . ."

She nods. "I'll get a to-go box for the cake." She gets up from the table as I pack my things.

A few minutes later, we've both put on our jackets and are walking down the street toward Thai Society. There's a light breeze from behind that pushes my hair into my face, and I have to keep tucking it back. Pepper wears a knitted rainbow hat with a fluffy white ball on the top, her dark hair hanging in loose waves around her shoulders. The tips of her emerald green shoes peek out from under her pants and clack against the concrete.

CHRISTINA

Persimmon Street is mostly restaurants, so there's a blend of smells swirling through the air. The neon lights from inside Brain Freeze make Pepper's hair look purple as we pass.

"Have you tried the ice cream here?" Pepper gestures toward the shop.

"I think it was the first stop I made when I moved into town, and I've been back regularly since." I laugh. "Everything is so good. And if you go in when it's not busy, they'll let you taste as many flavors as you want." Which is good for me. I can never seem to decide.

"Good to know," she says. "Although I'm pretty boring when it comes to my ice cream flavors."

"You're a vanilla girl. I knew there had to be something wrong with you."

Pepper laughs. "Strawberry, but still, I know. Boring."

"I think I've tried their strawberry, although I don't remember it very well," I say.

She pushes, then stumbles back as she attempts to open the door to Thai Society for me—the same way Cami did last time we were here. "Maybe I can buy you a scoop sometime."

The streetlight near us flickers, Pepper presses her back into the heavy wood door to hold it open, the strong scent of jasmine pushing its way out from inside, and a chill races up my spine. Something about this—the blinking light, the heavy door wide open, and the thought of ice cream—all feels familiar.

"After you," Pepper says.

I walk in past her, but I can't shake the feeling. Cami and I had been talking about ice cream the last time we came here,

---

CHRISTINA

too—it's right next door after all. I'm just being weird. I give myself a little shake and smile back at Pepper. "I hope you like it."

"I'm here with you. What's not to like?" She winks, and my heart takes a tumble of its own.

CHRISTINA

57 DAYS
UNTIL THE STORE CLOSES

Pepper

Between the time I spent reacquainting myself with Clover Creek and running into Christina "by chance," I was always at the store. Not just to keep up appearances, but because I enjoyed it. Every day my coworkers warmed up to me more and more. Not because they saw me as someone in a position of power—in reality, I didn't have all that much—but because these were genuine connections. Ones they'd forget once the season was over, sure, but they meant something to me. Having friends even for a short while made the small amount of time I had worthwhile—it made the times I wasn't here not lonely. Nothing could replace authentic human connection and how important it was to one's soul.

Was it always skeletons and candy (who needed sunshine and roses at Halloween)? No. Nothing in life was completely perfect; even I knew that. But truthfully it wasn't all bad—I'm sure there were others who were worse off than me. So I refused to look at it as the glass half empty when I could look at it as the glass half full. The Dead of Night staff and I were all in this together—each day a new challenge to overcome.

That day wasn't much different than any other. We were still nearly two months away from Halloween, and already The Dead of Night was selling out of certain items. It wasn't a new problem; every year it would happen for whatever the most popular costumes were for that season. This year there seemed to be a resurgence of the Addams family, particularly Wednesday, and something called a M3GAN costume, but I wasn't entirely sure what that was about. Then, of course, there was the ever-popular Spider-Man, and one called Bear, which wasn't an animal at all and seemed to be a chef. I needed to do more research about that, too.

"Tell me we're going to be getting more Ken wigs." Dewy had been poring over spreadsheets all morning, and the worry lines next to their eyes seemed to be growing deeper.

"Another shipment is coming this weekend, which will include headwear, but whether there will be 'Ken wigs' specifically, I don't know." Shipping lists from The Dead of Night were never very detailed; Dewy knew this.

They ran a hand over their head. "I'm going to get on the phone with corporate. How can they not be ready with costumes for the highest-grossing movie of the year? They must have a bunch of Barbie executives running the show over there." They laughed like this was a joke, but I was *not* picking up what they were putting down.

Instead of trying to explain why I didn't understand how a movie about a doll for children that was created well before I was born was such a hit for the adult market—a movie I had not seen—I laughed along with them. "Right?"

"Hey, Dewy." Caleb came around the corner. "Do we have the green light this year for . . ." He glanced around like he was looking for someone, which was silly. For the last three years we'd been surprising Lisa with a cake and a small party for her birthday.

"Yes. I've got it all ordered. Red velvet." They winked. That was the only thing that changed, the flavor of cake. "Just a little thing for one of the staff." Dewy looked at me. "It won't take away from business."

"I'm sure it's fine," I said. "And the wigs—"

"Don't worry. I'm on it, boss," they said, and walked away, pulling Caleb with them.

"Not your boss," I called after them. And *the wigs aren't a big deal*, but I didn't get to say that.

It had been almost two weeks, and Dewy was slowly opening up. I overheard them talking with Lisa—one of our Dead of Night alums—about their daughter, and it took everything in me not to squeal. They were planning themed family costumes this year, but they hadn't nailed down what they would be. I really wanted to ask to see a picture of the new little one but resisted again. Dewy didn't immediately clam up when they noticed me; instead they smiled and kept chatting. It was for sure a downside of being forgotten every year, but the upside was that no one remembered what had happened with me and the pumpkins either.

I finished up shifting some of the merchandise in the Roaring Twenties section. Each day the store got busier and busier—which was a great thing—but it was midafternoon, and most people were still at work. It wouldn't really pick up until the evening, and that was when I preferred to take my leave. Clover Creek in the evening was one of the most beautiful places in the world, and with Halloween around the corner, the whole town was getting ready for the month of October, when people from near and far would be flooding in. A West Coast Salem for those who couldn't make the trip across the country for the real thing. Storefronts were being transformed, and it was one of my favorite things to witness. There was so much that I missed because of the curse, but seeing this transformation made up for a lot of it.

I may not know about this year's highest-grossing movie or why that seemed so important, but I did get to see pumpkins being carved, and decorations being strung. The whole community coming together to make each year bigger and better.

However, the gray sky outside had been threatening to open up all day. I glanced out the high windows. It would suck to lose a night to the weather, but a little rain wouldn't kill me. Actually, nothing could.

Lisa dropped a box full of merchandise behind me. "New Guy is up to his boosheet again," she said as she pulled out more headdresses and jewelry to hang in our Greek Mythology section.

Our newest Dead of Night employee was making quite an impression, but not in the best way. "What's he doing now?" I grabbed some snake headbands from the box to help her.

"Alphabetizing the Funko Pop! figures." She rolled her eyes and adjusted the shell necklace of her costume.

That was another thing I didn't quite get. These little figurines had gotten more and more popular over the last few years, and while they were cute, I wasn't sure I understood the obsession with them. This year we had a full section dedicated to them. Little Corpse Brides and IT clowns, and Sanderson Sisters—okay, those I could get behind. "Well, that *is* a choice." I gave her a sympathetic look. He technically wasn't doing anything wrong so there wasn't much anyone could say to him. Being an "overachiever" wasn't exactly something to get written up over.

Today Lisa had dressed like Moana—her dark hair cascaded down her back and her brown skin seemed to shimmer, perhaps with sunblock since she also smelled of coconut. Her costume game had really stepped up. She'd totally be a shoo-in for this year's award. Maybe that was what the new guy was gunning for.

We continued emptying the box and shifting items around the section to make sure everything fit. The sounds of rain pounding on the roof and the Halloween soundtrack playing overhead filled the silence between us.

"Any big Halloween plans this year?" she asked.

I added more ear cuffs to the rack. "I'm probably just going to wander around—check out the town, that kind of thing." I shrugged like I hadn't been anticipating what hanging with my coworkers on the night of the greatest holiday would entail—like it had for the past five years I'd worked in this store.

"Some of us are going to get together after work and hang out if you're interested." She studied the goddess makeup kit in her hand. "It's kind of a tradition around here."

My insides vibrated at the suggestion. This was an event I

participated in every year. Once the store closed, we'd all pick a random costume that hadn't sold and make our way through town until we ended at the haunted house, where we would file through and point out all the things they bought for it from our store along the way. But I couldn't expect to be added to the group. Each year, I had to earn my invitation to tag along.

"Really? That sounds fun. Thanks."

"It *is* a lot of fun." She glanced around. "Last year, Caleb and this girl, Eliza—she went off to the East Coast for college, so she didn't come back this year—anyway, they decided to swap costumes halfway through the night, and Caleb was Sexy Nurse." She laughed. "I almost pissed myself. Seriously, best night ever." She continued to laugh, and all I could do was allow the scene to play out in my mind. Halfway down Fig Street, the pair hid behind a giant jack-in-the-box to make the exchange. Eliza was much smaller than Caleb, so his skirt didn't zip, and the legs of his boxers came out the bottom. The top of the costume barely covered his chest at all and stretched out the symbol on the front so much, it was unrecognizable. Lisa had spit her drink out when she saw him, complaining that it burned her nose—which was just as funny as, if not funnier than, Caleb.

I couldn't reminisce about it with her, so instead I said, "Sounds like quite the night."

"It was." She paused to catch her breath. "You should totally come out with us this year. And then maybe you'll get to come back to our store next year, too."

My chest squeezed. Most of the Dead of Night staff came back year after year, until things—like college for Eliza—kept them away. For everyone, this was their Halloween family. Everyone except for me, really. "Yeah, sounds like fun."

The new guy paused at the end of our aisle like he was inspecting what was going on, but when I stepped to the side and out from behind Lisa, he plastered on a smile and whistled away.

Lisa groaned. "He's not invited. So..." She zipped an imaginary zipper over her lips.

"Got it."

"Maybe we can get him fired or something?" She raised her eyebrows.

That was the thing I loved most about Lisa: She wasn't intimidated by me and didn't think she couldn't talk to me like just another person on staff. Maybe she'd already figured out that I couldn't personally fire anybody—I wasn't a part of the hiring process either. But whatever the reason, I really liked working with her. "I'm sure we could, but would that really be the best solution here?"

Lisa hung up the last of her snake earrings. "Yeah. I think it would be." She nodded.

"Or maybe you could provide him with some of your expertise and guidance as a seasoned worker with years of experience under your belt."

Lisa's mouth twisted like she'd just eaten a handful of Sour Patch Kids. "Or, counterpoint, we could get him fired."

I shook my head at her. "I'm going to let you think things over a little more before settling on a decision." I headed away from her and toward the *Beetlejuice* section of the store.

"No, I think I'm good," she called.

PEPPER

As I made it past an endcap of every color hair spray imaginable and rounded the corner at the vampire aisle, I slammed into someone. "I'm so sorry," I said before realizing who it was. "We really need to stop running into each other like this."

Christina stood in front of me, black silk blouse speckled with raindrops and her blonde hair slightly damp and limp. "At least this time you didn't catch me with any"—she paused—"interesting products."

I also didn't catch her alone this time. Behind her was a woman with brown hair, glowing brown skin, and a very pregnant belly. "No lube today, then, huh?" I whispered.

"Maybe next time." She winked, and I wasn't sure if she was joking or not.

Unsure what to say, I glanced past her, but there wasn't a cart behind her, and she wasn't carrying anything, so I asked, "Well, what brings you in today?"

"My friend Cami needed to get some things."

A twinge of disappointment hit me in the chest.

The pregnant woman held up a large hammer. "Peanut and I are going to be dad bod Thor." She rubbed her stomach.

I had no idea what that meant, but I didn't get a chance to ask as Christina giggled and then quickly introduced us.

"It's nice to meet you," I told Cami.

"Same," she said.

Christina twisted her foot—her black ballet flat squeaking on the linoleum—and propped it on the other one. "Since I'm here, you mentioned helping out . . . Said you might have some things and that I could stop by, and I was hoping maybe since I was here and all . . . ?"

"Yes!" I said a little too eagerly. "I'd be happy to help any way I can." I leveled my voice out.

"Good, because I was watching this YouTube video where someone dug a hole—or not really a hole, but used one of those wooden pallets and covered it mostly in dirt—and it looked like people clawing out of the ground, which seemed pretty cool, and anyway I was thinking that maybe you might have some of those lying around that you didn't need, seeing as you probably get pretty big shipments in." All the words kind of rushed out like a shaken soda that someone had popped the top off of.

I held back the smile that so desperately wanted to come out—she looked really cute when she was flustered. "I actually do have some of those."

A crash of thunder rattled the store, and the lights flickered.

Christina jumped. "Holy—!" But she didn't finish her statement. Teens swore all the time, but teachers were never allowed to in front of students, which was likely what made her hold herself back.

"Got those teacher reflexes working." I winked.

"Hey, I'll catch you later," Cami said. "I want to be home in case the power goes out. Plus, Peanut is hungry."

"Yeah, I'll see you tomorrow." Christina gave Cami a quick hug before she walked away. "She has one of the electronic doors. So no power means she can't get in her house."

I wasn't sure what that meant either, but I didn't want to ask since that could lead to questions about why I didn't know, and I couldn't exactly tell her. "Follow me if you want to take a look at those pallets." I headed toward the back of the store.

PEPPER

"How did that not scare the crap out of you? I'm honestly surprised I didn't leave a puddle behind."

Over the years, I'd had plenty of time to think about a lot of things. One of which was how fear was such a funny emotion when you really contemplated it. So many of the choices people made in life were rooted in fear. But when life doesn't affect you the same way it does everyone else, you kind of just lose that emotion. What exactly did I have to fear? "I'm not scared of anything." I decided to tell her the truth.

"Everyone is afraid of something."

"That's true for everyone but me." I shrugged.

"I'm not sure I believe you," Christina said as we stopped at the door to the back, which read **EMPLOYEES ONLY** in a horror-style font.

"Well, you should." Our gazes connected, and she seemed to study me, her eyes shifting back and forth. Her right one was just a little darker than her left. For a moment I wanted to know what she saw—what she thought—when she looked at me, but then again it didn't matter. She'd never remember this anyway. "Don't worry, I got you." I pushed the door open just as another crash of thunder rattled the building, and Christina jumped again.

She shook her head at me as she walked through.

Once we'd passed the tables that held Dewy's workstation and that the computer staff used for clocking their time, we headed down a hallway into a side pocket of the building that was used for storage. I flipped on the lights, and they flickered to life. Boxes we hadn't processed yet were stacked shoulder-high. Maybe we would find those wigs that Dewy had been so concerned about.

PEPPER

"Have you seen the *Barbie* movie?" I asked.

Christina gave me this look like I was wearing a chicken on my head. "Who hasn't?"

If it was still playing somewhere, maybe I should go and see it tonight, just so I knew what everyone was so wild about, and with the rain and everything, it could possibly be better than getting soaked.

"You are so beautiful," Christina said, and I stopped breathing.

I stopped moving. And time itself seemed to stop as well.

It had been years ago, when I was sitting at lunch at my very first job out of college, that my colleague made a comment about how straight women were more comfortable with the idea of two men kissing than two women. In that moment, my entire world changed—like its axis had shifted and begun spinning in a new direction. Because up until that point, I had lived my life believing certain fundamental truths about the universe. Water made you wet. Moonlight was just a reflection of the sun. Every woman who brushed off the dessert cart on the *Titanic* didn't die any happier than those that didn't—so always eat dessert when given the option. But more than any of those things, I thought every woman knew other women were beautiful. That everything about them—their bodies, the way they smelled—was just as good as, if not better, than everything about guys. That everyone at some point had thought about hooking up with women. When in reality, it turned out this was *not* the case. I had been conditioned to believe all the heteronormative messages, thinking I was straight because of society. But sitting at that café with my work colleague, it hit me—I wasn't straight at all.

And while I had thought about hooking up with girls and even maybe crushed on a few, I'd never actually been with one. After that moment with my actual straight friend, the realization that I was bi didn't really matter. I was already happily in a committed relationship. And after he passed away and before I had the chance to explore that side of myself, I got stuck here.

But now, standing with this adorable woman in front of me, staring at me with her stunning brown eyes—who had just told me she thought *I* was beautiful—I had no idea what I was supposed to do. The words *I think you're beautiful, too* were stuck in my throat.

"From the *Barbie* movie," she said like it was obvious. "At the bus stop with the older woman? Remember?" She scrunched her brows. "That moment was so touching."

My entire body got hotter than a Nashville chicken sandwich, and all I wanted to do was rip off the jacket I had on. "Oh yeah." I turned away from her to catch my breath. Oh shit. She was not hitting on me after all. If I could die, I wanted to do so right then and there. "Such a great movie." I forced a laugh as I moved deeper into the building and down a row of boxes where the pallets would be, and Christina followed.

"So iconic." If she noticed my embarrassment, she at least pretended she hadn't. But now I was acutely aware of the fact that I had a major crush on this girl, which meant I had no idea how to act.

I stepped away from her and tripped over the box of a giant mechanical spider. "This is what we've got." I motioned to the side.

"Careful there," she said. "So you're not afraid of anything, but you're clumsy, is that it?" She had this delightful smile on her face that said she wasn't making fun of me—more like friendly teasing.

"Pallets. You wanted pallets." A bolt of lightning flashed through the horizontal blinds on the large window we stood next to, quickly followed by the shake of thunder.

Christina jumped. "It's really coming down now."

"Sure looks like it." I shoved my hands in my pockets but that felt wrong, so I pulled them out, then ran a hand through my hair and shifted from side to side. "Will these work?" Electricity from the storm had invaded my body. My insides felt like a lit sparkler, and I had no idea what to do with my hands.

Christina came closer; the scent of roses, vanilla, and wood flooded my nose. She smelled as fresh as a spring day, and it had been forever since I'd experienced one of those. "Yeah, these are perfect, but . . ." She glanced behind me to the window.

"What are you wearing?" I asked, and Christina turned to me, those red cheeks of hers flaring. "The perfume or whatever? What is that?"

"It's Pretty Rosey from Betty's Bath Emporium on Carrot Street. Have you been there?" She sounded breathless.

I shook my head, inhaling deeply. "It's amazing."

The rain outside pounded the roof and echoed all around us, or maybe it was the sound of my heart thumping wildly against my ribs. Christina stood so close, and she had on that same cherry red lipstick she wore the first day we met—it would be so easy to lean over. Did she taste like cherries, too?

She licked her lips. Could she tell I was looking at them?

Another bolt of lightning flashed throughout the room at

PEPPER

the same time thunder rattled the building. Christina sucked in a breath and grabbed my arm.

"Don't worry. I got you." I placed my hand on top of hers. She was even closer now. Her body pressed up against mine. Her hand gripped me so tightly, it seemed like she needed something to ground her—to hold on to.

Her gaze flickered to my mouth and up again.

"Did you feel that?" Caleb barged into the room, and Christina jumped away from me. "Oh, sorry, I thought you were alone back here. Dewy was hoping you could help the new guy with something up front."

"Sure, no problem. I'll be right up," I told him, and he quickly exited.

"I guess we should do this another time," Christina said, and I wasn't sure if she was talking about the pallets. I hoped she wasn't just talking about them.

"I can bring them to you if that's okay."

"That would be very okay," she said. "I'll give you my number." She held out her hand.

Oh, my cell phone. It had been forever since anyone had called me—aside from people here at the store. I didn't even know the number myself, but it was on a paper at the register. "It's new, so I don't have it memorized yet," I said.

She took it from me and typed in her number. Her phone dinged a second later. "I just sent myself a text message. So now I have it." She handed the phone back. "You can save me as a contact if you want."

"Yes. For sure. I'll do that." I was sure I could figure it out.

Her cheeks flushed. "I will, too."

PEPPER

57 DAYS
UNTIL THE STORE CLOSES

Christina

I can't believe I forgot my coffee—but between stopping at The Dead of Night and getting sidetracked with Pepper and everything else, I must've put it down somewhere, because it's not here, and I'm freezing.

The AC inside the haunted house is blowing harder than gale force winds—like one of the kids messed with the thermostat. It's normally not this frigid in here. They are all running around, though, their sweaty little bodies—and the rain—making the air thick enough to drink and smell a little like a dirty locker room. And since we can't open the windows, all the painting for the day has been halted—putting us behind schedule. I should really go check the temperature if I don't want an astronomical electricity bill, but I'm currently buried in a pile of Halloween store bags, which should help ward off the cold but don't.

There are a few kids in the staging house working on costumes with sewing machines donated by parents, while others are here in the main house with me organizing all our supplies and separating them into the appropriate rooms—just to make sure we have enough of everything and to make a list of things we still need. I sit in the center of a mountain of Dead of Night bags with my student Hallee attempting to make a dent in the pile while Eli and Treyvon run from room to room distributing everything. There are usually more kids here, but it seems the rain has kept many of them away tonight—I don't blame them. I'd much rather be home on my couch wrapped in my new fuzzy hoodie blanket.

"You've done a really great job with supplies, Ms. L," Hallee says as she empties the contents of another bag and separates things into piles—a fake knife, some purple hair spray, and a Mardi Gras mask. Did I buy that? While attempting to get better organized a few days ago, I stumbled across some old bags from The Dead of Night in the staging house, but I have no idea how long they were sitting in that closet.

"That's nice of you to say, but if that were true, this list would be blank." I hold up the pad of paper I'm using to keep track of everything.

"No, really, I think this is a better haul than we've ever started with before. Even better than last year." Hallee's a senior and has been doing theater since freshman year, and she's been a patron of the haunted house since middle school—meaning she has many more years of experience with all of this than I do. "And you got the *realistic* fake blood. Dr. W used to say it was too expensive." She rolls her eyes.

CHRISTINA

When I originally picked it out, I hadn't thought about the fact I was going to need it in bulk, but I'm not sure mixing it is the best idea, so I've kept it the same. Who knows what kind of chemicals are in this stuff? I'm not a science teacher for a reason. I scribble down a note to go back over the finances again—and maybe buy stock in Mikey's Joke Emporium, since they obviously know what they're doing. Unlike me. Just like with everything else in my life, I'm feeling so in over my head with all of this. And the whole point of the event is to make a profit—not break even, and definitely not lose money. And with prices the way they are on everything these days . . . I let out a long sigh. Other school programs and the spring musical are counting on this. Maybe my parents are right, and I should move back home and get a much less stressful job in architectural engineering. God knows the pay would be better, and I could use my Chanel bag again without worrying it would get goo on it.

Eli comes rushing back into the room, ready for the next haul. "A severed head! Dope."

"Ms. L is the best." Hallee and Eli high-five.

"Well, I'm glad you approve." I let out a sigh. Just like Pepper said, they love it. Maybe she'll have some more cost-cutting ideas—aside from the deep discount she's already giving me and the other supplies she's offered at no cost. I scribble a note to myself to update my budgeting spreadsheet.

"This year's haunted house is going to be the most epic yet," Treyvon says as he comes back around the corner.

"Oh my god, you have the professional open wound kit,

CHRISTINA

too," Hallee says. "I totally call dibs on this one." She points to something specific in the package that looks like a giant gash. That I *know* I didn't purchase, but I don't mention it.

"Bet." Eli kneels down next to Hallee. "Oh, this one's mine, then."

"Nice choice," she says.

"What's the obsession with open wounds?" I have to ask. I still don't understand the fascination with who can have the grossest costume. Can't things be scary without also being disgusting? Like just the idea of the electricity bill is terrifying and there isn't any blood on it.

"We can't all have cool scars like you, Ms. L." Hallee gestures to my forearm where I'm rubbing. "How did that happen?"

The mark on my arm looks like a crescent moon, and for whatever reason, this time of year I always find my fingers tracing over the smooth spot without even thinking about it. "I don't remember."

"You sound like my mom," Eli says. "She's always got some random bruise she doesn't remember getting. Not in like a someone's-hurting-her kind of way. More like a running-into-the-coffee-table thing."

"Relatable," I say.

Treyvon picks up some face paint from the stack. "Does this stuff expire?" He studies the package intently, flipping it over in his hands.

"Maybe technically," I say. I've had an eye shadow palette since college, and I haven't had any issues with it, so a sealed package can't possibly be bad, can it? "Why do you ask?"

CHRISTINA

"The tag on this is from three years ago," he responds.

"Some of this stuff I found in the closet, so it could've come from there." The good news is that I'm not the only one that has overbought for this event. It seems like it's a systematic problem that previous teachers have faced. Everyone might end up with pink eye, but that's a worry for another day.

"It's never been opened. I'm sure it's fine," Hallee says.

I flip the page of my notepad and write down, *does makeup expire?* And also a note to myself to see how much those makeup kits cost. "I'll research it just in case. Put it to the side. And if you find any more old stuff, just pile it all together."

"Good idea," Hallee agrees.

A crash of thunder rumbles outside. The storm today has been wild, quieting for a little while, then coming back full force. I'm so ready for it to figure itself out and move on. Not that I don't love a good rainy day—just not when there's so much to do.

"It would be so epic if we could have sound effects like this in the haunted house," Eli says.

"Did you ever find out how to use the speakers?" Hallee asks.

"What speakers?" Treyvon asks.

She points to the corner of the room. It's one of those items on my ever-growing list of things to do that never seem to get checked off. Plus, we have access to Bluetooth speakers and cell phones, so it doesn't feel super important.

"Wait, we've had speakers all this time and haven't ever used them?" Eli asks.

"Dr. W didn't know where the equipment was to run them,"

CHRISTINA

Hallee explains. "But I know for a fact that they used them when my sister did this—before Dr. W got here."

"Well, I'm sorry to say I don't know about any equipment for speakers either," I tell them. "It's not like anyone left a user manual for this place." Although now that I say that out loud, it would be a good idea. I could possibly make one—in all my spare time. Okay, yeah, that's why it doesn't exist.

"Maybe you can reach out to the old teacher?" Eli says as he grabs another set of face paints to inspect.

"I could try." I make another note in my notebook. **Find out who the old teacher was before Dr. W and see if they can tell me how to use speakers.** "No promises." How important is it really to get them working? It's best not to get the kids' hopes up, especially when there are so many other important things to do.

"That would be really awesome," Treyvon says.

Another crash of thunder rings from outside so loudly, the whole house seems to shake.

"It would be cool." Eli throws another set of old face paints onto the outdated pile, and guilt gnaws at me from the inside. Maybe I could at least try. "Sound really has a way of elevating the experience. I love a good storm, don't you?"

"As long as we still have power, I'm good," Hallee says.

"You shouldn't tempt—" But I don't get to finish that statement as the power goes out. "Great."

Hallee, Eli, and Treyvon turn on the flashlight apps on their phones. Seriously, what did we do before the conveniences of modern technology? I grab my cell as well but don't turn the flashlight on just in case I need the battery for other reasons—

CHRISTINA

like making an emergency call because someone comes and murders us all. Being in this house surrounded by fake body parts and realistic blood isn't helping settle the nerves that are bubbling in my stomach like a witch's brew boiling in a cauldron.

Maybe we should get a cauldron for one of the rooms. Or are they too expensive?

"I guess I'll bring this stuff to the human torture room." Treyvon stands.

"This place is a tripping hazard even with all the lights on; maybe we should take a break from deliveries until the power comes back," I suggest. There's also safety in numbers in case that hypothetical murderer becomes a real possibility. A message comes in on our group chat saying that the people in the staging house are fine. I want to message back to lock the door—just in case—but I don't need to scare them unnecessarily.

"Fine." Treyvon plops down and pulls a bag toward him to sort.

"You know this store is actually run by demons, don't you?" Eli asks as he drags another bag his way.

"Oh, you saw Harper's post, too, huh?" Hallee says. "At first I was skeptical, but I have to be honest, they make some good points."

"What are you kids talking about?" After leaving my last job and now that I'm a teacher, I don't go on social media much. Aside from the fact that we're scrutinized by parents and administrators about what we post, seeing everyone have these curated versions of themselves feels unauthentic—and completely

---

CHRISTINA

unattainable. Occasionally I'll still save or bookmark a recipe I don't have time to make, but that's about it for me as far as any kind of social media is concerned.

"There's this account, Harper's Happenings, and they investigate ghost stories and conspiracies and then rate how plausible they are," Treyvon explains. That would be another reason why I've never heard of it before. Ghosts and conspiracies involving ghosts are definitely not my jam sandwich. There are enough real-world horrors; I don't need to know about the ones I can't see, too. "They reported on this theory a while ago . . . god, it was like at least five years," Treyvon says, and Hallee nods. "And since it's about Clover Creek, pretty much everyone here watched it when it came out. But it's totally not real."

"How can you say that?" Eli acts as though he's been injured—crossing his arms over his chest and clenching it as though he's been stabbed. "Harper rated it four skulls—which means it's more likely than not." He says the last part to me.

"More likely than not that a store is run by demons?" I ask. "Now, this I have to hear." I've been to that store more than any other in this town, and the people who work there all seem nice—normal—and then, of course, there's Pepper. She's so easy to talk to, and for whatever reason, she just gets me. Eli might have a flair for the dramatic, and I'm generally not one to fall for a conspiracy theory, but what if there really is something more here? I've never felt as comfortable around anyone as quickly as I have with Pepper—but her being a demon does feel a little extreme. And then, what would her end goal be? To eat my soul? What is it that demons do anyway?

CHRISTINA

"Well then, my good lady, allow me to pique your curiosity." Eli sits up like he's preparing for a monologue and points his flashlight so that it shines on his face. "I was once a skeptic like our good friend here, but when I started looking at the facts, I couldn't ignore what was right in front of me. The story goes like this . . . Years ago there was a man who wanted to be the richest man in the world. He thought if he were, people would respect and even worship him. That they would look at him and want to be just like him. But no matter what he tried, nothing worked and he was miserable."

"He shouldn't've tried to compare himself to others," Treyvon interrupts.

"Shhh," Hallee says.

"The story goes," Eli continues, "that one day he was approached by a demon. Of course, he didn't know it was one, but it offered the man whatever he wanted and in return he would have to provide a favor. The man thought he would finally get what he dreamed, so he wished to be rich, and the demon made it so.

"The man lived this way for years, flaunting his wealth and gaining respect from some and disgust from others. He didn't care. People knew who he was—they talked about him, and that was truly what he had wanted. However, he forgot what he'd bargained to get there. The demon didn't and came collecting."

"Yeah, yeah. And the rich guy lost his freedom because he thought money and power were more important, but in the end, money can't buy you everything."

"You're ruining the story," Hallee says.

CHRISTINA

"It's a metaphor for capitalism and how it's destroying the world." Treyvon shakes his head like the whole idea of demons and this story are ridiculous.

"You're missing the point," Eli says.

"And what's the point, man?" Treyvon asks.

"You know how it's the same workers there year after year? That's because they made a deal and are waiting for the demon to come collecting—unless . . ."

"Unless what?" Treyvon asks. "Someone destroys their master?" He rolls his eyes.

"Unless they can get someone to take their place. If they can sucker someone else into taking on their debt and adding a debt of their own."

Treyvon cocks his head to one side. "Really? And why would people do that?"

"Because they are greedy AF, man," Eli responds.

"So capitalism. Gotcha." Treyvon spreads his arms out in a "ta-da"-type style.

"Then how do you explain it when you buy something there and when you go to look for it, it's gone? You know you bought it, but it doesn't matter—you still can't find it until the next year, when you just stumble upon the thing you couldn't find the year before." He holds up an old Dead of Night bag like it's proving his point for him—and I have to admit it's pretty convincing. There are a lot of bags here, although I'm not sure they are all here because of some kind of magic—more like disorganization.

"There were a number of unused items in the closet," I say.

"Yes, but were they there because someone stored them

CHRISTINA

there or because that's just where they appeared? There's no way to know for sure, is there?"

Okay, he has a point—and a chill worms its way up my spine.

"I still don't think that means demons," Treyvon says.

"Maybe not, but it doesn't mean there *isn't* some kind of dark magic happening. They need you to have to come back into the store over and over."

"Still capitalism," Treyvon says. "Or maybe Dr. W just bought too much crap."

"Fine," Eli chimes in. "But it's pretty mysterious how the store randomly shows up one day and then, weeks later, it's gone."

"Just because no one's paying attention doesn't mean something nefarious is behind it," Treyvon says.

"And the fact that all the same people work there year after year. Demons. All of them." Eli nods.

Treyvon laughs. "You're reaching. They probably just like Halloween. I would've applied if my parents didn't want me to also do debate club. It would probably be cool to get to be around all the costumes and stuff. And I bet they work closely with the haunted house, too, right, Ms. L?"

"Yes, they do," I say. "They've been more than generous." And I don't think that has anything to do with them having nefarious reasons.

"See? Demons aren't generous." Treyvon crosses his arms like this is the end of it.

"That's just because they want you to trust them," Hallee says. "It makes sense to me. You don't have to believe it if you don't want to."

CHRISTINA

"I'm not going to," Treyvon says.

"Okay now," I try to redirect, "that was a fun story, but maybe we can focus on getting this all done so it's sorted when the lights come back on." Something about the tale tickles the back of my mind. Not that I think there are really demons working there—that's silly, isn't it? But I can see how someone could believe it. It's just realistic enough and at the same time has that little extra piece that could make a person feel smart for being able to figure it out. That's what makes conspiracies so enticing. But there is something else here—something I can't quite put my finger on—and I don't think it's the howling wind or the pattering of rain outside that has me feeling this way. My fingers find that special place on my arm and run over the scar.

"*If* the lights come back on," Eli says.

"We could tell ghost stories," Hallee suggests.

I bite my lip. Conspiracy theories, I can handle; monsters in the dark, not so much. That serial killer could be showing up here any moment, and the only things we have to defend ourselves are fairy wings, some makeup, and a magenta wig. We're all totally going to die. "I'm not—"

The lights flicker back on, and the three of them cheer. Thank goodness. I let out the longest breath. Not today, Zodiac Killer. Maybe I should look into taking some kind of martial arts class.

Eli jumps to his feet and shoves a piece of paper at me. "You don't have to believe me, but all I'm saying is don't be in this store at midnight on Halloween." He grabs an armful of things to distribute and he's off.

Treyvon leans my way. "Don't listen to him." He grabs a

CHRISTINA

couple of items and goes back to his job from before as well. "Race you back," he calls to Eli.

Hallee's phone rings. "I have to take this." She presses it to her ear. "Mom? Yes, I'm fine." And then she switches to speaking in Hindi and walks from the room.

The paper Eli gave me is a receipt from The Dead of Night. I fold it in half and my heart stops. On the back are a bunch of little flowers—simple, five petals, a swirl in the middle. I've seen them before. Gooseflesh ripples up my arms. I check the receipt again. This is from three years ago. A crash of thunder rattles in the distance and I drop the paper—those little flowers staring up at me.

CHRISTINA

54 DAYS
UNTIL THE STORE CLOSES

Pepper

I haven't had many relationships in my life. It wasn't that I started dating later, or because I was undatable. I've always been a serial monogamist. Once I'd chosen someone, that was it for me—and those relationships lasted a long time. (Some longer than they should have.) I might not have had a lot of experience with it even before the curse, but from the bits and pieces of media I picked up each time I came to town and from the things my coworkers told me—times were constantly changing.

And I had no idea what I was doing.

It hadn't been long since Christina and I were in the back room of the store. So it hadn't been long since I'd figured out I had a crush the size of a sequoia, or since I'd thought that maybe she wanted to kiss me. God knows I wanted to kiss her—and I'd been thinking about it every moment since.

She left so she could get to the haunted house, and I came

back here to my apartment—which was where I'd stayed ever since. I thought that a quick trip to get some food this morning would've helped clear my mind, except the smell of hydrangeas on my walk over to the coffee shop had me thinking back to the scent of her perfume. I wanted to see Christina so badly, and at the same time I was terrified, too. A galaxy's worth of emotions whirled around in my gut and threatened to suck me in like a black hole.

As much as I wanted to believe that I could have something normal even for a little while, part of me was starting to question that. My life, or existence, or whatever it was, was anything but normal.

But here in my apartment I was safe—here, no one could bother me. Here I could avoid the person I so desperately wanted to see. Because even if anyone tried to look for me, they'd never be able to find me.

Being Keeper had some perks, and this apartment that came with the job was one of them. Another thing I could thank magic for. It was decorated just the way I liked, and I could change anything by thinking hard enough. It was a design I wasn't sure I'd ever be able to pull off on my own in the real world, but for some reason it worked. Like magical interior decorators knew how to take my ideas and make them better. I always loved bright colors and bold patterns, and that was everything my space was. Not that anyone could ever come over and see it, but it was a place I was especially proud of.

I sat at the small table in my kitchen and looked out over the street in front of the store. No matter where The Dead of Night magically popped up, my apartment came along, attached like a second story. From my first night here, it felt like the coziest space in the world. Now it felt like home. If there was ever a reason I wasn't Keeper anymore, I'd probably miss it.

There were still a few things I missed about my life from before if I was being completely honest with myself. Like Mom and Dad. It seemed a little silly. I was a grown adult, and people lost their parents all the time—this wasn't much different from that, from losing a loved one—though mine were still out there. Out there not even thinking about me because to them I didn't exist. Yet, to me, they were still very much real and very much a part of my history. There'd been a number of times I wanted to reach out or go and see how they were doing—or like today, I wished I could call and talk to someone, anyone, about what happened with Christina—but I couldn't.

It was probably good I moved away when I did and this all happened here—in a place I didn't have a history with them.

And maybe it was a good thing the curse lasted only until a couple days after Halloween. So the time I spent wondering about these things—about them—wasn't for long. Plus, I'd never have to live through another Thanksgiving, my always and forever least favorite holiday.

It had to have been at least eight years ago that I celebrated it for the last time. The plates were all set out in the formal dining room—the good china and the real silverware. Mom had even bought a new tablecloth for the occasion. Thanksgiving had always been her favorite holiday—she loved to cook and feed people, but most of all, she liked the idea of "giving thanks." Although Mom wasn't a deeply religious person by any means, she believed there had to be some kind of higher power, and even if she wasn't sure what it was, taking time to be thankful once a year suited her. In fact, she embraced the challenge with gusto, making things from scratch and always trying something new. But that year it had been extra special to her.

The new diamond on my hand had been the reason—and she was extra grateful about that.

"What time is Mitchell getting here?" Mom called from the kitchen.

I stood at the large window in the living room, scanning the street out front. The Johnsons were hosting their family this year, and by the number of cars lined up at the curb, everyone had made it. But there was no sign of Mitchell's red Accord. He was late. Over an hour. "Soon," I said.

A flicker of movement down the street was just Mr. Holland moving his truck to accommodate another car. A car that wasn't Mitchell's. It wasn't that he didn't know how important this day was to Mom; I'd made that extremely clear. I'd even wanted us to drive together, but he insisted on going to his buddy's place for their traditional Friendsgiving—an event they'd been doing for years, just the guys. No one could bring a date, and they all had to do the cooking themselves—no store-bought already-prepared anything was allowed. Before, it wasn't a big deal that he had his midmorning with the guys and his afternoon with my family, but that was before he was my fiancé. So he promised he wouldn't eat, just have some snacks and a beer, and he would be here by three.

I was going to kill him when he finally pulled up.

PEPPER

"I'm sure the traffic is terrible," Mom said.

"What traffic?" Dad had abandoned his spot on his recliner and headed to the dining room.

"Teddy," Mom scolded.

"What?" Dad popped a black olive in his mouth.

I texted Mitchell again.

> ME: This is getting ridiculous! Where the fuck are you?!
>
> ME: Dad's eating from the relish tray he's getting desperate
>
> ME: At least pick up your phone and tell me you're too drunk to drive

Dad came up and put his arm around my shoulder and squeezed me into his side. "I'm sure he'll be here soon."

I laid my head against Dad's chest. "Thanks." He had always been my rock.

"Maybe we can keep something warm for him?" Dad whispered.

I looked out the window again. Yep, I was going to kill him. "Mom," I called. "Let's just keep something warm for him. I'm sure he wouldn't want us to wait."

"You think that'll be okay?" she asked.

"Yeah. Let's eat."

"That's my girl." Dad kissed the top of my head.

Mom carried a platter into the dining room, which looked like it could be on the cover of a magazine—fresh salmon with lemon spirals lined the top of the plate. Traditional turkey had never been her style—and we usually had it the week after when they went on sale. "I'm sure he just got caught up." Mom had loved Mitchell from the first moment I brought him home to meet her. "A ball of joyful energy," she had called him. Which was true. Mitchell had a way of lighting up a room. If I was an extraverted introvert, he was 100 percent extravert. He could make anyone his best friend by talking with them for five minutes. It was one of the reasons I had fallen in love with him—talking to him had been so easy.

"Have you two decided where you're going to settle down yet?" Mom kept her voice light as she started dishing out portions.

"Elaine," Dad warned.

"I'm not meddling, I'm just asking," she said. "You can go wherever your hearts take you." Those were her words, but she really wanted to hear we would be staying close by. I couldn't deny that the idea of being far away from them was difficult. But Mitchell's family was across the country, and we had spent the last four years in college close to mine. So maybe it was time to let him be close to his family for a while. I didn't want to be selfish.

After graduation we could go anywhere. "We were thinking Tahiti."

"For the honeymoon."

"No. To live, Mom."

"Very funny." She didn't think my joke was, though.

"We haven't decided. But I promise *you* will be the first to know."

PEPPER

"A white Christmas on the East Coast will be nice," Dad chimed in between scooping sweet potatoes onto his plate and then into his mouth. He was talking about the fact that that year we would all be going to Mitchell's family's house for the holidays. This way our parents could officially meet, and I could see what living in snow might be like.

"We're all going to need to get thicker jackets," Mom said.

"I'm gonna have to get my ski legs ready," Dad said.

"Oh, honey, I don't know if that's a good idea. It's been ages." Mom tsked. "But speaking of white . . ." Mom had been hinting at wedding dress shopping for a while now, but we hadn't even officially set a date yet.

"I suppose it couldn't hurt to start looking," I said.

Mom squealed like she was the one getting married. "There's this boutique I've had my eye on."

"Sounds great, Mom." From there, she sprung into all the other wedding research she'd been doing. It was a little overwhelming, but at the same time, I guess it meant I didn't have to do as much work, which wasn't a bad thing. Especially since the idea of wedding planning gave me a rash. It was all a little too much. Maybe Mitchell would be up for eloping?

As dinner progressed, Mom's excitement never faltered, and soon she was carrying a pie into the dining room. "Who's ready for dessert?"

Before I could respond, my cell rang—Mitchell's name flashed across the screen. "Where the hell are you?" I asked as soon as I picked up.

"Pepper?" the person on the other end asked—a voice that was most definitely not Mitchell.

PEPPER

I checked the screen again to make sure I hadn't misread who was calling, but no, it was Mitchell's name. My heart dropped into my stomach. "Yeah, it's Pepper, who's this?" I got up from the table and went back to the window. It was much darker out now, and the porch lights at the house across the street had been turned on.

"It's Ian, Mitchell's friend. There's been an accident."

A car horn outside my apartment window brought me back to my safe little kitchen in my safe little space, which was so many miles and so many years away from those memories.

I took a deep breath and popped another bite of apple fritter into my mouth. I had headed out earlier that morning to grab it and a cardamom hot cocoa from Glazed & Confused. The hot cocoa was a new flavor for me—it was warm and sweet with a tiny hint of spice that was a little unexpected. Peppermint hot cocoa was my usual go-to, but I would definitely be getting this one again before the month was over. The apple fritter, however, was one of my favorite things. A little crisp on the outside and warm and soft in the middle, with big chunks of cinnamon apples. And getting there close to opening meant they were fresh from the oven. But now as I chewed, it felt a little too gummy, so I wrapped it up for later.

That accident of Mitchell's changed so much about my life. It was how I ended up here in a place I loved. Meeting Christina had been an accident, too. And while it didn't seem like it at the time, maybe this one would also bring me something good.

Moping around was not an activity I was used to. I needed to shake myself out of this. I needed to find that bright side. There had to be one.

PEPPER

The antique cuckoo clock that hung between my kitchen and living room chimed. That was it. It was time to move forward to see what I could make with these lemons, and if I hurried, I could get downstairs for the first shift of the day.

With my argyle cardigan pulled tightly around my shoulders, I headed out my front door, down the steps, and to the other door. Thanks to the magic, I was connected to The Dead of Night, so when I left my apartment to go to work, I'd walk right inside the store. When leaving the store, if I thought about going home, when I walked out the back door, instead of actually being outside I'd be back in this special place, where I could climb the stairs to my apartment. It was the shortest commute I'd ever had to any job. Which was another benefit of my predicament.

As soon as the door to The Dead of Night closed behind me, Caleb rushed over, almost like he'd been waiting for my arrival. "It's all wrong!"

Maybe I should've gotten a shot of espresso in my hot cocoa this morning. "What's 'all wrong'?"

"The store! The medieval section is where the community helper section is, and some of the wigs are in the accessory section and vice versa like they started to get moved but it wasn't finished." Today Caleb was dressed as a boba tea, so it was a little difficult to take him seriously the way his "straw" bounced around when he spoke.

"Things don't just move around—"

"Exactly! New Guy was working last night, and we think he did it." It seemed the name Lisa made for our newest staff member had been getting around. "Molly was here, and she said that he said that he thought we had some 'efficiency issues.'" Caleb used air quotes.

No one did any actual labor setting up The Dead of Night. It appeared the way that would be best for the environment it was set up in. Stock had to be added to certain areas to give the illusion that it was all done manually, but that was all a part of the magic of the store. And the fact that New Guy—if everyone else was going to call him that, so was I—thought he knew better was more than a little comical.

"Is Dewy in yet?" I asked.

"No. Thank god. They would freak!"

That was an understatement. "Who's here already besides you?"

"Lisa, and Bryan will be here any minute."

"Okay, you all get started on moving everything back. Once Bryan gets in, I'll send her to help you, and when Dewy gets here, well . . . I'll figure out a way to stall them. But you're all going to have to work super-fast. Got it?" My time as a teacher, working on live performances, had taught me one thing, and that was to think on my feet. Curtain call came whether we were ready or not. There wasn't time to stress.

"On it!" Caleb scurried away as quickly as the skirt of his boba tea outfit allowed him to.

"Maybe take the costume off until you're done," I called after him.

He threw a thumbs-up in the air and started wiggling the costume over his head as he pushed through the door to the front of the store.

I walked over to Dewy's desk with its organized stacks of

papers and files and glanced at where Caleb had just gone. It was a necessary evil. With a swoop, I slid everything onto the floor. And not a moment too soon, as the back door opened and Dewy walked in. I quickly got down on my hands and knees. "Shut the door!" I called. It was showtime.

"What happened?" Dewy rushed over.

I shook my head. "Right as I came in, so did a big gust of wind, and whoosh. I've never seen anything like it. I think the door to the front of the store was open, so it created this kind of suction or something." I made a show, waving my hands in the air.

"I've told them time and again to keep that door closed."

"I know you have." I let out a dramatic sigh.

"Maybe I should put up a sign." If Dewy was flustered, they didn't show it.

I nodded. "That's a great idea. But first let's get this mess figured out."

Dewy and I got to work sorting all their papers and files as Bryan walked in. Last time she worked, a few days ago, her hair was a light blue, and now it was a mix of magenta and purple.

"Lisa has your assignment," I told her, and pointed to the front of the store.

She clocked in, adjusting her oversized heart glasses on her face. "You don't want any help here?"

"No, we've got this under control." I had to give the rest of the staff as much time as necessary to get the store back to normal even if that meant I had to do a little sabotage. "Wait, this pile is for receivables, right?"

"No. That's this one." Dewy pointed to another stack.

"That's right." I started dismantling the entire collection. I felt bad for creating extra work, but it was unavoidable.

"You know, I can take care of this if you want to make sure the doors get open on time," Dewy said, clearly annoyed at my incompetence.

"Are you sure? I don't want to leave all this for you, especially since I made the mess."

"It's not a problem. At all. Accidents happen." Dewy's lips were firmly pressed together. Yeah, I wasn't winning any points with them today, but the other Dead of Night staff would appreciate my sacrifice. Dewy was an amazing manager—they took their job seriously and cared immensely about the store and the people who worked there. This little stunt by New Guy would've been a punch in the gut—and we all loved Dewy too much to see that happen.

"Well, if you're sure."

"I'm sure," they said. "Oh, and Pepper? I'm glad you're feeling better."

That had been my excuse for not being here for the last couple of days. "Thanks." I got to my feet and dusted myself off. "You do whatever you need to do back here; I've got up front covered."

"And since Lisa's here, you can go to her with anything if there are issues," Dewy said.

"You got it, boss." I winked at them and walked away. Lisa would be glad to know that she was seen as the number two around here—that all her hard work was paying off.

PEPPER

In the front of the store, Lisa, Caleb, and Bryan were full out sprinting back and forth, getting everything put back in its original place. "I've bought you at least thirty minutes. How are we looking?"

Caleb braced his hands on his knees. "We should be good."

Doors opened in ten minutes, and since it was still early in our season, we wouldn't see many customers until later in the day. "I can help until opening. Tell me what to do." This was one of the best parts of working at The Dead of Night. People cared about one another. Well, most of the people. It wasn't looking good for New Guy, but that was okay; maybe one day he'd come around. Until then, we still made a good team.

"If you can start shifting the wigs back to their normal spot, that would be great," Lisa said as she ran by. "Let's go, Caleb."

He took a breath and sprinted off.

I spent nine minutes shifting things around, opened the doors right on time, and made sure to give Dewy an update that all was running smoothly up front, so they didn't come wandering out to check. No one complained about the extra work; they all just did what needed to be done.

There was never a dull moment in the store.

By midmorning the mess New Guy left us was completely undone, and Dewy was none the wiser. They also weren't as annoyed with me anymore since my little "incident" uncovered a report that had been misplaced. I chalked it up as another happy accident—which most definitely felt like a good sign.

My cell phone vibrated in my pocket. That was weird. I was already at the store.

PEPPER

> CHRISTINA: This is Christina... you know in case you didn't save my contact information... anyway... I was texting you about the pallets...

I imagined her cheeks turning their signature apple red color, and a bunch of butterflies flapped their wings excitedly inside my stomach. We'd exchanged numbers, but I wasn't about to be the first person to use hers. Not because I didn't want to—more because I didn't know what to say or even how to say it.

> ME: Yes, I know who you are.
>
> CHRISTINA: Right of course... I hope I'm not bothering you...
>
> ME: No it's fine.
>
> CHRISTINA: So the pallets??... When do you think you could bring them by?... Or I could probably find someone to pick them up if it's too much trouble...
>
> ME: It's no trouble at all.

This could've been the bright side I was looking for today. But I didn't want to seem too eager—worried it could possibly put her off.

> ME: Can I bring them to you tomorrow?

PEPPER

My stomach did a somersault as three little dots appeared.

> **CHRISTINA:** Yeah... That would be great... See you soon then... ♥

A heart. That had to mean something, didn't it? The butterflies in my belly busted out in a full-scale dance party. Oh crap. What was I going to wear?

54 DAYS
UNTIL THE STORE CLOSES

Christina

The last students leave, and the room hums with silence after sixth period. My cell phone buzzes before I even have a chance to take a breath.

DAD flashes on the screen.

He never calls. It's usually Emily, or Mom, or Ashley even, but never Dad. I snatch the phone up and press it to my ear.

"Everything okay?" I ask.

"Yes, Pumpkin, everything's fine. Just wanted you to know people are getting a little restless over here," he says, and I let out a breath. So this is the reason he's calling. Everyone else is complaining that I haven't officially RSVP'd to Emily's engagement party—and it's not that I haven't wanted to. I just need to know if I can take an entire day off and still be on schedule. Getting behind this early in the planning and preparation stage would be a disaster.

"It's looking promising, but I don't want to make any

commitments in case something comes up." I don't understand why they can't *understand* this.

"What's going to come up? Halloween doesn't exactly call for an emergency situation, and it's still way over a month out." His voice is light, but the comment cuts deep. This is the problem. They don't see what I do as something serious even though there are people depending on me—*lots* of people.

I clench my teeth and count to three—although I really need to count to ten. "It's an important event—"

"I'm sure it is. But it's your sister's engagement. Which is arguably more important, wouldn't you say." He says this like a statement, not a question, and I'm not sure why both things can't be equally important. "Can't you tell your sister you will be there?"

"I could, but I want to be one hundred percent sure first. There's so much to do, and I'm under a lot of stress—"

"I thought you took this job because it was *less* stressful," he tells me, or more specifically, he's using my own words against me. One of the reasons I left my last job was that it was too stressful—but that was only one out of a much more extensive list of things I didn't like about it.

"I did. It's just a different kind. They are counting on me to make this event really spectacular." And the school needs the funding, but I don't say that. It'll just get him started about how schools don't know how to budget, and blah, blah, blah, like he's ever worked in a school or knows anything about what we have to deal with on a daily basis. "It doesn't mean I don't want to be there; I've gotta figure it out, okay?"

"And no one else is more capable of doing an amazing job

CHRISTINA

than you are. You can do anything you set your mind to." He repeats the thing he's said to me since I was little for the gazillionth time. "I just wanted to let you know it's really important to Emily that you are there." The tone stays light. Dad has never been one to raise his voice—he doesn't need to—but the underlying message is loud and clear. I need to make this happen or I'll never hear the end of it.

"I know. She told me. Now I have to go if I want to stay on schedule."

"Love you, Pumpkin," he says. "And we'll keep this little conversation between us, don't worry." He says it like he's doing me a favor, and in a way he is. If Dad calls, that means everyone is talking—aka complaining—once again, about me. I will need to deal with this quickly, just not right now.

"I promise I'll talk to her," I tell him. "Love you, too, Dad."

My classroom door swings open, and Mia from my third period class walks in as I toss my phone back into my bag. I'm really not going to catch a break today, it seems. I've got so much to do, and I should've left seven minutes ago.

"Something I can help you with?" I ask.

"Mr. Kennedy was hoping he could borrow your key to the janitor's closet. This kid Brady's soda exploded in his backpack, and I guess the janitor is busy cleaning up some puke or something."

"I don't think I have one," I tell her.

"Can you check, please? Mr. Ecklers shooed me out of his class before I could even ask, and it's a huge mess."

I shimmy and yank open the top desk drawer—it hasn't worked right since my first day walking into this room. It's the

---

CHRISTINA

kind of desk that has seen some things, like it was used in detention or something before, with writing and marks all over it. All the drawer needs is a little beeswax to get it sliding smoothly in and out, but I keep forgetting to bring some.

I riffle through the pencil tray I shoved in here the first week I started teaching—to "stay better organized," ha! It's a mess of found pens and pencils and random knickknacks. With all the shaking and lack of care when tossing things inside, items have gotten shoved to the back, but since the drawer doesn't open wide enough, I pull the tray out. And there, right in the back corner, is a small set of keys that, now that I think about it, I remember being in the drawer and not knowing what they were for. "Are these them?" I ask.

Mia shrugs. "It's possible, and more than what Mr. Ecklers offered." She rolls her eyes. He's known to be quite the curmudgeon. "But I can ask Mr. Kennedy." She reaches her hand out, and I pass her the keys.

"Tell him to hold on to them. I've gotta get out of here."

"Oh. Are we going to get to spray-paint those skeletons today?" Mia wiggles her eyebrows like she is itching to get her hands on some cans of neon paint—because "it'll look so cool under the black lights."

Which, yes. Shit. I was supposed to pick some up at the store before heading over there today. "If I can get out of here, yes."

"Say no more." She rushes out the door.

Answering that call was the worst idea—I should've let Dad go to voicemail. Now I really have to hurry if I want to go to the library before I head to the hardware store. I'm about to

---

CHRISTINA

shove the pencil tray back into the drawer when I hesitate. Has this always been here? My fingers trace over a drawing of a flower. The same one from the back of the receipt. The same one that's on the wall in the staging house. A chill races up my spine and my scalp tingles.

I should know these—my heart, not my brain, is telling me, which is the oddest sensation. Do they remind me of something sentimental? Is that why my stomach is getting tight? It feels like something I should remember—but just like the wind, it's something I feel but I can't see.

Sirens whirl by on the street in front of the school and pull me out of my head. I need to go. I stop rubbing the scar on my arm, shove the tray back in, and grab my bag.

"Ms. Loring, to what do I owe the pleasure?" Mrs. Turner, our lovely librarian, calls out to me as I walk through the library door—the scent of old paper and her lavender aromatherapy air freshener greeting me.

"Need to do a little research, and I couldn't think of a better person to talk to."

Mrs. Turner pushes her ruby glasses up the bridge of her nose. "I'm your girl. What kind of information are you looking for?"

The flowers are the first thing to pop into my head, but instead I go with, "Dr. W left me some notes about the haunted house, but we're missing information about the sound system, so I thought maybe I could reach out to the teacher before him."

CHRISTINA

"And you came to me for yearbooks, since Mrs. Beckerstein isn't the most prolific with the computer." That was a kind way of saying the secretary was in no way a tech-savvy girl. She still took minutes with pen and paper at our staff meeting. But if I went to her with a name, she might be able to look it up.

"Exactly."

"Let me see what I can do," Mrs. Turner says. "Was it Mrs. Scott?"

"I'm sorry?" I ask.

She scans the line of books on a shelf behind the desk. "The teacher before Dr. W. I was thinking it was Mrs. Scott, but she left when our last principal retired." She grabs a book off the shelf. "Ah, here it is." She looks at the book in her hand, then grabs two more. "Just in case."

I'm not sure just in case of what, but I don't have time to ask. "Thank you. I really appreciate this."

"No problem, deary. Let me know what you find, though, will you? I pride myself on knowing all the teachers here and, well"—she taps her head—"maybe I need a little afternoon coffee." She chuckles.

"Sign me up for one of those," I say. "I just don't have time."

"Don't let me keep you," Mrs. Turner says. "Have a wonderful rest of your day."

"You too."

After spending the afternoon at the haunted house spray-painting skeletons, I settle onto my couch with all the yearbooks and a glass of angry water—seltzer is too nice a name for something so aggressively bubbled. Licorice decides now is a good time to inspect the new objects I've brought into his domain. He takes a few moments sniffing their glossy covers, then flops onto his back to lick his hind leg. Silly cat.

The spine protests as I open the first one. The task is simple enough, yet anxiety is swirling in my stomach, and my guava-flavored seltzer water isn't helping settle it like it usually does. Seriously, what's the worst thing I could find? My mind can't even come up with a worst-case scenario. Nothing about this task would call for one, and yet lingering dread tightens in my chest. I should've poured a glass of Moscato instead of an angry water before I started this. But then I'd probably spill it all over the books, and Mrs. Turner would never trust me again. Although white wine wouldn't stain, it would still be sticky and gross. I really should switch to red—there was that article about how it helps with blood pressure.

Focus, Christina.

I take a deep breath and search for the teachers' section, scanning each name and title, then flipping the page. I don't think I've met even half of these people, which tells me I need to get out more—but I don't have the time, especially right now. The next month and a half are full of work and haunted house stuff, aka more work. I should at least try to hit the gym, since I pay for a membership and it's easily been a few weeks since I've been there. My finger keeps scanning along the names. Ms. Wu—the math teacher—looks completely different than she does now, but dang, short hair looks good on her.

Wait. That's strange. I may not have been completely focused, but there wasn't a listing for the theater teacher. Did I

CHRISTINA

miss it? I go back to the beginning and scan again, this time more carefully. But as I get to the end of the teacher section for the second time, they aren't in here. Maybe they were sick that day? And couldn't make the time to do retakes? Totally possible.

No worries. They'll have to be in the back with all the photos from the theater department's many productions, and their name will for sure be listed there. It doesn't take long before I'm scanning photos from *Grease* and then candids from that year's haunted house. I wasn't at school with any of these kids so none of them are recognizable, but the feeling of the photos is the same. Smiling faces, grand gestures—big personalities—and of course, there are a bunch with kids covered in fake blood. At the very end of the section, there is a group shot out in front of the haunted house building, but unless the teacher that year looked young enough to be a high school student, they aren't in there. Not even their name is listed on the picture of the program from that year's performance.

That's super weird.

They couldn't have *not* had a teacher. That wouldn't make sense at all, would it? But then again, Mrs. Turner said she couldn't remember who it was, so maybe that's what "just in case" meant.

I grab the yearbook for the year before the one currently in my hand and do the same thing. And once again I come up empty-handed. Cami and I started teaching at the same time so it's not like she would have any idea. Could I ask Principal Wilkson? I really don't want to bother him. Maybe his secre-

---

CHRISTINA

tary could figure out how to look it up—but that's probably wishful thinking—or she would let me jump on her computer. Is it even legal for them to give out past employees' information?

It's not like I want to know for nefarious reasons. I just want to figure out how the sound system works and if any of them noticed those weird little flowers—or was perhaps the one who left them.

There's probably a completely logical reason why the theater teacher isn't listed in these books—even though every other teacher in every other subject is there, and most have more than one photo, posing with the club they are in charge of.

Witness protection?

Celebrity?

Is there a word for "fear of photography"?

My cell phone rings, and my little sister's name and face fill the screen. Shit. The call with Dad from earlier replays in my mind. I had planned on touching base with Emily, it just hasn't happened yet, but if I avoid her any longer, she'll probably think I'm dead, so I pick up—the picture of her replaced by her actual face, an expression of faux shock plastered there.

"Hey, Em. What's up?" I ask, knowing full well what this conversation is going to be about.

"You *are* still alive. I'll make sure to cancel that wellness check." Her scowl is softened by the grin she's trying to suppress. She's always been a terrible liar.

"Very funny."

CHRISTINA

"What *isn't* funny is that I still haven't gotten your RSVP yet." She presses her lips together. "Titi, you know you have to come. You have three weeks now to make it happen. I'm only going to get married once."

"You hope."

She narrows her eyes at me. "Now who's being not funny."

"I know, I'm sorry. I've just been—"

"Busy, I know." She shakes her head at me the same way Mom does—like she's disappointed. My stomach sinks. This is one of the many reasons I don't want to go. It's not that I don't love and support Emily—I do—I'm just . . . tired. Tired of the guilt from Mom and Dad, and Ashley, and now Emily, too. She gives me her best puppy dog eyes, and I crumble.

"I'll be there."

Her entire face lights up. "Promise? You aren't just saying—"

"I promise. I've just had a lot on my mind. This is a really big event, and the whole town is counting on me." It's a lot of pressure, and even if I'm not sure this is going to be my forever career, it's at least something I'm pretty good at, and right now—away from the pressures of home and my sisters—that's enough.

She leans back on her couch. "Antonio and I will totally come out and support you. I know it's super stressful. If you weren't so far away, I could help you after work."

"But I moved to the middle of nowhere—yeah, I know."

Licorice, obviously sensing my distraction, jumps from the couch to the coffee table to inspect the bubbles in my water. I give him a stern look and shoo him off. He's seriously the naughtiest kitty in the world.

CHRISTINA

"Titi." Her voice is light, not accusatory like Mom's or Ashley's. She means well. I really shouldn't give her a hard time. None of this is her fault. But all those words and feelings are rolling around in my brain and don't want to come out of my mouth, so instead we're both quiet.

She's in her robe—the one I bought her three Christmases ago. She always complains she's cold no matter what time of year it is. That's why that year it felt like the perfect gift. I remember it so vividly—almost as if it were yesterday.

I think it was the winter blues that had me down. Shopping had felt like such a chore. Getting out of bed started to feel like a chore, but I did it and braved the crowds and wandered store to store doing my best not to cry while picking out gifts for my family. I might have also been PMSing at the time.

Without even meaning to, I found myself in the PJ section at Nordstrom, and there it was—a gift that screamed Emily.

That Christmas morning was like any other in the Loring house. Mom always wanted the holidays to be special—an event that was special for "her girls." Even though we were adults by this time, Mom would wake up early to make pancakes, and the smell of maple syrup was the first thing to greet me. I wandered downstairs, where she stood at the stove in her PJs that matched my own—another tradition the Loring family was known for.

"You're up," she said. "Coffee is all ready." She tipped her head toward the carafe on the counter, which no doubt was already full of the steaming liquid of the gods.

As I fixed myself a cup, I asked, "Am I the last one?" A chatter of conversations came from the formal living room.

CHRISTINA

"We were about to send someone up," Mom replied.

"Sorry." I took a sip of the warm brew from my cup—creamy and sweet, just how I liked it.

"The kids already opened their gifts. They couldn't wait any longer." She meant my niece and nephew, and it hurt a little, but I understood. Christmas mornings when my parents made us wait to open gifts when I was the kids' age were brutal. I was sure to get the play-by-play later of what I missed anyway. She turned away from the stove toward me. "How are you feeling today?"

I took another sip of my coffee before responding. "It feels good to be home," I replied, which was true, but I still felt tired deep in my bones.

"I'm glad you came," Mom said, and I was glad, too. For a moment I'd said I would drive down for the day—since missing altogether would be out of the question—but Mom "persuaded" me to stay the night like tradition dictated, and there in the kitchen with the scent of coffee and maple and then pine from the fresh tree in the other room, my soul felt lighter than it had in the past two months.

"We will eat first and then we will open our presents," Mom said.

And true to her word, once the last pancake had been eaten, the rest of the family sat around the perfectly manicured tree with a stack of presents next to each of us—and over the next hour we would take turns opening each of them one at a time so everyone could see.

"Golf clubs? You shouldn't have," Dad said.

"Luke says they're the best," Ashley said.

CHRISTINA

"They should help with that bogey problem," Luke, Ashley's husband, joked, and Dad laughed.

"Oh, then you will love this." Emily stood and pulled a small box off Dad's stack and handed it to him. He looked to Mom since we were breaking the rules of order—one gift at a time—but Mom nodded, and Dad unwrapped it. "The Madison Club."

"Antonio got them," Emily said.

"You're going to love it," Antonio, Emily's fiancé, said.

"And there's something for you, too, Mom." Emily did the same—standing and sliding a small box off Mom's stack for her to open.

"I hope you don't think I'm playing a round or whatever it's called," Mom said as she unwrapped it, then she smiled. "This is more like it."

"And you can pick your own services, though if you want a massage, I'll get you the name of the person Antonio's co-worker recommends," Ashley said.

"I'll let you know." Mom winked.

This was what Christmas was in the Loring house. Who could outdo the others in getting the perfect gift. That year, though, it felt like it had gotten out of hand, and the gifts I'd picked out for everyone seemed to pale in comparison even though I had been very specific in choosing them.

"You're next, love," Mom said to Emily.

She picked up the box I'd given her, and I cringed. How was I supposed to follow golf clubs and a paid vacation? But before I could figure out a way to get her to stop, she already had it open, and she squealed, "This is perfect!" She yanked the robe out, clutching it tight to her chest. "This has to be the best gift ever. Thank you, Titi." She jumped up and hugged me before slipping the robe on and wearing it for the remainder of the day.

Ashley looked like she'd bitten into an olive with a pit still inside. Mom commented, "Well, isn't that nice." But those things didn't bother me, and I smiled for what felt like the first time in days.

Seeing Emily still wearing it now warms my insides.

"I get why you did it," she says, pulling me out of my thoughts. "I just miss seeing you more is all."

"I miss you, too." Which isn't a lie. It's just everyone else I'm not excited about seeing again. Clover Creek is just far enough away that a pop-in isn't possible, but it's not far enough to avoid the constant guilt trips of *Why don't you come home more often?*

"Okay, enough of that. Give me the tea. What's going on? Who's sleeping with who in the teachers' lounge?" Emily gives me a smile, the real happy one she's known for. She's good at this, at people and small talk, something I am not.

I laugh. "It's not that dramatic." Although Fran and Lotti have seemed to be a little extra flirty since Fran finalized her divorce. I could totally picture them going at it on the worn-out green sofa in the corner of the teachers' lounge—even with the mayonnaise grease stain. At least we all hope it's just mayo. Who else has braved the stain for some French lessons on that old thing?

"Oh . . . you've got something. Tell me." She brings the phone closer like she's leaning in for me to whisper in her ear.

"It's nothing." But Pepper's face flashes through my mind.

CHRISTINA

"You like someone. Is it that new coach? What did you say their name was?"

"It's not the coach," I say. But if she thinks it could be, does that mean I gave off that impression? Does anyone at school think— I shake my head. "It's not that big a deal. She works at the Halloween store and has offered to help with the haunted house is all."

"Hold up. She's providing free labor to hang out with you? She sounds amazing. Tell me more. What does she look like?"

How does one describe Pepper in a way that would do her justice? "A ray of sunshine on an otherwise cloudy day" could do the trick, but it really isn't something Emily could picture. "Dark hair, blue eyes, and her wardrobe spilled out of a box of Fruity Pebbles."

"Well, you could use a little color in your life." Emily laughs.

"Black is just easier. It goes with everything." And it's harder to stain.

"When are you going to see her again?"

"Soon, probably. I'm in the store all the time." I force a laugh. It kind of makes me sound like a stalker—which I'm totally not—but the sound is fake even to my own ears. Emily will never buy it.

"Bring her to the party," she suggests as if this were the most logical thing in the world. It isn't.

I stare blankly at her. "We barely know each other, and I'm supposed to be like, 'Hey, want to come to my baby sister's engagement party with me'?"

"Yes. That's exactly what you're supposed to do. What's wrong with that?"

CHRISTINA

"Don't you think it would be awkward for her? Meeting the family feels like something you do after dating for, I don't know, weeks or months even, not when you've just hung out a few times."

"Consider it a crash course. If she can't get along with the Loring family, you don't have to waste your time."

I purse my lips at her. She has a point. "I hate it when you make so much sense."

She gasps. "How dare I be so reasonable."

We both laugh. Why can't the rest of my family be this easy to talk to?

I take a deep breath. "I'm not like you or Ashley. So please don't be disappointed if I come alone, okay?"

"Oh my god. Never," Emily says. "I want you to be happy. No pressure. But if you're feeling it, just know it's okay. And I promise not to say anything to anyone, and if you show up with her, cool. If not, NBD. I'm just happy *you're* coming."

"And giving a speech."

"Yeah, and that."

"You're lucky I love you," I tell her.

"Yes, I am," she says. "Now, about me." She winks. "It looks like we are going into beta testing soon."

"Already? That's amazing."

"Our programmers are gods—at least that's what I'm telling everyone. But seriously, they're so excited, too. Profit sharing was totally the right thing to do. You're a genius, by the way."

"Says the girl who's about to be the next Bill Gates." My kid sister is literally one of the smartest women I know. Plus, she's

---

CHRISTINA

outgoing and not afraid of anything—like failure. Sometimes I wish I could be more like her.

Emily's cheeks flush red—a trait she shares with me.

For the next ten minutes, she gives me the rundown about her work and what's all going on—and to be honest, I understand only about half of what she says. Tech has never been my thing. I'm lucky I can get my phone or computer to work most days.

"But seriously, think about inviting this girl, okay?"

"I promise you I'll think about it."

"What's her name? I'm going to look her up on social."

I clench my teeth. "I'm not sure I'm ready for that yet."

She lets out a long sigh. "Fine. For now," she says. "Talk to you soon."

"Love you."

"Love you, too."

And then she's gone.

With my phone still in my hand, I log in to socials and look up Pepper White. I seriously can't believe I didn't think of doing this before. The list of people with the same name is surprisingly longer than I expected, but none of them seem to be her, so I try a different social media site instead. Not everyone has accounts on every platform; I keep contemplating deleting mine, but then what would the family say? I roll my eyes before searching for Pepper. But again, I can't find her.

My finger traces the scar on my arm. I have social media only for family reasons, and I don't really post anything. Maybe she's just incognito—like she's one of those accounts on private

---

CHRISTINA

without a photo of herself as the profile picture. Or maybe she doesn't have an account at all. I'll ask her the next time I see her.

On the screen is a post from my older sister, Ashley—a picture of a wrapped gift she can't wait to give Emily for her engagement. Seriously, she's already gotten them a present? And according to the description, she's already written her speech, too.

Ugh.

I close the app and grab my laptop. No way can I show up unprepared to this event. Maybe having someone with me wouldn't be the worst idea in the world. Maybe then my family won't talk about how I'm the last to find someone, and I won't have to explain a million times how I'm not dating anyone. Plus, it would be nice to have a reason to hang out with Pepper again.

But do I have the courage to ask her?

CHRISTINA

53 DAYS
UNTIL THE STORE CLOSES

Pepper

Nerves shook my body as I drove toward the haunted house to drop off the pallets Christina had asked for. The feeling was completely ridiculous. I was doing her a favor. Her little heart emoji in her text was because she was grateful, nothing more, and trying to assign some kind of deeper meaning didn't make it true. I was being ridiculous. Even though there was zero doubt in my mind that I was crushing hard on her, it would've been completely irresponsible to try and do anything about it. First—and actually most important—I didn't even know if she felt the same, despite that moment we had in the back of The Dead of Night. And second, I really had no idea how to pursue her even if I wanted to. Dewy had once told me it was called being a late bloomer—but I still felt like a dandelion in a garden full of roses.

I'd only ever dated men—a casual make-out session at a party didn't count—so this was all completely new territory.

My insides were all twisted up like a pretzel, and this thought, this feeling, made me burst out laughing. This wasn't a problem. Pretzels were delicious. I loved one with a little bit of crunchy salt and some mustard. I was being silly. Whatever was meant to be would happen. Sure, free will existed, but there was something called fate—which was how I ended up at The Dead of Night. Yes, some things you could control, but people weren't one of those things. As much as I liked Christina, I couldn't make her like me back. I just had to go with the flow and enjoy the butterflies dancing in my belly.

I pulled up to the front of the haunted house, and Christina walked out in black jeans and a black T-shirt, her blonde hair hanging loosely around her face, and I threw the car into park.

A beat passed—Christina looking at me, me looking at Christina. My heart pounding harder than a double bass drum.

"I hope this wasn't too much trouble," she said just before biting her lip—the signature red lipstick of hers made her already white teeth seem even brighter.

I cleared my throat. "No trouble at all. It's not really my day to be on shift anyway." It wasn't technically a lie since I was never technically supposed to be on shift.

"I had good timing, then, I guess." She brushed her hair away from her face and tucked it behind her ear.

"Seems that way." I opened the back of the hearse. "Where do you want these?"

Christina spun around and spread her arms out. "Anywhere here is fine."

"Perfect." I grabbed the first pallet and yanked.

PEPPER

"Let me help you." Christina stepped forward, hands outstretched.

"Oh yeah. Sure." *Oh yeah. Sure.* I wanted to kick myself. It had been forever since I'd felt so awkward around anyone. Why was it when you liked someone, it turned your brain into mashed potatoes?

"I'm sorry I was a little freaked out last time I saw you at the store," she said, and there were those cheeks bright as the sweetest cherry. "If I made you uncomfortable—"

"Me? Uncomfortable? No. Not at all."

"So you didn't think I was weird about being afraid of the rain?"

I shook my head. Christina, "weird"? There were a million words I could use to describe her—smart, beautiful, determined, driven—but "weird" would never be one of them. "No," I replied to her.

"Okay." She smiled. "You were just so cool and calm, I wasn't sure."

Me "cool and calm"? I wanted to laugh, but instead I slid the pallet forward, and she grabbed the other side. "Things seem to be coming along." I had no idea what else to say, and I especially didn't want to talk about me and how nervous I was just standing this close to her.

Christina nodded. "The kids really know what they're doing. Seriously, I'm not sure any of this would be done without them. They have it down to a science; I'm not even sure they need me here at all." She laughed but it wasn't the funny kind—it was a little sad, a little self-deprecating, and she didn't need to do that to herself.

PEPPER

"They're lucky to have you," I said as we hoisted the second pallet out of the car and laid it on top of the first one right outside the house's front door. "This is all a lot of work, and having someone they trust and depend on is really important. Don't sell yourself short." *I think you're incredible* is also what I wanted to say, but I kept that to myself.

"I guess. Sometimes I wonder if I'm cut out for all of this."

We grabbed another pallet and put it with the others.

"My family is a bunch of overachievers," she continued, "and sometimes I get the feeling this isn't good enough for them. That I'm just the odd one out."

"What about you?"

"What?"

"Is it good enough for you?" So many people looked at teaching like it was this easy job, but it wasn't. It was challenging and rewarding and frustrating and satisfying all wrapped into one—usually all happening on the same day. Christina seemed like someone who wasn't afraid of a challenge. She took on this job, built furniture, and jumped into this event with both feet. But today she seemed unsure. I hated that anyone made her feel less than what she was.

"I'm enjoying it more than I expected—not that I didn't think I would enjoy it—but I'm not sure it's something I'm passionate about, and I think that's really what the kids need, you know?"

"That's true." I'd had too many professors over the years who probably should've retired instead of trying to teach teachers how to teach when you could see they didn't have the heart for it anymore. But if Christina didn't think she could do this, that could mean she would leave, and I, for one, didn't want that to happen.

"My older sister got her law degree, and now she's a stay-at-home mom, but she's given my parents grandchildren, so . . ." She let out a long sigh. "And my little sister, she's designing this app that's going to revolutionize the way people connect with one another. It's hard to compare to those things."

"Right. You're just changing kids' lives is all. No big deal." I cringed at the sarcasm in my own tone. But teaching was hard, and more people needed to respect that. If there weren't teachers, there wouldn't be lawyers or people who could create apps. They all had to learn from someone. Teachers were the heart and soul of communities—and I didn't feel that way just because I was one. Plus, Christina needed to see how important she was in the grand scheme of things.

She stopped, her gaze shifting to the side. I wished I could look inside her head, see what she had going on in there. "You really think so?"

"I do. Teaching feels hard and thankless, but when you see your students grow and succeed, it makes it all worth it." She would see. This would all be worth it.

She raised her brows at me. "Have you been a teacher before?"

Damn it. She'd done it again—broken down my barriers and gotten me talking without thinking. There were too many things I couldn't explain, and I didn't want to have to try—especially when she was just starting to open up. "Ouch." I yanked my hand away from the pallet and shoved my finger in my mouth. "Splinter," I told her, but I was completely unharmed.

"We should probably be wearing gloves, huh?"

"That would've been smart." I slid the next one out of the back of the hearse, and Christina came to assist. "It seems like this Halloween thing might be rubbing off on you a little if you are watching videos about it," I said, mostly to change the subject again.

"Unlike some people, I don't particularly like to be scared." There went those brows again, like she was scrutinizing me.

We placed the next pallet with the others, and I spread my arms out, gesturing to everything around us. "It's not real, though. Dead people aren't really coming out of the ground."

"I suppose." She tipped her head back and forth. "'Do the thing you think you cannot,'" she said. "Sorry, Eleanor Roosevelt said that. Never mind."

I wasn't sure where she was going with that, nor did I know much about Eleanor Roosevelt, and since all the pallets were out of the car, I closed the back of the hearse.

"Thanks again for bringing these over," she said, her cheeks rosy again.

"It's like I said, I got you. It was no trouble at all." I stood there staring at her. She shuffled her feet from side to side. "I don't want to keep you."

"Oh. Yeah. Same." She looked a little surprised. And I immediately realized my mistake. I should've been thinking of a reason to stay, not leave, but it was too late.

PEPPER

"I'll see you around," I said, but what I really wanted to do was punch myself.

"I'll text you if I need anything else, then," she said. "Or you could text me."

"Yeah, totally," I said as I got in the car and drove away. Well, *that* was a disaster. If only there was a book on how to talk to hot girls. I really could've used one.

PEPPER

48 DAYS

UNTIL THE STORE CLOSES

Christina

While I haven't been as committed to my fitness routine lately, my mind won't stop racing with thoughts about the old teacher, those little flowers, the haunted house and everything that needs to be done, and of course what my sister and I talked about—Pepper. Emily wants me to invite her to her engagement party, which feels like a giant step. Sure, we'd been out a couple of times, but meeting the *entire* family?

Which is why I find myself shoving my duffle bag into a locker at Soul Sweat Wellness Center this morning before work—to get my sweat on and to (hopefully) take my mind off all of this, at least for a little while. It was the reason I got the membership to begin with—to attempt to disconnect from things. And since they take money out of my account every month for this place anyway, I might as well use it more often than I have, too.

One good thing about being here this early is that there

isn't any waiting to use the machines. My first stop is the elliptical to warm up, and there on one of them is Pepper. Her dark hair pulled up into a high ponytail, swinging back and forth with the movement of the machine. She's in bright pink leggings and a sports bra, and she has already worked up a nice sweat, which glistens on her body like glitter under the gym lights.

I am 100 percent not mentally prepared to see her—not that I don't want to see her. Did she notice me when I walked in? Should I risk it and leave now? My sister's voice echoes through my head—ask her—and I'm definitely not ready for that. But I'd also be lying if I said it wasn't nice to see her. Soul Sweat isn't a very large gym, and she'll for sure notice me just standing around, so I carefully climb onto the machine next to hers and lean forward to catch her eye.

She pulls out one of her earbuds. "Oh, hey. Working out before work?" It's the first time I've seen her fresh-faced—meaning without any makeup—and even without the eye shadow and perfectly tinted bronzer, she is stunning.

"Yeah. I used to be better about it, but lately . . ." I grimace. This is the first time she is seeing me without makeup, too. And unlike her, I need help in the eyebrows and eyelashes department. Being blonde has its drawbacks in that regard for sure.

"I don't think I've seen you in here before." She holds up her earbud. "Then again, I kind of just tune out." Her legs are still moving at a good pace, but she isn't even remotely breathless.

"I do whatever I can to distract myself from being on this

CHRISTINA

thing." I click a few buttons on the machine and get it going. "I've thought about taking up yoga."

"I don't really love cardio either."

"You could've fooled me. You make this look easy." I laugh, or try to. I'm already feeling it in my legs, and I just got started. Ugh. Kill me now.

"So tell me something. To keep our minds off of this." She glances down at the display. She must've gotten here right when they opened.

"About what?"

"I don't know," she says. "You're a teacher, right? I'm sure there are stories that go along with that."

I nod. "That's very true." But the only story that races to the front of my mind is the one that Eli told the other night—the one that has to do with where she works. Will Pepper see the humor in it? If she doesn't, I risk her avoiding me for the rest of time—which means I wouldn't be able to ask her to my sister's party. Call it a risk or self-sabotage, but either way I launch into the tale.

I don't do nearly as good a job explaining it, but Pepper has a smile on her face as I go on, which has to be a good thing. And when I get to the part about them all being demons, she straight up bursts out laughing—the sound of it buzzing through me like electricity. A shot of caffeine straight to my soul, and I'm already addicted and need to hear it again.

"I'd heard the store was *run* by demons, but that we're all demons is kind of hysterical. I can't wait to share this with the team."

"It is funny, isn't it?" The resistance level on my machine

CHRISTINA

kicks up, and I have to push harder with my legs. Pretty soon I won't even be able to speak; I'll be breathing too hard. At least the exercise is making my heart race and helps keep my anxiety about talking to Pepper at bay—like my body can't recognize it as anxiety anymore, just as physical activity.

"Do you believe at all in anything supernatural?" Pepper asks. "I promise I'm not a demon if you think that's where this is going."

I narrow my eyes at her. "Wouldn't only a demon say something like that?"

"It's possible." She plays along with my joke, which is nice in that she seems to really get my humor even though we barely know each other. Not everyone does.

I've never actually thought long and hard about it. "I don't believe in vampires or werewolves or anything like that. Mostly just because the idea that they could be real is terrifying."

"That's fair." She nods.

"But I suppose I'm open to the idea of, like, loved ones watching over you, and fur babies crossing a rainbow bridge somewhere. What about you?"

She takes a moment—her head tipping side to side like she's considering her answer. "I believe there are things that happen that we can't always explain, things that seem impossible," she says. "People will sometimes call things fate, or karma, or say that the universe has its way, but they are all in some way saying that they believe in magic. So I guess that's the long way of saying that I guess I do believe."

"I'd never thought of it like that before, but I think you're right. Someone cuts us off in traffic and then a couple minutes

---

CHRISTINA

later we end up passing them and think, karma. But it *is* kind of like magic, isn't it?"

"Are you, Christina Loring, saying that you believe in magic?" Pepper raises her brows at me.

"I suppose I'm saying that if you would've asked me that before, I would've said no, but the way you've put it now, I'd say that it's something I'd consider is all."

Pepper smiles. "I'm getting you to come over to the dark side, aren't I? Soon you're going to be saying how you love Halloween."

"Don't get ahead of yourself now. I'm just saying I would entertain the idea of *nice* magic." But definitely not the dark kind—again, too scary.

"Wait, so now there's nice and not nice magic?"

"You're the demon; you tell me."

And then we're both laughing, which is really hard to do on an elliptical machine. Sweat creeps down the side of my face, and I use my towel to brush it away.

"Now it's your turn," I tell her.

"What?"

"To tell me a story. Or not a story. Just anything." Now the incline on the machine rattles upward, and my quads start to scream at me. "This is brutal."

"My fiancé died," Pepper says, and I almost fall off the elliptical.

"Oh my—"

"Not recently or anything. It's been"—she glances up at the ceiling—"wow, it's been a while now. And I'm fine. We'd had a great time together, and part of me will always miss him, but

---

CHRISTINA

I've never really talked about it. Which is weird, right? It's weird."

"Grief is a weird thing." For the past few years right before the holidays, I think that's what I've been feeling, although my gram just passed away this year. Could the universe—or magic—have been trying to prepare me before I have to deal with this upcoming holiday season without her?

"That it is. My mom . . . she just lost it when it happened, and then I think I felt the need to be strong for her. Like she was crying so much, I thought if I cried, it would make it worse for her—so I didn't."

"You didn't cry?"

"Maybe a little." Pepper shrugs. "But she was devastated, and I had to hold it together for her," she says. "Too deep for an elliptical conversation?"

"No. This is good. I barely even notice that I'm working out anymore." I lean on my machine and let my tongue hang out of my mouth for a minute, which makes Pepper chuckle. "I know I've already mentioned my family to you before, and they're . . . complicated, too. So I get it. It's kind of why I moved. I had this great job and it paid me a lot, but I hated it and my family doesn't understand how I could walk away from something I worked so hard for."

"Yeah, it seems like the more okay I was, the less okay my mom was. Like she took it personally." Pepper shakes her head. "Why do parents do this? Can't they let us live our own lives?"

"It would be nice if they did, wouldn't it?"

"For sure."

CHRISTINA

"When I have kids one day, I swear I'm not going to do this to them."

She tips her head to the side. "You want to have kids?"

For a long time I didn't think I wanted to, but maybe since I'm getting older, or maybe because of all the time I've been spending around teens, I've been warming up to the idea a little. "Maybe. If I meet the right person."

She nods but doesn't say anything. The thrum of the machines and the music playing overhead fill the space between us. It's not the usual comfortable silence that sits between us but something a little tenser. Did I say something wrong? I've never asked her if she has any kids. Maybe she did and they died with her fiancé? Oh shit.

"I'm sorry if I overstepped."

"Oh, no." She shakes her head. "Nothing like that. Was I being weird?"

"No. You just kind of had this look."

She grimaces. "Sorry."

"If I had a dollar for every time I felt like I was acting weird . . . Well, I'd have *a lot* of dollars." Finally the resistance and the incline let up, and my pace increases for a moment before I slow myself down.

"If it means anything, I don't think you're weird at all. At least not in a bad way. Everyone is a little weird," she says.

"So there's a good way to be weird?" I ask.

"I think so."

"This I *have* to see."

Pepper raises her brows at me. "Challenge accepted. When you're free next, let me take you somewhere."

CHRISTINA

"You want to take me out?"

She nods. "I do."

My heart speeds up again even though my workout isn't as hard. "It won't be scary, will it?"

"Do you trust me?"

I slow down so much, I'm barely moving. Pepper's gaze is locked on mine like she isn't worried that she could fall off that machine at any moment even though she's not paying attention. It's not like I know her very well, but she makes me feel relaxed. I can talk to her in a way I'm not usually able to talk to anyone. As weird as it may seem, she makes me feel safe. "Okay, then. You're going to take me somewhere, and I'm just going to trust you."

She smiles—the simple act lighting up her entire face. "Don't worry, I got you."

CHRISTINA

47 DAYS
UNTIL THE STORE CLOSES

Pepper

I didn't need directions—Clover Creek and I had an intimate relationship—but that afternoon I was happy to have them. The honeybees that had taken up residency in my chest were in a full-on frenzy. I would be going on my very first official date with Christina. It *was* a date, right? That's what she thought this was, wasn't it? I shook my head, chasing away the intrusive thoughts that were trying to creep in. Of course she knew it was a date; what else could it have been?

I hooked a sharp right, almost missing my turn onto her street, and I slowed down so I wouldn't pass it. There it was—143 Maple Garden Drive. A cute little craftsman that looked as though it could've fallen out of the pages of any children's storybook. A large apple tree grew to one side, and a stone path snaked up the front around flower boxes that likely overflowed with bright colorful blooms in the spring—not that I would ever get the chance to see them to know for sure. The house itself was a happy blue with white trim and dark shutters.

As much as I wanted to jump out of the car, I was rooted to my seat. It had been so long since I'd felt this way about anyone. It had been years since Mitchell passed, so this whole idea of dating was so foreign to me. I'd never been on dating apps, and even when Mitchell and I became a thing, it felt so effortless. We'd had a class in college together—were partnered up on a project—and then things progressed. We'd probably been dating for longer than I even realized it was happening. And one day I didn't want him not to be around anymore. We had been officially unofficial forever. I'm not even sure who used the term "partner" first. It was all so organic, it seemed—or maybe that's just the way I'm remembering it because it was easier. No one ever remembered the bad things about someone after they passed—it was always the good and easy times. It was all their best qualities.

This whole thing with Christina kind of felt like that in a way—easy. But the difference this time was that I was so painfully aware of my feelings, they weren't something I could ignore. My situation now was so much more complicated than when I was a carefree college student. The stakes now were so much higher.

I was getting way ahead of myself.

Before I completely lost my nerve, I exited the car, walked up her front steps, and rang what looked like the doorbell but also seemed to have a camera on it. To say it had been a while since I'd been to anyone's home would've been an understatement.

PEPPER

"Come in," came Christina's voice from the camera-like doorbell thing. Fancy.

I cracked open the door. "It's me," I called. *Duh, Pepper, she probably already knew that since it was very unlikely she'd invite just anyone in her house.*

"I'll be out in a second. Feel free to relax." Her voice now came from somewhere in the back of the house.

Relax. Sure. "No problem." Try telling that to those darn little bees in my chest.

Christina's house did not reflect the same aesthetic she had in her wardrobe. Everything was bright. A combination of robin's egg blue and a sunshine yellow flowed from the living room into the kitchen. She had a gorgeous royal blue sofa, and to the side of it a pair of leather chairs sat with some adorable fuzzy white pillows. A glass coffee table with a few small cactuses was sitting in the middle. Light poured into the space from the enormous picture window in the front.

The kitchen cabinets were gray and the countertops white with a small bar area that had a couple of stools pushed up underneath. The table and chairs she'd made occupied a small dining area—and the craftsmanship of them was incredible. Near the front door there was a table with a few photos of her and two women who looked like her sisters, a few plants, and a bowl with a couple sets of keys. On the wall just above it hung a quote from Eleanor Roosevelt—THE FUTURE BELONGS TO THOSE WHO BELIEVE IN THE BEAUTY OF THEIR DREAMS.

For a moment I took the whole space in. It was like seeing

a completely different side of Christina than I had before. With a few more embellishments, it could've looked almost like my own little apartment—fun and inviting. Why did she wear black all the time when she also had this inside her as well? Christina was cake, for sure—each layer a new discovery.

Instead of snooping around—which I absolutely wanted to do to learn more about her—I sat on the couch, running my hand against the plush fabric. "I might need one of these," I said to myself.

How comfortable was I supposed to get? I had no idea, so I alternated between leaning back and leaning forward and crossing and uncrossing my legs. Maybe I should've sat in one of the chairs. Or on a stool by the kitchen island. I was completely overthinking this.

As I was adjusting the way I sat one more time, a black cat slunk out from underneath the couch.

"Oh, hey. Hope I didn't bother you." Yep, I should've picked a different seat. Here for only ten minutes and already I was messing this up.

The blackest cat I'd ever seen with the brightest green eyes seemed to study me in the way that cats do—judgmentally.

"Yeah, I don't know what to think of me either," I confessed to it. I'd never had a pet growing up—although I always wanted one. Mom said they shed too much fur to clean up, but as I gazed around, I hardly noticed any. I reached my hand down, and the cat just sneered at me—okay, maybe not sneered exactly, but clearly it wasn't impressed with me at all.

"You're gorgeous," I tried. In that moment it felt very important for me to make a good impression. This wasn't just any cat. This was *Christina's* cat. So I decided it would be my mission to gain its approval.

The cat, however, was not on board with this plan and continued to glare—its eyes turning into little slits like it was considering the quickest way to get rid of me or possibly kill me. Good luck with that, cat.

"You could try," I told it, "but it won't do you any good. So we might as well be friends."

"Who are you talking . . ." Christina walked out from the hallway mid putting in a pair of earrings and stopped. "You're kidding me."

Oh shit. Yep. I'd done something wrong.

The cat didn't seem bothered by its owner's creased brow, and it jumped onto one of the chairs and started kneading a pillow. Well played, cat. This wasn't over.

"For someone indifferent about Halloween, you have the perfect cat for it," I attempted. Wooing the cat had failed, but I wasn't giving up.

"The cat delivery service gave him to me, not the other way around, but I had thought the same when he chose me," she said, and I scrunched my brow—cat delivery *what*? Suddenly five years felt so much longer. "Licorice doesn't like anyone," Christina continued. "So don't be offended. I'm surprised he came out at all. He usually hides under the couch for hours if anyone even rings the doorbell."

I glanced at Licorice. Maybe he was on my side after all. "Well then, I guess I should consider myself lucky."

"Cats are so weird."

PEPPER

"So weird," I agreed.

The cat rolled over, exposing his belly, and Christina rubbed him down. She looked amazing in dark jeans and knee-high boots. Her cropped black sweater inched up as she leaned over, showing off a little skin at her side, and my heart danced.

"Ready?" she asked, and I quickly glanced away.

"Yeah, totally."

As Christina descended the front steps of her house, her blonde hair whooshed behind her—as if her own personal fan were blowing on her for dramatic effect.

We both got in the car and buckled up.

She turned my way, her eyes connected with mine, and she smiled so brightly, her teeth showed from between stunning red lips. My stomach did a back handspring. "Well, at least if I die today, the weather is nice."

I shook my head. "You're *not* going to die." I turned the key, starting the hearse. She seemed to enjoy using humor as a way to lighten the mood, which was something I could easily play along with.

"It's fine, really. It would save me a lot of trouble actually."

"Rough morning?" I asked as I pulled away from the curb.

She stared out the window ahead, nodding slowly. "Sometimes I think I should record her so she could listen to the way she talks to me."

"Your sister?"

"She's the older one, yet I have to be the bigger person. Why?" Christina threw her hands up. "Why can't she just be a decent human being for once? Why can't she have a normal conversation with me instead of acting like I'm some kind of burden on her—on the family?" She let out a sigh. "I'm sorry. I shouldn't unload all this on you."

"No, it's fine. I don't mind." That was true. The more Christina vented about her sister, the less time I had to be awkward and try to fill the space with small talk when all I could do was concentrate on the smell of her perfume and how dangerously close her arm was resting next to mine on the center console. Plus, I liked that she shared. I wanted to get to know this gorgeous woman, and hearing she'd had a rough start to her day meant I needed to help turn it around. And if there was anything I was good at, it was turning a negative into a positive.

"You're just so easy to talk to. Is that weird to say?"

"I don't think so. I think you're pretty easy to talk to, too." Too easy, in fact. I glanced her way and smiled. Oh, how I wanted to unload all my secrets with her in that moment, but at the same time I didn't want to risk scaring her away.

She dipped her chin to her chest. "So where is it that you're taking me anyway?"

"If I told you, I'd have to kill you." I took her lead and tried to infuse some humor into the situation.

"See, I knew I was going to die today."

We both laughed.

"But seriously," she said. "Do I get a hint?"

"Where's the fun in that?"

"I should've figured you were the type of person who enjoyed surprises."

"I'm going to take that as a compliment."

"You should," she said.

Ten minutes later, I turned the hearse through the iron

gates of Whispering Woods Cemetery. It had been here longer than the town of Clover Creek itself with headstones dating back into the early 1700s. Teens liked to tell tales about how the grounds were haunted, and at least once a year a group of them would try to sneak in and stay overnight. Once Clover Creek decided to lean into the spooky season, Whispering Woods became a well-known spot for Halloween enthusiasts. Next month this place would be packed daily with tourists. But today there didn't seem to be a single living soul.

"So you *are* planning to murder me," Christina said, but her voice was light so I could tell she was joking.

"Don't spoil the fun." I once again followed her lead as I looped the car around and parked it in one of the more secluded parts of the cemetery. It's not that I was killing anyone, but this was one of my favorite locations in all of Clover Creek, and I wanted to share it with her. "Ever dig up a dead body before?" I asked before cracking a smile.

"Can't say that I have." Christina continued this little game she'd started.

"Well then, how about a picnic instead?"

"Do we need a reservation?"

I winked. "Already taken care of." I exited the car and headed to the back of the hearse to pull out the basket and blanket I'd prepared for the occasion. The honeybees from before started buzzing in my chest again. I had mulled over what to do for this occasion for a long time. A restaurant seemed like too much pressure—the server could show up at inopportune times, it could be too loud to carry on a conversation, the food could end up not being good. Being somewhere without distractions or too many outside variables seemed the best choice. But now that I stood there looking out over the tombstones, I started to second-guess myself. This place is *very* secluded, and it would be extremely easy to kill someone and bury them here.

Christina got out of the car. Her head swiveled back and forth like she was really taking in our surroundings. Maybe this wasn't as great an idea as I'd thought. "Oh, we're really going to have a picnic . . . in a cemetery?"

"Yeah. Doesn't get more peaceful or private than this." I tried to sound reassuring. "We could go somewhere else if you want."

Christina seemed to hesitate. "No. I can be brave."

I let out a deep breath. Thank god. I had no idea where else to go. "Come on. There's nothing to be afraid of." I reached toward her. "I got you."

Her gaze shifted to my outstretched hand, and then my face, before she accepted. Her skin was cool against my palm, but as our fingers intertwined, a flash of heat raced up my arm and settled inside my chest, calming the swarm.

"What? You don't think dead people like company?" I asked, trying to get her back into her joking mood from before.

"Well, if you put it like that." She turned like she was about to get back in the car.

"Come on." I tugged her hand, and she followed along.

Whispering Woods Cemetery was expansive—much of its land preserved—but its rich history and family mausoleums were works of art. My family wasn't from here, I'd moved far enough away from them to breathe after what had happened with Mitchell, but after coming here the first time—since I couldn't go see Mitchell where he'd been buried—this seemed like the next best thing. This was where I wanted to end up one day. Not in the morbid sense of what that meant—to be dead. But in the way that as soon as I had walked through the gates and among the headstones, a serene feeling washed over me. Even before I stopped being scared, I was never scared here. If there were such things as ghosts, they never bothered me. Now being laid to rest here wasn't an option, but I still loved it.

"During Halloween, a number of residents will come out here and cosplay some of the more historic local residents, and the middle schoolers have to come out and ask them questions for a project on our local history," I said as we headed up a small hill. "At least that's what my coworkers tell me."

"Really? That's actually pretty cool."

"And the Sunday before Halloween at sundown, they do this massive town game of hide-and-seek."

"Okay, now that sounds terrifying."

I laughed. "It sounds like a lot of fun to me." And it was. I came every year for the event.

"Sure." She didn't sound very sure.

I squeezed her hand. "What, you wouldn't come with me if I asked you?"

"Are you asking me?"

"Maybe." I chewed the inside of my cheek. I really needed to get better at picking up when Christina was teasing and when she was serious.

"Then maybe I'll come."

I led Christina through some of the older headstones up

another small hill. The air was ripe with the scent of freshly fallen leaves, and when the wind blew, her rose-scented perfume flooded my senses and sent tingles through my body.

"This is one of my favorite places in all of Clover Creek so far," I said just as the view came into sight. From here you could see the entire city and beyond. A blend of buildings and trees in the distance, and if I tilted my head, the bright yellow banner for The Dead of Night peeked out from behind a towering evergreen. The town clock sat proudly in the center of the city. "I stopped by last week on a coworker's recommendation," I explained, because how else would I know about this place? I really needed to be more careful with what I said.

Christina's head swiveled back and forth like she was taking it all in. "It's breathtaking."

A flock of birds flew overhead, and Christina breathed steadily next to me—the sound of her sucking in deep breaths of the serene fresh air.

"It's so peaceful," she said, and I nodded. "You almost forget that there are hundreds of dead people underneath us." She squeezed my hand. There was that humor of hers again.

"Thousands even." I played along and squeezed back. "Help me with this?" I set the basket on the ground.

"Har, har." Christina took the corners of the blanket and helped me lay it out on top of the crinkly grass and fallen leaves. In the springtime, this place was green and lush with new flowers at every turn. Now, in the fall, the grass had browned, and the trees looked as though they'd been set aflame, with burnt orange leaves. She settled on the soft flannel as I pulled out the snacks I'd gotten earlier in the day—an assortment of cheeses and cold cuts along with some bread and jams. I figured you could never go wrong with cheese, but I hadn't considered the possibility of Christina being lactose intolerant until that moment. Luckily, I brought a lot of snacks.

"I hope Italian soda is okay." I held up the bottle. "I wasn't sure what you'd like to drink." Which was also why I had plain bottled water, too.

"It's perfect. I only imbibe occasionally. I'm not a big drinker. Sometimes when I'm out with coworkers, I'll get a soda water with lime, so it looks like I'm drinking with them even when I'm not, and it helps settle my stomach because, you know, social anxiety." She bit her lip like maybe she thought she'd said too much. At least it seemed like I wasn't the only one who was nervous.

"That's a smart idea."

She let out a breath. "Just don't tell anyone my secret, okay?"

"They won't hear it from me." I zipped an imaginary zipper across my lips. "Do you like hummus?"

She smiled and nodded. "I also love Havarti and Muenster," she said as she picked up the containers of sliced cheese. "No Swiss, though."

"No." My voice was tentative as I pulled out a sleeve of assorted crackers and opened it.

"Good. If you had any, I'd have to end the date right here and now."

"Not a Swiss girl, then?"

"Never." She smiled as she set a slice of Muenster on a cracker and placed it in her mouth.

I could get used to her humor.

PEPPER

We munched on snacks and drank as we chatted about the kind of topics that didn't seem important—comfort foods, hobbies, books we'd read, favorite movies—but they were all the things that made a person who they were. When we didn't speak, it was the type of silence you could soak in—the kind that felt like a cozy blanket in front of a roaring fire on a rainy day. Being with Christina was easy.

The clouds overhead floated by without a care in the world, creating pictures in the sky.

"I guess Margaret and Beatrice didn't get along." Christina broke the silence and motioned to the headstone nearby that read:

HERE LIES MARGARET LESTER
DIED THE BEST BAKER IN CLOVER CREEK—
TAKE THAT, BEATRICE.

That was another reason why this was one of my favorite spots. "You should see Beatrice's headstone." I raised my brows.

"Why, what does it say?"

"I can't tell you. You'll have to find it for yourself."

Christina narrowed her eyes at me. "You just want me lurking around the cemetery."

I shrugged. "Maybe." I pretended to grimace so she'd know I was teasing.

She took a sip of her soda and let out a long sigh. "I guess I have to admit, it really is peaceful here."

I settled back on my hands and gazed out at the towering trees and quaint buildings nestled between them in the distance—like I'd done so many times in the past by myself. Another light breeze swept by, and somewhere nearby a bird called out—singing a little tune. If I closed my eyes, I could believe it all was just a normal day with no boundaries or expiration dates or curses. It felt positively normal. Better than normal since I had someone to share it with. "Not so scary, is it?"

"No, I suppose it's not." She nudged me with her elbow. "But it's still light out."

"But it won't be forever." I winked. Maybe I was pushing the joking a little too much, but she had started it, so I thought it couldn't hurt.

"We aren't staying till dark, are we?"

"Live in the moment, Christina." I smiled at her. "Don't worry, I'll make sure you're home before dark."

"Well, I didn't say that either." Her red cheeks made my heart pound even harder.

For the second time that day, I wanted to break down and tell her everything—spill it out. Try to explain how curses were real and so was magic, and because of those things, I'm fated to forever be connected to that store and all that goes with it. A part of me didn't like keeping secrets from her. I wanted her to know every part of me, and I was dying to know every part of her. But past experience told me that my situation wasn't the easiest thing to explain and could potentially make everything worse.

The third year of my service with the store, I'd been so angry, I attempted anything and everything to get out of it. I tried to get fired. I told anyone who would listen about the curse—and they just laughed me off. Some of the kids in town ran with the lore and it expanded to a story about the store being possessed by demons. But it all didn't matter. When November second came along, the store vanished, and so did I with it.

By the time I'd come back, everyone had forgotten about me like always—but *I* didn't forget, and the rumor about demons was here to stay. And now I wasn't ready to give up my chance of being with Christina before it ever truly started by trying to explain it all over again.

All I had was this time—here, right now—to make it what I wanted. I didn't have that many days left before I'd be gone again, and no one would remember me.

What else was I supposed to do?

Either way seemed like such a risk. Attempt to live even a small amount of time as normally as possible or allow the inevitable to hold me back from what could be exactly what I've always wanted.

I had to take the risk because it was a risk worth taking.

"I like you—a lot," I blurted out. Not the smoothest way to tell someone, that was for sure, but my nerves had gotten the better of me. "And I was hoping maybe . . ."

But I couldn't finish. Christina's cheeks were the brightest red they'd ever been. She sat there staring at me, not saying a single word.

Oh shit. I had fucked up royally. Misread the situation. The good news was that in a very short time, she wouldn't remember this or me at all—both a curse and a blessing. But the next forty-seven days were going to be rough if I had to see her again. "I'm sorry. That was too much." I started packing up our snacks.

PEPPER

She placed her hand on my knee. "I like you, too," she said. "A lot, in fact."

Our eyes connected. My heart sped up to twice its normal rate. The space between us disappeared as we each leaned a little closer—like two polar-opposite magnets unable to resist the pull.

"I'd really like to kiss you," she said.

"I'd really like it if you kissed me," I replied. "But are you sure you're not worried about doing that here?" I raised my brows at her, not passing up the chance to tease her a little more. A risk perhaps, but I'd already taken the leap.

"Should I be?" Her warm breath tickled my cheeks. "You'll protect me if any rogue zombie comes along, won't you?" She smirked, signaling my risk was paying off.

"I got you."

"You keep saying that." She pressed her lips to mine, sending tingles down to my toes and back. I ran my hand through her silky hair and wrapped my fingers at the nape of her neck. Her tongue brushed against mine, the flavor from our blood orange Italian soda still lingering.

My entire body ignited as her fingers climbed up my arm and found a patch of skin where my cardigan had slipped from my shoulder.

When we finally broke apart, her red lips were a little fuller, a little redder, and her lipstick still completely intact. "I could get used to this," she said.

"The cemetery?" I teased.

Christina bit her lip. "Being with you."

PEPPER

46 DAYS
UNTIL THE STORE CLOSES

Christina

I'm going to do it. The last time I saw Pepper, not only did I not ask her about her social media accounts, but I also never even brought up the idea of going to my sister's party. But today . . . today is going to be different. And it has everything to do with the fortune cookie I opened with my lunch this afternoon that said, "You will never see the view from the mountains you don't climb," which I took as—Christina, stop being such a scaredy-cat and just ask the girl out!

What exactly did I have to lose anyway? The worst she could say is no, and if I don't ask, that's already the answer, right? Plus, after that kiss the other day, it's obvious she does like me—so maybe it won't be as bad as my worst-case scenario brain has conjured up.

My lip starts to bleed from where I keep worrying at it as I pull into the Dead of Night parking lot. That same new guy who Pepper had yelled at the first day I met her is racing around collecting carts—setting them up in one long line. He isn't a very big guy, though maybe he's stronger than he looks; otherwise, there's no way he's going to get those all to move at once. I don't need to be a physics teacher to know that.

But just watching this kid—and his clear determination to complete what seems to me to be an impossible task—gives me the strength to unbuckle my seat belt and get out of the car.

I. Can. Do. This.

I'm going to walk into that store, find her, and ask her. It's not weird at all. I'm just coming to see her, right? This all would be so much easier via text—and then I wouldn't have to look her in the face while I do it.

Christina, stop. A text is a terrible idea.

My brain is racing a million miles a minute, but my feet never stop moving forward, and soon I'm greeted by the same cackling witch sound that always goes off when I enter this store. The looming statues in the front welcome me inside with a wonky-looking arrow, pointing to where the shopping carts are, but today I don't need one.

I quickly scan the registers. She isn't there, so I resort to wandering up and down each aisle. They've gotten more stock in since the last time I've been in here, or maybe things have been shifted around a little—not that it's important. I'm not shopping, and I'm not *pretending* to shop today, so it doesn't matter. I'm on a mission.

By the time I make it halfway through the store, I start to lose my gumption. Maybe she isn't working today, and now I look like a stalker roaming around. I could get something for the haunted house, but I didn't bring my list with me. Oh god.

CHRISTINA

And now that I think about it, I left my credit card on the coffee table with my laptop. This was a terrible idea. A horrifically terrible idea. I grab the nearest thing off the closest shelf just to have something in my hand, and I turn into the next aisle.

Wham.

I collide with something—or rather someone.

The very someone I've been searching for.

My cheeks immediately get hot. "Funny bumping into you here." OMG. Could this have started any worse? I don't actually want to think of an answer to that.

Pepper laughs, a smile spreading across her face. "Wouldn't want to bump into anyone else." She gestures between us. "It is our thing after all."

The last couple times we ran into each other, we didn't actually collide, but all the other times it has been my fault, hasn't it? Is she trying to tell me I've hurt her? This really isn't going as planned. But when do plans ever go exactly the way they're supposed to? Maybe there's still a way to salvage this. Or not salvage—that's for wrecked ships, and I'm not wrecked, am I?

"Did I lose you?" she asks.

I shake my head so my thoughts go away. "Not at all. I actually came in to see you." Deep breath, Christina, you can do this.

She quirks up her brow. "Really? Well, I was just about to head out—"

"Oh—"

"—if you'd like to join me."

"Oh! Yes," I say way too enthusiastically, and put the skull

CHRISTINA

I'd picked up from the last aisle onto a nearby shelf. "Where did you say you were going?" I probably should've asked before being so enthusiastic.

"I didn't." A smile plays at her lips—daring me to accept this challenge. "Let's go."

"Hey, Pepper." A boy dressed as a scarecrow runs up. "You're coming back for . . ." He glances around like he's looking for someone.

"Yes. I'll be back before Lisa gets in."

He lets out a breath so forcefully, he practically topples over—making him look like he's actually made of straw. "Oh good, she's not here, because Dewy isn't back with the cake yet either, are they?"

"They're in the back finishing setting up. Everything is under control. Don't worry," Pepper says.

He flashes two thumbs-up. "I'm going to make sure there are enough streamers," he says, and then runs off.

Pepper turns to me. "One of our staff members has a birthday today. It's a tradition . . ."

"Yeah, totally." At school it seems like there's always cake in the teacher's lounge for someone's birthday. It's the best when they get it from Flour Power on Plum Street. Their Devil's Chocolate is to die for.

"Anyhow, are you ready?"

I take another deep breath. Surprises aren't really my thing, but so far Pepper hasn't done me wrong, so I relent. "Lead the way."

Ten minutes after walking into The Dead of Night, I walk

CHRISTINA

out, only this time I'm not alone. Pepper struts next to me in one of her signature outfits—a mash of colors and patterns I'd never have the guts to put together. We probably look like opposites. She's the Technicolor version, and I'm here in black-and-white—mostly black, that is. It's not that I haven't tried to incorporate some color into my wardrobe—but on a teacher's salary, it makes sense to buy things that are more versatile. And black goes with everything. Maybe it's time to get some new shoes. Something with a pop of color. That could be a start.

"What are you thinking about?" she asks as we head around the corner toward Plum Street, and I make sure to step over the loose cobblestone that I usually always trip over when I walk down this road.

"Shoes." I tell her the truth, which sounds much less pathetic than thinking about my complete and total lack of style.

"Yours are cute."

I don't have to look down to know what she's talking about. Like every other day, I have on black shoes—although today they are my ankle boots and not the standard flats I generally wear. Because today I wanted to look a little better than usual. Because today I have a mission. But since I'm not ready to go there yet, I reply, "Yours are so much prettier." And they are. Under her pink and red checkered skirt is a pair of rainbow-patterned tights, which lead to some fun red suede boots that match the red in her striped jacket. "How do you do that?"

She turns her head and has those brows raised at me.

Even in my corporate life, my choice of outfit was something I used to blend into a world dominated by men, not

---

CHRISTINA

something I used to stand out. "Everything you wear is bold and exciting, and, well, I'm—"

"Beautiful without even trying," she says, and immediately my cheeks heat up again.

"I don't know about that." I awkwardly laugh.

"You should." She steps ahead and stops right in front of me. "Wasn't it Eleanor Roosevelt who said, 'No one can make you feel inferior without your consent'? Well, you should know that you're gorgeous. This is a fact. No matter what you wear, you look beautiful. And anyone else's opinion of you doesn't matter."

It isn't just my cheeks burning now, but everything inside me tingles. Eleanor Roosevelt has some of the most inspirational quotes—she's one of my favorites. As much as I want to lean in and kiss Pepper, I'm frozen to the spot, scared I'll break the spell or whatever that has seemed to enchant this woman to say such a thing to me—about me—plain, boring, old Christina Loring.

"If you want some pretty shoes, let's go get some." She smiles in this way that isn't judgmental—more like she sincerely knows me, and this is exactly what I need to hear. I don't understand how she does it.

I smile back. "Let's do it."

She reaches her hand out. "I know just the place."

I take it, allowing her to pull me across the street and down another. Her hand is warm in mine despite the chill in the air. And everything about how we're connected has tingles racing up my arm. It's a sensation I've never felt before—not with

---

CHRISTINA

anyone I've dated, and Pepper and I aren't officially dating or anything, which means I like this woman more than I've even allowed myself to believe. My heart is thrumming now for a whole new reason that has nothing to do with the speed at which I'm walking.

"You sure I'm not keeping you from what you need to do?" My voice is a little wobbly in my throat.

"Nah. I'm always up for shoe shopping anyway."

She holds the door open to Sole Mates—a boutique shoe store that I've passed a million times but never have been inside—otherwise known as one of the two shoe stores in town. This one, however, doesn't sell sneakers. Here the shoes don't look like something a teacher would wear, and, well, that's what I am now. In the back of my closet, I have a pair of oxfords I haven't worn in years after almost ruining them in the rain, and a few pairs of neutral heels that I just couldn't part with even when I left my corporate life behind. But honestly, my feet don't hate the fact that I haven't worn any of them in a very long time.

I step into the modern space with an array of different types and colors of shoes that sit on little shelves along stark white walls. A few tables also have taller boots that don't fit on the equally spaced shelves. And there are plush chairs in peach, pink, and gray. A chandelier full of delicate crystal flowers is the centerpiece of the shop.

"Oh no, did those turquoise mules not work out?" The salesperson—with short wavy light brown hair and apricot skin, wearing a simple baby blue pantsuit—comes up to Pepper.

"They're perfect," she says. "My friend here could use your

CHRISTINA

expertise, though." Pepper turns in my direction. "Christina, this is Ainsley, and he is a shoe magician."

"Stop," Ainsley says before he takes my hand. "It's lovely to meet you."

"You're a regular here?" I ask Pepper.

"She came in for the first time a couple of weeks ago, and we've been, like, BFFs ever since, isn't that right, Pepper?"

"He's right. I have a weakness for fabulous footwear." She laughs, and Ainsley joins her.

"What is it that I can help you find today?" he asks. He has the fullest burgundy lashes, which make his brown eyes pop—maybe I need to get some colored mascara. But that's not what he asked.

The options here are endless. If I'd come in on my own, I'd probably walk toward the simple black flats, or if I was still working in the corporate world, I'd look at those patent leather slingbacks, though that isn't why I'm here. Except now, surrounded by all these different colors and styles, I don't know where to start. Black has always been my go-to.

"She needs something fun," Pepper responds for me. "But they also have to be comfortable and versatile."

I nod. How does she know me so well? "Exactly."

Ainsley ushers me toward a high-back chair. "Have a seat, and I'll work my magic." He winks.

He takes a moment to measure my feet—I haven't done this since I was a kid—making sure to get the exact length and width before parading around the shop plucking different options off the wall. He comes back and presents the first. "Gut reaction." It's a strappy wedge with a floral print.

CHRISTINA

"The shape is fine, but the pattern is a little much, and is it too high?" I grit my teeth. Am I being too picky? Should I try it on before I reach some of these conclusions? I love the way heels look—I just hate how they hurt my feet by the end of the day.

Ainsley nods like this was the answer he'd been expecting. "And this one is too plain, right?" He holds up another wedge in a brown leather.

I nod. "Yeah. I think so."

"I know exactly the thing." He stands. "I'll be right back." He abandons the pile of shoes and heads into the back. Do my feet stink? Is that why he ran away so fast? I didn't notice before when I took off my boots, but then again, I wasn't paying attention.

"This is just what he does," Pepper says. She's seated in a chair opposite me, legs crossed, hands poised on the arms like she's watching a show. She looks so elegant. My family will probably like her more than they like me. She has a confidence about her that I've never been able to achieve. "What are you thinking about now?" she asks.

I curl my toes against the hardwood floor, and tuck my hair behind my ear. "Is it that obvious?"

"You just get this faraway look in your eye, and you bite your lip."

My hand flies up to my mouth. "Do I?"

She chuckles. "It's not a big deal. It's actually kind of cute," she says, and my cheeks get hot. "Just like when your face gets all rosy like that."

I press my palms against my cheeks to try to cool them down—or cover them up, I don't know. "I could never be a poker player."

CHRISTINA

"Or a spy."

This time, I laugh. "Is that a real job, or just in the movies?"

Pepper shrugs. "I think they're called 'intelligence agents' now, but I'm pretty sure it's the same kind of thing."

"Makes sense," I say. "Did you always want to work in the costume industry?" That sounded bad. "I just mean you have such a way with fashion, it seems like that's something you would do." My hands against my cheeks do nothing to cull the heat continuing to rush to them, which isn't from the temperature in this place.

She smiles. "Actually, I always thought about teaching before I got into the costume industry, as you've so kindly called it."

"Really? And what's stopped you?" I ask. "It's the pay, isn't it?" It wouldn't surprise me if working at a Halloween store paid more than being a teacher.

"It's complicated." She shakes her head. "How are you liking it, though? Think you're going to keep it up?"

"I love the kids, and the administration is actually pretty reasonable—at least that's what the other teachers say, since this is my first teaching job ever. But my family doesn't get it. And the pay is criminal. All the extra hours, and with the haunted house . . ."

"It doesn't give you much 'you time,' does it?" She glances at the clock. Technically I should be at the house soon, and I need to go home and change first since I'm not about to ruin another outfit, but I have a purpose—there's a reason I dressed up and made the trip to see her to begin with. It's now or never.

I rub the scar on my arm. "I actually wanted to talk to you about something—"

CHRISTINA

"I think you're going to love these." Ainsley bursts out of the back room with a black box in his hands.

Pepper's brows are raised like she's curious what I'm going to say, but she leans back in her chair as Ainsley sashays our way.

He settles on the stool in front of me. "Comfortable, versatile, and fun." He opens the lid and pulls out a black cloth bag, and from it he slides out one of the prettiest shoes I've ever seen. It's a royal blue wedge—not as tall as the others. He lifts my foot and slips it on, and then he does the other. "Take them for a spin."

Heels really aren't my go-to anymore, but as soon as I stand, I remember why I used to wear them all the time. A powerful feeling rushes through me—it's like my back is straighter and my head higher, and not just from the couple inches the shoes give me. I parade around the few tables and chairs like I'm walking on a cloud. They don't pinch or rub, and in the mirror, I study them, turning each foot this way and that. They look—stunning. And they are prettier than any pair I've ever owned. More colorful, too.

Pepper comes up behind me. "You love them, don't you?"

I nod, but then I notice the same shoes that are on my feet on a shelf next to the mirror, and the price listed is well outside of my teacher salary budget. "I don't think—"

"I got you," Pepper says, then her tongue pokes out of her mouth to wet her lower lip, and the heat inside me rises about a million degrees.

"Your receipt." Ainsley comes up and hands something to Pepper. "Do you want to wear those out, or would you like me to box them up for you?"

CHRISTINA

I scrunch my brow. She did not. She absolutely *couldn't* have. But she did. She totally just bought me the prettiest shoes I've ever owned, and the backs of my eyes tingle. "You didn't have to."

"You're right, but the look on your face is worth it," she says. "Plus, I work in the lucrative costume industry, so . . ." She winks and fireworks erupt in my stomach.

"Thank you," I say to her, but it's not enough to express the immense gratitude I feel—and it's not about the price of the shoes or even the shoes themselves, but her words. The look on my face is worth it to her—*I'm* worth it. "I think I'll wear them out," I tell Ainsley.

"Excellent choice," he says. "I'll box your other shoes for you." He heads back to the chair I was sitting in.

"You wanted to say something," Pepper says. "Before."

My pulse is racing, and all I want to do is reach out and kiss this girl in front of me, but instead I blurt out, "Will you go to my sister's engagement party with me?"

Her brows raise and then they lower as she stares at me.

My heart stops. It was too much, too forward, too soon, I worry.

"On one condition," she says. "You wear those shoes."

CHRISTINA

39 DAYS
UNTIL THE STORE CLOSES

Pepper

Spending time with Christina was uncomplicated—or as uncomplicated as it could be with all her job and haunted house responsibilities and my faux work obligations. When I was with her, it was easy to forget that I was cursed, and that in a little over a month, I'd go into "hibernation" (which sounded better than what it was really like) until the following Halloween. Because being with her was the first time in years that I felt really, truly alive.

I hadn't actually thought about what that meant before. It was a whole gamut of emotions that danced across my skin each time the wind blew and a sense of presence I hadn't had since becoming Keeper. I was there, but not really. Being with Christina was a gift—a missing ingredient from a recipe that elevated the dish from good to delicious. It was something I hadn't realized had been missing, though now that I knew what it tasted like, I didn't want anything else.

For the past week we'd been stealing the little moments she had between all the busy things in her life to spend some time together that didn't require paint, or fake blood, or teens running around. Although it didn't mean everything Halloween related wasn't off the table. I'd slowly been converting Christina to the dark side—enjoying the upcoming holiday and all it had to offer that wasn't gore and human remains.

Today before Christina had to be at the haunted house, I let her introduce me to the Clover Creek farmer's market. To be fair, it had been a year since I'd last been to the event, which closed down Orange Street from sunup until early afternoon. Only I'd usually wander from booth to booth on my own, sampling fresh-made jams and sipping something warm from the coffee cart. It was different being here with someone. I really couldn't remember the last time I'd done it even with just a friend. But it was especially different being here with Christina.

"How do you feel about dill?" she asked, holding a pretzel stick with some kind of white creamy glop on one end.

"I feel very positive about dill," I responded. "Is this a trick question?" I was still getting used to the way she liked to tease me.

She popped the pretzel in her mouth, then produced one for me. "I'd have serious reservations if you didn't."

Christina had also become much more relaxed around me, so maybe that was why things felt so simple being with her. She didn't always have the most optimistic views, but once she let her guard down, she also didn't always take herself too seriously. Like today and snacking on things with strong flavors like dill, garlic, and blue cheese; she hadn't once covered her mouth as though worried about the smell of her breath. She didn't hesitate trying any of them at all—and I loved that for her.

She fed me the pretzel and watched intently as I chewed. Mrs. Dobbs' Delicious Dips were tasty, but if we walked just a few more stalls down, Stacy's Snacks were just a little bit better. Still, I pretended not to know these things as I slowly finished the snack and then swallowed.

A smile spread across Christina's face. "Good, right?"

"Yes," I agreed. "But maybe we should go around and try them all before we make any commitments."

"That's a great idea," she said. "Plus, that means more samples."

"Exactly."

She grabbed my hand and pulled me to the next tent, which was full of gorgeous handmade jewelry. The sign read, CHARMED, I'M SURE, where a woman with dark brown skin and wild purple hair pulled into a large bun on top of her head worked behind a small counter setting a stone in what looked to be an earring. She was mesmerizing to watch as she chatted with another woman, who was asking her questions about her work.

"Mrs. Stein," Christina said. "So good to see you."

The woman who was watching turned, and oh my, it was Mrs. Stein, the school counselor. It had to have been at least three years since I'd seen her last, but she looked almost the same with her wavy salt-and-pepper hair hanging loosely around her shoulders. She'd traded in her tortoiseshell glasses for a pair of red frames, which stood out against her pale cheeks, and her crow's feet had become a little more pronounced.

"How are you feeling?" Christina asked, concern coloring her voice.

Now that she mentioned it, Mrs. Stein didn't look as spry as she once did—although I wouldn't have called her old before, she wasn't exactly the youngest person on staff, at least not while I was there. And if I remembered correctly, she had become a grandma for the first time just before I took over as Keeper of the Store.

Mrs. Stein shook her head. "They're doing more tests. But I'm trying to stay optimistic." That sounded just like the Mrs. Stein I knew. She'd helped me find the bright side of things more than once when we worked together.

"That's good," Christina responded.

"The school is suggesting early retirement." Mrs. Stein shook her head. "Enough about me, who's your friend?"

"Pepper White. Pleasure to meet you." I held out a hand, not waiting for Christina to introduce me—it was an activity I was more than used to from years of experience, telling people who I was when I already knew them very well.

"Virginia," she said. "Lovely to meet you, too." Mrs. Stein's hand felt frail in mine as we shook. That was new. "Are you shopping for anything in particular today?"

"Just a little browsing before I have to head to the haunted house," Christina answered.

"Oh, that's right. How's it coming along?"

Christina bit her lip.

PEPPER

"It's going to be awesome," I responded for her. "Everything's on schedule." Okay, maybe I didn't know that for sure, but no one needed to think any differently. As wonderful as Clover Creek was, it was still a small town, and gossip was very much a thing. No need to plant any seeds of doubt, especially when Christina had been working so hard. And no matter what, the event would go on—those kids would make it happen—and it would be fantastic.

"That's great to hear," Mrs. Stein said. "Well, I'll let you get to it. My daughter's coming over later and she's got 'big news' to share. I think I'm going to be a grandma again, so I need to get some cookies, and I already got some other snacks." She held up a bag from Stacy's Snacks, and Christina slid a quick glance at me—likely thinking we needed to check that place out.

I said goodbye and let Christina and Mrs. Stein have a moment as I wandered around. At a special table with Halloween-themed jewelry on display, the scent of Christina's rose perfume announced she was there before she came up beside me.

"That's so sad about Mrs. Stein." She gestured with her head. "All she ever talks about are her kids and grandkids and wanting to see them grow up."

"What's wrong with her?"

"Cancer?" Christina shook her head. "I'm not totally sure, but she's been out of work awhile, and just now she mentioned she hopes she gets to see her newest grandchild before she's gone."

"That's sad," I confirmed. My heart clenched. It had been a long time since I'd seen my own parents. Even if they didn't remember me, it would've been nice to know they were still around—still happy. I think the reason I never went to see them was that I didn't want to know if something bad had happened to them or if one of them wasn't around anymore. It was easier to think they were living their best child-free lives—even if I was an adult.

"If there was only something that could help her stick around, you know?" Christina said. "Health care is such a mess."

It wasn't great before, but it only made sense it hadn't gotten any better, so I nodded as I scanned all the bat rings and potion necklaces. A pair of skeleton earrings caught my eye, each little metal bone a separate piece hooked together with some type of thin wire. When I picked them up and shook them, the little bones clinked together with a soft and happy little tone. "These are so cute," I said and jiggled them again for Christina.

"They look heavy," she said.

I shook my head. "They aren't really. Here."

She took them from me, dipping her hand up and down, testing their weight. "They'd look cute on you." She held them up to my ear.

My eyes locked with hers. "They aren't too scary for you?" I teased.

Her lips pulled up on one side.

I wanted to lean in and kiss them but instead said, "But what if they're cursed and make the person wearing them go on a killing spree?"

She broke out into a giggle. "I mean, I suppose it's possible."

"Or maybe they make the wearer fall madly in love."

PEPPER

Christina bit her lip.

I raised my brows. How I wished I could see inside that brain of hers.

"There's only one way to find out." She smirked before taking them up to the counter to purchase them.

"Someone's feeling brave." I nodded toward the little pink bag in her hand when she had finished.

"Oh, these aren't for me." She handed the bag over.

"You want me to test them out?" I laughed. "What if I go on a killing spree?"

"I'm sure there are some people who probably deserve it." She shrugged.

"Fair point," I said. She was so funny.

"Besides, not all curses are bad, right?" She leaned in and her lips brushed against mine. "I think we should test them out."

"You mean *I* should."

She smiled and nodded. "I knew you'd understand."

I leaned in and kissed her again; the dill flavor from earlier still clung to her lips.

The alarm on her phone went off, breaking us apart as she checked it.

"Thirty minutes," she said—meaning the amount of time she had left before she had to be at the haunted house. Time seemed to fly by so quickly when I was with her. I wished there was a way to slow it down.

"I could come with you."

"You don't want to spend your day off working." The lie I had told her earlier as to why I was available to hang out rolled off her tongue.

"It wouldn't feel like work. Besides"—I reached into the bag and shook the little bone earrings at her—"we have to test these out."

"And someone should be there just in case things go wrong," she said.

Or maybe if they go right. Those words were stuck in my throat as I held her gaze.

"Good idea," she said, and I hoped she was thinking the same thing.

"We'll need snacks." I pulled her in the direction of Stacy's booth.

"We will most definitely need snacks." She laced her fingers with mine.

At the haunted house, teens raced around and cursed when they thought no adult was listening. It was chaotic and wonderful.

The first time I helped out, Christina had been nervous it would be too much for me, but after I hung with her and the kids a couple times after school, she started to relax. Luckily, since it was both a school and a community event, and I was only there "after hours"—aka when classes weren't in session—I didn't need any special permission to be here. Who even knows what would've come up in a background check, if anything at all? Small-town living did have its perks like this, as I'm sure it wouldn't fly in a bigger city. I might not have been remembered, but The Dead of Night had always been a good partner for this event.

PEPPER

All the tree cutouts had been painted, so today we were screwing them into the wall to secure them in place. Small town or not, the kids weren't allowed to use the power tools, so I assisted Christina while all the students worked on other things. We'd never had anyone who could do these kinds of tasks before, and having Christina here really elevated the haunted house to a completely different level. What I would've given to have her around when I had been in charge of this event—she was so talented.

"People are really going to freak out when they see this," I said, and Christina stopped her drill. "In a good way," I clarified. "This looks amazing, and it's still light outside. Once it's dark and you get some cobwebs up on these things, and with the lighting in here, it's truly going to be incredible."

"You really think so?" she asked, her voice tentative. "I've never even been to this event before, so I'm not sure what people are expecting."

I had to remember that I hadn't been here either. That this was my first time seeing all of this. "Well, I've been to more than a few haunted houses in my day, and there's no way people won't be impressed," I said, but Christina didn't look so convinced. "Hey, Mycheal, is it?" One of the teens I'd been introduced to before was carrying in some paint for another room.

"Yeah. What's up?"

"You've been to this event before, haven't you?" I asked, and he nodded. "Can you tell Christin—Ms. Loring—here how cool this looks?"

"There's never been anything like this. And no one has ever

built us an electric chair. Last year we used some of Toni's patio chairs for one of the rooms, and their mom was pissed."

I had to suppress a laugh. Kids "donating" items without their parents' permission was a thing, so I always had to ask if it was okay before we used anything. "See?" I told Christina. "Thanks, Mycheal. You've been very helpful."

"Bet," he said, and continued on his way.

I shook my head. "I will never be up on the lingo."

"I've stopped trying. I once said something was 'cringe,' and from the looks I got . . ." Christina's eyes went wide, and her brows shot up. "You'd have thought I had clown makeup on or something."

"I can only imagine." I laughed. "Is this one good now?" I nodded toward the wall.

"Oh, sorry." Christina wedged between me and the cutout I was holding to finish screwing it into place. Her hair tickled my nose, and her shampoo smelled like fresh apples.

Her drill went *zziibbb, ziiibbb.* "Done," she said. "You can let go."

Doing so meant I could step away when all I wanted to do was press my lips against her neck—which of course I couldn't do with students around, so I complied.

She tried to shake the tree, and when it didn't budge, she nodded like she was satisfied.

"It's not going anywhere," I said.

"I just want to make sure. If someone got hurt, I'd never forgive myself." She studied her work, tilting her head from one side to the other.

"It looks great," I reassured her before grabbing a bag of

cotton spiderwebs. "Especially once we get these up." I pulled a chunk out, stringing it from one tree to the next.

Christina took some from the bag, too, and attempted to hang it with me.

"Really stretch it out," I instructed.

"Like this?" She tugged but still had too much in her hands.

"Here." I stepped toward her and showed her how to separate the cotton to make it look more like natural cobwebs. It was cute how she watched so intently, like she was really interested in getting it right.

"You make it look so easy."

"It's not like using power tools." I winked. She needed to know how amazing she was at this. That her contributions mattered, too.

"You're just saying that to make me feel better."

"Did it work?"

She stepped closer. "A little."

The back door to the house opened, and with it, a gust of wind blew all the cobwebs we'd just strung up all over us.

"Sorry, Ms. Loring," the teen said as they quickly closed the door.

"It's fine." Christina laughed. "At least we know we'll need some adhesive or something to make sure these stick on."

"Oh, I know where that is." The teen opened the door again, sending in another gust of wind and taking down more of our webs, and raced out.

Christina continued to laugh and shook her head, and I laughed along with her. "If these were real spiderwebs, I'd be totally freaking out."

PEPPER

"Well, you should know, then, that all our webs are made by a hundred percent natural spiders."

Christina kept laughing, obviously picking up on my joke. "You look like you have salt-and-pepper hair now. Wait, is that why you have that name?"

"Kind of," I said. "My mom said I was born with a full head of hair, and my dad said it was as dark as pepper, and the rest is history." I shrugged.

"That's adorable. This, however"—she plucked cotton from my hair—"not so much."

"Your hair is so light, it just blends in." I ran my fingers through her silky strands, seeing if I could catch any.

Christina's entire body shook. She was so close—with our bodies wrapped together in fake spiderwebs, it would've been so easy to lean in. Her gaze fell to my mouth. Was she thinking the same thing? My heart pounded so hard, she had to have felt it, too.

The door burst open again. "Got the spray adhesive," the teen who had run out before called, quickly shutting the door behind themselves. Christina and I jumped away from each other.

"Thanks, Dora," Christina said. "Maybe she can help you stick it on." Christina turned to me.

"Of course," I replied.

Christina's cheeks were glowing bright red as she busied herself with sweeping sawdust and helping collect the rest of the rogue spiderwebs. Dora helped me tug and pull and stick the stretched-out cotton to the trees, securing it with the spray adhesive, but all I wanted to do was be back close enough to

Christina to smell her apple shampoo and kiss her until my lips turned as red as hers.

This was her job now, but being here made me miss it—miss my old life. I was lucky, though, that I got to be here—to be a part of it again even for a short time. Too bad it couldn't be for longer—or forever. If there was only some way—someone—that would want to take my place, then maybe this thing Christina and I had didn't have to end.

"I'm going to move these." Christina held up the bags from our earlier shopping trip. The small one with the earrings was inside one of them.

Mrs. Stein came rushing to the front of my mind. She had a new grandkid coming—and while it wouldn't be ideal that they wouldn't remember her, maybe it would be enough for her to get to see them grow up.

For the first time ever, there could be a way to break this curse after all.

30 DAYS
UNTIL THE STORE CLOSES

Christina

I told Emily I was bringing someone to her engagement party today, so that's what I'm going to do. But now, as I stand in my bedroom looking at the dress I dug out of my closet for this very special occasion and the shoes Pepper bought for me, I'm starting to second-guess myself. I should've gotten something new. Not that the dress isn't nice. It's simple. It's elegant. It's Chanel. I wore it to a holiday party a million years ago so no one in my family has ever seen it before, but it also means it'll just remind them of all the things I used to be able to afford.

Licorice stops cleaning himself to stare at me from his spot on the bed.

"Ugh, I know. This is a bad idea." I rub the scar on my arm.

He goes back to licking.

It's not that I don't want Pepper to come with me. There's nothing I'd rather do since shutting down haunted house construction early for the day than hang out with the one person who has finally made this little town feel more like home than it ever has before. Since I moved here, it's been fine—it's a lovely place to live with just about everything anyone could need and nothing more—and while teaching is a struggle and not something I plan to do forever, it's all suited me well. It's been a way to make the world—my family—take a pause when it comes to me and all their expectations, and it's worked for a while now. But going to this party today, wearing this dress, and being surrounded by them will just put everything on fast-forward.

Emily promised not to say anything to anyone about me bringing a plus-one, and from the family group chat, no one seems to know, but part of me wants to keep it that way. Here everything is perfect and safe, and Pepper and I can exist in a space completely of our own creation. I can swim in this sea of joy, of being accepted as I am without any outside pressures. And to be honest, I don't miss spending stupid amounts of money on things. I like my comfortable clothes and flats. I like not having to put a full face of makeup on all the time. I like living in my little Clover Creek bubble. But in two and a half hours that bubble is going to burst.

Maybe I shouldn't go.

But unfortunately, that isn't an option. I can't let Emily down. Plus, I already bought a gift and had it professionally wrapped at the store with a big white bow, and it's presently sitting next to the door so there's no way I can forget it on my way out.

In my head, I've played out just about every scenario that could go wrong today. Forget the present—put it by the door.

CHRISTINA

Blow a tire—had Harold at the shop check the pressure in all of them yesterday. Spill something all over myself—wear a black dress. Hear how I shouldn't have worn black to an engagement party—well, there's nothing I can do about that. Anyhow, it's a dinner party, and black is always acceptable for an evening event, so hopefully I won't be the only one wearing this color. And having a plus-one will mean no one will ask me why I'm still single. At least I hope they won't. So I'm totally and completely prepared. Aren't I?

Everything needs to be perfect for Emily. I cannot be the one to screw today up for her.

Moths swarm in my stomach, eating holes right through the center of me.

There aren't any holes in my dress, are there?

I quickly flip the garment over, checking all the seams and everything in between. Luckily, it's fine. There's not even any cat hair since I lint-rolled it earlier, so I sit on the edge of my bed and take a few deep breaths.

My gaze lands on my shoes—the beautiful blue ones Pepper bought me. A smile tugs at my lips as my mind whirls with all the thoughts of what she'll be wearing. For sure it won't be black.

That's it. That thought is all I need to get me moving. I want to see her, so I put on my dress and finish getting ready.

The parking lot is already full by the time I pull into the restaurant where the party is being held. Pepper sits in the passenger seat next to me looking gorgeous in a light blue dress

---

CHRISTINA

that hugs her body—accentuating all her gorgeous curves. She even brought me a scarf that matches—like she knew I'd be in all black and could use a pop of color. We sort of match without matching. We complement each other in a way that people will likely assume we're a couple, but it's not like we've put a label on it—although I might be ready to do just that.

I glance at her again from the corner of my eye. Her legs are crossed, and her dress has ridden up, showing off her thigh. The perfume she's wearing is sweet with a deep undertone. I want to bottle it up and swim inside it.

But what happens after Halloween when Pepper's store closes?

The intrusive thought is there before I can stop it, but now isn't the time to fall down that rabbit hole of what-ifs, so I quickly push it away.

Luckily, there are still empty parking spaces, so I pull into one and cut the engine. Nerves bubble inside me like an overcarbonated seltzer. Tonight will be fine. It's just that there will be so many people, including my big, loud, well-meaning but intrusive family. That's the problem. With Pepper here, maybe they won't notice me so much and will instead have questions about the girl who's with me. She's stunning, and now that I'm not driving anymore, there's nothing stopping me from looking at her. She has swept her dark hair up and off her neck, highlighting a gorgeous statement necklace in contrasting blues and oranges. Tonight, she isn't in bold patterns like she normally wears, but the necklace is completely her. Bright—beautiful. She's the kind of person who commands a room.

They're going to love her.

CHRISTINA

"You ready?" She reaches over and squeezes my arm. "Or do you want to sit here for a few minutes?"

The anxiety I've built up inside my gut crashes together like spastic bumper cars. I take a deep breath and place my hand on top of hers—it's so steady, even though she's about to be in a room with my entire family for the first time. I wish I could be that calm. "I just need a minute."

She nods like she understands, because of course she does, and we sit there in silence—nothing to fill the space between us like there had been on the ride over with the music playing, but it's calming—the sounds of our breaths mixing together and falling into sync. Sometimes simply occupying the same space with someone can be the most intimate experience.

A few couples walk inside carrying gifts; one of the women I don't recognize is also wearing black. Thank god I won't be the only one. Pepper doesn't say a word, but she glances at me and smiles like she knows what I'm looking at—like she knows exactly what I'm thinking.

"There sure are a lot of cars here," I say instead of asking her how she does it—how she somehow sees right through me.

"Everyone is going to be watching your sister. It's her night after all."

She's right. Aside from Mom and Dad and Emily, most people probably won't even care that I'm here. Ashley will just make a mental note about my attendance so she can't hold it over me later.

"You're going to be fine," Pepper says.

I take one last deep breath. Whether she's right or not doesn't matter, and I've already stalled long enough. "Let's go."

CHRISTINA

Pepper is first to exit the car and comes around to open my door like she knows I need the extra help to really get me moving. She reaches out her hand, and I take it. Even though my heels are higher than hers, she's still taller than me. I'd never be able to stand in hers all night. I hope mine don't bother me. But on the list of all the terrible things to happen—spill something, mess up my speech, bump into someone and cause a chain reaction that makes a huge scene that somehow starts a fire, choke and need the Heimlich, or possibly just die from asphyxiation—pinched toes are basically nonexistent as something to be worried about.

"Thank you," I tell her, my hand trembling—hers is so steady like she's trying to pass along a little of her strength to me.

"I got you." She leans down and brushes her lips against mine. Little fireworks ignite along my spine and fizzle all the way down. They're like a shot of electricity to my soul, and now not wanting to go in is for a totally different reason, but I need to, so I pull away even though I don't want to, and I close the car door, pressing the fob to lock it.

"Forgetting something?" she asks.

I slap my hand against my forehead. "What would I do without you?"

"You'd have to come back out to your car." She smirks. "Plus, I need to get mine, too."

I press the button to open the trunk. "You really didn't have to bring a gift."

"I wanted to." She lifts her box out. "My mom always said

CHRISTINA

you never show up empty-handed." The little glimpses Pepper has given me into her family make me feel like this experience with mine won't be so far off from what she's dealt with herself. And knowing she's going to be okay in there—that she'll be able to handle herself—gives my raging nerves a sense of calm.

Once the trunk is closed and the doors are locked, I drop my keys into my purse, and we carry our gifts toward the front of the restaurant. My box is large and heavy. I had to get something that would be just as good as what Ashley bought or I'd never hear the end of it. *If you still had your last job, maybe you would've been able to afford to buy Emily something nicer.* No way was I going to set myself up for that.

"Do you want any help?" Pepper offers.

"No. I'm fine." I force a smile to prepare myself for having to smile through the next however many hours this dinner will take.

Stepping inside is like stepping through a portal directly into Italy. Not that I've ever been there myself, but the cobblestone floors, lanterns, and plush greenery make it feel as though we're standing outside a quaint little Italian town somewhere, not inside a restaurant in America. A sign at the front says the main dining room is closed for a private event.

"Ciao. Welcome to Casa Nostra," the host says. He's wearing all black with his name, JOSHUA, embroidered in white on his shirt.

"We're here for Emily and Antonio," I tell him.

"Of course," he says. "This way." He walks Pepper and me down the hallway, which looks more like a charming alleyway,

---

CHRISTINA

and into a massive room with a ceiling painted like the night sky and loads of tables all with red tablecloths. People mill around while waiters wander through carrying trays of hors d'oeuvres and champagne. Across the room are my parents and Ashley. Emily is talking with a group of her friends, and then there's Aunt Barbara and Uncle Donald, and my cousins Maggie and Joey. Wow, did *everyone* turn up for this event? How big is the wedding going to be?

"You can do this." Pepper nudges my side.

Maybe I can, but I'm not sure if I'm ready yet. "Let's put these over there." I head to the gift table, which is already overflowing with presents—Ashley's box with her big white bow sits prominently in the middle. Pepper sets hers down next to mine.

"It's your family; it's going to be okay," Pepper whispers. "They love you." She's right, they do, and they mean well. It's still not always easy being compared to my sisters, or hearing how even other family members besides them are better than me in some way. "How about I get us some drinks?" Pepper suggests.

"Maybe we should both go," I say, but then Aunt JoJo sweeps up and pulls me in for the biggest hug—immediately I'm wrapped in her arms and the smell of Chanel No. 5, her signature scent, which she wears way too much of. Her salt-and-pepper hair is set in curls that spring up and over her ears.

"Christina, darling," she coos.

I turn back, and Pepper gives me an encouraging smile, gesturing that she's going to the bar. She didn't even ask me what I wanted, and I could really use some angry water to help settle the nerves in my stomach before I drink any alcohol—but with a lime so people will think it's a cocktail and won't ask why I'm not celebrating.

"We were just having a discussion, and I need you to settle something for me," Aunt JoJo says. Her arm links with mine, and she navigates her way through the crowd. The silk skirt of her seafoam green dress is cool against my legs as she beelines to practically the opposite side of the room, creating her own wind in her wake. Her pale cheeks are flushed—or it could just be that she was a little too generous with the blush. She leads me straight toward a man who must be here from Antonio's side, because I've never seen him before.

"Christina, this is Daryl. He's one of the groomsmen and a lawyer. Daryl, this is who I was telling you about." She winks at him, and the impending sense of doom already settles in my shoulders.

Aunt JoJo doesn't have any debate she needs my help settling; she just wants to try and set me up. I should've seen this coming from a million miles away—and added it to my list of things to worry about for the night so I could've already thought of a way to kindly extricate myself from this situation. I should've just let Emily tell everyone I was bringing a date, and then I wouldn't be standing here right now. Should've, would've, could've—it's basically my life's motto at this point.

Luckily, it seems that Daryl looks just as uncomfortable as I feel. He runs a hand over his short black hair and stops at the back of his neck. His brown cheeks might even have taken on a rosy note of their own, or maybe that's wishful thinking.

CHRISTINA

"Don't hold the lawyer part against me." Daryl chuckles as he sticks out a hand.

I shake it in response. While there's no way anything will happen between us, he's my sister's fiancé's friend and so there's no reason to be rude either. He wasn't the one trying to set me up with a practical stranger—thanks, Aunt JoJo.

Under different circumstances, I'd probably say he's good-looking—not because I'm interested, but simply because it's a fact. He looks sharp in a navy suit and white button-up shirt—top button undone with no tie. The way he stands makes it look almost like a casual outfit; being a lawyer probably means lots of suits and ties, so perhaps for him it is.

"Excuse me," Aunt JoJo says. "It looks like I'm being summoned." And with that she's off again as quickly as she came.

"So you're Emily's older sister." Daryl takes a casual sip of his drink. It isn't the champagne that's being passed around. His glass is short, and the liquid inside is a honey color.

"One of them, yes," I say.

"That's right; there are two of you." He leans down to reach my ear. "Are you the nice one or the mean one?" A bold introduction, but then again, he did say he was a lawyer.

"I guess that depends on who you're getting your information from." I don't have to make it too easy on the guy, even if he does seem nice enough.

"I'll keep that in mind." Daryl chuckles again, the sound rich and warm. "Your aunt was saying something about architecture—" And there it is. Not even here for five minutes and already I have to deal with this. Why can't my family just accept who I am? It's not Daryl's fault, but I snap.

CHRISTINA

"You seem like a smart guy, and my aunt means well and all, but this"—I gesture between the two of us—"isn't going to happen. And it's not because you don't seem wonderful, you do, and you seem charming and are handsome and—"

"Gay." Daryl lets out a sigh, which I can only assume is relief the way his whole body seems to relax in the process.

Oh my god. I've been so wrapped up in my own feelings, not once have I considered how awkward this must also be for him.

"My boyfriend couldn't be here tonight. I tried to tell your aunt, but then she went to get you, and I didn't want to cause any drama."

A rush of relief washes over me. "I totally get it. You don't have to explain yourself. And same. Bi, but still." I gesture to myself. "I'm actually here with someone. She just went to get us drinks."

He nods like he understands. If I had a dollar for every time a well-meaning family member tried to set me up, I'd have a lot of dollars. "Not a champagne girl," he says.

"It gives me headaches," I tell him. "And also, I've got to be on my toes tonight, it seems."

"Yes, it does."

We both laugh.

"So you're Antonio's friend." I attempt to start over with him.

"Fraternity brother. We go way back."

I glance around the room for Pepper, but she's nowhere in sight. "That's cool. I've lost touch with basically all of my college friends. I graduated and started working, and there just

---

CHRISTINA

wasn't a lot of time, you know." I suppose we're still "connected" through the few social sites I still have accounts with, but I don't think that really counts—plus I'm never on there.

"Oh, I get it. If it weren't for Antonio, I probably wouldn't have any friends at all. He's the one that keeps us all in touch. Forces us to meet up at least once a month. Hell, if it weren't for him, I never would've met Jack."

"Your boyfriend?"

"Sorry. Yes." Daryl nods. "Antonio made us all do this ridiculous axe-throwing thing one night, and Jack was there with a group of his friends, and well, the rest is history."

"Met while axe throwing. That's a unique meet-cute." My mind rushes back to the moment I met Pepper in the Halloween store—some might also call that unique. I'm sure not many could tell the story about bonding for the first time while shopping for severed heads.

"And no one got hurt, somehow, or sued anyone." Daryl laughs. "It was a good time."

"It probably would've put a damper on things if someone had an arm cut off or lost a couple of fingers."

"I would've fainted. I don't do the blood thing." He shakes his head.

"Neither do I." Even the idea of all the fake blood lined up on a shelf in the staging house makes my stomach a little queasy. I have to constantly remind myself it's not real.

"I got you a seltzer, thinking it could help with your nerves," Pepper whispers as she steps up from behind me and hands me a glass. "With a lime so it looks like a cocktail." She winks.

I want to ask her how she knew exactly what I wanted, but

right now, I'm not even about to question it. "Perfect." I take a sip, and the bubbles immediately start doing their job. "Pepper, Daryl. Daryl, Pepper," I introduce them.

They exchange hellos and shake hands.

"I should probably . . ." he says.

"Yes, of course," I say.

He leans in. "For the record, you're definitely the nice one." He raises his glass toward who I assume is another groomsman—in an "I'm coming" kind of way. "It was nice meeting you both," he says before striding off.

I turn to Pepper. "Have I told you yet how glad I am you're here?" The seltzer water is exactly what I needed, but even more so, she is—her being here is already making this night so much easier. Although this thing with Daryl was never going to happen, at least now neither one of us has to explain why. I'm here with someone—who's looking at me like I'm the only person in the room.

Her brow scrunches together. "Someone was trying to set you up with him, weren't they?"

"Yep."

Pepper glances toward Daryl and back to me. "Had they never met a gay man before?"

I burst out laughing. "I didn't notice at first either."

"Christina?" She sounds aghast, and she totally should be. If I hadn't been so up in my feels, I definitely would've noticed.

"What? He's handsome." I try to defend myself.

"That's not what I'm questioning." But then she's laughing, too, and I put my hand on her arm like it's the most natural thing to do in this situation.

CHRISTINA

"We were taking bets on if you'd make it tonight." My sister Ashley comes up from behind me, and the mood quickly shifts. The light airy feeling I was just having with Pepper has evaporated quicker than water in a hot frying pan, and in its place the tension has returned. I take a big sip of my drink.

"Very funny," I say. "Why wouldn't I be here?" But even as I say those words, the hundreds of excuses I had not to be here race through my mind. Except at the end of the day, I didn't use any of them. Even with all the dread—and the worst-case scenarios I came up with—I made it. Considering not coming in my mind isn't the same as not showing up at all.

"I'm Christina's sister Ashley." She thrusts a hand at Pepper.

"This is my friend Pepper," I quickly say, but immediately regret it. Is "friend" the right way to introduce her? What would she have said if I had just kept my mouth closed? If only Ashley wasn't so passive-aggressive to subtly tell me I'm rude for not introducing her myself—forget that she didn't really give me any time.

"It's so nice to meet you," Pepper says, not commenting on my use of the word "friend."

Ashley hugs the elbow of the arm she's holding her champagne in with her free hand. "As in salt-and-pepper?" Her gaze runs up and down Pepper, like she's trying to figure her out—or figure out what she's doing with me.

"One and the same." If Pepper is offended by Ashley's comment, she doesn't show it. "When I was born, my dad said my hair was as dark as pepper, and that was all it took." She takes a casual sip of her drink—which is most likely sangria since there's fruit floating in her wineglass—seemingly not im-

---

CHRISTINA

pressed by my sister at all. Honestly, it's the perfect way to deal with Ashley.

"Cute," Ashley says. Maybe she's where I get my inability to communicate with other human beings, because she's terrible at it. I'm not sure how I never really noticed it before. Whether Pepper is a friend or something more, Ashley should be making her feel welcome, not being so snotty. Why is Ashley like this? "So how do you know my sister?" she asks.

"Christina and I met at the Halloween store."

"Oh, that's right, you have that little event or whatever." Ashley waves a hand in my direction, and I clench my teeth.

"The haunted house isn't just a little event. It helps fund all the arts programs at the school and brings in tourists to the community," I say.

"Plus, it's a wonderful creative outlet for teens," Pepper chimes in. "They get to be a hundred percent in control of their performance. No scripts. No expectations. It's really empowering for them."

I hadn't thought of it like that, but I'm not about to admit that here in front of my sister.

"I'm sure. And that's great for them"—Ashley gestures toward me with her glass—"but did my sister tell you she was set to be vice president at her last job?"

I hadn't, in fact, told anyone in Clover Creek about that part of my life. Because it didn't matter. I hated that job. No amount of money could've made me want to stay there. I loved watching things I designed be built—but I also love doing the building. And I couldn't stand the blatant misogyny in the office—it was so toxic. To hell with the patriarchy of corporate culture.

CHRISTINA

"And now she could be teaching the next vice president," Pepper says like it's the most obvious thing—the most important thing there could be.

"Of the United States." Ashley chuckles. "Or even president." She laughs harder.

"I don't get it," Pepper says without missing a beat.

Ashley glances from me to Pepper. "It was a joke."

"Yes, I assumed that from the laughing, but I was hoping you could explain the joke." Pepper casually sips her drink, a look of true interest in her eyes.

The brief look on Ashley's face is priceless—like she's bitten into a sour kumquat. "Well, anyway. I hope you remembered to bring a gift," Ashley says, ignoring Pepper's request completely.

"Of course we did," I tell her.

Ashley raises her brows in surprise. "You brought a gift, too? That's really kind of you." Why is she acting so shocked? She doesn't even know Pepper. My cheeks start to heat up for a completely different reason than they usually do. I'm not even sure why I'm feeling so protective.

"Of course I did. It's an engagement party." Pepper's tone is perfect—calm with a touch of "Isn't it obvious?"—and it hits Ashley right where it hurts. She squints her eyes at Pepper like she's trying to murder her with one look. Pepper seems completely unimpressed by Ashley's antics. And as much fun as it is seeing Ashley squirm, I throw her a bone, so she doesn't start an argument.

"Where are the kids?" My niece and nephew are the cutest

CHRISTINA

and, per the family group chats, are already geared up to be the ring bearer and the flower girl, so I assume they'll be here. Plus, seeing them would be preferable to hanging out with my sister.

"Avery has an ear infection, and Lincoln wasn't coming without his sister." She rolls her eyes like this is the most exhausting thing—she should try hanging out with twenty-plus teens at one time. "Which is fine. He'd be miserable as the only kid here anyway. So I got a sitter."

"I hope she's okay."

"She's fine. She's just milking it." Ashley waves her hand again, this time brushing away the comment. "I hope you have your speech ready, because Mom is freaking out." She gestures with her eyes across the room to where my parents are standing.

I shake my head. "I thought I'd just wing it," I say, and Ashley's eyes nearly pop out of her head. "Yes, I have my speech." I tap my purse. She really needs to learn how to lighten up.

"I thought this thing was supposed to start by now." She pulls out her phone and checks the time. It's 7:15 p.m.

"I'm sure it'll start any minute. There are a lot of people here," I say.

"And Antonio's parents paid a lot of money for this, so the least the venue could do is be prepared," Ashley continues.

I bite my tongue. Arguing won't do any good. "Do you know what we're eating?" I ask to change the subject.

"It's an Italian restaurant, so pasta, I assume." Ashley crosses her arms.

CHRISTINA

I exchange a glance with Pepper, whose eyes are screaming *Is this girl for real?* Instead of laughing, I take a sip of my drink. Explaining to my sister that I'm not the idiot she assumes I am is pointless. You'd think from her mood, she was the one who was getting married.

"I hope this isn't too much for you. Since you're the last one in the family who's still single," Ashley says.

Here for twenty minutes and already twice I've been reminded of this sentiment, first with Aunt JoJo trying to set me up and now this. I gesture toward Pepper. "It's not like I'm here alone."

"I thought you said she was your friend." The look on Ashley's face is a mixture of condescension and annoyance. If I'm not the only single sister anymore, that's one less thing she can hang over my head.

Pepper slips her hand into mine. "Of course, we're friends, too." Then she leans in and presses a kiss to my cheek. "You're friends with your partner, aren't you?"

"Yes." Her head pivots around. "I should go find him." And without saying another word, Ashley walks away.

"Oh my god, you were brilliant," I tell Pepper.

"She's awful. I know she's your sister and all, but come on."

I take another sip of my water. "She's exhausting."

Pepper holds her wineglass out to me, and I graciously take a swig—yep, sangria, and it's delicious. "I have one at the table for you."

"Titi!" Emily rushes up and wraps me in a giant hug. "I'm so glad you made it. And this must be Pepper. Thanks so much for coming." Emily, being Emily, wraps Pepper in a hug, too;

CHRISTINA

and Pepper, being Pepper, doesn't seem to mind, embracing her back with just as much ferocity like they're long-lost friends. She's good at this—at people—in a way I probably never will be. I really should ask her how she does it—how she seems to know people she's never met before. She has a sixth sense or something for sure.

"Thanks for having me. It's so nice to meet you, too, and congratulations," Pepper says.

"Have you seen Mom and Dad?" Emily asks.

"Did someone call my name?" Mom says.

"Did you just get here?" Dad asks.

I glance at Pepper, who doesn't seem fazed at all even though she's basically being accosted by my entire family at the same time. "I've been making my rounds," I say, and then I quickly introduce them to Pepper. This time I say she is my date instead of my "friend," and Mom's eyes immediately get glossy and her smile is enormous.

"It's so wonderful to meet you." Mom steps in and gives Pepper a hug. "I didn't know you'd be bringing anyone with you tonight," she says to me.

"It's not a big deal," I say, but that's a lie. It's a very big deal to my parents. They've always wanted me to settle down and find my person, especially these last few years—so even if this thing with Pepper is new, it gives Mom hope.

"I'm sure I mentioned it," Emily says, but the look she gives tells me that she didn't actually say a word about it. She's the best sister.

Tink. Tink. Tink. Tink.

Someone taps their silverware against their glass. "If I could

---

CHRISTINA

have your attention," Antonio says. "If everyone could take a seat, they're ready to start serving dinner."

"We'll catch up after," Emily says. "Oh, and I love your shoes." She quickly squeezes my arm and then rushes off toward her fiancé. The comment makes me smile. Of course she would notice.

"Oh no. Where are you sitting?" Mom asks.

"We have a spot over there." Pepper points to a place behind her.

"Maybe we could shift—"

"It's fine, Mom," I tell her before giving her a quick kiss on the cheek. "We will catch up later."

"Well, we'll want to learn more about you after dinner," she says to Pepper. "So no running off," she says to me, then she hooks her arm with Dad's and they head to wherever they're sitting.

"This way." Pepper squeezes my elbow and tugs me in the opposite direction.

I'm not sure how she did it, but she saved us the perfect seats. A couple of Emily's friends and their dates along with two of my cousins are already seated at the table. Mom and Dad are near Emily and Antonio, his parents are toward the front of the room, and Ashley and her husband, Luke, are on the exact opposite side from us.

"Thanks again for coming with me," I whisper to Pepper when we sit down.

"I got you." She reaches under the table and interlaces our fingers together; the warmth of her hand penetrates through my dress into my thigh and races up my leg to my center. My

---

CHRISTINA

heart stutters—those three words seemingly hold more weight than ever before. And I do feel safe. I do feel like she's got me. Our eyes lock, and I chew on the inside of my lip to stop myself from leaning over and kissing her with everything I have right now. I honestly don't know what I'd do without her.

CHRISTINA

28 DAYS
UNTIL THE STORE CLOSES

Pepper

The sun had barely made its appearance when I headed out for the day. The morning air was crisp with the sweet scent from Glazed & Confused, which for once wouldn't be my first stop today. I had other things I needed to get done—or more specifically, a person I needed to find.

I rounded the corner toward the front of the building when I nearly ran into New Guy. It had almost become embarrassing how I couldn't remember his name. But aside from Dewy, no one called him that. He was "New Guy" or "The New Guy" or, according to Lisa, "that 'Franken' guy." Which, in all fairness, fit him the best—especially since we all knew what Franken was a stand-in for.

It wasn't that he was a terrible person—he just wanted The Dead of Night to be something it wasn't. Namely, completely efficient and to 100 percent make sense. But there was nothing truly sensical about Halloween. There would never be radioactive bunnies who quadrupled in size and became hungry for human flesh—a costume we carried. And no one truly needed a collection of old-school lunch boxes with classic horror films on them. That wasn't the point of Halloween. It was a time to have fun, honor special people in your life both living and passed on, and celebrate hope over fear—by having the bejesus scared out of you because those scary things didn't kill you, and afterward you never felt more alive.

New Guy was concerned about profits and losses, he wanted it to be corporate and sterile, and that would never happen. His only good idea was that we should have a costume store that was open year-round. Now, that did make sense. The times I had to order things online for our non-Halloween-related productions for the year were numerous. Or I had to make the trek to the nearest shopping mall town, which was over an hour away. But again, that wasn't how The Dead of Night operated, and although I couldn't help thinking how wonderful it would be if I could be here year-round, it just wasn't an option.

"Oh, Ms. Pepper, good morning," he said. "Great day to be alive, isn't it?" He made a show of sucking in the deepest breath. That was the other thing that annoyed me about him. Calling me Ms. Pepper—like I was some kind of soda mistress.

"Pepper is just fine," I told him for the millionth time. "You're up early."

"I could say the same thing about you." He chuckled. For a college kid, he really had the dad humor thing down pat. "Getting in that morning workout?" he asked.

I glanced down at my long skirt, boots, and cropped leather jacket. "Yep. How'd you guess?"

PEPPER

"Well, the store doesn't open for another couple of hours," he said, clearly oblivious to my sarcasm.

"What about you?" I asked. His outfit—khakis and a hoodie—wasn't the typical workout attire either.

"I thought I'd get an early start and make sure the parking lot is cleaned up for the day."

"But you can't clock in yet." I narrowed my eyes at him. Being committed to your job was one thing but this just seemed over-the-top—which I supposed for New Guy was pretty much his MO. "You know. Never mind," I said.

He laughed like it was the funniest thing in the world. "That's a good one."

"You know me." Really, who was this kid? There were things like magic and curses, but the more time I spent with him, the more I started to believe that maybe possession was possible as well.

"Don't let me keep you. Gotta burn those calories." He pumped his arms like he was lifting imaginary weights.

"Totally," I said, and started to walk away.

"See you later!" he called after me.

I raised my hand in the air as a goodbye. Wow, that kid was something else. I could definitely see why the others didn't get along with him.

Did he just really love working at The Dead of Night, or was he this over-the-top in all the jobs he had? He wasn't that old, so maybe one day he'd figure it out that work doesn't love you back—even if you have a job you love.

Teaching was something I always knew I wanted to do—I loved it. It was also the reason I was now in this position. Not that I was mad about it, but part of me deep down still missed those days in the classroom—playing improv games and seeing kids bloom right before my eyes. Theater should've been a mandatory class. It taught kids so much about who they were—or who they could be—how to be vulnerable, and perhaps most important, how to support others.

As I continued down the street, my mind wandered to the possibility of being able to do all of it again. If my plan worked, I could have the perfect life—living here in Clover Creek with Christina, and possibly even teaching again. Maybe in some weird way, me being cursed was exactly what was supposed to happen so I could meet Christina and have this life with her.

Stranger things have occurred.

And sometimes we had to *make* things happen. Which was why I was out walking the streets this morning.

I'd yet to run into Mrs. Stein since after the farmer's market. It was just a matter of time, and I had to make myself available for it to happen. Which was why I made sure to go to all the places in Clover Creek—the grocery store, our one fabulous bookstore, the few gas stations, and of course, I'd been in the Halloween store as much as possible, since everyone in town showed up there at some point—and I hadn't lost hope.

It occurred to me at the market with Christina that Mrs. Stein had said something that could be useful. She had a reason to want to keep living even if no one remembered her. Now I'd gotten ahead of myself since I didn't even know for sure if she was dying or not, but still, it couldn't hurt to at least find out more about her predicament. And if she did have an impending expiration date, I could give her something no one else could. A way to stay alive so she could watch her grandchildren grow up. A little curse had to be worth it for that.

I made a promise to myself that I'd never trick anyone the way I had been. But what if they themselves wanted it? What if the person knew all the rules and stipulations ahead of time? That would be fair, and it would be something I'd be able to live with. My conscience would be clear.

It felt to me to be the perfect solution to both of our problems, so it only seemed right to at least give it a shot.

After walking the entirety of downtown a few times since sunrise, I headed to the corner of Rhubarb and Orange—a major intersection in Clover Creek—to see if I might be able to catch a glimpse of her. It was nearly impossible for anyone to go anywhere during the day without crossing this intersection at some point.

This was such a great idea, I was surprised I hadn't thought of it sooner.

If there was any opportunity of getting to be with Christina, even a sliver of a chance, I had to give it a try.

Two hours later, and not a single glimpse of the woman; I needed to refresh and recharge, and also get some sustenance. If it took me all day to find her, I'd do it, but I couldn't do it without snacks.

The bell rang as I pushed through the door at Glazed & Confused—the scent of sugar and coffee hung heavy in the air, and immediately my mouth started to water. Skipping breakfast had been a mistake, and my stomach roared like an angry lion—begging to be fed.

I complied with its request by ordering a chocolate coconut cronut and an iced coffee with extra cream and sugar, and then I went to sit down to shove it in my face as quickly as possible. But there at the table near the napkin dispensers sat Mrs. Stein. Once again, the universe knew better than I did—this was why I'd forgotten to pack snacks; this was why I'd skipped breakfast. This moment here was meant to be.

Mrs. Stein sat at the small pink table looking even frailer than she had the last time I saw her. The cardigan she wore hung off her, and she clutched a steaming mug in her hands, staring at something in front of her—but there wasn't anything else that I could see.

Now that she was in front of me, I wasn't exactly sure how to start off this conversation.

"Are you okay?" I started with. It seemed the most appropriate, given the situation.

She glanced up, dark circles under her glassy eyes. "I could be better."

"Want to talk about it?" I gestured to the seat, hoping she'd allow me to stay.

Her gaze slid back and forth like she was deciding if she wanted to engage or not. "You're Christina's friend, right?" More than that, Mrs. Stein and I had been colleagues for years before she couldn't remember me anymore, but that didn't mean I didn't remember her. Another benefit of this curse of mine, and one I was fully intending on using.

PEPPER

I nodded. "I am."

"Such a lovely girl."

"I think so, too."

Mrs. Stein smiled, then motioned toward the chair opposite her. "She must've told you that I'm not doing too well."

"She mentioned something briefly but didn't go into detail," I said as I sat down.

"Well, it's not looking so good." She fiddled with her coffee mug, pushing the handle from side to side.

"I'm sorry," I said, and I meant it. It didn't bring me any kind of joy to know this woman was suffering, and perhaps I could do something that could help her.

"Not as sorry as I am." She used a napkin to pat her eyes. "I don't think anyone realizes how precious time is until they are told they don't have much of it left."

"That's true." I broke off a piece of my cronut and ate it slowly, attempting to savor it—and along with it, savor the opening Mrs. Stein had left me. It was fortunate that sometimes it was easier to talk to a complete stranger about things. "What would you do, though, if you had all the time?"

She chuckled in the it's-not-really-funny way. "So many things."

"How is Lindsay taking the news?" It was a risk talking about her daughter, and if this were any other time or for any other reason, I wouldn't have done it. But I also needed to figure out a way to make sure Mrs. Stein believed what I was about to tell her was true.

"She took it as well as can be expected. Which was not well at all." She likely thought Christina had told me about her daughter—which was fair—so I needed another approach to make her really question how I knew things.

"That makes sense. I'm sure she's worried what she'll do without you," I said. "Kind of like how Mr. Olsen felt when he lost his father." It had been my second year at Clover Creek when the biology teacher's father had a terrible accident that forced him to leave the school mid-year. He'd been devastated—and completely inconsolable. He was still young himself, and like all accidents, it was completely unexpected. Not that losing someone important was ever easy. If we all spoke to and treated one another like it would be our last interaction, it likely would change so many things. We wouldn't let fear control us so much; that was for sure.

"How did you . . . ?" She scrunched her brows. "Christina wasn't at the school when that happened."

"She also wasn't at the school when Mrs. Agarwal brought in that hideous green couch for the teachers' lounge, or when that teacher's aide, Roberto, spilled his entire sub sandwich on it, leaving that gross greasy stain—that looked like it could be something else that was even more disgusting." It was all the teachers could joke about for the rest of the year, and at the time it was hysterical.

"I don't understand," she said, but I had to give her credit for not looking or sounding scared.

This was it. My opportunity to tell someone my secret. Past experience said she could react in a number of different ways, so I was prepared. "What would you say if I told you we knew each other—worked together even—in the past, but you can't remember me?"

PEPPER

"I think I'd say it sounds ridiculous." She wasn't wrong. I was sure that was exactly how it sounded.

"But not impossible."

She narrowed her eyes at me. "I'm not sure I believe you."

"And that's fair. Hell, I wouldn't believe me either. But how would I know all of this? How would I know, growing up, your family used to call you Maisey—and I know that because your mother came to visit you at school the year before she passed away." I held my breath, waiting for her reaction.

Mrs. Stein folded her hands softly in front of her. "Maybe it's the illness talking, but are you some kind of guardian angel?"

I shook my head. So far this was going better than expected. "Nothing like that, no. But I might have something that could help you. If you're willing to listen." I chewed on the inside of my cheek. She might not go for it at all, but I at least needed her to hear me out.

"Let me refill my coffee and we can chat," she said.

"Here, let me get that for you." I grabbed her mug and headed for the counter, my heart thrumming in my chest. This was my chance.

PEPPER

26 DAYS
UNTIL THE STORE CLOSES

Christina

When Ashley called me two hours ago and left a message saying there was a family emergency, and that I needed to get to my parents' house ASAP, I didn't have time to think. I ran into Principal Wilkson's office—luckily he said he'd cover my last class of the day—canceled everything for after school, and jumped in my car to race down there as fast as I could. A million thoughts blur together like the scenery whizzing by my car. Fortunately, I've done this drive so many times, I could practically do it with my eyes closed, because my mind isn't on the road. I had just seen them all at Emily's engagement party, and everyone was fine. What could've happened that they couldn't just tell me over the phone?

Someone is dead. That's the worst case that my mind can conjure, and it makes sense why they wouldn't tell me until I get there.

But who could it be?

The leg I'm not using for the gas pedal bounces ferociously, shaking the entire car, and the hand not holding the wheel worries at the scar on my arm as I turn onto my childhood street.

I throw my car into park and run up the driveway past Emily's new Beamer and Ashley's Range Rover and push through the front door without knocking, with a little more force than usual. "I'm here. Now, what's wrong?"

My entire family sits in the living room mid-conversation. The scene is so similar to what it was like back in high school coming home to find them all after getting off my shift at the local pool as a lifeguard. Dad in his recliner. Emily on the floor messing with the cat. Ashley on one side of the couch, and Mom on the other. The only difference this time is that Mom's foot is in a rather large plastic boot that's propped on a pillow on the coffee table.

"Oh, honey, you didn't need to race all the way down here," Mom says. Her words are a little slurred like she's had a few drinks—or, considering the circumstances, likely some very strong painkillers.

My ears burn. No one is dead. I should be happy that no one is dead. Although I'm about to kill someone right now. "Ashley said it was an emergency. No one was picking up their phones." Why, for the love of all in the universe, did no one pick up their phone? I'm ready to scream, but instead I press my fingernails deeper into the palms of my hands.

At that, everyone but Mom scrambles for their cells.

"It was on silent." Ashley flips her phone in her hand like it's not a big deal.

CHRISTINA

"Left it upstairs." Dad chuckles.

"Battery died," Emily says—her teeth clench in that embarrassed emoji kind of way.

"You are a tech genius, and you didn't charge your phone?" My voice is shriller than I mean it, and I shouldn't take it out on Em, because she's always been the one I can count on, but today I really needed her.

"It wasn't on purpose," she says, and she does sound sorry, which is more than anyone else.

I let out a long breath—both relieved and angry that I'm standing here right now. "I canceled my entire day because I thought someone was dying." I give Ashley a death stare. She could've made it clear in her message. She could've told me everything was okay and not to worry. Why does she have to be so terrible to me all the time?

"Mom needs surgery," she blurts out like this somehow makes up for her complete disregard for me and my feelings.

"What?" I ask.

"It's a funny story really," Mom says. "I was carrying the laundry down the stairs, and Baxter, that mischievous little feline, was trying to help, and I fell." She giggles, actually giggles, at this.

"You fell down the stairs?" I must've misheard because there isn't a single thing funny about that story. Those are some strong painkillers for sure.

Dad shakes his head. "Your mother shattered some bones in her ankle, and she's going to need surgery to repair it, but they want to wait for the swelling to go down—"

"And make sure the insurance will pay for it." Emily rolls

CHRISTINA

her eyes. Her disdain for the sick care system, as she calls it, is palpable.

"Yes, I'm sure they also want to make sure all the paperwork is in order," Dad says.

I flop down in one of the chairs. "Okay, no one is dying, and Mom is having a surgery some other day that isn't today, so why was it that I needed to rush down here?"

"Mom's going to be out of commission," Ashley jumps in. "And Dad has a business trip coming up next week." She cannot possibly be suggesting . . . "So someone needs to be here to help her out."

Of course she is. Because this is who Ashley is—this is what she does. Or what she doesn't do. She never thinks about me. But getting loud has never been effective, so I take a calming breath and keep my tone level. "I have a job. In Clover Creek. And a huge event I'm planning." And once again this all could've been communicated with me over the phone. It didn't require a panicked call for me to race all the way down here; not that I add that, even though I really want to. I'm already feeling completely ganged up on.

Ashley humphs. "Yes, and Emily is getting ready to launch, and I have kids—"

"That go to school during the day. Which is where I *have* to be. And Emily works from home." I pull in another deep breath, this time counting to ten.

"I have a lot of meetings," Emily says, and to her credit, she does look like none of this was her idea. It's not as though she planned her very important launch event at the same time Mom fell down the stairs—but also it isn't like I planned mine at this same time either. I don't want to take this out on Em, and it totally isn't her fault, but why does my whole family not see the value in what I do?

Ashley tips her head to the side. "We thought—"

"I can't believe you," I snap; my voice is louder than I intend, but I don't care anymore. "I get that you all don't think my job is important, but it is. And I'm sorry, but I don't have the flexibility to work from home. And I may not have kids, but for fuck's sake, Ashley, can't you be here during the day when Luke's at work and the kids are at school—"

"Just because I don't have a job doesn't mean I don't work," Ashley says.

"I never said you didn't. But god forbid the laundry doesn't get done for a couple days, or *gasp*, Luke does some."

"We know your job is important," Emily says.

"Maybe you do, but they don't." I point to the rest of my family. "No, I'm not some big-time architect, but I'm pretty good at my job, and it doesn't make me miserable, and shouldn't my happiness mean something?" I stand. "You know what? I'm done trying to convince you. Because it doesn't matter. I'm happy. And, Mom, I'm sorry you're hurt, and I will do what I can, but I won't be shirking my responsibilities to *my* kids and my community."

Dad clears his throat. "You're right, honey, and even before all of this, your mom and I had been talking and we've been meaning to chat with you, but it's never felt like the right time, and now, well . . . It probably isn't the right time either, but the Fishers are willing to rent out their barn, and Mom and I thought it could be a good place for you to do your woodworking and maybe sell some of your creations to local folks or whatever you want."

A moment ago, I was ready to storm out the door, and now I'm frozen in place. "You want to support my art?"

"We've realized we haven't been as supportive of your passions as we should've been. And we didn't really understand when you took this teaching job, but we saw that chair you made for Mrs. Vasquez. You're very talented."

I made that chair three years ago when my depression hit right after Halloween. I needed something to focus on and Mrs. Vasquez's daughter-in-law was having a baby, so I offered to make the rocker. I didn't even know my parents knew about it. "What's the catch?" Maybe it's wrong to be so judgmental, but this feels too easy.

Dad fiddles with his wedding ring—his nervous tell. "No catch. But if you could help out a little just until your mom is back up and going, that would be really appreciated."

"You've got to be kidding me," Ashley pipes in.

"Why do you care?" Emily says. "You don't want to take care of Mom."

"You want me to quit my job to live at home and take care of Mom and you will pay for me to have a space to work on my projects just like that. No other strings attached?"

Dad looks at Mom, whose head has fallen back on the couch cushions and she's fast asleep. "You'd really be helping us out. And we really think you could do something with your skills."

I can't say I'm not tempted. No more early mornings or grading papers or parent-teacher meetings, and I'd finally have

---

CHRISTINA

the time to do the thing that I love. "I'm going to need to think about it."

"Of course," Dad says.

Before anyone else can say anything, I walk back outside, down the driveway, and get into my car.

As I head onto the freeway, back toward Clover Creek, the conversation with Dad plays over and over in my mind. If I did it, I'd be giving them what they want, but I'd also be getting what I want. Deciding to teach was a way for me to "take a break" and rethink my life, but I've been so busy, there hasn't really been time. Yes, I'd be moving back home, which isn't ideal, but would it really be so bad? Mom won't be hurt forever, and I've got a little money saved up, so who knows, maybe I could open a shop in town. I'd save money on rent and covering the cost of prosthetic scars and warts for the haunted house until my reimbursement comes in—*if* it comes in. Maybe once Halloween ends, I won't feel as bad as I have the last three years if I have a plan in place.

The tires thrum against the concrete, drowning out the low volume on my stereo, and I think about what my life could be if I took a leap. This one can't be as impulsive as the last. This time I need to consider all the pros and cons and really consider the worst-case scenario.

A light on the dash comes on, and even with my foot on the gas, the car starts to jerk forward. No. Not now. I release the pedal and throw my blinker on. I'm still at least an hour outside of Clover Creek, and there's nothing around here for miles. When I try to press the accelerator, nothing happens, so I move to the side of the road and park the car.

CHRISTINA

The temperature gauge isn't that high, and while the gas tank isn't the fullest, the light isn't on. I've never made that trip home and back so quickly before, so maybe she needs a little break.

My head falls back against the headrest. What is this supposed to mean? I feel like the universe is trying to tell me something. Is it saying don't go back to Clover Creek? Or maybe it's trying to tell me to stop and really think about what I want and if this would be the best way to get it? Quitting my last job had been the easy way out. I could've stayed and fought for what I wanted, but I didn't. I cut and ran. What else could I lose if I give up on everything now and take the easy road again?

Lightning flashes in the darkening sky above. I turn the ignition. Nothing. It'll be dark soon, and I'm stuck.

Shit.

Okay, universe. What am I supposed to do now?

I reach for my purse to get my cell, and my take-out bag from earlier falls on the floor, spilling a couple packets of ketchup and a few of those salt-and-pepper packets.

This hint from the universe I understand.

CHRISTINA

26 DAYS
UNTIL THE STORE CLOSES

Pepper

The rain was steadily coming down as I drove out of Clover Creek and toward the location Christina had given me. I wasn't sure how technology had gotten so advanced even in the past five years that someone could share their location and the phone would give you exact directions, but here I was. Granted, I hadn't used the company-issued phone much in the previous years, other than to receive calls or texts from other employees, so it might not have been that much of an advancement. But with the last rays of sunlight quickly disappearing, I had hoped it would allow me to find Christina even in complete darkness.

Luckily there weren't many cars on the road, likely because of the incoming storm. Maybe she thought she'd be able to get ahead of it when she decided to go out, but it seemed luck wasn't on her side today.

The farther I drove away from Clover Creek, the denser the tree line became. What color was her car again? Would I even be able to see it among the shadows of the trees? She was counting on me, so I needed to find her.

An hour and fifteen minutes into my drive, and I worried I might've passed her, but the app on the phone told me to keep going. My wipers were working on overdrive, and I was about to pull off the road to try and call her when my headlight caught the glint of something on the other side of the road. While visibility wasn't great, I was pretty confident no one was coming in the opposite direction, so I quickly passed and turned around, pulling the hearse to a stop behind what I hoped was Christina's car and flashing my headlights.

> CHRISTINA: Is that you?
>
> ME: Yes
>
> CHRISTINA: Coming . . .

A couple minutes later, her car door opened, she quickly climbed out, closed the door behind her, and ran toward me, throwing herself into the passenger side of the hearse. "Thank you so much," she said as she pulled the jacket from over her head. In the time it took her to get from her car to mine, she had gotten completely soaked.

I handed her the towel I'd brought just in case. "Here."

"You're my hero." She kicked off her oxfords and stuck her feet up and under the dash, where the hot air was blowing.

"It's fine. I got you," I said. "What happened?"

She used the towel to squeeze some of the water out of her clothes and hair. "I don't know. It just decided to die on me.

Hopefully Ned can come and tow it back to town tomorrow and tell me what's wrong. I should look into getting some kind of roadside assistance."

The rain was really coming down. "I'm not sure it would help much in this."

"Maybe not." She flipped the visor down, inspecting herself in the small mirror. She must have had on waterproof mascara, because it was perfectly intact along with her lipstick—which never went anywhere. Satisfied, she flipped it closed and pulled out a package of mints. "Want one?"

"Are you trying to tell me something?"

"Maybe." She smirked.

"Well, I guess I need one." I smiled back.

She held the package out to me, and I took one, popping it into my mouth, and Christina did the same.

"These are strong." I wouldn't have been surprised if steam came out of my mouth.

"They're the best." She reached over and played with the amulet attached to my key ring. "This is pretty."

I almost laughed. To her, it was just a silver circle with an engraved star and a red stone in the center that had a way of always catching the light just right, making it sparkle. The symbols around the star looked like pretty adornments, not the words spelling out my curse in a language no mere mortal was capable of reading. It was, in a word, pretty, but it was also powerful.

"Where'd you get it?" she asked.

I shrugged. "It came with the keys to the car." Which wasn't completely a lie. The keys came with the curse. I just decided to put the two together—since it was never possible to lose the amulet, I never lost my keys. Win-win. "Ready?" I asked. I didn't want to rush her.

She dropped her bag to the floor and buckled her seat belt. I did my best to check my mirrors to see if anyone was coming before taking my foot off the brake and slowly creeping back out onto the road. The rain poured down in sheets, and my wipers couldn't work fast enough to get rid of it. I made it right past where her car was parked when the hearse started sliding.

Christina gripped the door handle. "Whew."

I pulled back off the road and put the car in park. "Maybe we should wait it out a little?"

"Yeah, I think that's a good idea." Christina typed on her cell phone and held it out to show me. "Looks like this storm is going to be around awhile."

I checked the gauges on my dash. "I should've stopped for gas."

"But then you might not have made it to me before this." She gestured to the window. The world was a complete washout beyond. "And I'd be all alone out here."

"True. But I don't think I can leave it running for the heater." I gritted my teeth. While the hearse appeared and disappeared with the store, it didn't have a magically filling gas tank. On the bright side, it also never broke down.

"How bad is it?" She leaned over and looked herself. "Oh yeah, you better turn it off."

I hesitated. "But you'll be cold."

"We'll both be cold," she countered.

I glanced to the back of the hearse. "Not necessarily."

Her head swiveled in the direction I'd just looked. "How is that going to help?"

"There are blankets back there." I paused. I had a feeling she wasn't going to like this idea, but it might be the only way to make sure she didn't freeze to death. "You could take off your clothes, and wrap yourself in a blanket," I added quickly, "and we could lay them out to dry here on the front seat." I wasn't sure how efficient that would be, but at least she wouldn't get sick. If it had been me to get soaked, we wouldn't have this issue. Sure, I'd have been cold, but no harm done.

"Why do you have blankets in the back of a hearse?" She raised her brows at me, which was fair. It was super weird.

I said the same thing when I opened the hearse's back door a couple days ago. "There's this new guy at the store, and he thought it would be a good idea to put a 'body' back there. Not a real one, of course, and he loaded in a bunch of padding and blankets. It's a terrible idea, especially since I'm the only person allowed to drive this car, but right now, I'm not mad about it. Especially if it's going to keep you from getting hypothermia." Good thing he never got around to cleaning them out like I'd asked him to.

Christina glanced at the dash, then to the back of the hearse, lifting herself up to peer over the seat and through the little red velvet curtains. "It does look pretty comfortable in there." She nodded. "All right, I'll do it." She took off her shoes, climbed into the back, and a moment later the jeans and shirt she'd been wearing were thrown into the front seat. "Okay, I'm set."

I wrung as much water as I could from the clothes, laid them on the seat, and turned the engine off.

PEPPER

"It's almost like a bed back here," she said.

"I think that was the point. Honestly, no one really understands what the new guy is trying to do most of the time." The temperature seemed to immediately start dropping.

"Well, I'm glad he did this, I suppose."

"Me too." I wrapped my arms around myself, wishing I'd grabbed a cardigan before I ran out the door. The fit-and-flare skirt and top I wore were cute, but they weren't built for warmth. However, when Christina called, there wasn't time to think, I needed to get on the road quickly, and it was a good thing I did. A couple more minutes and I'm not sure I would've made it.

Her damp towel lay next to me, and I grabbed it to cover myself. Since there wasn't anything else around, it was better than nothing. "What were you doing out here anyway?" I asked. Maybe if I didn't think about it, I wouldn't be so cold.

She let out a long sigh. "I had to go to my parents' house, and let's just say things were interesting as always."

"You don't want to talk about it?" I started to shiver.

"Not really," she said. "I could play some music on my phone or something, or no, I should probably save the battery, shouldn't I?"

"Uh-huh." The towel seemed to make me colder than I was without it, so I threw it onto the floorboard and tucked my hands in my armpits.

"What do you think it's like to be tall?" she asked.

"What?" The cold must've been affecting my ears. I couldn't have possibly heard her correctly.

"We're probably going to be here awhile, and we don't have

any entertainment, so I thought we could talk about something."

I chuckled. "And you thought we should talk about height?"

"Yeah." She poked her head out from the back. "Oh, it's cold up here."

"I didn't really notice."

"Pepper," she said, "your teeth are practically chattering."

"It's fine." Which was a lie, but I'd survive, and that was all that mattered.

"You should come back here."

I turned around and finally met her gaze. Brown eyes framed by long black lashes stared back at me.

"It's warmer, there are a ton of blankets, and with these curtains closed, it'll help keep the heat in."

I had to admit it sounded nice. The windows didn't exactly keep the cold out like heavy velvet could. "Are you sure?"

She nodded.

If she was sure . . . I kicked off my shoes and joined her in the back. She had a plush black blanket wrapped around her and was lying underneath another one. After some maneuvering, I slid under, too. She'd already closed all the curtains over the windows, so once she tugged the one to the front closed, it was completely black. Only a small amount of light that had come from a nearby streetlamp came through at all. It took a moment for my eyes to adjust to the new darkness.

"See? Isn't that better?" Christina lay on her side, her head propped up on her hand.

"It really is." I turned on my side and matched her, resting my head in my hand propped up by my elbow. "Now, what were you saying?"

She laughed, and the scent of mint tickled my nose. "I was asking what you think it must be like being tall. Like can you imagine what it would be like to, you know, actually see everything while you're walking around?"

"I'd never really thought about it."

"It was a question in this game the kids were playing the other day in class, and I haven't stopped thinking about it. About how one's perspective can be so different based on their height."

We never played any games like that when I taught, but since I couldn't say that, I thought about my answer. "I could see what was on top of the refrigerator; that would be one thing."

"Exactly. That's what I mean. Like, the world must look so different." She was clearly very excited about this discovery.

"And what does it look like for you?" I asked. While I wasn't exactly what one would call tall, I wasn't as short as Christina either. She was petite.

"I see a lot of chests." She locked eyes with me, and we both started laughing.

"Shoulders and necks for me, so it's not much better."

"But people probably don't try to pick you up," she said.

"No! Stop it." Was she serious?

She shook her head. "I wish I could tell you it's not a thing. It happened a lot in college."

"Guys?"

"Guys," she confirmed.

"It's not all guys, but it's always a guy. Why is that?" I've had the pleasure of knowing a lot of great men in my days, but the ones that weren't great sure ruined it for the rest of them.

"I wish I knew," she said.

And then it was quiet. The rain pounded the roof of the hearse, and here I was lying next to this beautiful woman. Her damp hair hung halfway to her elbow, and there was a strawberry-shaped birthmark on her shoulder, next to her black bra strap. I wet my bottom lip with my tongue.

Thunder crashed somewhere in the distance, and the wind began to howl.

"You *did* lock the doors, right?" Christina's voice sounded tentative. Which wasn't surprising since she had made it abundantly clear that she didn't enjoy being scared.

"I did," I assured her. "There's nothing to be afraid of."

"What about serial killers?"

"I don't think they would be out in the rain like this. Too much hassle," I said. "I mean, how would they hold their umbrella and a knife? It isn't practical," I joked to help lighten the mood—something she had done on numerous occasions.

She scooted closer. "And werewolves?"

"It's not a full moon."

She came even closer, her leg touching mine, and butterflies took off in my stomach. "Plus, you'll protect me if anything scary comes along, won't you?" Her gaze dipped to my mouth.

"I got you."

"You and that saying." She cracked a smile.

"Everyone needs a catchphrase," I said.

"So what's mine?" She tipped her head to the side, her damp hair tickling my arm.

PEPPER

I shook my head. "You have to figure that out yourself."

"Well, we'll need to do something to pass the time." She ran her finger down my arm, giving me goose bumps.

"Did you have something in mind?"

She smiled even brighter than she had before. "I do." She pressed her lips to mine, and there was something bolder and more intense than the kiss we'd shared before. A longing, or a deep desire, drew me in like a vacuum. Heat rushed from my lips down to my toes and back. I brushed the damp hair from her face and held her cheek in my hand. She tasted like mint and smelled like roses.

The blanket she'd been cocooned inside slipped down as she lifted herself up, and I lowered my head onto the soft cushions around us. She took the lead, and I willingly followed. My heart was racing in my chest.

I wrapped my hand around her exposed bare back, pulling her deeper into me. The satin lace of her bra was smooth and cool. "Is this okay?"

"Uh-huh. What do you like?"

"This is all a little new to me," I admitted.

"I'm no expert either, so just let me know if you're uncomfortable, and I'll do the same, okay?"

I nodded.

Her fingers found the place where my shirt and skirt met, and she slid her hand up, my skin igniting under her touch. She cupped my breast as I kissed her neck, tasting the rain on her skin.

I couldn't get enough of her. Time slipped by as we explored each other, and our breathing got heavy. She pulled my shirt over my head, and our hearts beat against each other—skin on skin. The car rocked with the howling wind, but the storm outside was nothing compared to what was raging between me and Christina.

Not only had it been too long since I'd been with anyone, but this was also my first time with another woman, and it felt right, so natural, and even better than I ever thought it could be. Her hand slid between my legs, and I gasped, rocking my hips forward, encouraging her to keep going.

Somehow along the way, I lost my skirt and bra, and sweat began to bead up along my lower back, but I didn't want to stop. Now that I had a taste of Christina—of what it was like being with her—I completely drank her in. I was drunk off the way my body tingled as she touched me, and the moans that escaped her luscious lips were the most beautiful sounds I'd ever heard.

Completely spent, I laid in Christina's arms as the rain quieted. Being with her like this would've made it impossible to be without her, but I had a plan. I had found a way to hopefully break the curse my way—so no one would have to get hurt. This may have been the first time with Christina, though it didn't have to be the last—I'd make sure of it.

PEPPER

22 DAYS
UNTIL THE STORE CLOSES

Christina

There's so much to do, and I still haven't given my parents an answer to their proposition yet. It's all so much more complicated than I originally thought it would be. Leaving Clover Creek means leaving all that's here, and my heart is telling me I need to stay, while my head is saying maybe I should go. Luckily, I still have a little time before Mom's surgery, and Ashley has surprisingly stepped up in the meantime, and I can't help but wonder if she doesn't want me to move back at all.

As far as the haunted house, it's coming down to crunch hour for the big event. The kids have done an amazing job—I'm so proud of them—but they also keep coming up with things they need for their respective rooms to make it "the best." Which is why I bought six ashy blond bob wigs and white lab coats—special-rush-ordered from The Dead of Night to make sure I'd have them in time. It's not a huge deal.

I have the budget for them—since each room has an allocated amount, and they haven't spent all their money yet—but it's the time that isn't on our side. Pepper assured me they could get what we need, and I had practically jumped for joy this morning when she told me the order came in with their shipment.

Unfortunately, that joy seems to be short-lived as I currently stand in the back room of the Halloween store waiting to pick up said order.

Pepper peers over her boss's shoulder as they scroll through the computer. "The order came in, I'm sure of it."

"I agree. It says so right here." Dewy taps the screen. "Which means it should be right there." They spin around in their chair and point to an empty corner of what they call the office, but it's really just an open space with computers on folding tables.

Pepper glances at me with apologetic eyes. "We need to find this order," she says to Dewy.

"I'm so sorry," they say to me. "We're going to do everything we can to make this right."

"Is there even enough time to order more?" I ask.

Dewy glances at Pepper, who is shaking her head. "The order *has* to be here. The items haven't been scanned into inventory, so they can't be sold. It's around here somewhere."

I gesture to the space behind me where stacks and stacks of boxes sit. "'Somewhere' meaning . . . ?" There's panic in my voice. I can't let the kids down. I already promised them that the order was coming—a mistake I won't make again until I have whatever I need in my possession.

CHRISTINA

Pepper takes my hands in hers and looks me straight in the eye. "Even if I have to stay up all night and open every single box in this place, I will find them. I promise. I got you, okay?" Her words calm the gremlins in my stomach.

I nod. "Okay."

"I can help you get started." Dewy rises from their chair with a box cutter in their hand.

They slice through the tape on the lids of several boxes, and Dewy and Pepper get to work.

"Is there anything I can do to help?" I ask. "There's still a little time before I have to head over to the house."

"Not really," Pepper says.

"This is like opening a can of worms." Dewy pulls the lid of one box open and starts digging inside. "If the staff finds any of this stuff, they'll think it's fair game, so we have to be careful and retape all the boxes."

I chew on my bottom lip. That's a lot of work. A lot, *a lot* of work. And Pepper and I have plans for later tonight. Even with all there is left to do, tonight is a quick shift to make sure the kids are getting home and to sleep at a decent hour—not that many of them use the extra time for that, but the school thinks it's important. Which means I won't be completely spent at the end of the day and can actually spend some alone time with her.

Pepper digs through a box, then sets it aside.

Dewy yanks something out of one, and I hold my breath for a moment, but it's not my special order. "Pepper."

"No way," she says.

"Ken wigs?" I ask.

CHRISTINA

"Dewy told me this story..." Pepper shakes her head. "You had to be there."

It's torture watching them do this. I should leave and wait to hear from Pepper later. Maybe even come back and help once we're done at the house for the night. It's not the alone time I'm hoping for, but it'll be better than nothing, I suppose. I open my mouth to tell them goodbye when another Dead of Night employee walks in and starts typing on the other computer.

"Where do you want me today, boss?" she asks.

Dewy steps away from the box they're working on and heads back to the computer. They click around and then say, "Registers. But before you go, you wouldn't happen to know where the stack of boxes that was right there went, do you?"

The girl, whose name tag reads LISA, rolls her eyes. "Someone was 'making improvements' again last night." She uses air quotes around the words.

"You've *got* to be kidding me," Dewy says.

"What is wrong with that guy?" Pepper straightens up from the box she's been bending over.

"Did you see where he put them?" Dewy asks.

Lisa shakes her head. "As soon as he started talking, I turned around and walked out. I told him I didn't want anything to do with it."

"Is this guy someone important's relative or something?" I ask.

"You'd think so." Lisa crosses her arms over her chest. "Can I go now?"

CHRISTINA

"Yes, and if you see Kev, can you send him back here, please?" Dewy asks.

"He's on shift tonight?" Lisa whines.

Dewy nods. "Caleb called out."

"Son of a witch," Lisa says.

Dewy's cheeks puff out like they're holding in a laugh, then they say, "He's on cleanup, so—"

"So he could be anywhere, but he's not on register with me. Got it." Lisa turns to head toward the front of the store. "Thank you."

"You're welcome," Dewy calls after her.

"Why does he still work here if no one likes him?" I hate to ask the question, but . . .

Pepper presses her lips together. Maybe I shouldn't have asked.

Dewy rubs the back of their neck. "Not liking someone isn't grounds for termination."

"We'll find him," Pepper says. "We'll find him, and he'll show us where the order is, and then I'll murder him."

"Pepper," Dewy says, but there's no conviction in their voice.

"Fine, then; no murder," she says. She looks at me and mouths, *Maybe a little murder.* "You used to be fun," she says to Dewy.

Dewy smiles and shakes their head. "I'll take the front; you take the back." They head off in the same direction Lisa went, leaving Pepper and me alone.

"Your boss seems pretty cool."

CHRISTINA

"Not exactly my boss, but yeah, they're great. It just takes them a while to warm up."

My cheeks get hot. "Sorry."

Pepper steps away from what she's doing and stands in front of me. Today she has on pink suede wedges, so I have to angle my head up even further to look at her. She tucks my hair behind my ear and presses her cheek against mine to whisper, "You don't have to stress about this. We'll find it, and then the murder option is always open. Just say the word."

I'm engulfed in the scent of her perfume—it's intoxicating. "You'd murder someone for me?" I know she's joking, but the sentiment is sweet regardless.

She pulls back and looks me in the eye. "You know I got you." She leans down, pressing her lips to mine. This is the thing I've needed. It always seems like teens are around anytime we're together—and kissing in front of them is a strict no-no. I reach my arms around her and slide them up the back of her shirt to pull her closer—needing the skin-on-skin contact and wishing it was so much more.

She nibbles on my bottom lip, and it takes all my effort to keep my knees from turning into mashed bananas. When she pulls away, it's not only my cheeks that are warm but my entire body.

"If this guy lost them, you can kill him," I tell her.

Pepper laughs. "Done."

Voices grow louder, and the door to the back of the store opens as Dewy and the guy I assume is Kev walk through.

"It's not more efficient if I have to come and find you for an

---

CHRISTINA

order when I knew where it was less than twenty-four hours ago," Dewy is saying.

"But actually, it is," Kev says. "We should be rotating our inventory going from the oldest boxes to the newest ones. Then we won't be stuck with popular items coming out years after they were popular and then having to donate them instead of making a profit."

"He did not just *well, actually* Dewy, did he?" Pepper whispers to me.

"You heard him right. And I'm thinking lost or not, murder is still on the table," I whisper back. I don't know this guy, but already he's gotten on my nerves.

Dewy pinches the bridge of their nose. "Just where are the boxes?"

Kev lets out a long sigh. "Like I said, they're right over here."

Pepper lifts her brows at Dewy as they pass, and Dewy clenches their fist, shaking it at Kev's back as we all follow him deeper into the rows and rows of boxes. It seems like Dewy might also be thinking about murder right now, too.

"Like I said, they're right here." Kev waves his hands out, making a show of where he's rearranged things.

Dewy slices the tape on the top box and peeks inside. "Yep. This is yours."

I let out the deepest breath of relief. "Thank you so much."

"You're welcome," Kev says at the same time Dewy does, and I'm not sure how they don't strangle that boy right then and there.

Dewy hands my special order over to me, then turns back to Kev. "We're going to have a talk about putting everything back to the way you found it." They start walking off, Kev right on their heels.

"You're missing the point," he's saying.

"All good?" Pepper asks me.

"All good," I confirm. "I guess this means we can still hang out tonight."

"I wouldn't miss it." She leans down and kisses me again.

"I can't wait."

Nerves chew through my stomach like hungry termites as I get ready for Pepper to come over. Yes, she's been to my house before, but tonight is different. At least I hope tonight will be different. For weeks we've spent a lot of time together, but the amount of that time that we've actually been alone has been minimal—so tonight I'm kind of hoping for a little more.

That's one of the only reasons I agreed to this movie night when she gets to pick, no questions asked. Her goal has been to "turn me over to the dark side," so to say I'm anxious—no, terrified—by her potential pick of films is an understatement. I requested not too much gore, and knowing Pepper, she will at least take this under consideration, but it still leaves a lot of choices on the table. That all said, this Halloween season has so far been my best one in years—but usually the blues don't hit me until after it's over, so I guess I'll see if it holds out. If Pepper is still around—which I'm hoping she will be—she might turn me over to that dark side and take Halloween off my three least favorite holidays of the year list.

I really should've put some stronger requirements on this

CHRISTINA

movie we'd be watching. How does one get in the mood for a serious make-out sesh after witnessing someone get disemboweled? Is that even possible?

Movies aren't real, is what Pepper would say, but will she still be saying that if I'm puking up popcorn? Blood and guts are gross. It's why I didn't ever consider being a doctor. No thank you. It's enough that I have to deal with my own bleeding issues once a month—which is complete bullshit. Periods are bullshit.

Maybe I could convince her not to watch the movie at all? Would that be weird? *Hey, come to my place and we can watch a movie together, except when you get here, instead of actually doing that, I plan to try and get you naked.*

Okay, yes, that sounds terrible, which is another reason I'm glad people aren't able to read my thoughts, because how embarrassing would that be? However, now with that visual in my head, I can barely concentrate on what still needs to be done.

My cheeks are hot as I slip into some comfy sweats—can't appear like I'm trying too hard—but I also made sure to use the lotion Pepper said she likes when I got out of the shower, because I don't want to appear like I'm not trying at all.

It was such a good idea to let the kids go a little early tonight, so I'd have time to come home to clean up and change before Pepper gets here.

In the kitchen, I heat up some oil to make the popcorn. Would a Riesling pair well with it? Or maybe a Moscato? Salty and sweet seem like a good balance. The kernels in the pot go *ping, ping, ping* against the metal as I pull the cork on a bottle of wine to let it breathe. Which also conjures up a silly image

---

CHRISTINA

in my head of a wine bottle actually taking deep breaths, and I laugh. Licorice just looks at me.

"What? It's funny," I tell him, but he isn't amused. He plops down on the floor and rolls onto his back. "Don't get too comfy. That doorbell is going to ring soon."

Shit. That doorbell *is* going to ring soon. I spin around.

Wineglasses? Check.

Napkins? Check.

Super-cozy blanket that's a little small so we'll have to snuggle? Check.

I dump the popcorn into the bowl, and as I'm sprinkling on some salt, the doorbell rings. Licorice skitters under the couch. "I tried to warn you," I tell him as I open the door.

Pepper has also changed from the outfit she had on earlier. She's in yoga pants and a cropped sweatshirt that shows a little bit of skin. She's holding a box of Red Vines and a bag of dark chocolate M&M's. "I brought snacks."

"I made some, too," I say as I let her inside.

"I can smell." She takes in a big whiff and closes her eyes. "Smells better than a movie theater."

"You won't get gum on your shoe here either," I tease.

"That's good." She takes her Birkenstocks off and leaves them by the door. It's the first time I've seen her in anything other than heels. She's wearing rainbow socks.

"Should I even ask what we're gonna be watching?" I wrinkle my nose.

"Don't look so scared. I thought a lot about it, and while this is technically a horror movie, it's also considered a comedy, and it was made so long ago, it's not that scary, I promise.

CHRISTINA

We've come a long way in special effects that this movie just doesn't have. But it's a cult classic nonetheless and a complete must-watch."

"Um, okay." Horror isn't so great, but comedy could be fine. "I'm not sure how something can be both scary and funny, but I'm willing to have an open mind. 'Joe's head was ripped off, LOL.' I don't think I get it."

Pepper laughs. "I don't know, Joe probably deserved it," she says, and now I laugh, too. "It was one of my dad's favorites. And if you hate it, we can turn it off."

I take a deep breath. I *did* ask for this. Or maybe I should ask her to get naked now. Stop, Christina. My cheeks get hot again, so I quickly turn toward the kitchen. "Okay. You get us set up, and I'll get the popcorn. Remote's on the table."

"Perfect." She turns the TV on, and I attempt to turn my hormones off by taking a deep breath and a drink of ice-cold water.

Wait. Popcorn gets stuck in your teeth. Why didn't I think about this before? Yes, it's the perfect movie snack, but sticking your finger in your mouth to get kernels out from between your teeth is not cute. I should've gotten chips. But then our fingers would've gotten all oily. Unless I'd also gotten us wet wipes. I really should've thought through this whole snack situation better.

"Did I lose you?" Pepper asks as I set the bowl of popcorn on the table.

"Just having snack anxiety," I admit.

"I should've guessed." She smiles. "This is perfect." She gestures to the small spread of items on the coffee table before she sits down.

I take a step to get ready to join her when Licorice slinks out from under the couch, and I'm so surprised, I can't move.

"Hey there, little fella." She reaches down, and Licorice headbutts her hand, allowing her to scratch him behind the ears, then he jumps up on the couch and starts making biscuits on the blanket Pepper is under. "Is something wrong?"

I shake my head. "No. I'm sorry. It's just he, Licorice, doesn't like anyone. It took him a couple years to warm up to my family."

"Cats are weird," she says, then picks up the side of the cozy blanket that Licorice hasn't claimed for himself and holds it up for me to get under. "Now, come on. The show's starting." She's right, cats are weird, especially my little scaredy-cat, so I should be glad he senses something good about Pepper.

I can't help but smile a little as I sit next to her. "*Tremors?*" The picture on the screen is kind of ridiculous. There are three people huddled together, and in the ground below them is this extremely giant monster worm-looking thing with a lot of teeth. It's comically ginormous. I might understand this horror comedy thing after all. "This doesn't look too bad."

"It's not, I swear."

I tug the blanket a little and scoot a bit closer so that our legs are touching. She grabs the bowl of popcorn, holding it between us, and presses play. Licorice is contently lying on Pepper's other side, pressed up against her opposite leg.

A little over an hour later, half the bottle of Moscato is gone, along with the Red Vines; Licorice has abandoned the

---

CHRISTINA

couch for a spot on his favorite chair; and Pepper spoons me from behind as we lie on the couch together, her body curled around mine, the heat of her breath on my neck. The smell of her perfume—vanilla and incense—blends together with the fabric softener from the blanket we're cocooned inside. The movie is just as ridiculous as Pepper said it would be—even if I have jumped a few times. But she is always there, a solid presence, telling me it's going to be okay. It's almost hard to be scared with Pepper so close. It's also hard to concentrate on the movie at all. I'm hyperaware of all the places her body is connected to mine.

I'm honestly not sure where the guy in the movie is going with this last worm thing. The whole group seems royally forked. But the way it comes full circle from the beginning—which is also very clever—feels really satisfying for a scary movie. I still don't completely understand where the worms themselves came from, but talking isn't what I'm interested in at the moment.

The credits roll and so do I, so I'm face-to-face with Pepper. Her expression is soft, her cheeks flushed to a pale rose. Her makeup tonight is simple—a little mascara and some brassy liner that make her eyes really pop.

"So . . . ?" she asks.

"Okay, it wasn't terrible. But I'm not going to be watching *Halloween* or Jason Krueger or whatever anytime soon."

"It's just Jason and then Freddie Krueger, for your reference, but that's totally fair."

"That was only like an hour and a half, too, so it was pretty

---

CHRISTINA

quick." I rub her foot with mine. Neither of us has socks on anymore. "You don't have to go yet, do you?"

"I didn't have any other plans tonight, no." She reaches over and rubs her thumb against my bottom lip. "Did you have something in mind?" Her lips curl into the most mischievous grin.

And that's all it takes.

I'm not sure if she leans in first or if it's me, but we're kissing with the fierceness of lovers who have been apart for ages—not able to get enough of each other. Her hands are in my hair and up my top, and my hands are fighting with the band of her leggings, needing to touch, to feel every inch of her.

There are moments in life when the stars align and the universe provides exactly what you need, and for me that moment is now—here—on this couch with this beautiful woman. My body is on fire with every caress of her hand, with each nibble of my neck. Her hands are so steady, never second-guessing or hesitating to touch me in all the places I need to feel her. There aren't many things that are perfect in life, but Pepper and I fit together seamlessly. It's like a dance—an effortless balance of back and forth—like she can anticipate my every want, my every desire, a moment before even I do. It's as though we've done this a hundred times before, but it's all so new, with so much of each other still needing to be explored.

Pepper brings me to the edge—a place so vulnerable—but I trust her, and soon I'm breathless, and she's grinning at me, her rosy cheeks much brighter now. Those blue eyes of hers focus on me with such intensity, I can feel it in my soul; and

---

CHRISTINA

it's in this moment, without even meaning to or knowing that I've taken the leap, that I know I've completely fallen for her.

"I . . . I . . ." But I can't bring myself to tell her, not yet. Will she think I'm cliché? Will telling her here, now—like this—scare her away? We haven't known each other long, but I also feel like she knows me—the real me—and that I know her, more than I've known anyone else.

She smiles at me like maybe she can read my mind. "It's okay," she says. "I got you." But I don't think she really understands that she unequivocally does.

Whether she realizes it or not, she now holds my heart, and I don't ever want her to give it back.

CHRISTINA

19 DAYS

UNTIL THE STORE CLOSES

Pepper

Outside, the wind whirled as if Dorothy herself would be careening by any moment, but inside Take It Cheesy, tucked in a corner booth, it felt as if the outside world didn't exist at all. While the place was packed, and the roar of conversations around us rose above the sound of the pop music playing overhead, it was just Christina sitting across from me, blonde hair hanging loose above her shoulders. She tickled my knee with her fingers under the table. I pressed my foot up against hers, wishing we had been that couple who sat on the same side of the booth instead of across from each other.

This—being with Christina—had become such an essential part of my life, and now that I'd talked to Mrs. Stein, I had a plan—there was a chance I'd get to stay. So even with the approaching holiday, I didn't worry about the after. I thought about all the things that could be—not how it would all work since I'd essentially been suspended in time. Those issues didn't seem as important. There would be nothing we couldn't overcome together. If I let my mind wander into negative spaces—like the chance of not being with Christina—it was hard to breathe.

I hadn't felt this way since even before Mitchell, because Christina was different. No two relationships could ever be exactly the same, and they shouldn't be. They each had their own uniqueness—and with Christina, I had been more myself than I'd ever been before. Like I'd finally gotten my wings and turned into the butterfly I'd always been underneath. This was what it must mean to be your true authentic self.

"Have you decided?" I asked, quirking my brows up at Christina.

She shyly shook her head at me. "I really don't think it's necessary."

I gasped—which, to be fair, was mostly for show. I wasn't actually aghast at her response. "Christina Eleanor Loring, how could you possibly say such a thing? After all we've been through." I clasped my hands over my heart to really push my performance over the top.

"It's just . . ." she started. "Won't it look silly if I dress up, too? Isn't it the kids' special day?" She had this adorable look on her face—lips pressed to one side, forehead slightly creased; I wanted to reach across the table and press them out with my thumb.

For a few days now, I'd been asking Christina what she planned to be for Halloween. Most of the really good costumes at the store were long gone, but it wasn't completely a lost cause for her. Plus, it was just plain fun, and with all the hard work she'd been doing, she deserved a little of that. "Yes, which is why you're there to support them, and one way to do that is to join in on the festivities."

"What if I look silly?"

"That's the point! It's a day you can be anything you want to be."

"I just want to be with you." She reached across the table and took my hands in hers. She had painted her nails a combination of orange and black, and I had to give her credit for taking a step in the right direction. She'd come a long way from when I first met her—that was for sure. She hadn't watched any Halloween movies with me yet, but she would get there.

"And I will be there. Every night if you want me to," I said.

"You have to work, too. I bet those last days before Halloween are your busiest." She wasn't wrong about that. The store would be packed full of people who waited till the last minute to get their costumes or those looking for a deal—even though the deep discounts didn't come until the day after Halloween.

"It doesn't matter. I can still be there." Which was true. As long as no one called out sick, the store was always staffed appropriately, and even if someone did, the store could always find someone else.

"Come over when you close. Okay?"

"Okay."

"And maybe stay the night with me after." She chewed on her bottom lip, and I wished I could do that for her.

"Absolutely." I squeezed her hands. "On one condition."

She narrowed her eyes at me—suspicious as always. I suppressed a laugh.

PEPPER

"You at least wear a witch's hat or something," I said.

She tipped her head to the side like she was really considering the idea. "I *could* be a witch." She smiled.

"You could." I nodded.

"And I could get some ruby red shoes to go with my outfit."

I nodded again. "Now you're speaking my language. I might even have some you could borrow."

She laughed. "Because of course you do."

I had a thing for pretty shoes—like that was a bad thing. "Watch out. I might start rubbing off on you."

"You'll know it when I start buying shoes other than black." Her smile was smug, but she'd come around one day. It would just take time.

"And when you do, I'll buy you your first pair."

"I'm gonna hold you to that."

"I hope that's not the only thing you'll hold me to." I winked, and her cheeks flushed red-hot again.

She took a long sip of her ice water and glanced to a table close by full of teens. "Do you think it's going to rain?" she asked, obviously trying to change the subject. Not because she wasn't interested—those cheeks told me otherwise.

I took a drink of my cherry Coke before answering. "It might." We were safe and warm, and if we had to hide away in this booth forever, I'd be okay with it. Although a little more privacy would also be nice. "Why do you ask?"

"It just smells like rain."

I scrunched my brows. "What does that even mean? What does rain smell like?" It wasn't that I was impervious to the idea that things had a certain odor—like after school, Christina always smelled a little like hand sanitizer, but usually she smelled like roses. And the Halloween store always smelled a little like rubber from all the masks.

"Worms." Christina's voice was so firm, so sure, I almost couldn't tell if she was being serious or not.

"Wait. So is it the rain that smells like worms, or the worms that smell like rain?" I'd never heard this before in my life, and obviously Christina had strong opinions.

She bit her lip, as though pondering my question carefully. "Both."

I laughed and shook my head. "How do you know this? Do you smell a lot of worms?"

"All the time." She squeezed my knee, making my foot kick. "No, of course I don't go around smelling creepy, crawly critters." She laughed along with me.

"I don't think you can say that worms crawl."

"But I can say that they are creepy."

"They might not be the cutest, but they're harmless. Unless, of course, they were some kind of mutant worm."

"That's what I could be for Halloween. A mutant worm," she said.

"Now, that's the spirit." Mutant worms made me think back to Dad's favorite Halloween movie of all time. I really needed to watch it again.

She shook her head and laughed even harder. "No." She kept laughing as the server set our order down in front of us.

With the weather outside so blustery, it was the perfect time for grilled cheese and soup—which was what both Christina and I had ordered. The difference being the type of grilled cheese. I went with their cheesy maple bacon, and Christina got the bruschetta grilled cheese. Between us sat a bowl of tomato soup (which had cheesy croutons, of course) for dipping.

Christina glanced at my sandwich and then at her own.

"You're having order FOMO, aren't you?"

"Is it that obvious?"

I pulled my sandwich apart and offered her half. "We could do splitsies."

She followed my lead, handing me half of her sandwich and then taking my half from me. Her whole face lit up as she took a bite.

"That good?" I asked.

She nodded, making that OMG-this-is-amazing moan. "How do you always know the best thing to order?" she asked around a mouthful.

"It's my superpower." I winked. Plus, I'd eaten at this restaurant long enough to have tried just about everything on the menu.

I stared at all the carvings in the booths—it was a time-honored tradition in this town to leave your mark behind—and practically memorized them all. One day I'd be able to leave my mark without it being erased from existence—and maybe, just maybe, this year would be my last one tethered to that store.

"What are you looking at?" Christina asked, pulling me out of my thoughts.

I hadn't even realized I'd been zoning out. "All the names," I told her, which was true.

Christina bit her lip and smiled, quickly digging in her

purse and pulling out a ballpoint pen. She leaned over and used the tip of it to dig into the wood, carving out a little *CL + PW* with a heart around it. "What do you think?" she asked.

I reached out my hand and took the pen from her, adding a little flower next to it—nothing fancy, just five petals and a swirl in the middle. My own kind of signature to mark the occasion with. "It's perfect."

Butterflies danced in my stomach. It was as if Christina had looked inside my soul and done the thing that I'd been dreaming about. It had to mean that this would all work out. And now this moment was immortalized—forever imprinted in this place—and that made it all the more real that this was truly it for me. This had to be a sign that we were going to get our forever.

"I love you," I said, because I did—it was my truth that I could tell her right now that had nothing to do with breaking curses.

"I love you, too."

PEPPER

18 DAYS
UNTIL THE STORE CLOSES

Christina

Halloween and horror movies are scary—even bone-chilling sometimes—but it hit me while stringing up spiders in a tree outside the haunted house that there's nothing quite as terrifying as being in love. The vulnerability of putting yourself out there basically saying, I think the world of you, I hope you like me back. And it's not that I think Pepper will hurt me—it's that I've been in this place before and I've ended up hurt. Having faith in something you can't see or hold or even quantify seems like the worst idea, but it's also the greatest feeling in the world. Knowing that someone has your back, regardless of all circumstances.

Love is so powerful. Nothing can make you feel so good and at the same time crush you so indefinitely—and yet we seek it out over and over again. The thrill of it, like the thrill of a good scare, keeps our hearts racing. I never quite realized how close these feelings actually were before, and now that I see it, I can't unsee it. Halloween might not be as terrible as I once thought.

With the days rushing to get us there quicker, it's crunch time at the haunted house, meaning all hands on deck—or for me, it means spending all day at school and then coming here and spending late hours, sometimes after all the kids have gone, just to get everything done in time. My handle on time management isn't so great when one whole page of to-dos gets stuck to another. Not that I regret the "time off" I've taken. It has been worth it.

Pepper is my powerhouse, spending all her free time here with me, helping with every task without complaint. It's like having another set of hands—like a clone of myself, because she doesn't need much direction or explanation at all. She also somehow stumbled upon this hidden sound system, and the kids are thrilled we'll have haunting sounds playing as people walk between rooms. I'm still not clear on how she even found it, but I don't care—I no longer have to hunt down some mystery teacher. Although Mrs. Turner, our librarian, is now on the case of trying to figure out who it was.

"Let's move the gurney at an angle so it's clearer what's going on when people walk in," I tell Chloe, who's working with me. Pepper is in the room next door helping them get the last touches in order.

"The mural looks great, don't you think?" Chloe says as she helps me move the hospital bed Clover Creek Medical had donated to us. They were getting rid of it anyway and even

CHRISTINA

came to me first to see if I could use it for the haunted house, which of course I jumped at. Any free items, we will find a way to incorporate into the show.

I get the bed in the right position and spin around. The scene on the wall looks like a window inside a medical facility with a group of escaped patients pressed up against it. The story is that the people who are in this room have captured the doctors and now the patients are performing experiments on them, so they're there to watch. It's gruesome and disgusting, which means it'll probably be one of the favorite rooms of this year's haunted house. "Skylar did an amazing job."

"She's so talented," Chloe says.

"I couldn't agree more."

Boom. What sounds like thunder hitting the wall makes me jump. "What the . . . ?" I stop myself from saying more in the presence of a student.

"Holy shit," Chloe says and then quickly covers her mouth. "Sorry."

"It's fine. I almost said something worse. What do you think that was?" I ask.

Pepper rushes in. "Everything okay in here?" Her head swivels around like she's trying to understand the source—that makes two of us.

"Is it raining?" I ask her.

"Is that what it sounded like to you?" she asks as she walks in and up to the mural, placing her hand on the wall. "Oh no."

"What?" I put my hand next to hers, and the entire wall is vibrating. "What does that—" Before I can finish, water starts pouring out of the electrical outlet.

CHRISTINA

"What's happening?" Chloe races out of the way of the stream that's flooding into the room. Luckily the ground is concrete, and there are drains in each room to make cleanup easy at the end of the event, but it doesn't spare the box of costumes and props.

"A pipe burst," Pepper says.

"But how? It's not freezing out or anything." And isn't that the only reason a pipe would break? Aren't they made of metal? I race to get things out of the way—the cardboard is already turning into a mushy mess. It's not like all these costumes are made out of the best material either. This is a catastrophe. "What do we do?"

"We have to shut the water off," Pepper says.

Shut the water off, yes, okay. But shit. "I don't know how."

Pepper lets out a long breath and runs from the room.

"Chloe, can you help?" My arms are ten times heavier with all the wet fabric.

"Won't I get electrocuted?" She points to the outlet.

"Shit." I jump out of the stream. "You didn't hear that," I tell her.

Chloe doesn't say a word; she stares at the ground like she's ready for it to turn into fire or start sparking—since water conducts electricity, doesn't it? Other students start gathering outside the door, craning their heads to try and get a peek at what's happening.

"What's going on?" one asks.

"Fuck," one of them says.

Language, I want to respond, but words are clogged in my throat. This is a disaster. Worse than a disaster. All their hard

---

CHRISTINA

work is literally washing down the drain in front of me, and the only thing I can do is stand here and watch. Are the other rooms flooding or only this one? How long will this set us back? Will we have to cancel this year's event? All these questions are crashing through my head as boxes break apart and the drain starts to clog, but water and electricity don't mix, and I'm not about to risk it. I'm lucky nothing happened to me before when I was standing in the flow.

I scoot back toward the wall as the water level starts to rise. So this is where I die, huh? In front of my entire theater troupe. There's too much water to jump over, and if I'd been smart, I would've climbed on the gurney like Chloe, but now that's also out of reach. "Kids, you need to—"

The water stops. And even clogged the way it is, the drain still works—admittedly much slower than it should.

There's a ruckus by the door, and Pepper comes in, her feet sloshing through the water, and she starts clearing the drain.

"Be careful," I say, and point to the outlet.

"It's fine. They're built to handle this." In no time, the water is gone, but the damage is done. "I shut the water off, but we're going to need a plumber," she says.

I nod. If I try to speak right now, I might cry. Nothing like this ever happened in the corporate world. Fire drills were a norm—a project that was supposed to be finished wasn't, or an email that shouldn't have been sent went out—but this feels a hundred times worse. Those things usually affected only a few people—this affects the kids, the school, and the entire community. Right now, I'm sad for them.

CHRISTINA

"My dad's a plumber," one of the kids says from the doorway, but I'm still taking in all the mess and don't register who it is.

"Good. Call him," Pepper says. She glances my way, but I'm too busy calculating all that will need to be done to fix this to really focus. It's ruined. It's all ruined. I drop the items I had collected to the ground and rub the scar on my arm. "Sammy," Pepper says. "Get three other people and pull out the costumes and lay them on the grass outside to start drying. River, you get some people together and collect the props and separate them into piles—things that are salvageable and things that aren't. Make a list of the items that aren't. Let's go." She claps her hands, and the kids scatter, doing exactly what she's told them to do. Pepper walks up to me and takes my hands in hers. How is she so calm right now? "Are you okay?"

I shake my head. "I don't know where to start." The event is ruined.

"We're going to get this fixed. It's going to be okay." Her voice is so reassuring, but my stomach has wrapped itself up in a knot so tightly, I want to throw up. "Hey. This isn't a big deal. Everything will be fine. I promise."

"You think?" I want to feel as positive as she does about this situation, but the kids' work is ruined, and I'm starting to feel like the soggy remains of the cardboard boxes, easily defeated by a little water.

"I do," she says. "Do you trust me?"

I finally meet her gaze. Blue eyes fiercely staring into mine. Her hands so steady, so sure, grounding me in place. I nod. I do trust her. There isn't anyone in this world I trust more.

CHRISTINA

"I got you," she says, and I nod.

"My dad's on his way," someone shouts.

"Perfect," Pepper says, but she doesn't turn away. "Don't worry. It's all going to work out, and we'll be back on schedule before you know it." She squeezes my hands, and the tension slowly seeps out of my body.

"Thank you," I tell her.

Pepper smiles. "Now, let's get you some angry water and maybe a snack. You've been nonstop all day."

"I think we are all going to need a snack if we're going to have enough energy required for this job."

My phone pings in my pocket not once but three times. Principal Wilkson already knows—is the first thought that races through my mind. How am I going to explain this? I pull my cell out as it pings again. It's not the principal, but it's almost as bad.

> EMILY: Just wanted to check in on you
>
> EMILY: Mom's doing okay
>
> EMILY: Ashley not so much LOL
>
> EMILY: But you should consider coming home
>
> EMILY: I think you could push it until after Halloween and then who knows . . . maybe your friend Pepper could come too ☺

A lump the size of a grapefruit forms in my throat. On top of everything else, I'm not ready to deal with this right now.

CHRISTINA

> **ME:** Can we talk later . . . Just had a major issue at the haunted house that I have to deal with
>
> **EMILY:** Yeah of course
>
> **EMILY:** Call me whenever
>
> **EMILY:** Love you Titi
>
> **ME:** Love you too

Three hours later, a massive hole has been cut into the wall, right through the mural the kids worked so hard on, and a giant industrial fan is blowing at it. Mona's dad was able to fix the pipe, but he won't be able to repair the wall until it's completely dry.

"What a day," Pepper says as she picks up the last of the costumes from the lawn. We're going to bring them back to my house so they can dry the rest of the way. Most of the props luckily are salvageable, and the kids said that even the rougher-looking ones have more of an authentic quality now, so they aren't upset at all. From a budgeting standpoint, we should be okay. Mona's dad's company is doing all the work free of charge. But the mural is ruined, and who knows if there will be enough time to fix it. Plus, I don't even know how to break it to Skylar. She'll likely be devastated. I'm devastated for her. Today has been a lot. More than the kids should ever have had to deal with. And I'm exhausted to the bone.

"I don't know what I would've done without you today," I tell Pepper.

She shakes her head. "It was nothing."

CHRISTINA

"No. It was everything." And it really has been. Not once was she flustered by the events of today. Not when she was ankle-deep in water—likely ruining her shoes. Not when she had to scrape up what looked like bloody vomit from the floor—but was likely just some of the gross-looking paper masks the kids made. And not when Eddie cried that he was worried the event would be canceled. The kids saw weeks of their work literally wash down the drain, and Pepper was infallible.

She stops and looks at me, and that's when the tears come. "Hey, it's okay." A moment later I'm in her arms, and she's holding me tight. My face is pressed into her neck, and I'm engulfed in her comforting scent of vanilla and incense as she rubs my back. I'm feeling both heartbroken for the kids but also so incredibly lucky at the same time.

"I know," I say. "I feel so terrible for them."

"The kids will be okay. Just like you will be okay."

"I know," I say again because I do. "And I really appreciate you. No one has ever done anything like this for me. We are so lucky to have you here. *I'm* so lucky." And it's the truth. For the first time in my entire life, I feel completely loved and supported. I wrap my arms around her and hold her tightly back.

CHRISTINA

17 DAYS
UNTIL THE STORE CLOSES

Pepper

There were times in life when the thing you least expected became the best thing to ever happen to you. It was that way with me and this curse. If it had never happened, I never would've met Christina. She may never have come to Clover Creek. And there would never have been an us—a her and me.

Not all things that on the outside seemed terrible were, in fact, terrible. There would always be a bright side, even if it wasn't obvious at first. Sometimes life needed patience. Even after the darkest nights, the sun would eventually rise. You only had to believe.

For me, that light came while I'd been on aisle thirteen. I'd been placing discount stickers on sets of face paints when Mrs. Stein found me.

"They want me to come in and talk," she said, not "Hello," not "It's good to see you." Her eyes were focused—determined—and her voice was so steady. She had mentioned when we chatted before that they never broke bad news on the phone—that they always wanted you there in person just in case you took it poorly. This had to mean that her doctors didn't see any other options for her, that her time was coming to an end.

My heart tightened in my chest. I'd never wish this upon anyone. "I'm—"

"No. It's okay. I've been preparing myself for this, and now thanks to you, I have another way." To her credit, she held it together quite well. She didn't seem upset or angry. If anything, she seemed assured.

Part of me wanted to cry for her—and for me, for two totally different reasons. I wanted to scream. I wanted to jump up and down. I wanted to hug her so tightly, but instead I said, "So you're a hundred percent in?"

"I'm in," she said. "I'll meet you here two days after Halloween at midnight."

This was it.

I would be able to stay.

Christina and I were going to get to be together—forever.

PEPPER

16 DAYS
UNTIL THE STORE CLOSES

Christina

Three years ago, after Halloween, I was hit with what I call the "blahs." A feeling that sat in my chest like a boa constrictor slowly tightening, a sensation that would last well into the spring, and each year it has gotten worse, with last year being the worst of them all. It wasn't until this past summer that I started feeling normal again. I'd been living in survival mode.

Now, thanks to Pepper, I'm happy. With no hint of the "blahs" at all.

This Halloween is different.

The energy in the classroom today is like a mirror to my own feelings, buzzing like a busy beehive. All the kids are gathered around the stage playing a game that's essentially freeze tag but while acting—where two kids are onstage acting out their scene and someone in the audience yells "Freeze" so the two onstage stop moving, and the new person comes and tags one out and starts a new scene in the same position as the tagged-out person, which the other person onstage has to follow. It sounds more complicated than it actually is and only took me watching for about five minutes to get the hang of it the first time. It's a classroom favorite, and since I'm in such a great mood—regardless of the impending issues still needing to be fixed at the haunted house—instead of teaching, I'm letting the kids play improv games. It also lets me work on other things instead. Sue me.

A burst of laughter comes from the front of the room, which means I'm going to get another note in my box about "loud noises," but at the moment, I don't care. Kids should have fun. I think other teachers are jealous that this is one of the kids' favorite classes, and that we actually get to have fun and laugh, not like in math. What's fun or funny about quadratic equations? Nothing. At least theater makes you think on your toes, gives you confidence in public speaking, and allows for creativity. Not many other classes can have all those claims to fame.

However, maybe if I made friends with one of the math teachers, these spreadsheets wouldn't be giving me such a headache. I didn't major in accounting for a reason. We should be right on budget, even with our little pipe incident, and if all goes well, turn a nice profit. Or I could've messed up the formula, and we're royally screwed. Either way, I need to make sure I have everything in order to get my reimbursement for the year. My personal bank account is hurting.

The bell rings, signaling the end of the period, and loud groans followed by applause come from the group before they scatter off to grab backpacks for their last class of the day—

CHRISTINA

seventh period—which also happens to be my prep period, so I have another hour and thirty minutes before I have to be at the haunted house to greet all the kids.

That includes the five minutes I have to drive over there and have a quick daily freak-out—just normal panic about all the things we still need to do and that could go wrong—before they arrive. I'll be so glad when this event is over.

"Bye, Ms. Loring," someone yells as the door closes, and the once boisterous classroom falls into complete silence.

It takes a moment for my ears to adjust, and I slouch back into my chair. Maybe a ten-minute nap first wouldn't hurt. As soon as I close my eyes, the classroom door opens.

Cami pokes her head in. "Have a moment, Ms. Loring?"

"Of course, Ms. Alvarez." It's always weird to be so formal, but on school grounds it's expected for everyone to address one another the way they want the kids to address them.

Her growing stomach makes an appearance before the rest of her slides in the door, and she closes it behind her. "Monster wants tachos. Do you have time?" She rubs her belly. I love that she makes up silly names for the newest member of the Alvarez family, insisting she won't know their name until they come out to meet her. Cami already has her purse—which is just a giant canvas bag like mine these days—flung over her shoulder.

I glance at my mess of spreadsheets. "And maybe an adult fruit punch for me." I close my laptop, slip it into my bag along with the piles of receipts I've been keeping, and hoist the giant thing onto my shoulder. I think teachers carry more crap around than the students.

CHRISTINA

"I won't tell," she says.

I circle back to my desk to grab my cell phone before I forget it—again—and head out the door with Cami. At least this time I didn't leave my wallet at home.

Less than fifteen minutes later, we've placed our order at the counter of Take It Cheesy and search for a place to sit.

"Are they giving food away today?" I ask as I follow Cami, who waddles through crowded tables.

"I'll be glad when October is over," she says, then glances back at me. In front of her is the only booth available—the one we never sit in.

"Doesn't look like we have another choice," I tell her, and she gives me a sympathetic grin. I don't know why but something about this booth gives me chills. Maybe because it's a little darker and tucked in the far corner away from everything. Like it would be easy to be murdered there and would take hours before someone found your body.

Cami sighs with relief as she slides across the vinyl. A few more weeks and she'll have to move the table to make room. "I could kill those women who are nothing but baby. I feel like the Marshmallow Man."

"I told you about this table."

She laughs. "Okay, there might be some relevance to your murderous theory, or it could be that this table is smaller than all the others. Or I'm just bigger." She gestures to her stomach as if it were some kind of giant balloon that's ready to burst.

"You're beautiful." Which is true. Her dark brown hair is pulled back into a ponytail and her brown skin practically glows, even in this low lighting. Cami has always had a sense

---

CHRISTINA

of style I could never pull off; she's wearing a flower dress that curves around her baby bump, a chic denim jacket, and Adidas Superstars instead of flats or heels—which are probably more comfortable, too. They aren't the technical "business casual" we're supposed to wear to school, but she said she's never had a problem with anyone complaining even before she started showing. Maybe I should get myself a pair instead of always wearing these black flats that make my feet smell terrible. That's another thing I need to pick up—foot powder for these shoes.

"I don't feel beautiful," she says.

Once she's settled with her feet stretched out to rest on the opposite bench, I take a seat, setting our order number at the edge of the table. This booth isn't as bad as I thought. Not that I assumed I would immediately die if I sat here, but the feeling I usually have about this space has waned even if Cami has made it so there's less room on my side—not that I'm complaining. I'm not in the process of trying to create another human, so she's welcome to all the room she needs.

Like all the other tables here, there are things carved into the wooden top, like people's names, or—my finger slides along the grooves—here someone took the time to etch in a picture of Taylor Swift. It's really quite impressive. And, of course, to keep things "cheesy," lots of people have carved their names with someone else's and big hearts—it's actually encouraged here.

"Thanks for coming with me. I know you're slammed with all the haunted house stuff." She takes a long drink of her chocolate milk. "I promise I'll help you next year."

"If there *is* a next year." I take a gulp of my sangria—the

CHRISTINA

sweet red wine and fruit juices with a hint of cinnamon ease some of the tension out of my shoulders.

"Don't say that. You're doing amazing." But the reality is she has no idea how I'm doing. She hasn't seen the mess at the house, or the damage from the burst pipe, or my disastrous spreadsheets.

"I don't know if I'm going to be able to pull it all off." Will this be the first year in history that Clover Creek doesn't have a haunted house? If we don't get back on schedule and get the final room put back together, it's possible.

"At least it's not the end of the semester. You've got that going for you."

"I'm sure my students love that they don't have any assignments, but how do I grade them if they're playing theater games?"

She takes another big gulp of her milk, finishing half the glass. "Just give them all A's."

"If it were only that easy."

We both laugh. Teaching is great but also the hardest job I've ever had. At least I don't have to deal with the parents like some of the other staff do.

I take a deep breath. "It's crunch time, and there are still a million things to do. I'm sure you heard about our attempt to make a swimming pool in one room."

"What about your helper?" Cami raises her brows at me, and my cheeks are immediately set on fire. "You seem happier these days, even more so than when I first met you."

"Pepper is good. Better than good." I take a drink to cool

CHRISTINA

my face down, but it doesn't work. Nor does Cami say anything—meaning she's not letting it go.

"I bet she is." Cami's brows bounce up and down.

"Stop." I bite my lip. "But I really like her." Which is not a lie but also . . . "Actually, I think I'm totally in love with her." The words escape through my lips, and it feels good to finally say them out loud to another person—even if that person isn't Pepper.

"OMG. Have you told her?"

"No. Not exactly." I grimace. It's complicated.

Cami throws her hands in the air. "Girl, what are you waiting for?"

"I haven't really dated a girl since college." And that was more like messing around. "What if it's too soon?" It's only been, what? Not even two months?

"Who cares? And she'd be an idiot if she didn't feel the same way. You're a catch."

Am I? "Maybe she knows how to format a spreadsheet," I say to try and change the subject.

"You know, I'm sure she'd format anything of yours that you wanted." Cami's eyebrows dance again.

"Oh my god. Stop."

"All I'm saying is that you'll never know unless you put yourself out there."

But that's what's so terrifying. It's been years since I've had that shaken-up-soda-in-my-stomach feeling for anyone, and Pepper and I haven't even dated for long. What if she doesn't feel the same? What if I screw it all up before it even has a

---

CHRISTINA

chance to ever really start? My relationships never seem to work out, and I'm not ready to let Pepper go.

"So you have a million things to do," Cami says, changing the subject for me. That's one of the best things about her, she never pushes me too far. But she's right, I have to at least try to make a move. And maybe I will. "You're going to be fine. And if you're missing anything, send one of the seniors off for it or something. They'll think it's cool to help run errands."

"Because errands are so much fun." My list of things to do is ever-growing. Like the pile of clothes by the door that I need to take to the dry cleaner, and if Cami hadn't asked me to grab some food, I'd likely be eating pickles and crackers for dinner. I really need to get to the grocery store.

"They are for kids who never have to do them."

"Do you think I could get one of them to go grocery shopping for me?"

Cami laughs. "I mean, I bet they would, but if you're picky about your laundry detergent or anything—be specific because you never know what you'll get."

"Good point."

A server shows up with our tachos—tater tots covered in cheese, pico de gallo, pulled pork, sour cream, and guacamole—and an order of their Cure for Your Hangover Mac 'n' Cheese—which is their signature macaroni and cheese with hash browns, bacon, a poached egg, and lots of jalapeños—and two plates.

Cami takes a big sniff of the tachos. "Whoever said 'Let's make nachos but use tater tots instead' is my hero." She scoops a mound onto her plate and then goes for the mac and cheese.

"They really are delicious. I've never had them with the

CHRISTINA

pulled pork before so I'm excited to try it." I take some of the jalapeños from the other dish and add them to my tachos.

"Oh, that's a good idea." Cami copies me by putting a jalapeño on her bite of tachos and then adds some of the bacon and mac and cheese, too. "Can you pass me the Cholula?" she asks around her bite.

I slide the container of condiments her way, and my breath catches. While Cami happily adds hot sauce to her plate, I'm staring at the spot behind where the condiments just were. A place that says *CL +* in the exact way that I loop my letters—like I had been the one to do it—with a giant heart around it, and next to it there's a flower. The same flower that I keep seeing over and over.

I close my eyes, and I can picture myself using the tip of a broken pen to etch my initials, laughing and glancing across this very table, but there's no one there with me.

"Earth to Christina," Cami says.

"What?" I shake my head and the vision fades away, but there's gooseflesh all over my arms.

"Are you okay? You look like Mr. Wilkson just assigned you to watch over Saturday detention."

"Have you ever done something and then not remembered doing it?" I ask, but I already know the answer for myself is no. Or was no until this moment. Now I'm not so sure.

Cami shrugs. "All the time." She laughs, but I don't join her. There's nothing funny about this, is there?

"No, I mean . . ." I point to my initials, to the heart and flower, and to the blank space where it looks like someone else's initials should be but aren't.

CHRISTINA

"Whoa. That looks like your—"

"I know."

"And you didn't—"

"Not that I remember." Panic creeps into my voice. This is beyond weird. It's almost downright scary.

"Whoa," she says again. "You haven't even dated anyone seriously since you've moved here, have you? I mean, aside from right now?" For the second time, Pepper flashes in my head.

"Yeah, in all my free time I'm swiping up and down or whatever."

"I think it's left and right."

"Who cares?" I snap. "Why are my initials here?" I finally peel my gaze away from the wall and make eye contact with Cami. "I'm sorry. I'm kind of freaking out."

"It's okay. I would be, too. This is seriously creepy." She picks up a tater tot and pops it into her mouth.

"It has to be someone else, right?" Someone else who has the exact same handwriting as me. Doppelgängers exist, so maybe it's possible two people write exactly the same.

Cami nods. "It has to be."

I pick up my fork and create the perfect bite, but before I put it in my mouth, I glance back over at the wall. "Have you seen this flower before?" It cannot possibly be a coincidence.

Cami shifts on the bench to try and get a better look. "It's cute, but it's not, like, super artistic or anything." She shakes her head. "I don't know."

I turn away from the wall, and instead of the perfect bite, I take a long drink of my sangria. It doesn't help.

CHRISTINA

"I'm sorry," Cami says.

"It's fine. I'm sure it's just a coincidence." I finally take the bite, and it's the perfect blend of cheese and heat, and the pulled pork is really delicious, too. "Good choice," I say even though I'm having a hard time truly enjoying it.

"Thanks," she says, but her voice seems tentative.

This is totally fine. I'm totally fine. "So, yeah, I'm not sure if I have everything I need for this weekend." I attempt to get us back on track, but my gaze keeps shifting to the wall.

"Right, you were saying that."

I swallow another bite of my tachos. "You think I should tell Pepper how I feel?"

Cami's brows rise. "I think it would be worth a shot." She sips her chocolate milk, looking at me from over the top of her glass. "And she's cute, right?"

"That's not the point."

Cami shakes her head. "No. Of course not," she says. "But what if she feels the same? That would be good, right? And then maybe she would stick around."

She's making a lot of sense.

"Maybe I should take another trip over there—to The Dead of Night—and tell her."

"I think you should." Cami douses more of her food with Cholula sauce. "This weekend, I get to go stroller shopping."

"One of those *fun* errands."

"Exactly." Cami half smiles and goes back to mixing everything on her plate together as she glances at the wall. "We're never sitting at this table again."

A chill runs up my spine. "Never."

CHRISTINA

13 DAYS
UNTIL THE STORE CLOSES

Pepper

Opening night for the haunted house was a massive success, and the line for it was wrapped around the corner. The whole town was full of tourists for the season wanting to get a glimpse of the spectacular job Christina and her students had done. At least that's what I'd been told all evening from people coming in and out of The Dead of Night while I worked.

They said that "Haunted Woods" by Clover Creek High would probably be the highest-grossing event the school—and the town—had ever seen, all with a little help from an app called TikTok. I guess there had been some rumbling about them trying to shut the app down earlier in the year, but it never happened, and luckily so, because I'd never seen so many people in the store—and in the town—before. Teens really had figured out social media, and it was working for them.

The store was also flooded with new customers, and New Guy was nowhere in sight, so as much as I had wanted to get over to the house before it closed for the night, it wasn't going to happen. The store wasn't exactly my priority, but these people would be remembering me this time—thanks to Mrs. Stein—so I needed to make a good impression. Not because I was worried about working here again. Soon, I'd be living in this town, so I couldn't start off on the wrong foot. The possibilities of what I could do when I was no longer tethered here, however, were endless—well, maybe not endless in a small town, but it would all work out; it had to.

I had quickly texted Christina between helping at the register and finding last-minute items for customers, and we agreed to meet up for a celebration drink at Tipsy over on Kiwi Street when we were both finished.

A couple hours later, once we closed the store and encouraged a few lingering customers to come back tomorrow, I walked into Tipsy. Even though there was still almost two weeks left before Halloween, and with the house and most of the town closed for the night, the bar was packed. Christina waved me over to where she had somehow managed to get two stools. She picked up the witch's hat saving my seat and placed it back on her head. Her "witch costume" was a simple black pleather skirt and knit sweater, but still I was happy to see she put herself out there like that and was having fun. Slow progress was still progress.

"I thought you'd never make it," she said to me, and then gave me a quick peck on my cheek.

"New Guy really messed everything up. He was so adamant about being on the schedule and then—poof, he vanished." I sat next to her, and she slid a drink my way.

PEPPER

"Like he ghosted?"

"Yep." I took a sip of the martini Christina had ordered for me. "Oooh. What is this?"

"It's called Witches' Brew and has blackberries and prosecco and something else. It sounded sweet, so I thought you'd like it." She leaned in and nudged me with her shoulder. Sitting in front of her was likely her usual—Sapphire and tonic with a lime.

"Enough about me. Tell me how it went."

A smile brighter than the full moon lit up her face. "The kids were amazing, and we ended up having to shut the line down." She took a sip of her drink—her red lipstick still perfectly intact.

"No way."

She nodded—her eyes wide and full of pride—and she should be proud. This event was no easy task, and she handled it like a seasoned pro, not a teacher who was in her first year.

"That's amazing. You're totally going to break your goal for fundraising this year." I placed my hand on her leg—right below the hem of her skirt—and leaned in to kiss her. She tasted like gin and lime.

"Thank you, but that's why I'm going to have two of these tonight." She raised her glass and clinked it against mine.

My hand caressed her knee and found a little spot of prickly hair. "You're amazing."

She placed her hand on mine. "Stop playing with my survivor patch." That was what she called the place on her leg where the hair survived after she shaved. "Why does that happen anyway? I swear I get it all."

PEPPER

"It's cute," I said.

"It's annoying," she told me, and then she laughed.

A little while later, I ordered us another round, and Christina talked about the finer details of the events from the night. I couldn't wait to get to see the house for myself this year. The plan was still for the crew at The Dead of Night to head over there on Halloween after we closed. It had been so hard not to talk about what I'd already seen when helping Christina out. But I wanted it to be a surprise for everyone at the store, and they wanted it to be a surprise for them, too. I could hardly believe it would be our last time going as a group of Dead of Night staff. That next year at this time when I was at the store, they would remember this trip we'd taken together, and I'd get to laugh along with them. I'd be in on the inside jokes, and they'd know that. It was all so overwhelming, I almost wanted to cry. All thanks to . . .

And there she was—across the bar, Mrs. Stein sat at a high-top table with who I assumed was her daughter, Lindsay. She looked so different from the last time I'd seen her. She'd cut her hair short, and it wasn't brown anymore, but colored fiery red.

"What are you looking at?" Christina asked, and then followed my gaze. "Celebrating probably," she said, and then took another sip of her cocktail.

Celebrating? My head swiveled in Christina's direction. Did Mrs. Stein tell people she would be taking on my position at the store? I supposed that could be something worth celebrating, considering her condition—if they believed her. "What do you mean?" I asked, wanting to know what she had said that made people this excited for her to go out drinking and not running off to get an MRI of her head.

"Oh, it's all over town. Mrs. Stein is going to be okay. There was some big mix-up at the hospital." Christina raised her brows at me. "I think she can sue."

"Be okay"? She could sue the hospital, because she was *okay*? I couldn't wrap my head around those words. She was supposed to be preparing to meet me in a few days. She was supposed to be living it up and saying her goodbyes. Maybe that was it. Maybe this was the story she wanted to leave everyone with before they forgot all about her. That had to be it, didn't it? But what if it wasn't?

There was only one way to settle this. I told Christina I'd be right back and headed toward where Mrs. Stein stood across the room with a champagne flute clenched in her hand.

"Pepper." She said my name without reservation. "I've got great news. I'm going to live!"

The group she was with cheered, but a pit opened up in my stomach.

"You're just saying that, aren't you? Because we—"

"I'm sorry," she said as she pulled me into her. She hugged me like we were old friends—which I supposed we were. "They sent me off to a specialist, but there had been some kind of mix-up with my file. I just got back. I was going to tell you. But they say I really am going to be okay."

"And we're going to sue their pants off," someone in her group yelled.

My body started to quiver. Sadness, disbelief, and even a little anger all fought for the upper hand. I was a cyclone of emotions, passing through all the stages of grief simultaneously. "You promised." My voice was nothing but a whisper. This couldn't be happening. This had to be some kind of cruel joke.

"I know, but I'm sure there's still time to find someone else," she said.

She had no idea what she was talking about, but there was no use saying any of that to her. "Congratulations," I squeaked out. "I have to go." I pushed myself through the crowd as it became harder and harder to breathe.

This was where I was supposed to finally get what I wanted. It was supposed to be *me* who was celebrating. She was ruining everything. Yes, it was selfish of me, but this was supposed to be *my* time. The anger that was only a mild sensation before took full control and heated me to my core.

I was halfway down the block when someone grabbed my arm.

"Hey, what was that all about?" Christina stood there holding our coats, staring at me with concerned eyes.

The rage inside me couldn't be contained anymore. "This messes everything up," I shouted. Luckily, the streets of Clover Creek were empty. I was angrier at myself for getting my hopes up than at Mrs. Stein. It wasn't her fault, and I honestly couldn't blame her for not wanting to do this. It just sucked—for me.

"What does? I don't understand."

"Of course you don't," I said. "Because I didn't think I needed to tell you. I thought I had it all worked out." My hands shook at my sides. This couldn't be happening. This absolutely *could not* be happening. But of course it was.

PEPPER

"Pepper." Christina took my hand—her skin so cool against mine. How many more times would we get to do this? Hold hands before she forgot about me completely? "Whatever this is, you can trust me. I got you," she said, and my throat got thick. The words I'd spoken to her a hundred times punched me in the gut, and I doubled over. "Hey, that's what you say to me all the time." She tried to sound comforting, which only made it worse.

"I'm cursed," I was able to push out without crying because I wouldn't, I couldn't—I had to be strong for Christina. I couldn't upset her.

"Come on. Whatever it is, it can't be that bad."

"No, Christina. It *is* that bad. It's not some figure of speech. I am legitimately cursed. And when the store disappears, so will I, and you won't even remember I exist." Speaking the truth didn't make me feel any better. It only made me want to throw up.

The usual pink flush in Christina's cheeks faded. "Are you breaking up with me?"

"What? No! The stories about the store are real—well, kind of, and it takes a human soul for it to work, mine in this case. And two days after Halloween, it will all vanish. Me included."

"You're moving away? I thought you wanted to stay in Clover Creek." Maybe it was the alcohol or maybe she really didn't understand. Either way, the timber of her voice had gone up a notch, and it made my chest tighten harder, quickly squashing down my anger like I'd had a bucket of ice water thrown at me. "If you don't want to be with me anymore, you could just say—"

"That's not what I'm saying at all." I grabbed her hand and held it to my heart.

"Well, you aren't making any sense," she said, the redness returning to her face, and her eyes filling with tears. "And if this is your way of trying to not feel guilty about leaving or something, you could just tell me."

I locked onto Christina's gaze. There was something so vulnerable about her face—about the way she looked at me. It was no use. Like it had been before when I'd attempted to tell anyone about my situation, Christina didn't *want* to believe me. I couldn't blame her. Just like I couldn't blame Mrs. Stein for not wanting it. If it hadn't happened to me, I probably wouldn't believe it either. And now we were so close to Halloween and then I'd be gone. I'd disappear, and Christina wouldn't remember anyway. Did I want to spend the last few days I had with her fighting? No. Of course not. So I did what I needed to and plastered on a smile. "You're right. I'm just kidding. I thought it would be funny, but I can see I was wrong." I pulled her toward me, wrapping my arms around her and burying my face in her hair. "I'm sorry. Can you please forgive me and forget all of this happened?"

"So you don't want to break up with me?" Her voice was muffled by my shoulder, but the way it shook shattered my heart. Never in a million years did I ever want to hurt her.

"No. Breaking up with you isn't something I *ever* want to do."

She dropped our coats and wrapped her arms around me. "Good. Because I don't know what I'd do without you." She sucked in a breath.

PEPPER

"Please don't cry," I said. "I never want to leave you. Okay?"

She nodded. "Okay, good. Because I never want to leave you either."

It had been a long day, and she hadn't slept much since the haunted house started, and she probably shouldn't have had that second gin and tonic. "Let me take you home."

"I'd like that." Christina pulled back, wiped her eyes, and kissed my cheek. "Can you stay the night?"

"Anything you want." I kissed her forehead. "I got you."

PEPPER

12 DAYS
UNTIL THE STORE CLOSES

Christina

The days blur together in a mix of school, haunted house, and spending time with Pepper. A perfect blend of sweet and hot—a recipe that I would never get tired of. I didn't mention the thing that happened at Take It Cheesy. I don't know how to even bring it up without sounding completely bananas. Plus, we're coming down to the final days—finishing up projects and getting all our last preparations in order for the big show.

Today Pepper is helping me and two of my students put the final touches on the mural—the one that got destroyed by the pipe bursting—in the "examination" room.

I envisioned Skylar being devastated when I told her what had happened. But she shrugged it off and said she'd fix it as soon as she was allowed—which is today.

The plaster is finally completely dry, so she's been hard at work quickly turning disaster into art. She's a born leader as well as talented—this kid will be going places.

Skylar and her friend Tawny lead the charge, instructing Pepper and me in exactly what needs to be done. Pepper cleans up some of the white lines since she has a steadier hand than I do. She focuses so intently on her project, the tip of her tongue pops out of her mouth from time to time, and I can't help my mind from wandering into dangerous places—like last night when she did things with her tongue I had only read about in romance novels.

Pepper glances at me from the corner of her eye and smirks like she knows exactly what I'm thinking. My cheeks heat up immediately, announcing to her that she's correct. She lifts her brows and shakes her head at me.

What? I mouth.

You're bad, she mouths back.

Paint runs down my hand and arm from holding my brush up too long. "Crap." I drop it by my side, and the paint runs back in the opposite direction.

"Someone's going to need a shower when we're done." Pepper winks at me, and the thought of her in my shower with me pops involuntarily into my head. How much longer until we can clean up and head home for the night?

"Oh my god. Same," Tawny says. "I don't know how anyone paints and doesn't get it all over themselves." She has on a pair of overalls that when we started preparing for this event months ago looked almost brand-new, and now they are covered with paint and fake blood and god knows what else.

"Some of us don't have that problem," Skylar says. She's in leggings and a T-shirt, but she doesn't have even a speck of paint on her, and she's the one who's done the most on this

---

CHRISTINA

project. I'm not sure how it's possible. I've just started and already am close to ruining another shirt—luckily this one isn't designer—even with this skeleton apron on. I learned that lesson a long time ago.

"Not all of us are professionals," Tawny shoots back. "Even Ms. L has paint everywhere." Tawny's red hair is pulled up away from her face, and there's a mixture of blue and black paint smeared across her cheek and onto her ear. The shirt she's wearing also has a rainbow of colors from all her time working in the house, much like the overalls. That's what most of the kids do, wash and wear the same clothes over and over so they don't ruin everything.

"What do you think, Ms. L?" Skylar asks as she steps away from her work.

"It's impressive. You can't even tell the wall has been cut out and put back together." It's like there was nothing there before at all. It'll be a shame when we paint over this for future Halloweens to come. At least I probably won't be here to see it happen. I've been thinking about Dad's proposition, and with everything going so well with Pepper, it feels like it could be the best time to take the next step in my life. I need to talk to her about it.

"Do you think something is missing in their eyes?" Pepper steps back and inspects the piece with us.

"I could add the fluorescent paint, and then when the black light hits them, they'll really glow," Skylar says. "I can't believe I didn't think of it."

"I just posed the question," Pepper says. "It was your idea."

Skylar nods—a huge smile on her face.

CHRISTINA

Pepper has a way with the kids that even I haven't mastered. I honestly think she might have missed her calling—she would be an amazing teacher. Much better than me, that's for sure. Maybe she could take over for me here, and then when things are more settled at home and I've built up a little inventory, I could come back up this way and open a store on Artichoke Street. We wouldn't be too far away from each other for too long—the drive isn't terrible. It could be perfect.

Skylar goes back to painting the eyes with some of the glow paint, and Pepper bumps me with her hip.

I want to throw my arms around her and tackle her to the ground, but of course I don't. "That was really sweet of you," I whisper instead.

"I don't know what you're talking about," she says. She really is too modest.

"You'd make a great teacher," I tell her, to plant the seed.

"You should autograph this," Tawny is telling Skylar.

She glances at me then back at the wall. "Don't you think that would be weird?"

I shake my head. It's her masterpiece. "I don't think so." She should be proud of what she's done—twice now.

"I don't know," Skylar says.

"You could do it in black paint in the bottom corner, so it's there but isn't totally noticeable and doesn't take away from your design," Pepper suggests. Another great idea.

"Maybe if everyone who worked on it gets to sign it, too." Skylar looks at me again. "Would that be okay?"

"Yes, of course."

CHRISTINA

Skylar crouches down and paints her name in the far corner, then she hands the paintbrush to Tawny. "We need to find Hallee," Skylar says, a big smile on her face.

Tawny finishes and hands the paintbrush back to Skylar. "I'll go find her." And she runs out of the room.

"Your turn." Skylar goes to hand me the paintbrush.

"Oh, that isn't necessary." I shake my head. It's so sweet, but this is her masterpiece. I've barely done anything.

"But you have to," she says.

Pepper presses her lips together and gestures toward the corner with her head—like I shouldn't argue.

"Fine," I relent. There's plenty of room down here for my whole name, but instead I paint my initials with an extra little heart looped into my L.

"Supercute," Skylar says. "Now you."

"Me?" Pepper says.

"Yes, you," I agree, handing her the brush. If I have to do it, so does she.

Pepper crouches down as Hallee comes into the room. "Wow," she says, inspecting the finished product.

"Right?" I say.

"And when we turn the black lights on, their eyes will glow." Skylar goes over and points at them on the wall.

"I believe you're next." Pepper hands the brush to Hallee.

"This is such a cool idea," Hallee says as she bends down to where we've all already signed.

The alarm on my phone goes off, pulling my attention away from Hallee. "Cleanup time," I announce.

CHRISTINA

It's a rush to rinse brushes, put things away, and make sure the kids get picked up—the ones who don't have their own cars or aren't walking home.

Thirty minutes later, Pepper and I are doing the final walk-through of the night to make sure paint cans are closed and no one left any snacks out.

"I think it was a successful day, don't you?" she asks.

"I do." I wrap my arms around her waist and pull her close. "And I think you said something about a shower earlier."

"You caught that, did you?" She brushes her nose against mine before kissing me. "Are you ready?"

Ready to get out of here and get her naked? Yes. I pat my back pocket. "I just need to find my phone."

Pepper laughs. "I should've known you would lose something while we were here."

I walk to the other side of the room and check around the spot where I hung some intestines on the wall. "And I wanted to talk to you about something, too."

"Oh really," she says as she starts searching for my phone, too.

"You know how I went to my parents' house a few weeks ago, and how my mom hurt herself?"

"Yeah, is she okay?"

"She'll be fine, but my dad had an idea, and seeing how great you are with the kids and everything, it got me thinking..." I go on to tell her everything Dad said about moving home for a while and supporting my art as Pepper follows me from room to room searching for my phone. She doesn't interrupt me—which is so sweet. My thoughts are racing a million miles a

---

CHRISTINA

minute, and I need to get them all out. I tell her how she could take my job here—how she would be so great at it, the way she handled Skylar and the kids tonight.

That's it. "I remember where my phone is," I tell her without looking her way. "It's in the mural room." I remember when the alarm went off, I left it on the paint table.

I tug her hand, and we head in that direction.

She waits by the door as I walk in to grab it. "You want to move away?" Her voice is so light, I almost don't hear her. It's sweet she's worried. That she cares as much as I do. But she doesn't have to be concerned. I have a plan.

"It's not like that. I wouldn't be that far, and it wouldn't be forever. Plus, it's a way for me to finally pursue my true passion. I was never supposed to teach here forever." I chuckle. "I'm actually surprised I've lasted this long." Three years. It's already been three years, although it hardly seems that long the way time flies by.

The mural really turned out great, and painting our names was such a sweet touch. I still can't believe Skylar wanted me to be a part of that, and Pepper, too. That's why she'd be perfect here with them. That's why Pepper needs to consider this idea.

I glance down to the corner, and my breath catches.

No. It can't be.

There, next to Skylar's name, is a PW and a simple little flower—a swirl in the middle of five petals. I glance at Pepper and back to the wall again. The same one that I've seen over and over. The one that's been following me like some kind of sign.

CHRISTINA

"You can't leave," she says, but I can barely hear her over the ringing in my ears.

My gaze is glued on the corner. "Do you know where that came from?"

"What?" she asks. "Let's talk about this plan of yours. You can't move away from here."

"I need to know how that drawing got here." I point.

"The little flower? Does it really matter?" She pushes out a loud breath. "I guess I did that when I painted my initials. It's kind of like a habit anytime I have any kind of writing utensil in my hand. But this is serious, Christina. We need to talk about you wanting to leave Clover Creek."

"You did that?" She told me she did, but I don't understand. It's just not possible.

"Yeah. I'm sorry. Was that not okay? I can paint over it if you want."

I race out of the room and grab my bag, pulling out the folders. It's in here somewhere.

"Hey, wait!" Pepper rushes after me. "We need to talk."

I snatch the old receipt and hold it out to her. "Did you do these, too?"

Her gaze floats to the paper in my hand and back to me, and she nods. "I must have when you were at the store." Her voice is tight. "Christina, you *can't* move away from here."

My head moves up and down, but words get clogged in my throat. This isn't possible. It doesn't make any logical kind of sense.

"Say something, please," she says, but I'm still staring at

CHRISTINA

her—the girl who I thought I met the day the Halloween store opened for the year—and the air gets so thin, I can't breathe.

"Have we met before?" I croak out.

Pepper's face morphs like she's been punched in the stomach. "What do you mean?"

"What do I mean?" I thrust the receipt toward her. "How is it that you drew on this?" My voice is getting louder, and Pepper is shaking her head.

"It's just a habit—"

"This is from three years ago!" That's the date on the receipt. That's when I purchased these items myself—it's the last four digits of my credit card number printed here.

Pepper's face loses all its rosiness.

"What aren't you telling me?" I'm yelling now because this is more terrifying than ghosts or zombie patients.

"I can explain." She puts her hands up and slowly walks toward me.

"Explain how you drew on this three years ago, but also we somehow just met two months ago?" It sounds too wild to be true—and if I weren't looking at her and didn't have this paper in my hand, I wouldn't believe it. "How did you do this?"

Demons. The story Eli told in this very room weeks ago rushes to my mind.

"Because we *have* met before. You just don't remember." Her voice has changed into something calmer, and she sounds like normal confident Pepper—so sure of what she's saying, but how could that be?

Tears sting the backs of my eyes, and I shake my head again.

CHRISTINA

No. That's not right. "Whatever you're playing with, I don't like it." I grab my bag and sling it over my shoulder. I need to get out of here.

"No. Please don't go," Pepper says. "You can't move away. You can't leave me. I can't lose you again." Her breath hitches. "I can't lose you forever!" She wraps her arms around her stomach like she's shielding herself from some kind of terrible beast as she crumbles to the floor. Pepper, the woman I've come to know that isn't afraid of anything, looks so small and scared. My heart cracks wide open.

She reaches out to me. Her hand trembling. Her eyes pleading. I may not know everything about her, but this feels vulnerable and real. This is a side of Pepper White I haven't seen before. I find myself taking her hand and kneeling next to her. She draws me closer and runs a finger along the scar on my arm. "I know how you got this," she says.

A chill races up my spine. I don't know the story; just one day I woke up and it was there. "Tell me."

CHRISTINA

0 DAYS
UNTIL THE STORE CLOSES

Pepper

After what happened at the bar, I did my best to act normal. I spent my time at the store, met Christina at the haunted house, and pretended there wasn't a giant ticking clock above my head. Christina never brought up the conversation again either, which was probably for the best. We only had so much time left together, so I did everything I could to make it as good as possible. Because if this was it for us, I wanted Christina to know she was loved. Even if she didn't remember me, maybe, just maybe, she'd be able to remember the feeling—and maybe that would be enough to make her not want to see anyone else before I returned, or do something worse, like move away. It was selfish of me, but the thought of coming back to her being with someone else, or not in Clover Creek at all, was too much to handle. And I had to stay positive. I had to find the bright side in all of this. What else was there?

Halloween night came, and the haunted house was a

smashing success. The school and the kids were in excellent hands with Christina. One night as I watched a line of excited patrons waiting their turn to get inside, it dawned on me that it could've been Christina's dislike for the holiday that made her best suited for this job. She had no thoughts or expectations. She didn't need to do things "her way." She let the kids run with their imagination. That was something I should've done more of, perhaps—not that it mattered now. But I'd hoped that seeing their faces, and the sense of accomplishment that came from the event, would have her sticking around another year—or more.

Just as planned, all the Dead of Night employees dressed up with leftover costumes and we partied the night away. New Guy, of course, wasn't included. Not that any of us missed him. I'd be surprised if he made it back next year. For all his trying to change things, The Dead of Night was how it was. All its staff was perfectly imperfect—and that was the way we liked it.

Although it had hit me that this was supposed to be the first time I'd be remembered after this event, I plastered on a smile because there wasn't any other choice. I couldn't leave Christina with a frown. She deserved all the happiness in the world, so I did all I could to give it to her while I still had the chance. Time may have worked differently when I wasn't here, but it still felt like being away forever and coming back to everything changed. I didn't wake up each day and go through the motions in solitude, but I was left with the lingering feeling that days—weeks—months—were passing by. My memories of Christina and my hope she'd be here when I returned would be the only things that would get me through the time away from her.

When she wasn't paying attention, I memorized the way she looked. The curve of her Cupid's bow above her cherry red lips and how she'd bite them when she was concentrating. I memorized the way her hand felt in mine. The calluses on her palms from working with wood. The chips in her polish on her short, manicured nails. The sound of her voice, and how she sometimes hummed to herself in the shower. I memorized the moments in between the big things because they were just as important. Every second with Christina was precious.

Before I knew it, and before I was ready, November second came, and I spent the day with Christina doing all the things she loved the most. I wanted to capture the sound of her laughter and bottle it up to listen to when I missed her. I wanted to slather myself in her favorite perfume so I could pretend she was next to me even when she wasn't. I even bought some of her favorite lipstick in a different color so I could always carry something around that made me think of her.

That night—our last night together—the stars kept us company as I took my last walk through Clover Creek with Christina by my side. She didn't ask or complain about why I wanted to stroll through town—a completely mundane thing—she happily accepted we would be together. That was another thing I'd miss about her: the ease of just being together. My chest clenched so tightly, my whole body ached.

It would be ten months until I saw the stars, the streets, the people of Clover Creek again, so I relished the crisp air, the wind whipping my hair into my face, and the hoots from owls perched high in the trees. The scents of fireplaces and dead leaves and the possibility of rain hung heavily in the nightly breeze, and I had to blink continually to stop myself from crying. This feeling was worse than losing Mitchell. With him, I didn't know it was coming—I had no time to prepare—and this was categorically so much harder.

Christina and I had been strolling right near The Dead of Night when the first clap of thunder sounded, and we made it inside the store right before the rain exploded from the clouds above.

"That was close," I said as I shut the door and locked it behind us.

"We won't get in trouble for being here, will we?" Christina asked. Her head swiveled around, like she was taking it all in—the quiet stillness of a place that hadn't been still since we opened seventy days ago.

"No, it's fine," I told her. It was the last place I wanted to be on the final night I had in this town, but we'd left her car near the restaurant, and when the big sale started, I'd misplaced the keys to the hearse. They'd show up magically on the hook in my apartment in less than twenty-four hours, and unless someone else was holding them inside this very empty store at the stroke of midnight, it didn't matter in the slightest.

Even with the lights off, The Dead of Night looked almost exactly the way it had earlier in the day. The 60% OFF signs still hung on mostly empty racks. No one could resist a sale, and when people clocked out for the day saying *Goodbye* and *Hope to see you next year*, no one asked about what else needed to be done because that was it. The store did all the hard work itself, and no one ever seemed the wiser.

"It's kind of spooky being in here, isn't it?" Christina pulled herself tighter into my side.

"I suppose," I said, even though I didn't really see it that way. This place, as much as I was angry with it, at times was home. It was all I had. "There are some chairs in the back from the party earlier; we can sit back there until this dies down a little." As if on cue, thunder crashed and rain assaulted the roof, making Christina jump. "Plus, it's probably quieter. And there might still be cake." I had to speak louder over the sound of the storm as I held out my hand to Christina. With the store empty, every noise was amplified tenfold.

"I thought for sure that jump scare the kids had at the haunted house would've gotten you, but nope, you really aren't afraid of anything, are you?" Christina took my hand and together we pushed through the door to the back room.

Like I'd said, a bunch of chairs and a table were still set up from the early closing party that afternoon, and half a sheet cake—chocolate with vanilla frosting—sat in the middle.

"I didn't know you were allowed to drink on the job." Christina pulled a White Claw out of a tub of melted ice.

"Last day. It's tradition," I said.

She placed the can on the table and moved farther back into the store—among the stacks and stacks of boxes. The Dead of Night was never short on inventory. "There's still a lot of stuff left."

I shrugged. "It'll get used next year." Most of what was left were costumes and wigs and larger lawn decorations. The things that could expire were what always went on sale and got snatched up in the days before we closed.

"How long do you have until it all gets cleared out?" She continued deeper into the maze of boxes—deeper into the back of the store—and I followed.

"It'll all be gone tonight." It was the truth. It would all be gone, including me, in only a few hours, and Christina wouldn't even remember having this conversation. The backs of my eyes burned, so I quickly looked up and blinked.

"How's that possible?" she asked.

"Do you really want to talk about it?" I closed the space between us and held her around the waist. We didn't have much time left, I didn't have to pull out my phone to know that exactly; I could just feel it. It was like a gentle tug that continued to get stronger the closer midnight got.

"Not really." She licked her lips.

Light filled the room with a flash of lightning, and then the thunder quickly followed.

Christina sucked in a quick breath. "It's really coming down."

We stood next to the only window in the back—it overlooked the parking lot, but with the blinds pulled up, we could watch the rain fall. It sparkled in the light from the lamppost that was nestled among the tall evergreens outside, the individual drops falling like glitter into the dark murky puddles on the blacktop.

"I wish it were snowing," I said.

"It probably will this winter."

I nodded but couldn't say anything. For me, there would be

no snuggling in front of a fire, or watching flakes fall from the sky, or studying how the snow would sparkle in the sun. There would also be no shoveling or dealing with trying to drive in the stuff either—which I supposed I should've been happy about, but being happy about anything at the moment was getting increasingly more difficult. I clenched my jaw and swallowed the thickness at the back of my throat.

"This weekend we should relax, now that Halloween is officially over for both of us," Christina said.

I stared out the window. The rain was getting harder, faster, and I couldn't make out the individual drops or the puddles anymore. The anger in this storm was palpable, and I couldn't help but relate. "Yeah, sure," I squeaked out.

"What's wrong?" Christina asked. "You've been kind of off all evening."

Had I been? I didn't mean to be. I thought I'd been doing a great job at keeping my feelings tightly bottled up. I wanted this to be a night to remember, even though it wouldn't be. "I'm sorry." I forced a smile.

"See, that's not the real you. What's going on?" She tilted her head at me, and took a moment before tentatively asking, "You don't still think you're cursed or something, do you?"

I turned away from the window to face her. "What would make you think of that?"

"To be honest, I haven't stopped thinking about it." She let her gaze fall to the floor. "I keep thinking that I'll wake up one morning to a text that you decided to leave."

I took her hand. "I would never do that." Not on purpose anyway—leaving, however, was inevitable.

PEPPER

"I know, but . . ." She shook her head. "I guess I'm just being—"

Lightning flashed and thunder crashed simultaneously. A shadow passed right over Christina's face.

"Look out." I leaped forward, wrapped my arms around her, and spun Christina away from the window as one of the giant trees from outside came crashing through. Something pressed against my back as our legs got tangled, and we both hit the ground, glass raining down around us.

Her chocolate peppermint breath from the Andes mint she'd eaten earlier caressed my cheek. "You're a superhero; that's your secret to not being afraid," she said, but her voice wobbled a bit.

"Just call me Captain Reflex," I tried to joke. "Are you okay?"

She was quiet for a moment, her gaze scanning my face. "You're holding me a little tight."

"Oh right." I released her and scrambled to my feet.

Christina stood, and a small gash on her forearm dripped blood onto the ground. I grabbed a costume package nearby, tore it open, and pressed the fabric of whatever it was to the open wound. "Is it a bad thing that it doesn't hurt?" she asked.

"Not necessarily. I bet your adrenaline is pumping." My heart was pounding, too, but for a different reason. Everything about tonight was already so unfair—and now this? Why was the universe being so cruel?

A branch hung through the window, and jagged shards of glass were scattered on the floor—one of the pieces larger than a headstone. It was amazing she wasn't hurt worse. I had to at least be grateful for that. "The Dead of Night will pay for all of your medical expenses." I pulled the cloth away to get a look. The cut wasn't terrible, but it likely needed stitches, and there would definitely be a scar.

Christina stared at the ground. "If you hadn't . . ." But she didn't finish her thought. She didn't need to. If she had been standing where she had been before I stepped in and pushed her out of the way, a huge pane of glass would've hit her. "Are *you* okay?" she asked me this time.

"I'm fine. But we should get you—"

"No. Maybe you don't feel it either." She tugged my arm to spin me around, and she gasped. "Your jacket. Oh my god." She pulled it off, jamming it in my hands. The back of my leather jacket had a diagonal slash from shoulder to waist, and from the feel of her cool fingers against the skin on my back, it had also torn through my shirt. "There's nothing there. You're fine."

"Don't sound so disappointed," I said to try to lighten the mood.

Her hand gripped my arm, chilled fingers against my warm skin that sent ripples all the way up and into my chest. "It's not funny."

I shook my head. "No, it's not." There was nothing funny about tonight at all.

"That thing should've sliced you in two." She was right. That was exactly what it should've done, but I had to be in top physical health at all times for the store, so this was the blessing that came with my curse. Nothing could hurt me. Physically at least—inside my chest, my heart was slowly cracking in two.

PEPPER

"I guess I got lucky. Turned at the right time." There was nothing else I could say. The truth would've been harder to believe.

She flinched and let go of me, instead wrapping her hand around the cloth still pressed to her arm.

"You should get that looked at."

She nodded.

"You'll be okay." She had to be okay. I needed her to be. There was no other option.

Her eyes locked with mine. "Because you got me, right?"

I swallowed the lump in the back of my throat. "Yeah. I got you."

But she didn't move. Her gaze flickering back and forth between me, the broken window, her arm, and my torn jacket, which was now on the ground. Rain flew in on the wind through the gaping hole where the tree had smashed the glass, getting us both wet.

"This whole thing is really real, isn't it?" Christina asked. "That's why you aren't hurt."

I just nodded. There was no reason to say I told you so.

"But I don't understand," she yelled over the howling wind.

I took her hand and led her away from the window and the rain, and to the seats we'd passed on our way into the back room. When the store vanished tonight, it likely would fix the window, or it didn't matter. It would be an empty building—ready for the next tenant to move in.

Christina's whole body shook as I set her down and got her that White Claw. "What's this for?"

PEPPER

"I thought maybe you could use a drink." I pulled a chair up in front of her so that our knees were touching.

She cracked the can open and took a healthy swig. "Tell me everything."

"Are you sure you want to hear this?" I asked. She hadn't wanted to hear it the last time I tried.

She nodded, and I pulled her arm toward me, securing the fabric over her cut. It wasn't exactly a short story, so it would take me a while to get through it all, but that's exactly what I did. I took a deep breath and explained my story from the beginning—about how I'd been tricked, and the years I've been attached to the store, so that's how I knew so much about the town and all the best things to order whenever we went out. I told her about Mrs. Stein and how I thought I'd found a way to break the curse but failed. Christina leaned in and listened with her whole body, never interrupting me. It was the first time I'd ever talked about all of it, and I actually felt heard.

"What's going to happen?" she asked when I was finished.

"Once midnight hits, this will all disappear." I waved my hands over my head.

"Just like that." She snapped her fingers, and my heart broke a little more.

"Yep."

She glanced around at the mess from the party, all the boxes, leftover decorations, and everything else around us. "What about me? What happens if I stay here with you?"

I shook my head. "I don't know."

"Maybe I'll come with you," she said. My sweet, kind

Christina. I didn't know what I would do without her—she was right in front of me, and I already missed her.

"Is that really what you want? For everyone to forget about you? What about your family? Your sisters?"

"I don't know. I just know I don't want to lose you."

I swallowed hard, not once but twice. This was so much harder than I ever imagined. "You won't remember." But I would. As much as I tried to ignore all the feelings of the last few days, they all came crashing into me. The inevitable was here. Now. This was really happening. She finally was ready to listen to my predicament, but it was too late. Tonight, I would lose her, and there was nothing I could do to stop it.

"I don't want to forget you." A tear slipped down her cheek.

"I don't want you to forget me," I confessed, and the backs of my eyes burned something so fierce that no amount of blinking could stop it.

Thunder rumbled the walls—like a warning, but we both seemed to ignore it. "I'm not leaving you." She grabbed my hand and wrapped her fingers with mine, squeezing tightly.

"I don't think it works that way." While no one had ever been with me inside the store since the time Kitty tricked me—I'd always been the only one to get pulled away. I didn't even have to be here for it to happen. Once midnight hit, no matter where I was, I'd be gone.

"We have to try, though, right?" Tears continued to slip down her cheeks.

I reached up and used my thumb to brush them away. It was wrong and selfish. I had no idea what would happen once midnight struck if Christina was still in the store. Part of me wanted her to be sucked away with it—with me—but the other part knew what she would be giving up if she did and I prayed that didn't happen. She deserved to live. She deserved to wake up tomorrow with her future wide open in front of her. Her family, her students, this community needed her.

She gripped my hand tighter and leaned forward, pressing her forehead against mine.

"I'll be back," I told her.

"But you said I won't remember you." Tears dripped onto our fingers.

"You won't."

"Then you have to make me remember. Promise me you'll make me remember how much I love you."

I leaned away to look her in the eyes. "I can try, but I can't make you feel things for me if you don't want to."

"But I *do* want to. I want to be in love with you. I don't want to live without you at all. I don't want to know a world without you in it."

The tears I'd held back all day rushed from my eyes. "But that's how it has to be. Because very soon this will all be gone and so will I, and you won't remember me—but I'll be left remembering you and what we could've had together. You'll just see me as this girl that works at the Halloween store, but I'll know what it feels like to hold your hand, to kiss you, to be with you, and I won't be able to."

Her cheeks flushed red. "Then remind me. Tell me all of this on day one. Come and find me no matter where I am and tell me, and then we'll have two months to break the curse together, not only a few days."

PEPPER

"You're angry with me."

"Damn right I'm angry. I'm mad at myself for not listening to you. I'm mad at you for not telling me sooner. And I'm mad I finally found my person, and you're going away."

I shook my head. "You won't remember any of that." I tried to sound reassuring, but reassuring for her or me, I didn't know.

"But *you* will. You'll know how much you mean to me. And you owe it to me to try again. You have to tell me."

"And what if it doesn't work? What if you don't believe me? What if we can't find someone to break the curse?" I didn't know if I could put her through that.

"I don't know. We do it again."

"How many times?" I asked. This was already so hard, saying goodbye. I didn't know if I'd be strong enough to repeat it—especially multiple times.

"What?"

"How many times do we try—do *I* try? Because it's my heart that's breaking right now—and it will each and every time I have to leave you. Your feelings will be spared, but mine..."

"Just promise me, please," she begged, and then she pulled me into her, gripping me so tightly like she was scared to let go. I held her back, just as scared, and I memorized everything about her. The way her breath hitched as she cried. The way my body shook against hers as I sobbed.

This was why it was called a curse and not something else. Losing someone in this way was worse than death. She'd wake up tomorrow and would never think of me again, but I'd spend the next ten months thinking of nothing but her.

"I got you," I said. "You won't remember, but know that anytime I say 'I got you,' what I'm really saying is 'I love you.'"

And that was it. That was how I lost Christina. I held on to her until the clock struck midnight and then everything around me went black.

PEPPER

12 DAYS
UNTIL THE STORE CLOSES

Christina

My finger traces along the scar on my arm. Some wounds you can't see—but this has been there. A reminder of something, of someone I'd been forced to forget. Part of me always wondered how it happened, but I'd also always felt silly for not knowing.

I still remember it was a few days after Halloween, and as soon as I opened my eyes, something was off. It was the first time I remember feeling just blah. This fogginess—a cloud of uncertainty—clung to me that I couldn't shake off. In the shower that morning, I noticed my arm. It wasn't a cut or even fresh looking, but a scar that's still on my arm right now. I couldn't remember ever seeing it before, but that didn't make sense, so I let it go. But maybe I should have questioned it. Maybe then I could have remembered or figured something out.

Pepper sits in front of me on the cold concrete floor of the haunted house. Her story of how it all happened races through my mind—like puzzle pieces that have no true form or shape of what the finished product should look like and yet they are coming together. Her story—our story—gives me clarity on so many things I've been feeling since I met her. She's always felt comfortable. It's always felt like she's known me better than I know myself. From our first time together, it felt like coming home, and now at least I understand why. "How many times have we done this?" I ask.

"You and me?" Pepper takes a breath, hesitation in her eyes. "Three. This is our third time. Our third Halloween."

Now it's my turn to take a deep breath. Three. Wow. I guess I should be glad it hasn't been longer—that she hasn't had to do this more times than that. "What happened last year?" I rub the scar on my arm again, assuming it had to be different than our first.

"We failed. I did exactly what you wanted. You should have seen your face that first day you came into the store and I told you we'd already met. You didn't want to believe me." She grins a little with this faraway look in her eyes. "But then I started telling you all the things I shouldn't have known. I think you thought I was a stalker, but you came around, and then . . ." She shakes her head. "You became so determined, so obsessed with breaking this curse, you were miserable. And with the added stress of trying to put this event on, it was too much. You weren't eating or sleeping. You were constantly crying. And when we couldn't figure out a way to break the curse, you were devastated—inconsolable. I was so scared for you. It was heartbreaking. I couldn't do that to you again."

I remember last November was when my depression was

CHRISTINA

the worst. It wasn't until summer that I felt semi-normal again. I didn't even know why I was so upset—but this all makes sense. "That's why you didn't tell me."

She nods. "You seemed so happy this time. Almost like you did the first time I met you. So I figured maybe it was better this way. I'm sorry."

"No. I'm the one who's sorry. I'm sorry I didn't let you think there was another way. I'm sorry you had to suffer through this again all on your own." A tear slips down my cheek, and Pepper brushes it away. She's been so strong through it all—I couldn't do it if it were me. Just the thought of saying goodbye to Pepper has my chest clench so tight, I can barely breathe.

"You're worth it." She holds my gaze so steadily with her own. I understand why I wanted to break the curse so badly last time—because I don't ever want to live without this feeling; I don't want to live without her.

"What do we do now?" I ask. My mind is whirling, but I don't have any ideas. I don't know what we have or haven't done before.

She grabs my hand and laces her fingers with mine. "We enjoy the little time we have left together, and you make yourself the promise that you won't leave Clover Creek, and we will get to be together every year. Even if it is just for a little while."

It's not enough, I want to say. But that isn't fair to her—after what she's been through. And it's not like I have a plan or know any more about what it is that we're fighting against. "Maybe this time we'll find a way to break the curse," I say.

She smiles—but it's forced, the way her eyes don't crinkle in the corners. "Yeah, maybe."

CHRISTINA

"Don't do that. You don't have to pretend for me." I know I'm not as strong as she is, but she doesn't have to carry all this weight alone.

She lets out another long breath. She must be so tired—tired of fighting and losing and having to do it all over again. "I'm not pretending."

"Bullshit you're not." I release her hand and stand up. "It's okay to be mad. Because I'm mad." I just don't know who or what to be mad at. Not at her—this isn't her fault. But this situation is bullshit. I finally find my person, and I only get her for ten weeks a year and then I forget her. This isn't what I want. I want her every day of the year. I don't want to have to live like this.

"It won't change anything."

"Maybe not, but it's okay to be angry. What's happening with you, with us, it's not okay." I pull her to her feet, so we're both standing. "I love you," I tell her without hesitation. I've felt it in my bones so long, and now it all makes sense as to why.

"I love you, too."

"So I'm not giving up." We may have tried and failed before, but that doesn't mean we'll fail again. There has to be something we haven't thought of yet.

"Is that what you think I'm doing? You think I'm giving up? Because I can tell you it's not easy being seen as a stranger to the person I love. From the moment you walk into the store, I want to wrap you up in my arms, but you have no idea who I am, and it is heartbreaking."

I can only imagine, and I don't want to disregard her

CHRISTINA

feelings or what she's been through. "Then let's do something about it."

"What?" She throws her hands up and walks in a circle. She's obviously frustrated, and I can't fault her for that. She's lived with this truth longer than I have. But I'm glad she's riled up. I'm glad she isn't trying to turn this into a positive, because it's not. "What do you want me to do?"

"I want you to fight for us." Maybe it isn't fair for me to say that or ask, but it's the only thing that feels right. I'm ready to fight.

"Fight who? Or what? Do you think I haven't tried?"

"That's not what I'm saying."

"Then what are you saying? Because we've tried everything I'm willing to do. I refuse to trick someone the way I was tricked. I won't do it. I can't do it. It's not fair."

"And this . . . this is fair?" I yell back at her.

"No. It's not. But it was *my* mistake, and I'm paying for it."

"You mean we." She isn't in this alone anymore. She needs to realize that.

She shakes her head. "It doesn't have to be this way for you. Just say the word and this doesn't have to happen." She gestures between us.

My chest clenches so hard, it's like the wind has been knocked out of me. "Can you so easily walk away?"

"No, of course not," she yells. "It kills me every time I have to say goodbye to you. Because I remember. I remember you." A tear slips down her cheek.

It isn't Halloween yet, so we still have a chance—I still have

---

CHRISTINA

a chance to convince her we can try again. "Then let's not say goodbye this time. Let's break this curse."

She shakes her head. "I don't know how."

"Let me help you."

"We already—"

"I don't care," I say. "I don't care what it takes. I'm not losing you again." I wrap my arms around her and hold her tightly against me, burying my face in her inky black hair, which smells like vanilla and incense and home. She is my person, and when you find someone who truly gets you—like Pepper gets me—you hold on to them with everything you've got. I won't let her go.

"I don't know how much longer I can keep doing this." Her breath hitches, and she holds me back, as if, without me, she wouldn't be able to stand.

I don't know what we've tried before, but we're going to do it all again if it means we can be together. Pepper might not be up to tricking anyone, but I don't know if I can make the same promise. "I got you," I tell her, and she bursts into tears.

CHRISTINA

11 DAYS
UNTIL THE STORE CLOSES

Christina

How to break a curse.

I type this into the search engine as I settle into the teachers' lounge for lunch. Ever since Pepper gave me the rundown on what happened, I haven't been able to think about anything else. She said we already tried everything, but have we? The only way I'll be sure is if I try it all—again, I guess. And luckily the internet is amazing. Literally every ridiculous idea is right at my fingertips. The trouble is . . . where do we start?

The suggestions that come up are wild. The first post is a poem about boiling lemon balm and drinking it with hummingbird bones. Where would I even find such a thing? I open another tab and type, Can you buy hummingbird bones, and surprisingly it's possible. I jot it down on my list to discuss with Pepper later.

Another post suggests that the curse is there because the

person allows it to have power over them—which is entirely unhelpful and obviously written by someone who has never been cursed. And then there are a number of posts that suggest the only way to break a curse is by accepting Jesus Christ into your life. I'm not anti-religious or anything, but I have serious doubts about following a book that was written years after this person supposedly walked the earth and then it was translated and edited a million times over by mostly men. Call me a skeptic, but it would feel no different than accepting Peter Rabbit into my life—which also probably wouldn't do anything to help break this curse.

"What are you doing?" Cami pulls the chair out next to me and struggles to sit down. Her due date is coming up fast. She glances at my screen. "Occults? Are you already thinking about next year's theme?" Thank god there's a reasonable explanation for my very suspicious online activities.

I set my phone down and open my leftover take-out container. It'll be a miracle when I can get back to the grocery store. "What are your feelings about witchcraft?"

She opens her lunch and pulls out a sandwich. "I know we were taught to fear witches when we really should've been worried about the people burning them. Why do you ask?" She takes a bite, crunching through something.

"What are you eating?"

"Ham and cheese with mayo and Oreos," she says, and I frown, not on purpose, but because, *what*? "Don't knock it till you try it," she says around a mouthful.

I hold up my hands. Pregnancy cravings are weird, and I know better than to question her, especially when she's hungry.

CHRISTINA

"You just caught me off guard. It sounds interestingly delicious." I try to make up for the fact that my face does not hide my emotions about her lunch choice.

"What's with the witch questions?" She moves the conversation along, thankfully.

I could attempt to explain Pepper's situation, but we only have twenty minutes before we have to get back to class. "Just haunted house stuff. So what would you do if you thought you were cursed?"

"Okay, I'll play along." She leans back in her chair and sets a bag of jalapeño kettle chips on her stomach like it's a table. "I guess I'd try to figure out who I pissed off to get cursed in the first place and then see if I could get them to reverse it."

"And if it wasn't a person per se but, like, a place or a thing?"

She munches on a chip thoughtfully. "Can you destroy it?"

That's an excellent question. "I don't know."

She grabs another chip from the bag. "Then I'd start there." She pops it in her mouth before taking a bite of her sandwich.

Destroy the thing that's cursing you. It's not a bad idea, but how? Trying to burn down the store seems like it might be a little too risky—especially since arson is a felony—but it's not completely off the table. How would one go about researching how to commit arson and get away with it without getting caught? Does incognito mode work for that?

"I've lost you," Cami says.

"Sorry. It's opening night, and I'm a little all over the place." I swirl some chow mein noodles on a fork. I could heat them up, but that would take too long.

CHRISTINA

"Oh shit, that's right. How'd I forget it was tonight?"

"Probably because you're busy making a whole-ass human being." I nod toward her belly.

"I think I lost my mucus plug."

This time I make sure I don't make a facial reaction, but again, *what*? "Is that bad?"

"Nah. It means I'll probably go into labor soon." She takes another bite of her sandwich like this isn't a big deal.

"What the hell are you doing here, then?" For someone—me—who has never had a baby and doesn't want to see what it looks like to have one, it seems like a very big deal, and one she should have a plan for that isn't eating a weird sandwich in the teachers' lounge.

"I haven't had any real contractions, only some Braxton-Hicks. Plus, I don't want to waste any of my maternity leave until it's absolutely necessary."

I shake my head. Our country is super messed up. "That sucks. I'm sorry. But I guess I don't have to worry about you needing to use . . ." I gesture to the old green couch.

"Not your fault. And I'd have the baby right here before I sat on that thing and delivered it." She makes a face like the couch is the grossest thing in the world—and she's correct about that. "Back to your curse question, though. There's a psychic out past that taco truck. You could always go check it out for ideas."

"How do you know that?"

"I went and got a reading last week," she says. "I wanted reassurance that everything was going to be okay." She rubs

---

CHRISTINA

her belly. "It's silly, I know, but the power of positive thoughts and all that. Plus, maybe they could be fun to have out for next year or something. Do some readings outside on the lawn."

There's power in positive thoughts—at least that's something Pepper would say. "I'll go check it out for future ideas. Thanks."

"I can't wait to see what next year's theme is, because it's already sounding really cool."

If she only knew.

CHRISTINA

11 DAYS
UNTIL THE STORE CLOSES

Christina

There isn't time to do any research on psychics after lunch and before needing to hurry over to the haunted house after school for our first official night, so it gets added to the list of things to do for later.

The hours before "curtain up" race by in a frenzy of activities—you'd think Taylor Swift herself would be coming to the show tonight, not that it's opening night to the general public. The rush of excitement is really what makes this event all worth it. It's a feeling that I can't even describe—a euphoria that pulses through each and every person as props are set out, makeup and hair get done, and costumes are put on.

There's already a line when we open the doors at six o'clock sharp.

I position myself with my walkie-talkie headset at the exit. The screams coming from inside tell me things are going according to plan. Once the event has started, I never walk through. Even though I know it's all fake—it's too much for me. The kids really get into character, so with the sounds and the darkness, the scary factor increases by a thousand.

The first group of ten people exits—a bunch of teens laughing and pushing one another as the door opens, then closes. Four of them are alumni who worked on the event and graduated last year.

"That was amazing!" one of them says.

"I almost peed myself," says another.

"Let's do it again!" a third one calls out.

"Hey, Ms. L," they all shout at me as they rush back off to the front of the house.

If the rest of the night goes like this, we'll be in great shape. I press the talk button on my headset and give the front of the house an update—letting them know the first group is done and how enthusiastic they were.

"Things are great up here, too," Steffi says over the headset. "We are almost out of tickets for tonight, and the art booth is on fire—in a good way," she quickly adds. "Like, the line for it is superlong."

Out in the front of the house there are activities like pumpkin painting, simple carnival games—like throw the ring on the bottle—and some much less scary Halloween characters wandering around for the little kids who aren't quite ready to go inside the house, and this year our art teacher, Mrs. Fuller, suggested her students paint faces and give temporary tattoos. We splurged on some pretty pricey markers that can be used on the body and last a few days—but it sounds like it's worth it.

CHRISTINA

A few hours later, twelve hundred people have come through already. We should have at least two thousand more before the night is over. These numbers are better than last year—assuming we can keep up this volume for the rest of the week—and history is on our side for this.

Overall, the event is running smoothly, and we've only had to do one hard stop to get someone out who decided it just wasn't for them. That's when we have to turn all the lights on and one of the kids who isn't in costume but dressed all in black and generally unseen during the show assists someone who gets a little overwhelmed. It's rare, but it does happen.

The exit door opens again, but it isn't a group of rowdy teens who spill out but my family.

I have to do a double take. I almost can't believe my eyes.

Mom pushes her scooter forward while her other foot is propped up, Ashley is as pale as a sheet of printer paper, and Emily, Antonio, and Dad are laughing hysterically. I officially told them that I was turning down their offer. Without knowing what is happening with Pepper, I can't commit to leaving. Even if I forget her, I have to make the promise to stay. To give us another chance to be together. I can't leave now, knowing what I do and what I could have. While they were supportive of my decision, I'm not sure they completely understood, so it's surprising to see them.

"What are you doing here?" I have to give them credit that this year they said they were going to come out—something they haven't done yet since I started teaching—and then actually followed through.

CHRISTINA

Emily is the first to race up and give me a hug. "That was fantastic." She squeezes me so hard that for a moment I can't breathe.

"Thanks," I'm barely able to respond.

Mom hugs me next—which is only a little awkward with her scooter—followed by Dad. "This is quite the event," Mom says.

"And quite the turnout," Dad adds.

"It's really impressive," Ashley says, and I'm ready to fall over. A compliment from my big sister? Did someone get a recording of that? I should keep it tucked away in my back pocket forever. Ashley saying nice things to me doesn't come often. I wonder how those words tasted coming out of her mouth.

"Great job, sis." Antonio squeezes me into his side. I have to admit, he's going to make an awesome brother-in-law. And he's good to Emily, which is most important.

"I guess I'm just surprised to see you all here," I say.

"And it shouldn't be like that," Mom says. "We should've come sooner. We should've been more supportive. We're going to try more from here on out." She reaches over and hugs me again.

"Thank you," I tell her, because coming back with something dismissive—like, "It's no big deal," or "You don't have to do that"—would be disingenuous. And saying something like, "Yeah, for real" would just be inappropriate. "It feels good to be here," I tell them, which is true, "and the kids are great."

"They seem like it," Emily confirms.

"If you like this, you'll really love our spring production." I'm probably pressing my luck, but I don't care. They *should*

CHRISTINA

come out here more—they should make the effort to be a part of the things that I find important even if they don't think they are.

"Will there be as much blood?" Ashley asks with a sour look on her face.

"We're doing *Alice in Wonderland*, so it's unlikely," I tell her.

"We're really proud of you," Dad says. It's been years since he's said that to me, and it means a lot—he's not a man of very many words, but he always means what he says.

"She's really amazing, isn't she?" Pepper comes up and hip-checks me.

"You're here early." I pull her in for a hug. I'm so excited she gets to witness this historic event for herself, so I don't have to tell it to her later.

"Someone finally decided to show up for his shifts, so I got to cut out," she says.

"Pepper, it's lovely to see you again," Mom says.

"Likewise. Did you enjoy the performance?" she asks.

"We were just telling Christina how we'd never seen anything like it," Mom says.

"Or seen anything as disgusting," Ashley adds.

"A lot of people don't understand horror, but I like it. It helps us dissect things that are wrong in our society without being preachy. Wouldn't you agree, Christina?" Pepper turns to me and winks so that no one else sees. Now I understand how she knows how to deal with Ashley so well. She's had practice.

I nod. "That's a great way to put it." I still don't like all the blood, but the way Pepper gets under Ashley's skin is poetry in motion.

CHRISTINA

"Well, we won't keep you," Dad says.

"We have a long drive back," Ashley adds.

"I'm glad you all made it," I tell them. And I really am. I hope this means they will attempt to come this way more often, so it isn't always me going down to them.

We all say our goodbyes, and finally I get a chance to talk to Pepper about my conversation with Cami earlier and her idea to go and see a psychic. She listens so intently, and I have to give her credit for not making faces or interrupting or laughing—which all seem like they could be reasonable reactions.

"I don't want you to get your hopes up," she says. "But we can try it if you want."

I squeeze her hand. This could be it. The thing we need. I lean in and kiss her cheek quickly since I'm technically still on work duty. "You'll see," I say. "You'll see."

CHRISTINA

7 DAYS
UNTIL THE STORE CLOSES

Christina

I've never been one to believe in psychic powers or the power of tarot or whatever, but this whole thing with Pepper has me seriously reconsidering my stance. It's completely possible that someone has the ability to sense things that are outside the realm of a normal human being—at least it should be possible if curses are real, right? And if it means the difference between breaking said curse or not, I'm willing to believe 1,000 percent.

The psychic Cami recommended had an opening per their very user-friendly online appointment setting app, so I'm heading out to get a feel for them for myself before Pepper shows up—which is why I asked her to meet me there instead of us driving together. There's no reason to subject her to it if I don't get the vibe they'll be able to help. She gave me the extensive list of all the things we tried in the past—hiring an exorcist is a real thing, it seems, and something she allowed herself to be subjected to on my behalf—and I don't want to torture her like that again, so it feels like a little caution could be helpful.

But I'd be lying if I didn't have a little faith that this could work. The psychic was right about Cami's delivery going well. Ariella Camilla-Sofia Alvarez arrived three days ago without any complications, and she is just as beautiful as her mother.

I drive past Holy Guacamole—the place Pepper and I had our first date, which actually wasn't my first date with her at all. It all makes sense now why I found her so easy to talk to that day, how she knew exactly what I'd want to eat, and knew all the right things to say. It had been so easy to brush it off at the time—or chalk it up to fate—but that wasn't it at all. She made it happen.

She's put on a brave face for so long that now it's my turn to make things happen. It isn't fair to her to keep having to do this.

My GPS tells me my destination is ahead on the right, but there's just a bunch of trees. I don't know what I should be looking for until an old Airstream trailer comes into view. It's shiny silver, and a sign in front reads: SPIRITUALIST AT WORK AND PLAY. And another says: WEDNESDAY TWO FOR ONE SPECIAL.

According to Pepper, we've never been here, and according to the internet, they've only been open since mid-May, so it seems like it could be worth a shot, or at the very least it can't hurt to try and hear what they say. Sailor has a decent enough Yelp rating, so really how bad could this be?

My tires slide to a stop on the gravel out front, and I throw the car in park. The sun is behind me, and my car casts a shadow over the trailer like an omen. I'm not generally one to

CHRISTINA

believe in signs, but something about the way the dark form looms heavily over the shiny silver has chills racing through my body. I'm not sure what to make of it. Or if I should make anything of it at all.

I take a deep breath.

Here goes nothing.

I grab my wallet from my bag and head up to knock on the trailer door.

A man in a red plaid shirt and jeans answers, and for a moment I think I might be in the wrong place.

"Sailor?" I ask.

"One and the same," he says. "You must be Christina; come on in."

His scruffy beard and shaggy blond hair make him look more like a lumberjack than someone who deals with the supernatural, but either way, he doesn't immediately give off axe murderer vibes, so I follow him inside.

The scent of patchouli hangs heavily in the air. There's a little foyer—if you can even call it that—with a small table full of leaflets. The connecting room is covered in rainbow scarves and twinkle lights. One wall is filled with shelves loaded with an assortment of candles, rocks, and books. In the center of the room is a leather couch, a coffee table with a small rock fountain in the center, and two chairs.

"Come have a seat." Sailor gestures to the setup. "If you hear any banging or grunting, my husband is out back chopping wood, so don't worry."

"This isn't at all what I expected," I confess as I choose one of the chairs and settle into it.

CHRISTINA

Sailor plops down on the couch and props a foot on the opposite knee—he's wearing pink socks with kittens on them. "I get that a lot. Which is why I decorated a little, and that does seem to help some, but"—he gestures to himself—"there's nothing I can really do about this. And my husband hates it when I shave my beard. But enough about me. What's troubling you?"

The online form wasn't very specific when I made this appointment. Do people only come to psychics when they are bothered by something? "How did you—"

"Psychic, remember?"

Okay, well, either this guy is the real deal or he's extremely good at guessing. The jury is still out, but regardless, I'm here and going to give this a chance. "I actually have a question for you."

"Shoot."

"What's the fastest way to break a curse?" I figure I should cut to the chase. Either he'll have answers or suggestions or he won't, and Pepper should be here soon, so there's no reason to waste any time.

"Whoa." He leans forward, dropping his foot to the floor and propping his elbows on his knees. "Why do you think you're cursed?"

"Not me. My girlfriend. It's a long story, but I really just need to know if you can tell me how to break one or not. She's on her way here, but she's already tried everything, and I don't want to get her hopes up." Actually, Pepper doesn't want me to get *my* hopes up—she already has her doubts—but since this is a new lead, how can I not be a little hopeful?

CHRISTINA

He steeples his fingers. "It's slightly more complicated than that. What's the origin? What was used to create the curse? Is there anything tied to it—like a talisman, or idol, or totem?"

Oh. This *is* much more complicated than I thought. Maybe I should've gotten more information from Pepper before coming in on my own. "I'm not sure." I bite my lip. Wait. That last thing. "I think there is some kind of amulet, though. Does that count?"

"Okay, now we're getting somewhere. Many times if you can destroy the thing that's holding the curse, you destroy the curse." He makes it sound simple—like, why didn't I think of that?

Why didn't I think of that?

My heart rate speeds up. That's basically what Cami said, except this isn't burning down an entire building. This seems possible. "Can you do that? Can you help destroy the thing—the amulet?"

He leans back and props his foot up again. "My rates for that are a little higher."

Costs be damned. I don't care if it takes every dollar from my 401(k). "But you can do it?"

"I should be able to, yes," he says.

Oh my god. Could it actually be this easy? It almost feels too good to be true. Which has a twinge of doubt creeping into my thoughts. "Not to sound whatever, but how do I know for sure? Do you have some referrals or something?"

"A skeptic. It's okay. A lot of people are. Let me see if I can help ease your worries." Sailor leans forward and narrows his eyes like he's really looking at me, then he takes a couple of deep breaths. "You work in some kind of arts," he says.

CHRISTINA

"Yes. I'm a theater teacher, and—"

"Shhh..." he says. "You have a lot of pressure on you right now. And... and you have a big change on your horizon. But don't worry, I'm getting the sense it's going to work out." He opens his eyes and leans back once again.

Holy shit. I don't know how he knew all of that about me, but he's completely spot-on. People online said he is legit. Maybe this is the answer we've been looking for. Maybe Sailor is going to be our hero today.

"Now how do you feel?" he asks.

"Great. You're amazing. My girlfriend will be here any minute, and she'll have the amulet with her."

"She carries around a cursed amulet?" Sailor rubs his beard.

"It's attached to her car keys." That does sound weird, now that I think about it. "I'm not sure if it's cursed, though, or if she is or how it all works. You would probably know better than me." A nervous giggle escapes my lips.

He nods slowly like he's considering what I said. "I guess it's harder to lose that way." He chuckles. Okay, so he gets it. I can't believe I was lucky enough to find this guy.

There's a knock on the door.

"Oh, that has to be her." I jump up and yank open the door to a surprised Pepper staring up at the trailer. I take a step outside to greet her.

"So this is it, huh?" she asks.

"This is it," I tell her. "He has an idea that might work. You have your keys, right?"

She pats her pocket. "Can't drive without them."

"Perfect. Let's—"

CHRISTINA

She grabs my arm before I can turn around. "Christina." My name is an exhale, like she's exhausted to the bone. "I don't want you to get your hopes up." She's sweet, but she hasn't talked to him yet. She'll see he's the real deal.

"I know." I lean in and kiss her cheek. "I just want to try, okay?"

Pepper glances at the structure behind me and then nods. "Yeah. Okay."

I take her hand and pull her inside.

Sailor is in the same spot on the couch, but as soon as Pepper steps in behind me, his friendly smile changes into a contemplative expression—narrowed eyes, tight jaw. He must be concentrating.

I pull Pepper toward the chairs, and Sailor leans away from us. Maybe he's in the zone—or this is part of the process—like he has to build up the mental energy to do what he's about to do. I sit, and Pepper eyes me before she settles in next to me—he's not making the best first impression.

I clear my throat, ready to get this all started. "This is who I was telling you about," I say. "She's the one who's cursed." I gesture toward Pepper.

He eyes her—scanning her from head to toe—and he crosses his arms over his chest. "I can tell." His voice sounds tense now—completely unlike the way it was before.

"I promise I don't bite," Pepper offers.

"It's no offense, you're just projecting some really strong vibrations," Sailor says.

Are vibrations good or bad? Based on his attitude and body language, I'm going to go with not a good thing right now, but

---

CHRISTINA

we're here and he seemed confident before that he could help, so we have to try, right?

"She has the amulet we talked about," I say to try and move things along. This isn't going as smoothly as I'd hoped. "Give him the keys," I tell Pepper.

She pulls them out of her pocket, and Sailor jumps up from the couch and slams into the shelves, knocking potted plants and crystals to the ground.

"Put that away!" He throws his arms up like a shield and crouches down next to the couch.

Pepper glances at me before she complies and slides the amulet back into her pocket.

"What's wrong?" I ask.

"I can't help you," he says. "I'll refund all your money. I need you to leave and take that thing with you."

No. This can't be right. He said he could do it. He had an idea that we've never tried before. He's supposed to be what makes this better. "But you said you could help," I say, my voice taking on a desperate edge—because I am, in fact, desperate.

"This is above my skill level." He jumps on the couch, races past us, and opens the door, hiding himself behind it.

Oh my god. He's kicking us out. I shake my head. "I don't understand—"

"Come on." Pepper stands next to me, holding out her hand.

"But he's supposed to fix this. He's supposed to . . ." What? What is he supposed to do?

"He can't." Her voice is so calm, it makes me want to scream even louder, but instead I let her pull me to my feet.

CHRISTINA

"I'm sorry," she tells him as we pass and head outside.

"You seem really nice, I'm sorry I can't help you," Sailor says as he closes the door behind him and the lock clicks.

I stand there staring up at the trailer—standing in the hope I had as it burns up and dies inside me. The dark shadow is still there—looming—mocking. We never should've come here. I never should've gotten my hopes up. For a fleeting second, I truly thought this was our answer. I can't believe how wrong I was.

Tears slip down my cheeks, and Pepper wraps me in her arms.

"It's okay," she whispers in my ear.

"No. No, it's not okay." I cry into her shoulder. "He knew things about me that he shouldn't have. I don't understand. He was supposed to help. This isn't okay at all."

"I don't know what he told you. And I'm sorry, but there's nothing we can do."

"We can't just give up." I want to run back in there. I want to ask him why he seemed so sure before and then he kicked us out. I step away, and Pepper grabs my hand. I still have leftover spray paint on my fingernails. My heart sinks a little more. I feel like such a fool.

"This is what I didn't want to happen. This is why I didn't tell you this time around. You get so obsessed—"

"Am I supposed to do nothing?" I shouldn't yell. I'm not mad at her—I'm just mad, which is why I'm crying, and that makes me even angrier. But crying is better than punching people, and I'd really like to punch someone right about now.

"That's not what I said."

CHRISTINA

"You might have given up, but I haven't. I won't. I will fight for us." Sailor might be a really good scam artist, or maybe this curse is more powerful than anything he's ever seen. But I'm not going to run scared from it.

"And you will drive yourself into an anxiety-induced panic attack."

I want to tell her she's wrong—but she's not. I'm just not going to let this slide. I can't let her go through this again. "Then help me. We'll figure out how to destroy that amulet without him," I say. "Please, Pepper. Please."

There's still time before I have to get to the haunted house for the night, so Pepper takes me to the one place that always cheers me up—Brain Freeze. The neon sign outside is a greeting on any day that's been "just one of those days"—and that sure as hell has been today. The look of sheer terror on Sailor's face when Pepper pulled out her keys is forever engrained in my mind. Or maybe it'll disappear just like she does in seven days.

I don't know what is worse, the knowing it's going to happen, or the knowing there's not a damn thing we can do about it.

Pepper holds the door open for me, and I step inside. The scent of freshly baked waffle cones is my greeting. "Do you know what you want to get?" she asks me.

What is the perfect flavor after my soul has been crushed and needs to be reconstructed so I can keep on living? Is it cherry? "I don't know."

"Maybe you'll have to taste a few." She gives me an encouraging smile. She knows me better than anyone in the world. How am I going to live without her? But the answer is I just will. I won't remember her. My throat gets thick even without trying any of the frozen milky creations.

"I do like to sample." I struggle to put on a brave face. She's trying and I need to, too.

"I know." She squeezes me into her side, and it feels like coming home.

There are two people ahead of us, so I scan the board.

"You know, there are no less than two cups of sugar in a gallon of ice cream," the boy in front of us is saying.

"Kevin?" Pepper says, and the boy spins around.

He looks vaguely familiar—the traditional college frat boy type with shaggy hair and khaki pants.

"Hey, Pepper." The boy holds his hand up like he wants to high-five, but Pepper doesn't move.

"Where the hell have you been?" she asks.

"Is this your mom?" the boy with him asks. He looks almost exactly like the first except he hasn't shaved for a long time.

Pepper deadpans, "Hell no. I don't want any part of . . ." She gestures to Kevin's entire being.

"Damn," the boy says.

"I've been doing some very important things for the store," Kevin says, ignoring his friend. "There's this company that can create custom costumes. Just think if we could offer that service."

That's it. He's the guy who reorganized all the boxes and pissed Dewy off. The one who almost lost my very important order.

CHRISTINA

Pepper shakes her head like she can't believe the words coming out of his mouth. "It's a retail job, Kevin. The only important thing you need to do is show up and help the customers."

"You'll see. It's really going to revolutionize things," he says.

His buddy hands him his cone. "Let's go, bro."

"We expect you to be there tomorrow," Pepper yells after him as they walk out the door.

"What was that all about?" I ask.

She stares after them. "Just someone who shouldn't be working at the store."

"I remember. He seems really enthusiastic." I grimace. That's the kind way of putting how annoyingly arrogant that guy seems to be. I can't imagine what it would be like to work with him. "Wasn't murder on the table before? What happened to that?"

"I haven't forgotten. Timing is key," she says, then gestures to the ice cream case and the attendant who's waiting for us, a smile on her face.

"Ready?" she asks. Her multicolored hair is piled on top of her head, and her pink visor matches her lips. Her bedazzled name tag says SALLY.

"She's going to need to taste a few," Pepper answers.

"Of course," Sally says. "What can I get for you?"

Pepper gestures with her head like, *Go ahead*, and since there's no one behind us, I taste at least six flavors before I settle on Fruity Pebbles. It's the happiness I need in my life put into an ice cream flavor. She pays for my cone and her cup of strawberry, and we head outside to sit on a shady bench.

CHRISTINA

The boys from before are down the street chatting in a larger group of college students. They don't act much different than high school boys, pushing one another around and being loud enough so their jeering is easily heard from where I'm seated.

"I know we talked about murder, but maybe that guy wants to take your job." I gesture toward them.

"I won't trick anyone," she says.

"Even if they deserve it?"

She looks at me like I know the answer, and I do, but that doesn't mean I think it's fair.

"What if he *wants* it?" I ask, and she raises her brows in response. "Come on. That guy wants to be important. I'm not saying trick him, I'm saying that you could tell him it's the most important job at The Dead of Night, and that isn't a lie."

She tips her head from side to side like maybe she's actually contemplating my suggestion. "I don't know."

"Just think about it, okay?" I reach over and squeeze her knee. "For me."

"I won't lie, but if he wants it, I'll gladly hand it over."

Noted. I smile in response. Now I just need to find this guy and slip him the word that a big promotion could be up for grabs if he's willing. I get Pepper's stance, and it's honorable, but I didn't make that promise to her or anyone else—and I will do whatever I have to do to keep my girl.

CHRISTINA

2 DAYS
UNTIL THE STORE CLOSES

Christina

When trying to locate college-age boys in the town of Clover Creek, one only has to understand the inner workings of a college boy to know exactly where he'd be. That's why Gamer's Galaxy is the first on my list of places to hit up in the small moment of time that I have during my prep period before getting to the haunted house for our final night.

Did I try several other places in days past? Yes. I went back to Brain Freeze, then I tried the bookstore (and of course he wasn't there, but I did get a new book about a girl named Amanda Dean on her wedding day), and I took a walk down Orange Street (also known as the busiest street in town)—but nothing. I then tried the grocery store to kill two birds with one stone—and because college kids eat, don't they? (Apparently not.) I finally wised up and asked my students. Which was what I should've done in the first place, but live and learn, I suppose.

Now that I'm here with the neon lights, bells ringing all around, the pool tables, and even a bar with a line of beers on tap, I realize I should've known to try this place first. It's basically Vegas for kids who can't gamble the real way, only by swiping their card in exchange for the hope to win tickets instead of cash. It's also the closest to gambling in Clover Creek.

I weave my way through the standup arcade games, and by the ones with plastic motorcycles you "ride" to play. There are basketball hoops, spinning wheels with flashing lights, and a whole little store where people can exchange those precision tickets for cheap junk—like giant stuffed monkeys.

With most of the schools still in session—high school the first to get out in the next thirty minutes, followed by elementary, then middle school—the place is pretty empty except for some older men at the bar, the people who are working, and the college kids. Bingo.

A group of four boys are hanging around *Mario Kart*—two of them playing while the other two watch. Their bodies move left and right while the two who are seated turn the wheels this way and that, and they all yell at the screen. One of the drivers hits something in the road and goes spinning. By matter of deduction, two of them could be Kevin—they are both white, have shaggy blondish-brownish hair, and are wearing cargo pants. One of them is playing the game, and the other is standing behind.

"Look out for the Spike Bomb," one boy standing behind the players—the one who is definitely not Kevin—says.

"Banana peel. Banana peel!" The other points and jumps.

"Did you know that a banana is scientifically a berry, but a

CHRISTINA

strawberry isn't?" One boy who's playing jerks the wheel to avoid the hazard. That's got to be him. Even from the brief interactions at the Halloween store and the ice cream shop, it seems the most likely.

Though I prepared ideas of what to say to him, I probably should've thought a little more about how to approach him before I walked through the door. Now I'm just awkwardly watching a group of young guys playing a video game. Does this count as stalking? I make a mental note to look it up later to be safe, but for the time being, I'm going to embrace it.

There's a flash on the screen, and the guy playing who isn't Kevin punches the air while Congratulations is illuminated in big bright letters.

"GG," he says to Kevin, and the two slap hands—front to back and then fist bump. The winner stays seated, but Kevin gets up and one of the other guys slides into the seat he's just left vacant. As he comes around to the back of the seats to presumably watch the next racers, he catches my eye, and I wave.

Here goes nothing.

He smiles and scrunches his brows, likely trying to figure out where he knows me from as he walks my way. "Hey," he says. "Do I know you?"

"Not really. But you know my girlfriend, Pepper."

"That's it. Brain Freeze." He hits his hand on his leg. "She didn't send you to come looking for me, did she?"

"No. Why? Are you supposed to be at work?"

He shrugs. "It's possible. So why are you here?"

This is my chance. "You seem like the kind of guy that doesn't like to do menial tasks. I know we don't know each

---

CHRISTINA

other, but you give off the vibes of 'upper management.'" I spread my hands out to make a show of the title—to make it seem much grander than what it actually is. I've got to sell this.

"Totally," he agrees.

"So what would you say if I knew how you could get the most important job The Dead of Night has to offer?" I try to keep my voice casual, but my adrenaline is racing.

He narrows his eyes. "I'm listening."

I look around like I'm pretending I don't want anyone to overhear me, but what I'm really worried about is that he'll hear my heart ricocheting in my chest, or maybe be able to tell—even in this low lighting—that I'm starting to sweat. Focus, Christina. You can do this. "I'm ready for Pepper to do something else, but in order for that to happen, she needs to find someone willing to take her place."

Kevin rubs his chin—either to try and look smart or maybe he has an itch. "Her job does seem pretty cush. She's not even ever on the schedule—comes and goes as she pleases."

"Exactly," I say. "Which is perfect for you so you can do all your other company research, am I right?" Okay, it should not be this easy, should it? Maybe I need to tone it down.

"Does it come with benefits?"

"So many." It just depends on one's definition of "benefit." Eternal life might be exactly what he's looking for—who am I to judge?

"What's the catch?" he asks, and I'm glad that before I walked in the door, I'd practiced ten different ways this conversation could have gone, even if I didn't know how I was going to start it.

CHRISTINA

"See, I knew you were a smart guy." Everyone loves to be complimented—especially guys like Kevin. "The catch is you have to come and say you want the job before midnight at the store on November second."

"Midnight?"

"Yep." I nod like this is more than logical. "Corporate policy." I wink. "They need to make sure the person is truly dedicated, and what better way than to see if they'll show up at that specific day and time."

He bobs his head up and down. "Okay. Yeah. Makes sense."

"So you'll take the job?"

He rubs his chin again—maybe he has a rash. "Can you even offer me her position? Doesn't there have to be, like, interviews or something?"

Well, shit. Maybe this kid isn't as gullible as I thought. "Nope, she just has to pick her replacement. And she picks you."

"Why isn't she telling me this, then?"

That's a really great question, and although she said she would talk to him, I wanted to get to him first—I wanted to sell it, whereas I'm sure she wants to be ethical about the whole thing. Oh, how I love her. "She didn't want you to feel pressured. Look, she's going to downplay it, and tell you a bunch of weird things to make sure you really want the job."

"Like a test?"

"Exactly like a test. See, I knew you'd get it," I say. "So when she talks to you, no matter what she says, just tell her you want the job."

"That's it?"

CHRISTINA

"That's it." My heart stops as he stares at me. He has to say yes. He just has to.

He holds out a fist, and it takes me a second to realize he wants me to bump it, so I do. "Thanks for the heads-up. Wait. Why are you helping me?"

"No. That's where you're wrong. *You're* helping *me*. I need her to get a different job, so really this is all just selfish of me." Sometimes the truth is stranger than fiction.

"Yeah. Cool. Well, you're welcome, then." He laughs.

I laugh with him. "Yeah, thank you. And don't forget you have to be there before midnight on the second for her to hand the position over to you; otherwise, they won't let you take the job." Literally.

"I got it." He taps the side of his head. His friends hoot in the background, and he swivels in that direction. "I should—"

"Go." I practically shoo him away.

He turns and heads back to the game without even saying goodbye, but I don't care. I rush out of the arcade, hop into my car, and head for the haunted house. I did it. I actually did it. And now we have a chance to finally break this dumb curse, and maybe I wasn't completely forthcoming about what would happen, maybe it's selfish of me, but I could argue that Pepper hasn't been selfish enough. Sometimes you have to do things you don't like for the person you love—and I love Pepper. She's done her time; now someone else can deal with the curse.

CHRISTINA

0 DAYS

UNTIL THE STORE CLOSES

Christina

Two nights ago, the town of Clover Creek celebrated Halloween. Two nights ago, we had a record number of people come through the haunted house. So many, in fact, that we blew past our fundraising goal, and we ended up staying open later to accommodate everyone. The kids were hyped, and since we'd done such a great job, Principal Wilkson said we could delay starting breakdown for a couple of days—and that he'd even come to help.

As glad as I am that the event is over, part of me wants to rewind time to do it all again. Putting on shows or events like this is difficult and stressful, but there's nothing like the rush of the final curtain call. This Halloween will go down in the record books for sure. Or at least it will in my own mind—as long as I get to keep all these memories.

As she promised, Pepper talked to Kevin. The way she told

the story of that interaction implied she was a little skeptical that he would show up—even though he had seemed to say he wanted to do it. "He's unreliable," she told me. Which may be true, but he's our only hope.

That's why on the last night, Pepper and I are having a picnic in the store—complete with candles and wine, and a circle of monsters leering at us from the shadows. Not real ones, of course, just the decorations from the store that have been shifted around. Today is the official last day it's open, but still, there's something spookily romantic about being watched over by a ten-foot-tall skeleton.

"This reminds me of our first date," she says as she pours prosecco into two stemless plastic wineglasses.

"Really?" I say. "Tell me about it." My idea and her idea of our first date will be totally different, won't they? For me, I'd probably count the time we went and got tacos, or maybe that time I ran into her at Déjà Brew—which she has since told me was no accident.

She smiles and sets the bottle down. "I took you on a picnic in Whispering Woods."

"And I let you have a second date?" I tease. The idea of me agreeing to a date in a cemetery is laughable, but with Pepper asking, I could easily see how I was persuaded.

"To be fair, I didn't tell you that's where I was taking you."

"That makes more sense." I take a sip of my wine, the flavors of green apple and honeysuckle flooding my mouth while little bubbles tickle my tongue.

"I didn't bring wine, though, just Italian soda."

CHRISTINA

So she was being chivalrous—didn't want to make assumptions or make me feel pressured in case I wasn't a wine girl. Smart. "What flavor?"

"Blood orange."

I scrunch my lips together. "I would've preferred straw—"

"Strawberry," Pepper says with me. "Yeah, I know that now. But you still kissed me."

"I kissed you on our first date?" I pretend to be aghast, but I could see how I'd want to get lost in her stunning blue eyes, or just be closer to her. Even now, sitting here, knees touching isn't enough. Pepper has this aura, a spirit that pulls me in, and I want to be caught up in her orbit. "You must've done something right."

"I was so nervous. I had no idea what I was doing. But"—she shrugs—"it ended up okay. Better than okay actually."

"I'm glad you asked me out."

"Me too."

I reach over and lay my hand on top of hers. "What do you think will happen tonight?"

Her lips pull to the side in a kind of sad half smile. "I don't know. We've been here before. It was the first year, and we weren't waiting for anyone exactly—just happened to be nearby when the rain started to fall and, well . . . you know."

I finger the place on my arm where the skin is smooth. "And last year?"

"We were at your place. You made fettuccine Alfredo, and we lay on the couch watching some rom-com you'd picked out. I admit I didn't pay much attention to it because I wanted to memorize the way we felt there together, you in my arms. The

CHRISTINA

way your chest shook when you giggled. Then we went to bed and . . ."

She doesn't have to fill in the details. Even without my memories, I know what she's going to say. I might not have remembered her, but I do remember waking up one morning in early November and feeling incredibly lonely just like I had felt the year before. It was as if I'd lost something—but I could never figure out what it was. As the days passed, the ache in my chest eased, and then before I knew it, it was August and I met Pepper and, well, here we are—again.

She takes a sip of her wine and sets the glass down. "What do you want me to do if it doesn't work out this time?" She's not looking at me—her gaze fixed somewhere on the blanket we're sitting on, maybe on the amulet that's attached to the hearse keys that are lying next to the bottle of prosecco. They look so insignificant, and yet they hold so much power. Our fate, more specifically.

"Why are you asking me that?"

"Because it's your life, too. Your parents made you an amazing offer, and I . . . I don't want to stop you—"

"We try again." My voice is clear and strong.

Her gaze connects with mine—eyes glassy. "Are you sure that's what you want?"

"I'm sure." Because this is the kind of thing you fight for—a person who's willing to watch you fade away and keeps coming back no matter how hard it has to be for her. That quote—if you love something, let it go—rushes through my mind. I've never given it much thought before until this moment. That's what Pepper has had to do—she's had to let me

CHRISTINA

go over and over—but she's had so much hope, determination, and most importantly, love to help us find a way back to each other. She has sacrificed so much for me, and I'm willing to do the same. "I won't tell you how to do it, but if there's a way we could have more time..." I don't blame her for how she's handled this. I don't know what I would do in her position.

"I'll do my best."

"I know you will." I lean forward and kiss her—under the watchful eyes of a giant werewolf, a space alien, a grim reaper, a ten-foot skeleton, and a large tree with an empty swing that moves when you get too close to it—and it's the most romantic thing ever. I want to memorize her lips, the taste of apples on her breath, the smell of her perfume. I don't want it to be our last kiss, but if it is, I need it to be perfect. For her, since she will have to remember it for us both. I reach up to stroke her jaw, and a loud bang has me jumping back before I get the chance.

I quickly glance at my phone. If that isn't Kevin coming in, I don't know what's about to happen, but we're really close to midnight. How did I lose track of the time?

"I'm surprised he showed," Pepper says as she stands.

"Hello." Kevin's voice echoes through the darkness. If I didn't know the monsters circling us weren't real, I'd be terrified right now.

"We're in here," Pepper calls back.

The light from his phone comes into view before he does. "So this is one of the perks, huh? Can I bring dates here, too?"

"Probably," I answer.

"It's not all fun and games," Pepper says.

"Cool. This gives me even more ideas." He stumbles over to

CHRISTINA

one of the giant monster statues—the werewolf with glowing red eyes and ripped jeans, claws extended like it's ready to attack. "Did you know that giraffes are thirty times more likely to get struck by lightning than people?"

"What does that have to do with anything?" Pepper asks, and I'm thinking the same thing.

"Just a cool fact." He bops the monster on the nose. "I'm going to make some changes around here."

Pepper gives me the look—like I-can't-believe-this-guy. I can't either, but I take a deep breath and steady my nerves. He's about to make it so Pepper and I can be together forever, so the least I can do is be nice.

"It's not your problem," I whisper to her.

"Do you hear that?" he yells at the monster. "I'm going to be your boss." He punches the monster statue, and it rocks back and forth.

"Hey, come on, don't do that." Pepper goes to step forward, but I grab her hand. "Are you drunk or something?" she asks him.

"Celebrating my promotion," he says, walking toward another monster statue before punching it, too. It's not super aggressive or anything, more like he thinks he's playing a game—plus he's been drinking, so there's that. I take a step behind Pepper just in case. If this is how he is when he's happy, I don't know if I want to see him if he's upset. Oh shit. Will we have to move away from here? He *will* remember us, but we won't remember him, will we? I didn't think this through well enough—or leave myself proper notes that would be big enough clues without breaking any of the rules.

CHRISTINA

"I told you, it's not exactly a promotion," Pepper says.

"But it's *not* not a promotion either," I say, even though my adrenaline is pumping. We need him—need this. It's a necessary evil.

"I said I wouldn't trick him." She pivots so that her gaze can connect to mine.

"And you aren't. It's not really anything. So we're both right." It's a slippery slope, but I'm not letting this opportunity go. I snatch the keys off the blanket. "All you have to do is take these." I hold them out to him.

"You hear that, big guy? I. Am. The. Boss. Now." He punches the plush statue again, and the plastic nose caves in. "Holy shit." He laughs and spins around, but his feet tangle up, and he slams into the monster's legs, making the statue fall on top of him.

Oh shit.

Pepper and I rush over. Kevin is knocked out cold.

I grab his arm so I can shove the keys in his hand.

"He has to be awake," Pepper says. "He has to agree to take the job."

"What?"

"It's a rule. He has to agree," she tells me.

My heart stops. She never told me about this before. "But he did. He's here." I yank on his arm, and a snore escapes his mouth. "Wake up!" I yell at him, but it's no use. He smells strongly of alcohol and weed.

"I'm sorry." Pepper holds her hand out. There is sadness in her eyes. She tried to warn me this wouldn't work, but it was so perfect.

CHRISTINA

"No." We have only a few minutes left, but I'm not giving up. I glance at the amulet still clutched in my hand.

"Christina, give me the keys."

Something so small, and yet it holds so much power. It's not fair. This is my life. And I should get a say in how I live it. I shake my head. "No. I won't do it. I'm not going to lose you again." A rush of anger surges through me.

"So what? You're going to take my place? Don't be ridiculous."

"Why is it ridiculous? You've done it. Maybe it's only fair if I take a turn, and then we can switch back and forth until we figure out how to break it for good." That's an idea we haven't tried before, I bet. It could work. Couldn't it?

"I can't ask you to give up your life—"

"You aren't asking me. I'm choosing to. I agree to it—for you. I agree to take the job. I agree to keep my memories of you. They're all I'll have, and I'm tired of them being ripped away from me." I say the words out loud in case it matters, which I am guessing it does.

"You have a family."

"So do you. I bet they'd love to see you."

"It's not the same," she says. "I've done it before. I promise I will find you again. I can't let you leave all of this behind for me. I will take the job," she says even louder, her voice echoing around us.

I cup her cheek. "Don't you get it? I'd do anything for you."

She cups my cheek back. "And I would do anything for you." Then she kisses me with a fierceness she hasn't before—or at least I haven't remembered. She pulls my body into hers

---

CHRISTINA

and runs her fingers down my arm, grabbing my hand that's holding the keys. The ring is still looped around my finger, and she closes her hand around mine—so we're both holding on.

I wrap my other arm around her waist. "I won't let you go." I don't want to. And we were so close, it's cruel that it won't work out for us.

"I'll see you again soon." She presses her forehead to mine.

A tear slips down my cheek. "It's not enough." My chest clenches so tight, I can barely breathe. A sadness so intense overtakes me that I don't know how I'll ever recover.

"It'll be okay," she says. "Just give me the keys."

The keys. These stupid keys. I clench them tightly in my hand. I want to chuck them across the room. But that won't stop what's coming. "I'm coming with you." That's all I want. To be with her no matter what. I can't lose her. Not again.

"Christina—"

"No. I'm coming with you." I squeeze her hand tighter. "I won't give you the keys, but you can hold on to them with me, and we can see what happens." I have no idea how the magic works or how it will choose which of us to take or if it will take both of us, but I don't care. I have to try.

"Together? Are you sure?"

"I got you," I tell her as more tears slip from my eyes.

"I got you," she says back.

This time I take the lead, and I kiss her with everything I have. My heart slams against my ribs, and my skin tingles. *This* is love. It's sacrificing everything, and I'm ready to do it. Pepper has already had to do it more than once. She is my person, and

CHRISTINA

no matter what happens, we will find our way back to each other. I have to believe that.

I hold on to that thought, that hope, and all the love we share as the world seems to vortex around me—and while we stand there, hands, bodies, and hearts connected, it must become midnight, because everything goes black.

CHRISTINA

363 DAYS
UNTIL HALLOWEEN

Christina

When I open my eyes, I'm still in the Halloween store, except it's different. The monster circle that surrounded our picnic spot is gone—and so are the discount signs, and Kevin is nowhere in sight. The racks are stocked again with costumes, but instead of Halloween, the store's theme has changed to Masquerade. The one thing that is the same is that Pepper is still with me.

"What's happening?" I ask her.

"I don't know," she says, her gaze shifting back and forth—her hand holding mine even tighter than before.

"What do you mean? Is this not normal?" She has done this more than once, so what does it mean that she doesn't know what's going on?

"This has never happened before—"

Smoke rises from the floor, and a scroll appears in front of us. My heart is pounding now for a completely different reason. I pull myself closer to Pepper, and she wraps her other hand around my arm, securing me in place.

"This is how I got the rules my first year," she says.

"So we did it? We're stuck together?" My voice shakes. I don't know whether I should be happy or sad. I'll miss my family, but at least I have Pepper. At least we can be together.

The scroll unrolls.

It reads:

Congratulations.

You've done it. You've broken the curse of The Dead of Night Emporium Incorporated. While we are sad to see you go, we are impressed with the sacrifice you were willing to make, and to show our appreciation, we are gifting you this store. As with all The Dead of Night stores, it will be kept properly supplied, but after you read this letter, your memories of how you were able to break this curse will be removed. You have to understand, we have a business to run, and we can't have you spreading the word.

Christina, because of your willingness to sacrifice yourself for Pepper, you will have your memories of her returned. Another gift from us. You can't say we aren't giving, now, can you?

We appreciate your service, until next time.

Upper Management

A puff of black smoke, a flash of light, and it's gone. I blink a few times, allowing my eyes to adjust. Everything

---

CHRISTINA

is the same. The store with its stocked shelves, and Pepper is here with me—her hand holding mine—and I remember her. I remember *everything*. Three Halloweens' worth of memories flood into my head, making me so happy, I could cry again.

"What just happened?" Pepper asks.

"We did it." I turn to face her, and she has shock in her eyes. "I don't know what we did, but we did something." We broke the curse. I can feel it just like I can feel a set of keys clenched in our hands—cold metal against warm skin.

She glances around again like she's taking it all in and then pulls me toward the front window. Outside is Ginger Street. Across the way is Déjà Brew. We're still in Clover Creek, and the clock tower that peeks out from behind the buildings says 12:03. "We did it," she repeats.

I nod, and she holds me to her. I hug her back with all my strength. She is here with me, and now I never have to let her go.

She pulls away and looks around again. "And now we own a costume store?" She laughs.

It's my turn to look at everything. It's all so much to take in. "And now we own a costume store," I confirm, and laugh with her. "It feels surreal. Almost too good to be true."

"Because now you get to work in the ever-lucrative costume industry with me."

"Well, there's that," I say. "But more importantly, I get to be with you. Which means you're stuck with me."

She laughs again. "Oh, no. *You* are the one who's stuck with *me*."

I kiss her cheek. "That's fine. Because you got me."

She kisses my forehead. "I got you, forever."

CHRISTINA

ACKNOWLEDGMENTS

I did it again! I can hardly believe it.

And like before, I first would like to thank you, the reader, for taking the time to read Pepper and Christina's story. There are so many books out there, and you chose to spend your time with *these* characters. That means more to me than you will ever know. (And if it isn't too much to ask, I'd be honored if you would consider leaving a review—that's the best way to help other readers find this book, and it's so helpful to us authors. I've also heard for every review you leave an author, you'll have a mind-blowing orgasm. Now, I don't know if that's true or not, but either way it couldn't hurt.)

Halloween has been one of my favorite holidays for as long as I can remember. Many of the things Pepper says about Halloween mirror my own thoughts about the season. I love dressing up and getting together with friends! And what isn't fun about fun-size candy? Nothing. Exactly! Getting to write this story has been an absolute dream.

I'm so grateful to a lot of people who made this novel

ACKNOWLEDGMENTS

possible. To create a book it takes a team, and I've been lucky to work with the best.

First is my agent, Eva Scalzo. Girl, I love you! Thanks for always being there when I've needed you!

At Berkley publishing, a GIANT thank-you to Esi Sogah (editor), Genni Eccles (editorial assistant), Ariana Abad and Kaila Mundell-Hill (publicists), Elisha Katz and Kalie Barnes-Young (marketers), Caitlyn Kenny (production editor), Susanna Gentili (cover artist), Colleen Reinhart (cover designer), Alison Cnockaert (interior designer), Jennifer Wong (production manager), Christine Legon (managing editor), Joan Matthews (copyeditor), and Lindsey Tulloch and Pam Feinstein (proofreaders).

Maurine Trich, you did it again, too! Thanks for our lunch talks; they helped so much!

A huge thank-you to my girls in the group chat—Beth-A, Heidi, Jenn-A, and Jodi. I love you more than words will ever express. Empowered women empower women—and that's what you do! Everyone should be as lucky to have friends like you!

Thank you to my Rosebuds authors and #TeamEva authors! Having a safe space to talk about all bookish things, good and bad, is something every author needs.

And last but not least, thanks to my family for putting up with me on deadline, when I'm there but also not because my characters are having conversations in my head, and all the times in between.

A Hexcellent Chance to Fall in Love

ANN ROSE

READERS GUIDE

DISCUSSION QUESTIONS

1. The first and most important question: What do you love about Halloween? How would you feel if you were trapped in a Halloween store like Pepper?

2. Which POV was your favorite, Christina's or Pepper's? Why?

3. Did their romance feel believable to you?

4. One of the themes of the book is "What are you willing to give up for the sake of love?" Do you think one character or the other was willing to risk more? What would you have done if you were in Pepper's situation? Do you think her actions were justified? What about Christina's?

5. Did any part of this book evoke a particular emotion in you? Which part, and what emotion did the book make you feel?

6. Was there any part of the plot, aspects of the characters, or structure of the story that frustrated or upset you? If so, why?

7. Speaking of structure, this novel has the reader possibly believing we are reading a linear story, but we eventually find out that's not the case. How did you feel about this structure, and do you think it worked? Why or why not?

8. When did you sense there was something off about the structure? Were there any particular clues that gave it away for you?

9. Do you think the setting and atmosphere of the novel affected the romance in any way?

10. How did you feel about the heat level of this book?

11. When we found out that Pepper had been sacrificing her own happiness just for her short time with Christina, how did that make you feel?

12. What do you think happens to Pepper and Christina after the book ends? Where does their story go from there?

ENHANCE YOUR BOOK CLUB DISCUSSION

- Throw a Halloween-themed event—even if it isn't Halloween!
- Have everyone wear a costume.
- Ask everyone to bring a Halloween-inspired dish to share.
- Have everyone bring their favorite candy to share.

Keep reading for a preview of

THE SEEMINGLY IMPOSSIBLE LOVE LIFE OF AMANDA DEAN,

out now!

APRIL 2019

It was totally normal to be terrified the day of your own wedding, right?

Maybe *terrified* wasn't the right word. Mandy was nervous. Anxious.

Petrified.

Her stomach seemed to shimmy its way further and further into her chest as she sat alone in her private hotel suite, staring at the long gown hanging from the curtain rod. All Mandy had to do was slip into the first—and last—white dress she would ever wear. Well, that and do her makeup and get her hair done and about a million other things. But she hesitated. More specifically, she couldn't move even if she wanted to. Had she really been so lucky not only to find the love of her life, but also to be getting married?

This was a good thing. Something she'd always wanted.

And now, she was mere hours away from walking down an

aisle sprinkled with rose petals in various shades of pink—why couldn't she breathe?

No.

Today was going to be fine.

Better than fine.

She took a deep sip from the coffee mug death-gripped in her hand, the steam fogging her vision as she continued to stare at her dress. There wasn't anything particularly extraordinary about the garment hanging there. It was simple, understated—except for the small train. It was definitely not something Mandy was used to picking out. She had always been known for her affection for black—or shades of black—in all her clothing choices, but that day, as she stood on the little podium in front of the three-way mirrors and felt the buttery silk lining caressing her skin as she was zipped inside the cream-colored gown, she never wanted to take it off. Except now, putting it on seemed impossible.

Or maybe it was that *today* seemed impossible.

On the surface, it all seemed simple—small tasks she needed to complete to get to her moment of walking down that aisle—but there was nothing simple about getting married.

It wasn't that she thought she was making the wrong choice. No, that wasn't it at all. This was a day Mandy had dreamed about for years—even decades, if she thought hard enough about it. The lace dress hanging on its satin hanger. The pink and white peonies tied together with gold ribbon. The light blue Chuck Taylors with *I DO* written on the soles. They were all a part of this perfect vision she had for herself on this day, and they were all waiting for her.

Soon over two hundred people would be waiting for her too. But here—*now*—in this hotel room, it was Mandy alone with her thoughts. And this, being alone, stirred memories inside her belly like ice cubes in a blender, sending gooseflesh rippling all over her skin. She'd kill for a margarita right about now. The hotel minibar was looking quite tempting—even at fifty dollars a miniature bottle—not as small as the airplane ones, but also not full-size, completely overpriced, and a terrible choice this early in the day . . . even if it would dull the nerves raging inside her.

Mandy had been in love more times than she wanted to count. Her heart had been broken just as many. Would this wedding mark the last time she'd put her whole soul into someone? Or was this the inevitable beginning of the end, and she'd be left scooping up the shattered pieces of her heart yet again? Mandy both knew it was different this time and struggled with the sense of impending doom as if the other shoe— a black Chuck with *I DON'T* emblazoned on the bottom—was about to drop and crush all the dreams she'd been constructing for as long as she could remember.

These were *not* the kinds of thoughts someone should have on their wedding day, but they spun through her mind and stuck like melted marshmallow. A cobweb of white gooey uncertainty that she needed to clean away.

The Belgian waffle she special-ordered sat untouched in front of Mandy as she took another long drink of her coffee and watched the pulp in her orange juice drift to the bottom of her glass. Edmund hated fresh-squeezed orange juice, said juice should be sipped and never chewed, but Mandy loved to catch the little bulbs of fruit flesh between her teeth and bite down. Little explosions, like nature's Pop Rocks. But she couldn't bring herself to drink it today, or even take a bite. Instead, she alternated between staring at her dress and staring at the uninspired artwork hanging on the wall. It was the basic bulk buy most hotels did—some cheap reproduction they put in a gaudy frame in an attempt to make it look expensive. Mandy could've painted something better with her eyes closed.

Thankfully the bed was comfortable enough, and the coffee was hot—unlike her shower. She tried to convince herself it wasn't a sign of how things would go today. But the fact that she had woken up late, and the icy water, and then room service forgot the bacon with her order, well, things weren't off to a great start. She sat in the hotel-issued bathrobe, towel wrapped around her wet hair, trying to get warm—willing herself to believe all those things were not omens or harbingers of doom, and that they, in fact, had nothing to do with each other. They were all just flukes. One-offs. Not the universe's way of preparing her for what was to come. She really should go down to the desk and complain, but that would be one more thing to add to Mandy's to-do list, and she couldn't move.

Why was there this great importance placed on weddings anyway? One day in a relationship blown out of proportion compared to all the other days a couple proved their commitment and love for each other. Why today and not last Tuesday? Not to say that Mandy hadn't bought into the hype. Hell, she *was* the hype. Teen Mandy could've looked at bridal magazines for hours. Adult Mandy just had to have the ever-fashionable s'mores bar at her reception complete with miniature chalkboard signs that named each individual ingredient even though it was an additional charge. Add-on packages were Mandy's Achilles' heel. They were literally made for her. She needed everything to be perfect. But why? And for whom?

It was just a day, wasn't it?

Marriage was for a lifetime, right?

"The Imperial March" blasted from Mandy's cell, and she quickly swept it up. "Yes, I'm up, and I have food."

"Good," her mom said. "We don't want you passing out during your vows."

"That can't really happen, can it?" There was a reason Mom's ringtone was what it was. Mandy's mother was the queen of giving others just one more thing to worry about. If Mandy actually made it down the aisle without slipping on one of the rose petals, now there was a possibility she'd end up on the ground in a dead faint, embarrassing herself more than she had in the fifth-grade talent show, and *that* was beyond humiliating. How many people there would be repeat audience members? Isa would laugh her ass off. Aunt Mary would snap the world's worst candids that would haunt Mandy at every family event from now until the end of time.

"Not if you eat something." Mom tried to sound reassuring, but once the anxiety train got rolling down Mandy's track, there was little that could slow it. "Have you talked to Isa today?" It was like Mom knew exactly what Mandy needed. Her best friend. The person she'd been able to count on for anything and everything since kindergarten. Just hearing her name seemed to calm the swarming hornets in Mandy's stomach.

"I texted her, but she's probably not awake yet." Mandy

used the side of her fork to slice off a piece of waffle, dipped it in the now-cold maple syrup, and shoved it into her mouth. She was not fainting today. No way. No how.

"Well, I'm sure you'll hear from her soon."

Mandy hoped. Isa was the only one who would be able to convince Mandy she was just being silly with her thoughts of "signs from the universe." "You picked up the programs from the printer, right? And have the box of favors to give to the caterer? Oh, and did you get a chance to call—"

"Everything is taken care of. There's nothing you need to worry about right now except for making sure *you* get ready," Mom said. "Don't forget the hairstylist will be there within the hour, so you need to get a move on if you're going to be on time for pictures."

"Yes, Mom," Mandy said with a mouthful. Despite not being hungry, she thought the waffle was delicious—crisp on the outside, and soft, still a little warm in the middle.

"Now don't get angry," Mom said, and Mandy's heart started pounding. Nothing good ever came after those words. Like the time Mom took Mandy to get a perm. Or the time Mom threw out Mandy's entire seashell collection. "But I bought those shoes just in case you wanted to have them for the pictures."

Mandy shouldn't have told her mother about the baby-blue tennis shoes she purchased—but she had been so excited about them. Mom reacted exactly as expected. Creased brow. Puckered lips like she took a bite of expired yogurt. "I *have* shoes." Mandy attempted to keep her voice level, but she should've seen this coming. *This* was Mom's MO.

"I know. I know. And you can do what you want. But you

really can't wear those shoes for a proper ceremony, and I think you'll really like these. They have blue soles and everything." Mom sounded much too cheery.

Mandy was getting a headache. She couldn't deal with this right now. "I'll look at them."

"That's all I'm asking," Mom said. "Now hurry up, and don't forget *not* to wash your hair. The stylist said dirty hair is easier to work with."

Too late. Mandy hadn't forgotten, she just didn't want stinky hair on her wedding day. "I remember."

"And eat," Mom said.

Mandy shoved another bite in her mouth. "On it."

"Don't talk with your mouth full. You'll choke, honey."

Mandy *was* thinking about choking someone.

They said their goodbyes, and Mandy checked the clock. Somehow an hour had passed since she'd gotten out of the shower. Her stylist would be there any minute, and Mandy was supposed to have her makeup done before she arrived. This was not a sign. But the conversation with Mom about the shoes played over in the back of her mind. Who was she to tell Mandy what she could or couldn't wear to her own wedding? Or what was "proper" for her special day?

In less than five hours, she was set to marry the love of her life. Who saw her for who she was—flaws and all—she was sure of it. And it was going to be wonderful, and perfect, and there was nothing that was going to ruin this day.

She shoved waffle in her face like she'd been starved for a week—not even taking the time to enjoy her favorite breakfast food—and raced into the bathroom for her makeup.

ANN ROSE is a typical Taurus—loyal but stubborn, which means being an author is the perfect career for her. Growing up, she thought everyone told themselves stories in their heads, so imagine her surprise when she found out this wasn't true. While asking the private group chat for ideas on what to include in this bio, Ann was reminded that some of her greatest qualities are her awesome best friends from high school—a fact she couldn't argue with. She loves dark chocolate, sarcasm, her family, tacos, and her cats—obviously not in that order. Ann likes to write stories that have a balance of humor and heart, and while she thinks she's hysterical, she'll let you be the ultimate judge of that. Ann also writes young adult novels under the pen name A. M. Rose.

VISIT ANN ROSE ONLINE
AnnRoseAuthor.com
X AnnMRose
◯ ⓢ ♪ Totally_Anntastic

Ready to find
your next great read?

Let us help.

Visit prh.com/nextread

Penguin
Random
House